"Please, Mr. Blackheath,"
she said low. "Don't."

"Ian," he urged her in that silky-hot voice. "Call me Ian." His other hand swept up to trace the lower curve of her lip. "I'm a dangerous man, Emily. Dangerous. You would do well to remember that."

He leaned so close to her that his breath wisped, hot, across her tingling lips. "I'll try to keep from acting on my . . . *impulses."* His voice was low, rough-edged. "It won't be easy, with those eyes of yours . . . all soft and amethyst, but I'll endeavor to be strong. However, if I were you, I would stay in the nursery . . . as far away from the east wing of the house as possible."

"The east wing?" Emily asked unsteadily.

"It is my private domain. Forbidden. I promise you, you would not like what you find there."

"You'll find me patently difficult to shock, Mr. Blackheath," she said.

"Oh, I could shock you, I'd wager, Emily Rose. And take the greatest of pleasure in doing it."

Hot, firm, moist, more heady than any juice brewed of poppies, and far more addictive, his lips brushed hers with a carnal mastery that made Emily weak, left her shaken, wanting. . . .

Books by Kimberly Cates

Crown of Dreams
Only Forever
To Catch a Flame
The Raider's Bride

Published by POCKET BOOKS

KIMBERLY CATES

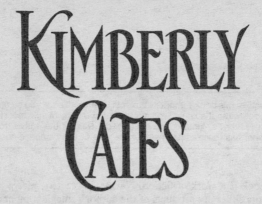

The RAIDER'S BRIDE

POCKET BOOKS

New York   London   Toronto   Sydney   Tokyo   Singapore

This book is a work of fiction. Names, characters, places and incidents either are products of the author's imagination or are used fictitiously. Any resemblance to actual events or locales or persons, living or dead, is entirely coincidental.

POCKET BOOKS, a division of Simon & Schuster Inc.
1230 Avenue of the Americas, New York, NY 10020

ISBN: 0-671-75508-0

First Pocket Books printing February 1994

10 9 8 7 6 5 4 3 2 1

POCKET and colophon are registered trademarks of Simon & Schuster Inc.

Cover art by Ken Otsuka

Printed in the U.S.A.

The RAIDER'S BRIDE

Prologue

$\mathcal{T}$he hunger was inside him again—dark and wild.

Pendragon leaned low over the neck of his stallion, the wind tearing at the silvery folds of his cape and penetrating the thin layer of his silken mask.

He was consumed by the danger, bewitching and seductive—as primitive as the release found in the wet heat between a woman's thighs. For only when fencing with death itself did the legendary patriot raider feel alive.

He glanced over his shoulder to where a dozen of his horsemen ribboned out behind him, lit by the torches clasped in their hands. The rebel band was as deadly as an assassin's stiletto. And tonight they had done their work well.

Pendragon's mouth curled in a feral grin as he regarded their quarry.

A man, bound and gagged, rode belly down over a bay gelding, his nightshirt flapping like a banner in the wind.

He seemed a laughable captive at best—one whom no one would have judged worthy of the attention of a notorious rogue whose legend stretched a hundred miles up the coast of the colony of Virginia.

But that was what had made the captive, Lemming Crane, so useful to the English. He was intelligent enough to follow orders, yet had the appearance of a fool, so that no one would ever suspect him of being a spy.

When Pendragon thought of how close Crane had come to discovering the truth . . .

The raider's jaw knotted. No, it didn't matter. They had discovered Crane's treachery in time. And tonight Pendragon would make certain no other English spy would dare to challenge him again.

Crystal blue eyes shimmered with violence between the slits in the raider's mask. There was only one way to crush a nest of spies once and for all. And that was to obliterate one of them with such horrifying finality that the others would wake up a dozen years from now still drenched with the sweat of their terror.

The raider's mouth hardened as he saw the flicker of light through the trees—a glowing eye born of darkness and demons.

He tightened his knees about his stallion, and reined Mordred through a break in the woods. The sinister glimmer of light became the entry to a cave illuminated by the torches of the raiders who waited there. A single support post shored up the cave's crumbling entry. The thick length of wood was the only thing keeping the arch from collapsing beneath a hillside of earth and rock.

It had been called Brigand's Cave for a hundred years. A haven of dark legends that clung thick within the chamber of stone, pooling in the craggy shadows.

If ever there had been a site fashioned to inspire terror, this was it. As Pendragon wheeled his mount to face his captive, he was certain that Lemming Crane had heard tales of the spirits said to walk here—victims of Indian massacres, of murder and witchery. Spirits the wigmaker was no doubt afraid that he would soon join, courtesy of Pendragon's sword.

There had been a time when the raider might have felt pity for the terrified man. A time when Pendragon might have shrunk from what he was doing, though aware it was a painful necessity. But whatever compassion had once remained in his black heart had been deadened long ago,

2

leaving a ruthlessness that terrified not only his enemies but sometimes his allies as well.

In a fluid motion Pendragon swung from the saddle and turned to watch as two of his men dragged Crane from the bay. They hauled the wigmaker between them, flinging him into the glaringly bright interior of the cave. Despite the cords binding him, Crane attempted to scrabble away from them, but his back slammed up against a fallen boulder.

There was a soft sound of boots against the cave floor as Pendragon's second-in-command, Sir Tristan, came forward and unfastened the gag from the wigmaker's mouth. Sir Tristan kept one steadying hand on Crane's shoulder as the man coughed and sputtered.

"Welcome to my corner of hell, Tory spy," said Pendragon, the raider's voice velvet soft. "Can you feel the devil watching you?" A wave of grim laughter rose up from Pendragon's men, and Crane's pasty features whitened further.

"P-please," the wigmaker begged. "I've done you no harm!"

"Not for lack of trying, I am told. It was really quite an inspired plan, Mr. Crane. You playing the honest colonist in desperate need of aid from Pendragon's raiders. Your shop ransacked by British soldiers, destroyed because of rumors you had guns stored there. If it hadn't been for a certain Private Louden's love affair with the bottle, we might have ridden straight into the trap you had set for us tonight."

"You would believe a drunken fool?"

"A dozen armed men were hiding in the area surrounding your house. If Tristan hadn't set the guardhouse afire to lure them away, we might have been hangman's fodder, and you would be counting out your thirty pieces of silver."

Pendragon paused. "Tell me, Crane, just for curiosity's sake, how much am I worth to the Crown at the moment? What would they pay the man who fits a noose around my neck?"

Crane hesitated. "A thousand pounds. And any lands or assets in your name."

"Blood money. An ugly way to make a fortune. Much

cruder than, say, gambling or abducting an heiress. Of course, with the regrettable lack of morals these days, I'm certain you're not the only one hungering for the king's purse." His voice grew paralyzingly soft. "Tell me, Crane, who else scurries like a rat in the night, wanting to feast on my flesh?"

"How should I know? I've no interest in the others. We are competing for the same reward money, and they would only rob from my purse."

Pendragon turned and paced back to the support post, caressing it with one white-gloved hand. "Crane, have you ever wondered what it would be like to be buried alive? Entombed with your eyes still open, your heart yet beating?"

A strangled sound came from Crane's throat.

"If this length of wood should be ripped from its place, allowing the mouth of the cave to collapse, sealing you off from the world, how long do you suppose the air in this little antechamber would last before your lungs began to burn? How long before starvation clawed at your stomach? Or thirst consumed you until you licked at the cave walls to drink what moisture clings there? How long will it take for madness to devour you as you sit alone in darkness waiting to see Lucifer's face?"

A piteous sob racked Crane, and he fell to his knees, groveling before Pendragon. "You cannot do this! I know nothing!"

Pendragon planted his glossy boot on Crane's shoulder and shoved him away. "Search your memory. Surely you must have heard something. A bit of information about someone else in your despicable profession. At the very least you could tell me who you run to with your scraps of betrayal."

"I go to Atwood, the garrison commander, or to Major Glendenning, whoever will give me the largest purse, and they pass the information on to . . . to someone."

"To *someone?* That is distressingly nonspecific, Mr. Crane. Surely you know this person's name?"

"Do you think they would tell someone like me? I just do what they tell me and ask no questions."

"Crane, Crane, you are supposed to be a spy, someone whose profession is discovering information disastrous to those he betrays. And yet you tell me nothing I don't already know. It is extraordinarily trying."

Shaking his head in mock regret, Pendragon crossed to where the wooden support post was a slash of black against the torchlight. With great deliberation he stripped off one glove and ran his fingertips over the rough wood.

"Perhaps you have heard of my regrettable lack of virtue, spy. Patience, in particular, is an attribute I lack." Pendragon leveled Crane with the piercing gaze that had made far braver men quake. "My stallion is tethered to a tree outside. All I need to do is bind a rope about this support and tie it about the beast's saddle. The slightest pressure of my knees would make him strain against the rope, tear the length of wood free."

"No! No, please!"

"It is very simple to stop me. You just have to give me the information I seek. Who else takes Captain Atwood's blood money? Who else slinks through the dark to play Judas for this mysterious man whose name you do not know?"

"If I knew anything, I would tell!" Crane vowed. "I swear by God and all the saints I would."

"An oath from a spy?" Pendragon gave an ugly laugh. "I'd wager it holds the same value as a whore's vow of faithfulness."

"P-please, milord Pendragon! I—"

Pendragon held up one hand, and Crane choked into silence. "Sir Tristan, it appears that our guest is determined to be difficult. I'm afraid we shall need the rope."

Tristan stepped away from the crescent of men, coils of hemp bundled in his arms. Pendragon felt a surge of almost certain triumph as Crane's face turned green.

With great deliberation, Tristan knotted the cord about the length of wood, giving the knot a tug to secure it. Then he turned to the man staring up at him in horror.

"The Crown cannot help you now," he warned. "Atwood will just find someone else to take your place. He'll cast you aside with no more thought than he'd spare for a soiled glove. Tell us what we need to know, and perhaps I can persuade Pendragon to show mercy."

Crane turned pleading eyes to Tristan, clutching at his arm. "I would tell! I would, if I knew anything at all!"

With the slightest movement of one hand, Pendragon signaled, and two burly men stepped forward, their hands closing on Crane's shoulders.

"Pendragon, this man is a cowardly dog to the very marrow of his bones," Tristan said. "If he had the slightest bit of information, he would give it to you. I'd swear it on my mother's grave."

"It is not your mother's grave we gamble upon." There was an edge to Pendragon's voice, an answering spark in Tristan's green-gold eyes. "If you should be mistaken, Sir Tristan, the forfeit paid would be the death of every man here. Since Crane cannot or will not give us the names we need, our only way to terrorize the other spying bastards is to make our vengeance against him so grisly no other would dare to continue hunting Pendragon or his raiders. Now bind the end of the rope to Mordred."

A sick light darted into Tristan's eyes, tension rippling off of him in thick waves—a tension all too familiar of late.

"But to bury the man alive . . ." he reasoned. "I'm telling you I don't think this is necessary. The bravest of men would have broken by now, and this pathetic wretch is far from—"

"Bind the rope to my stallion."

Tristan stiffened as if Pendragon had struck him. Crane struggled to reach Tristan, all but incoherent in his desperate quest to reach his unlikely ally, yet his captors held firm.

Pendragon's jaw clenched as Tristan, on the brink of outright defiance, cast one more glance at the wigmaker. But at the last possible moment Tristan turned with an oath and disappeared through the mouth of the cave.

Pendragon released a breath from lungs that burned.

"Gawain and Dinadan, you will loosen our guest's bindings so that he may free himself when the cave is sealed. We want him to be able to embrace the demons when they come for him."

The two men who held Crane swiftly completed the task, and the wigmaker crumpled to the ground, his sobs unintelligible against the cave's floor.

Pendragon took a torch from the grasp of one of his men, then, with a jerk of his head, signaled them to leave. They filed out, some hastily, as if fearing they themselves would be caught in their leader's trap, others slowly, as if dazed. Pendragon watched them go, his mouth twisting with sardonic amusement.

"I'm afraid my men have less stomach for meting out justice than I do. However I do not tolerate disobedience. They know it well."

The raider jammed the torch into a crack in the cave floor. "And now I fear I must bid you adieu, Monsieur Wigmaker. When you meet with the devil, request that he save a particularly blazing spot in hell for Pendragon. God knows I've labored hard enough to earn it."

Sketching Crane an elegant bow, Pendragon wheeled around in a cloud of silver and stalked out into the night.

"I know nothing!" Crane's screams echoed behind him as he crossed the clearing. "Have mercy!"

Tristan stood holding Mordred's reins, and in spite of the mask covering his friend's features, Pendragon knew how they must appear—angry, almost betrayed.

"You're going too far, man," Tristan grated, his voice raw with disbelief. "Don't do this, for the love of God."

With gloved hands Pendragon pulled the reins out of his friend's clenched fingers. "It is already done."

In one fluid movement the raider swung astride Mordred, the slightest pressure of his knees ordering the mighty stallion to surge forward. The rope hissed as it uncoiled. Then the hemp snapped taut, the mighty stallion hesitating only an instant before straining against it.

With a horrible sound the support snapped free, thudding

dully across the ground. The stallion shied, rearing and plunging in an effort to free itself, but Pendragon soothed him into submission, reining the animal around.

The raider stared at the cave's entry, lit with glowing orange from the single torch that remained inside. For long seconds the stone arch hung as if balanced by the devil's hand. Then, with a hideous sound, an avalanche of stone and earth crashed down, sealing the English spy in Pendragon's gateway to hell.

1

*C*andlelight splintered in a sea of prisms, flinging miniature rainbows across the room aptly named the *chambre d'amour* at Blackheath Hall.

It was a room intended to tempt angels away from heaven's gates—a sensual banquet of texture and color. Mythical lovers were painted in carnal ecstasy from floor to ceiling. Thick white furs were scattered near the hearth, while imported candies called Nipples of Venus waited on a silver tray to be tasted by tongues hungry from loveplay.

Countless women had been entertained in Ian Blackheath's notorious den of sin at house parties as decadent as any Roman orgy and at gambling fetes in which a king's ransom had been won or lost on the turn of a single card.

Yet beneath this seeming decadence even more sinister affairs had taken place. Blackheath—that ruthless speculator whose loyalty was said to reach no deeper than the bottom of his own purse—had enriched his treasury here with patriot coin.

Contraband weapons had been bartered in the dark of night. Precious guns and black powder that had been smuggled into the colonies on Ian's fleet of ships had been sold to desperate men eager to fuel the fires of revolution—a cause so noble that everyone was certain a soulless opportunist like Blackheath could never understand it.

But tonight there would be nothing so amusing as love-play or so exhilarating as a revolution happening in these opulent rooms. Rather, Ian could sense another type of battle brewing, if the expression in Anthony Gray's hazel eyes was any indication.

Ian supposed he should consider himself lucky that Tony had waited for the servants to scatter to the far wings of the house before beginning his tirade. But the footman who had served refreshments after they'd arrived at the plantation house had disappeared moments before, and it seemed Ian's brief reprieve was at an end.

Resigned, he lounged against the back of a crimson divan, and stretched his long legs out before him, a generous glass of brandy cradled in one hand.

He sighed. "I suppose it would be useless to point out that you could have followed the example of the other men and been indulging in your lady's charms at this very moment instead of wearing a rut in my Oriental carpets and peeling the paint off my murals with the heat of your scowls."

"What I'd like to do is wring your bloody neck!" The violence in Gray's usually reasonable tone made Ian grimace. "You cold-blooded son of a bitch!" Tony raged. "I practically begged you not to entomb Crane alive. Damn it, there was no reason to do it."

Ian skimmed his fingers beneath the thick fall of his dark mane, kneading an area where the knot of his mask had chafed hours before. "I should have guessed what your fierce insistence upon trailing me home from our raids meant—a lecture in brigand etiquette."

"Damn it, Ian, this is no jest! I—"

"Have mercy, Tony. Have mercy," Ian groaned, interrupting him. He leaned his head back against the red cushions. "The brandy has not yet taken effect. I assure you, there is no reason to stir yourself up into a tempest, especially over Lemming Crane."

"Oh, no," Tony blustered. "Nothing to stir myself up

about. You just made me party to murder, for God's sake! Nothing at all out of the ordinary!" Tony's face washed red with fury. "I don't mind thievery. Robbing tax collectors has been tolerably amusing. And I've never balked at teaching some tyrannizing ruffian a lesson for tormenting someone weaker than himself. I've even grown fond of wearing those ridiculous masks and playing Robin of the Hood! But this business with Crane . . . it makes my blood run cold! I should have told you to go to bloody hell!"

"That would have made things a bit awkward, don't you think?" Ian observed idly. "Insubordination can be dashed inconvenient."

"Inconvenient!" Gray let out an impressive string of oaths, driving the toe of his boot into the leg of a mahogany table. A statue of Zeus in the guise of a swan seducing Leda teetered precariously, threatening to tumble into the tray of sweetmeats.

"There's no need to attack the statuary, Tony," Ian said, reaching out to steady the statue. "I can assure you that your soul is no more blackened by what happened tonight than it ever was. Lemming Crane will be Pendragon's guest only for this one evening. Then, when he is sufficiently miserable, I shall slip into a rear entrance of the cave and lead him back into the light—along with a list of others foolish enough to serve as English spies."

If anything, Tony's face grew more thunderous, almost sick with betrayal. "You never intended to leave him there?" Tony gripped his own glass of brandy so hard Ian expected it to shatter. "All this time you planned to let him go?"

Ian raised one dark brow and nodded in assent.

"You bastard!" Tony hurled his glass against the wall, scattering shards of crystal across the room. "You could have told me what you were about!"

Ian cast a dismissive glance at the bits of glass. "I didn't know I was required to consult you."

"You always have before! From the moment we conceived the idea of Pendragon—"

"We were both as drunk as lords that night, if I remember. A condition I intend to seek out tonight with great fervor."

"Ah, yes. Get bloody drunk! That way you won't have to deal with anything or anyone. You won't have to be responsible for your goddamn stubborn—"

"How I choose to deal with my life is none of your concern," Ian said, cutting him off. "I know that you think I can't get along without your advice, Tony, but we'll both have to get used to some changes. When you wed the virtuous Miss Mabley three months from now I can hardly be running off to your bridal bower to discuss the most expedient way to extract information from a spy."

"Why the hell not?"

"You know why!" Ian snapped savagely. "On the night we decided to take the path of rebellion, we agreed we'd involve no women or children in our lives. We're hunted men, Tony. And a knife blade held to the throat of anyone we loved would jeopardize not only the two of us but the entire band as well. Tell me, if Atwood or Glendenning had your Nora trussed up in a cozy little cell, what would you sacrifice to save her? How far would you go to—Hellfire, what's the point in hashing through all this again?" Ian bit off a curse. "It's for the best that you leave the raiders anyway. Any man as infatuated with a woman as you are with Nora can hardly be expected to summon up devotion to any cause except bedding her."

"You don't understand, do you?" Tony asked tightly. "I love her, but that changes nothing about how I feel regarding freedom. Independence. Because of Nora I have more to fight *for*. I want to start a family with her someday, Ian. A future—"

Ian gave a dark laugh. "And to think everyone considers you the rational one between us. Ah, well, I've resigned myself to the fact that I can do nothing to sway you from this marriage, any more than I could stop you from getting into that duel with Manderly where you almost got your head blown off."

"You *would* compare love to that! By God, there are times when I think you've succeeded in forcing ice to flow through your veins in place of blood. Just two weeks ago you received a letter telling you that your only sister was dead, and you didn't show so much as a flicker of emotion. You merely tripled your wager and tossed out the dice."

Ian looked away as images rose unbidden in his mind. His sister, beautiful, selfish Celestia Blackheath, forever seeking love from any man who would pay attention to her, from their dancing master to their father's aged friends.

Ian had been just fifteen when he'd last seen her, but he would never forget how her eyes had shimmered with hate. She had loathed him, and he supposed he couldn't blame her. He had been Maitland Blackheath's only son, worthy of their father's constant albeit negative attention, while she was a mere daughter, to be shoved aside as if she were invisible.

There had been a time when Ian had wanted to mend things between them. Wished that they could share the grief over their mother's death, their father's selfishness.

But there had been no room in Celestia's heart for forgiveness. No common ground for them to forge even the most fragile tie. There had only been the end of any illusion that a family had once existed in Maitland Blackheath's elegant Boston home.

And now Celestia was dead.

Ian had lounged at the gaming table after he received the news, knowing that he should feel something—sympathy, understanding, grief—for this woman who had shared his blood. Instead, he had tightened a hard shell around his emotions, and had cast out the dice. . . .

He drove away the memories and let his mouth curve into an arrogant grin, masking his feelings from Tony's perceptive gaze. "I won the wager that night, if I remember. Quite a handsome sum."

"Damn you, Ian, stop this!"

"You must forgive me if I don't have your reverence for the sacred institution of family, Tony. My father was a selfish bastard hungry for sons and my mother was a gentle, if weak, woman, desperate to do her duty by him."

Ian drained the brandy in a fiery gulp, the liquor loosening his tongue as he told about the childhood he'd barely spoken of in his fifteen-year friendship with Tony

Gray. "I watched my mother waste away through three miscarriages and two stillbirths. I saw her bury three children who died before their first birthday."

He twirled the stem of his goblet in restless fingers, staring at the candle fire dancing in the cuts in the crystal. "She was bedridden when I was fourteen, and the doctor said there must be no more children. When I was fifteen, I watched her stomach start to swell, and I knew my father had refused to keep his infernal breeches buttoned."

Tony's face whitened with compassion. "I'm sorry."

Ian winced, uncomfortable as always at Tony's uncanny ability to see past his carefully guarded facade to the man beneath. He forced a bitter laugh. "My father was sorry, too. But he was far too virtuous a man to seek his pleasure in another woman's bed. Rather than condemn his immortal soul to hell for a dalliance, he condemned my mother to a slow, torturous death. That is what love means to me, Tony."

Ian stiffened, the words he had spoken suddenly seeming to penetrate the haze of brandy and bitter memories, making him aware of just how much he had exposed to his friend, just how vulnerable he'd allowed himself to become.

"It doesn't have to be that way," Gray said quietly. "Before I met Nora I wouldn't have believed that—"

"Enough, by God's blood," Ian snapped. "I don't think I could endure listening to another litany of Miss Mabley's virtues. If you've finished lecturing me about my mistreatment of Lemming Crane, I'd appreciate it if you'd go off to woo your ladylove at once."

Tony started to protest, stopped. "All right. No more about Nora. But as to Crane . . ." Tony paced to the window, shattered glass crunching beneath his boots. "Ian, I was not the only one among the raiders who was troubled by what happened tonight. I could feel their horror at what you were doing. They were afraid of you. Sickened by what you had made them a part of."

"Fear of the demon Pendragon is the most effective weapon we have against the English. I'm certain that by morning half of Virginia will have heard of the fate Crane supposedly suffered. Any spies left in this vicinity should be fleeing from Williamsburg in terror."

"But your own men *believe* you murdered someone in cold blood."

"It's possible that their fear of me is the most important of all. It will keep them from questioning my orders at times when the merest hesitation might cost them their lives. I don't doubt it will save their necks one day."

"Either that or force them to betray you!"

"Does it really matter whether it's one of the Crown's wolves who unmasks me or one of my own men?" Ian stared meditatively into his brandy, swirling the amber liquid around the crystal bowl of his glass. "I suppose there are those who would say it should. I fear I am far too cynical to trouble myself over such vague distinctions. No matter who brings me to face the king's justice, I will end up just as dead."

"Sometimes I think that is what you want."

Ian gave a shrug edged with an unaccustomed weariness. "Even the most brilliant gambler eventually faces ruin, Tony," he said. "We cast the dice every time we put on our masks and ride. Someday, my friend, even Pendragon will have to lose." Ian finished the last of his brandy, grateful to feel it smoothing the rough edges the night's hunt had left inside him. "Of course," he observed, "I have read that death is the greatest adventure of all. What do you think, Tony?"

Ian levered himself to his feet and crossed to where a decanter glistened on a rosewood stand. Removing the cut-glass stopper, he poured himself another drink.

He drank deep of the brandy, hoping to dull emotions that were too sharp and cutting. Emotions he had escaped so often at the bottom of a bottle or in the arms of a beautiful woman.

But tonight he sensed that even those familiar remedies would not ease the restlessness inside him. He glimpsed Tony regarding him with those eyes that reminded him of a spaniel's—soulful and caring, with an odd innocence despite years of hell-raking almost as distinguished as Ian's own.

Ian stripped off his frock coat and waistcoat, flinging them on the *siège d'amour,* a piece of furniture designed for entertaining multiple ladyloves at once. But even the sight of the damask-covered *siège* increased Ian's vague sense of loss, for it had been a gift from Tony, given as a jest one Christmas, in the days before Gray's devotion to the innocent Nora had dulled his thirst for such scandalous adventures.

With impatient hands Ian ripped free the neckcloth that had fallen in cascades of lace down his chest. "I think I preferred it when you were ready to call me out for a duel, rather than having you stand there with the look of a father confessor on your face."

"Then I'll leave you in peace—just as soon as you tell me when we are to release our friend Mr. Crane from the cave."

"We?"

"Ian, until I place my ring on Nora's finger, you will not be rid of me. Crane must be half crazed by now, and a madman is a dangerous thing."

Ian forced a low chuckle. "Don't be an old woman, Gray! Crane will be so shaken after a brief stay as our guest that I could hold a loaded pistol to my heart, and I doubt he could manage to pull the trigger."

"In your current state you'd probably let him try it!" Tony snapped, but Ian could see him battling valiantly against the smile that threatened the corners of his mouth. "Tell me when you're leaving, or . . ."

The words died in Tony's throat, Ian tensing as well as they caught the sound of running feet hastening toward the chamber.

"I thought you gave orders we were not to be disturbed," Tony said, his gaze narrowing on the door.

"I did. Unless the blasted house is burning down, my servants should know better."

One hand strayed to the hilt of the dagger concealed in Ian's Russian leather boot, while Tony's fingers rested with deceptive negligence on the hilt of the dress sword that hung at his waist.

With instinct honed in countless nights of raiding, Ian took up a place favorable to defense and struck a casual pose, while Tony did the same.

At that moment the door flew open, revealing a black youth of about sixteen dressed in silver livery. Obsidian eyes that had always snapped with fierce loyalty were filled with distress.

"Sir, beg pardon to disturb," Priam stammered, "b-but it's the most awful thing . . ."

Ian's gut clenched at the stricken expression on the youth's face. "Out with it, man," Ian snapped. "What the devil is amiss?"

"Some—some person is here, sir, and I wasn't sure what to do about it."

"Soldiers?"

"No! It—it is a . . . a *vicar,* sir!" Priam said in a tone one would have used to describe the Four Horsemen of the Apocalypse.

"What the blazes?" Ian's hand fell away from his knife as he gaped at this young man who had distracted whole companies of soldiers with an icy calm and had suffered the even greater danger of juggling lies to Ian's more temperamental mistresses when his master was using the excuse of a romantic tryst as an alibi.

A vicar. Priam's words echoed through Ian's mind. Fury rushed in to replace the tension of moments before. By God's blood, hadn't he endured enough? Ian thought. Crane's wailing, Tony's temper fit, his own grim memories? Now he was to be accosted by a vicar because Priam had failed to fling the man out the door?

"Let me make certain I understand this," Ian said with quiet rage. "You raced down here, making me think half the English army was storming the gates, when it was nothing but that idiot Dobbins plaguing me?"

The servant's Adam's apple bobbed in his throat. "Yes, sir. I mean, no, sir. It's not Mr. Dobbins, sir. It's someone I've never seen hereabouts. A Mr. Edric Clyvedon."

In spite of the tension of moments before, Tony gave a low chuckle. "Clyvedon? I've never heard of him, praise the saints. Dobbins must be recruiting holy men from other parishes to battle for your soul, Ian."

"All the more reason to hurl this Clyvedon idiot off my property at once. Priam, you tell this bloody vicar the same thing I've told Dobbins for the last fifteen years. Let him go to the devil in his own way and leave me in peace to go in mine."

"I tried to tell him that, sir," Priam insisted. "Well, I didn't speak to him *that* way, but I told him you were otherwise engaged and that you had an aversion to vicars. But the child . . . Mr. Clyvedon said you must receive her or he would come and haul you out of this wing himself."

"Child?" Sweet Christ, could this abominable mess get any worse? "What the devil—"

Tony's face glowed with a touch of his old amusement. "Some former mistress staking her claim upon your purse, *papa?*" Gray inquired so sweetly it set Ian's teeth on edge. "And after all the time you've spent lecturing the rest of us about taking precautions. To think that you might have grown careless."

"Close your mouth, Gray, or I might decide to shoot you—that is, after I clean up whatever disaster has just landed on my doorstep." Ian started to stalk from the room, but Tony stopped him, pressing the glass of brandy back into his hand.

"You'd better take this with you," Tony said, his eyes twinkling. "I have a feeling you're going to need it."

"What I need is to be left the bloody hell alone." Ian snatched the glass from his friend's hand. "Do me the courtesy of being halfway to Pennington Grove when I return to this chamber."

"I am, as ever, your obedient servant." Tony sketched him a mocking bow. "That is, as long as you tell me what time we are to meet tomorrow."

"At dawn, then, if it's the only way to be rid of you," Ian snapped. "See to it that Mr. Gray is gone when I return,

Priam, or it will go the worse for both of you." Ian spun around and stormed out of the room, Tony's chuckles echoing behind him.

Ah, yes, this was so blasted amusing!

All Ian needed was more damned upheaval! One time in his whole benighted life he had wanted to toast his feet at his own hearth, drink his own brandy, and spend the night sleeping in his own blasted bed.

Alone.

But no. He had to be pursued to his very doorstep, tormented first by Tony and now by this vicar.

Ian could only hope the man possessed a strong instinct for self-preservation. Because if he did, one glance at the master of Blackheath plantation would send the man scurrying away as if the hounds of hell were about to devour him.

Ian glimpsed a housemaid whispering behind her hand to a serving wench, and the fury tightened in his chest, growing fiercer with each curious pair of eyes he passed.

By the time he reached the withdrawing room in which Priam had placed the visitors, Ian's head was throbbing and the brandy Tony had given him was nothing but fragrant fumes at the bottom of the glass.

With the palm of his hand, Ian banged open the door. A remarkably short man of about fifty shot from his perch on a spindle-legged chair as if he'd been fired from a cannon. The man, presumably Clyvedon, looked as if he'd been tossed around hell on the devil's own pitchfork.

Circles of sweat marked his frock coat. His wig was askew His fingers twined almost frantically about a plain linen handkerchief while his eyes were round and somewhat alarmed, as if the man feared that someone was about to set his coattails on fire.

His unkempt appearance was an astonishing contrast to the child who was enthroned on the settee, her azure satin slippers resting upon a velvet footstool, her tiny figure resplendent in a gown of rose-colored satin so elaborate it could have clothed the finest lady at King George's court.

Honey-gold curls threaded through with strands of taffy color were arranged with amazing intricacy about her small face, while her chin tipped up in an expression of haughtiness that seemed out of place on a child who could have been no more than eight years old.

Ian felt his brows knit as his glare brushed over the girl, but her cornflower-blue eyes showed not the slightest bit of childlike unease. Rather, she regarded him with the disdain of a queen.

"A gentleman does not present himself to a lady without his frock coat on," the child announced, delicately pinching her turned-up nose. "Especially when he smells of brandy."

"My dear Miss Lucy," the vicar protested, mopping the fresh sweat off his brow with the damp kerchief. "Please! You must not begin by displaying bad manners!"

The child merely shook out the lace on her petticoats, as unfazed by the vicar's reproach as she had been by Ian's glare.

"I have a fractious nose," the child proclaimed, staring down that offended feature at Ian. "My mama always said so."

"Then you can carry your fractious nose off and bury it in your mama's skirts," Ian snapped.

The child's rosebud lips pressed together, her brows lowering over thickly lashed eyes. "My mama is dead." The words were flung out not in childish grief but rather in the manner of a duelist slapping the face of his enemy with a glove in challenge.

Ian stiffened as if the child had done just that, a sick sense of regret flooding through him.

"I'm sorry." He tried to gentle his voice, but the child would have none of it. She continued to scowl back at him, her chin thrust out.

"I heard Mokey, the groom, say that my mama died in jealous fits. She tried to shoot Mr. Avery, and he wouldn't let her, so she got shot instead. I don't believe Mokey, though," the child said almost to herself. "Mr. Avery wouldn't shoot Mama. He brought me sweetmeats."

"Merciful heavens." The minister gasped. "How many times have I told you that you must not speak of such ugly things?"

"It is the truth, isn't it? About my mama? And you and Mrs. Clyvedon are always saying I'll roast in hell if I don't tell the truth."

The child spoke so calmly that she might have been discussing a play she had seen rather than the murder of her mother—a tragedy of such magnitude that most children would have been in hysterics.

More unnerved than he cared to admit, Ian scoured his memory for all the mistresses he'd had through the years. More than a few of them had exhibited the type of dangerous temper the child's story seemed to imply.

Dear God, *could* this child be his?

He searched her face for anything familiar—his eyes, Maria Hobart's mouth, Angelica Mardinet's smile—but there was no physical resemblance to Ian or to any of his former lovers.

He should have been relieved. Instead he merely felt more off-balance.

And yet there was a certain toughness in the child's face that nudged at Ian's heart. He set the glass on the table and searched for the right words to say. "I'm very sorry about whatever misfortune has befallen you, Miss Lucy, but I cannot see what this could have to do with me."

Those wide blue eyes leveled at him like the twin barrels of a gun. "You have to take care of me now."

"Me? Play guardian to a child? Impossible!" Ian's gaze flashed from her to the vicar in disbelief. "Clyvedon, what kind of trick are you trying to play here? I'll not tolerate—"

"It's not a trick!" Lucy cried, and for the first time, a flicker of something vulnerable entered her eyes. "My mama is dead, and you have to take care of me."

Ian rounded on the vicar, furious, confused. "You tell me right now what the hell this is about. Who is this child's mother, and what the devil claim does she have on me?"

The vicar started to loop his arm instinctively about the

child's shoulder, but at Lucy's glare he snatched it back as if he feared she'd bite it off. He cleared his throat. "This is Miss Lucy Dubbonet, sir. Your sister Celestia's child."

"Celestia?" Ian gaped at the little girl, feeling as if his soul had split, plunging him into the dark, cold places inside him. He turned back to the vicar. "What you claim is impossible. My sister couldn't have carried a child. She made certain of—"

He glanced at the child and bit off the words, but they went on, relentless, in his mind. Celestia had been so frightened by what had happened to her mother that she'd made an old Indian woman deaden her womb when she was just sixteen. . . .

"I assure you, Miss Lucy is indeed your sister's child," Clyvedon insisted.

"Well, what about the girl's father, then? The child didn't just appear beneath a cabbage leaf, did she? Believe me, Celestia was not the type to receive the honor of an immaculate conception."

"Captain Dubbonet's ship was lost off the Gold Coast when the child was five. Your sister, it seems, made haste to get on with her life."

"My sister was always able to adapt when it came to men." The caustic words slipped out before Ian could stop them.

"At any rate, sir," Clyvedon rushed on, "I was given the responsibility of taking Miss Lucy away from the home of her mother's . . . ahem . . . protector in Jamaica after the unfortunate incident that led to Mrs. Dubonnet's death."

"Well, you can take the girl right back to Jamaica on the next boat," Ian said. "Surely in your travels you must have heard that I am a bachelor of notorious reputation. People from Barbados to Boston know of my tremendous appetites for gambling and drinking and . . . other sports of a kind that should not be mentioned in a child's hearing."

Clyvedon all but choked on his embarrassment, but Lucy's gaze sharpened, as if she understood what Ian was hinting at far better than the holy man did.

Ian felt his own cheekbones heat beneath her too-wise gaze. He grimaced. It had been a hell of a long time since anyone had summoned a blush from the rakehell Blackheath. If Tony were here, he'd have fallen into paroxysms of laughter by now.

Ian shook himself inwardly. "Mr. Clyvedon, even if I had a more acceptable way of life, it wouldn't change the way I feel about this matter. My sister and I had been estranged for years. Celestia would not have entrusted a worn pair of slippers to me, let alone her child. Surely there must be someone else who can see to Lucy's needs. Someone better suited than I am."

Clyvedon mopped his jowls with the kerchief. "If there had been *anyone* else, do you think I'd have come *here?*"

"I see. Then perhaps I can help solve this dilemma," Ian suggested. "You could take the child to my uncle Fowler. He's a respectable sort, as far as Blackheaths go. Or my cousin Elisabeth Merriton."

The vicar tugged at his neckcloth as if it had suddenly grown too tight. "I regret to—to inform you that your uncle broke his neck falling from a horse eight years ago."

"That was disobliging of him," Ian snorted in disgust. "No doubt Fowler was drunk. The man's horsemanship always was execrable when he was in his cups. What about Elisabeth? Surely she would be a stable influence on the child."

"The word 'stable' is a particularly . . . ah, unfortunate choice, sir. You see, Miss Merriton ran off with her papa's postilion and has never been heard from again."

"Blast it, the girl always did have the most inconvenient weakness for a well-turned thigh." Desperately, Ian named every blood relation he could recall, no matter how remote or removed, while Clyvedon continued to list their unsavory fates.

At last Ian gave a pithy oath, defeated. By God, the poetic justice that had been served on the Blackheath family might even have been amusing if he had not been faced with the small, increasingly indignant person before him.

"Everyone else has died," Lucy's voice cut in, as affronted as if they had done so to irritate her on purpose. "I think it was very rude of them to leave me all alone."

"The Blackheaths always did have abominable manners," Ian muttered. He heaved a deep sigh. "Well, I suppose there is no hope for it, then, Mr. Clyvedon. She will have to go back to the vicarage with you."

"The—the vicarage?" Clyvedon thrust his hands behind his back, his face mottled red.

"I won't go back there!" Lucy cried. "You cannot make me!"

"No!" the vicar shrilled, equally alarmed. "She—she belongs with her own family!"

"But your home would be the perfect place to raise a child from such a tainted family—far from worldly temptations. Of course I shall give you an earthly reward as well. I'll pay you a fortune—"

"I would not take that girl back home if you gave me a king's ransom!"

Ian's eyes glinted with mockery. "Come now, Clyvedon. How much trouble can such a small child be?"

"Keep her and see for yourself," the vicar challenged, then turned and fled.

Ian started to hurry after him, but at that instant he glimpsed a flurry of rose-pink skirts. A small hand seemed to bump accidentally into a table, sending it flying against Ian's legs.

Never in his life had Ian been caught so unawares. But between the effects of the brandy and his own confusion over Clyvedon's reaction, he stumbled. Pain jolted up Ian's shins and slammed into his elbows as he crashed to the floor. He rolled to his side in an effort to regain his feet, but he could already hear the vicar's carriage thundering away at a pace that would have challenged Tony's matched bays.

"Son of a bitch!" Ian shouted. "Priam! Damn it, somebody stop that accursed—"

But his words were cut off by the slam of the door. Lucy braced her back against it, her face fiercer than any Ian had seen across a dueling field. "I won't go with him!"

"You can't stay here!" Ian bellowed. "Didn't you hear a word I said?"

"Yes. You don't want me!" The words were so cold that Ian stilled, his gaze locked on the child's face. "Well, I don't want *you* either."

"Lucy, you must try to understand," Ian began, feeling an unaccustomed twinge of guilt. "It's not possible for me to keep you. I have very important business to attend to." He raked his hand back through his hair. "I can't have a child underfoot."

Those blue eyes were merciless, spearing him with hate and just a hint of fear. "My mama said you were the wickedest man in the whole world. She despised you, and I do too."

"At the moment I don't have a particularly high opinion of *myself.*" Ian sagged until one shoulder rested against the settee, his hand rubbing at his throbbing head. "Oh, what the devil. It's too late to do anything about this mess now. I suppose you'll have to stay here, at least until some other arrangement can be made."

Lucy said nothing. She just stood there, rigid, the tiniest quiver in her lips.

Ian winced at a sharp pang of guilt.

"We'll make the best of it, shall we?" He made a feeble attempt to cajole her. "We'll have a holiday before I find a nice school to send you to, with lots of other girls."

"I don't like other girls. They don't do what I tell them to and don't 'preciate my dresses enough. But I guess that won't matter, because I don't have any dresses anymore. *You* made Mr. Clyvedon run away with my trunks."

Ian bit off a curse. "You mean that imbecile dumped you on my doorstep without so much as a nightgown? What the devil am I supposed to do? Dress you in sackcloth?"

"If you try it, I shall tear them into rags and smear soot on my cheeks. And I'll tell everyone that my wicked uncle threw away my gowns!"

"Bloody hell!" Ian clutched his throbbing head between his hands. "I'll get you some other dresses!"

"It'll be very 'spensive. I like lots and lots of lace." Her shrewdness made Ian wonder if there was more of Celestia in this daughter than he had first believed.

"Fine." He surrendered. "I'll buy you oceans of lace if that will make you happy."

The hard triumph in Lucy's eyes seemed out of place in such a little face. She pressed her rosebud lips together, a certain wistfulness clinging about her features. Ian barely caught her whisper as she turned away.

"I am never happy."

The chimes of the clock as it marked the hour of four seemed to drive white-hot nails into Ian's skull.

Exhausted, frustrated, and feeling the full effects of his encounter with the brandy decanter, he made his way through the corridors of Blackheath Hall, a single candle clenched in one hand.

The whole house was blanketed in the eerie silence of a battlefield after combat was done. The servants were probably cowering in their beds, still shaken by the uproar of the past five hours, while Tony, unforgivably amused by the night's proceedings, had tarried about the plantation house, drinking Ian's wine and laughing that unholy laugh until it had grown too late for him to leave at all.

It had been the night from hell. Ian could only be glad that it was almost daybreak.

But that would hardly be the end of this disaster.

He could scarcely expect Lucy Dubbonet to vanish the way his throbbing head and churning stomach would the next morning. He could hardly fling her out the door the way he would Tony Gray once dawn arrived.

No, come morning Lucy would still be there, demanding to be dealt with, muddying up his infernal life. Sweet Jesus, what he wouldn't give to face more mundane problems—a simple sword fight or an exchange with pistols—a slash to the shoulder or thigh, a pistol ball that failed to pierce a vital organ. Something he could stitch up and poultice and summarily dismiss.

But there would be no easy escape from this night's

disaster, no simple solution to the dilemma of Miss Lucy Dubbonet.

Ian was surprised to find himself hesitating outside the doorway of the gold room, his devilishly handsome features more wary than they had been when he faced a regiment of soldiers. The child was inside, asleep in the amber-velvet splendor of the huge tester bed.

Ian stepped into the room and looked down at her—a surprisingly tiny figure curled up on the tumbled sheets, her gold curls tossed across the pillow. The Mechlin lace collar of Ian's finest shirt was fastened beneath her chin in lieu of a night shift, the child's fingers knotted in the delicate web that tumbled down her chest.

He couldn't suppress a rueful smile as he remembered the fuss the little hellion had kicked up when faced with the indignity of wearing a man's shirt to bed. Only when Ian had remembered her penchant for lace and fished this one from beneath his valet's horrified gaze had she quieted.

She had taken the garment as if it were her due—no gratitude, no flicker of pleasure in her eyes. Just a hard satisfaction as she went regally to bed.

"Is she sleeping?"

Tony Gray's soft question made Ian turn. Damnation, did the man have to follow him everywhere?

Ian shrugged. "She appears to be—praise the saints. I was beginning to consider giving her lemonade spiked with rum to knock her out. What's more alarming," he added wryly, "is that my housekeeper was so desperate, I think she was ready to let me." His gaze intensified on the child. "What the devil am I supposed to do with a little girl, Tony?"

"She's a tiny thing. She can't eat much. As for clothing, I admit she has extravagant tastes, but you're used to that, what with the flock of mistresses you've kept over the years. I imagine you two will get used to each other in time."

"Surely you can't be suggesting that I keep her? Here, in the middle of this nest of treason?" Ian's fist knotted around the candle. "Even during the brief time she stays, we'll have to make adjustments. No new plans for entertaining the

English except in emergencies. There is the shipment of playthings coming up for Chalmers of Boston, and some powder for that Connecticut farmer. Those business dealings will have to go forth as planned."

"We'll manage. It will be easier than you think."

Ian gave a bitter laugh. "No self-respecting Blackheath ever did anything the easy way. And from what I see of her temperament, this child is pure Blackheath. Blast her to blazes."

"She's your sister's child, Ian. You are her only living relative. She needs you." Tony's words twisted inside Ian, releasing something that felt disturbingly like fear.

"I don't have time to play nursemaid!" Ian objected, taking a step nearer the bed. "I'll have to enroll her in some sort of school as far away from Virginia as possible. Maybe that place your sister went to."

"Miss Witherton's Academy? It's a fine establishment, but it won't accept any new pupils until the next term begins three months from now."

"That's not soon enough! There must be some way I can get rid of her immediately!"

Tony's mouth curled in disgust. "I suppose you could blacken her cheeks and sell her at the next slave auction. Or you could indenture her to some tradesman in town. She could be a milliner's bond servant, stitching from dawn to dusk for her keep."

"You know that's not what I mean! I have responsibilities, Tony."

"Of course. To your *cause*. And that takes precedence over a lone child who has no one in the whole bloody world except you."

"Don't play at bleeding heart, Tony! It doesn't suit you."

"I can't help it. Look at her, Ian. The poor little mite. Orphaned and then dragged here all the way from Jamaica. She must have been so afraid."

"That child wouldn't be afraid if she were invited to luncheon by a school of sharks!" Ian said, with a grudging admiration for Lucy's stubborn bravado. "At any rate, even if I were sympathetic to her plight, it wouldn't change the fact that it's far too dangerous for her here."

Ian fell silent for a moment and pressed his fingertips to his throbbing temple. Suddenly he brightened. "Tony, you have numerous acquaintances who are far more respectable than my own. Surely there must be some among them who would love to have a pretty, biddable little girl to keep them company."

"Biddable?" Tony stifled a chuckle beneath his hand. "You and I may be masters of subterfuge, my friend, but even we couldn't conceal this child's willfulness for more than a heartbeat."

"What about your sainted Nora? The Mableys have six children already. No one would even notice if we slipped an extra one in amongst 'em."

"Nora and her mama are off visiting in Charleston. Nora's bosom friend is about to deliver her first babe, and Nora is most anxious to get into practice—" Tony broke off, his cheeks reddening.

He cleared his throat gruffly. "At any rate, Ian, in spite of what you might believe, children are not interchangeable. I have it on highest authority that Nora's mama counts them up every night at suppertime." The teasing note left Tony's voice, and Ian felt hot irritation at the solemn light that suddenly shone in Gray's eyes. "Ian, for the first time since you bloodied my nose at Hargrove's Boarding School, I'm going to abandon you and force you to cope with a disaster by yourself. It might just be the making of you."

"I hate it when you play the self-righteous bastard," Ian said with quiet venom.

The corner of Tony's mouth ticked up in a grin. "Why do you think I do it so often?" he asked, then turned and left the room.

A drop of hot wax splashed onto Ian's hand from the candle he held, but he barely felt it as he edged closer to the child.

Damn Tony. Damn Celestia. Damn himself.

He wasn't a fit guardian for a little girl. Why the devil

hadn't Celestia considered the child's future and made some other arrangement? No doubt his sister had been far too busy having jealous hysterics over her current lover to bother with such a trivial matter. Ian sighed. There was nothing to do about it now except muddle through somehow. Perhaps he could find some relative of the child's father to take her until Tony could get her into the academy. Or . . .

Damn, he couldn't think about it anymore. He'd go to sleep. Things would look better in the morning . . . wouldn't they?

He started to leave, then stopped, frowning as he saw that the shirt Lucy was wearing had slipped askew, leaving one of the girl's narrow shoulders exposed. She gave an almost imperceptible shiver—all the more wrenching because Ian could tell she was attempting to stifle it. He gritted his teeth and pulled the coverlet over her bare skin.

At the brush of his fingers, Lucy whimpered and jerked away from him, as though even in sleep she tried to keep a distance from anyone who would touch her.

The gesture was all too painfully familiar. Ian closed himself against it.

He stepped back, wanting to stalk from the room. Wanting to forget about how small her hand was, curled beside her rosy cheek, how fragile the slight stirring of her breath was as it riffled her golden curls. But he stood there for several long minutes, looking down into Lucy Dubbonet's innocent face, wondering which of them was more bewildered by this sudden familial bond—him or the little girl who lay frowning in sleepy defiance into the lace of his shirt.

2

*I*an jammed his clenched fists into his frock coat pockets in an effort to keep from throttling the child sashaying along before him, her pert nose thrust skyward in an attitude of total disdain.

Disguised as Pendragon he had survived numerous encounters with pistol and sword. He had fought, outnumbered six to one, and had escaped dozens of traps by his wits alone. He had traded weapons for the coin of hard-eyed zealots, men who made it no secret that they would have liked to kill a speculating cur like him.

But he would have faced all these enemies at once, armed with nothing but his own bare hands, if it had meant that he wouldn't have to endure another minute in the company of Lucy Dubonnet, eight-year-old daughter of Satan, the scourge of the civilized world.

They had come to town to order up a few necessities—a simple enough prospect, one would think. He was rich enough to pay whatever was necessary to rig her out, and he had felt so guilty about the way he'd received the girl that he was willing to give free rein to her childish extravagance.

After all, Ian had reasoned, how difficult could it be to clothe one little girl?

He shuddered, remembering all too well.

In the space of three hours the child had managed to insult everyone from the burgess's daughter to the servant girl dipping out water from a barrel in the town square. Lucy had taken up huge chunks of the seamstress's time in choosing materials. And then she had tossed her curls and declared she wouldn't wear such provincial fashions for all the world.

In the last shop they assaulted, Ian had told Lucy that he would not put up with any more of her nonsense and had ordered the shopkeeper to make the gown anyway. But Miss Mudden had snatched up the dress goods and said she'd rather stitch clothes for Crawley's fighting cocks, for they'd be far less likely to claw her eyes out if the garments failed to suit them.

The look of triumph Lucy had cast at Ian had made him want to shake her, but she'd already managed to make enough of a spectacle in that particular shop. Even the rogue Pendragon knew when to retreat.

But when they entered this last shop, Ian resolved, things would be different.

He glanced at a newly painted sign that swung above his last hope—the only milliner's shop that had thus far escaped Hurricane Lucy. A spread fan bearing the likeness of a shepherdess was overwritten by swirling black letters: Mme. Emily d'Autrecourt, Fine Gowns and Millinery.

Ian's jaw set, hard. This time he would get this whole ridiculous task over with once and for all, even if he had to borrow Mme. d'Autrecourt's needle and sew his niece's mouth shut in the process.

"Lucy, tell me something." Ian said in the tone that had made countless English soldiers back down. "Do you intend to live long enough to wear any of these clothes you claim to want so badly?"

The child sniffed in disdain. "I haven't wanted any of them!"

"My point, exactly. I'd suggest you remedy that situation in this shop, or I shall order an entire wardrobe for you in the ugliest colors I can imagine and then I'll truss you up in it myself."

The child glowered at him, hands on hips. "I won't wear black," she bellowed in a voice that would have done a sailor proud. "It's des-picable. I like blue."

Ian banged his hand against the shop door, sending it flying.

"Then *choose some bloody blue cloth* before I have to kill you!"

The door crashed against the inside wall, and Ian could feel the room shake. The cries of the other customers echoed in his ears as the women wheeled to face him.

A half dozen ladies flattened themselves against shelves full of silks and laces, their faces as stricken as if the first cannonball of the threatening revolution had just exploded in their midst.

Ian felt hot blood rush to his cheeks as Lucy pushed past him in high dudgeon and stalked to a box of glittering buttons. The silence seemed to stretch out for eternity as the women gaped at him—the rakehell who was supposed to be far too lazily arrogant ever to lose his temper. Ian groped for something to say, but before he could diffuse the uncomfortable situation, it grew worse by half.

"Ian!"

He winced as he heard the amused cry of Flavia Varden, Tony's onetime mistress.

Despite Flavia's thirty-some years, no hint of gray streaked the guinea-gold hair tucked beneath a most flattering bonnet, a buttercup yellow confection from the days before Tony had fallen under the spell of spritely Nora Mabley.

Flavia hastened over, taking Ian's hands in a fashion that left no doubt that she would be happy to entertain him in a bed still warm from her current lover.

"To what do we ladies owe the unexpected honor of this visit?" Flavia cooed. "Don't tell me. You've come for some colored gauze for the Roman fete you are hosting in two weeks."

His face grew even hotter at the mention of the upcoming

party—an affair so scandalous that even the most suspicious Tories would never suspect that an arms deal was being transacted in Blackheath's wine cellar at the same time.

Ian stiffened, acutely aware of Lucy's unwavering gaze over the edge of the button box. She had fallen silent for the first time in the entire day.

Why the devil couldn't the girl drive off Flavia the way she had everyone else, Ian thought in irritation. It was just like her to be so damned contrary.

He cleared his throat. As the host of such a notorious entertainment, he could hardly act disturbed. "Ah, yes. The fete. I'm anticipating it with great relish."

Flavia gave him a playful slap. "I don't doubt it, you naughty man! Dressing up like centurions and gladiators and carrying ladies off for your own personal org"—Flavia glanced around slyly from beneath fluttering lashes, a dimple dancing beside her painted lips—"er, entertainments."

With a gasp an outraged mama swept her three daughters out of the shop. Another shy-looking woman skittered out in their wake.

Flavia tittered. "Look at the silly fools scatter. You positively terrify them, Ian! The mere idea of such a wicked, wealthy, deliciously handsome rake stalking their precious virtue is far too enticing for them to bear. I vow they'll dream of being ravished by you before their heads strike their pillows tonight! But I'll be able to do far more than dream, won't I?" Flavia teetered forward on the toes of her slippers, displaying her bosom to best advantage. "Who knows what might happen when I fling myself at the feet of my Roman conqueror?"

"Are you his mistress?"

Ian stiffened at Lucy's acid-sweet inquiry.

And he had actually *wanted* the child to speak? Now he was tempted to tear off his neckcloth and use it as a gag.

"Lucy, what a question, for God's sake!" Ian snapped.

But, as usual, the child ignored him. Eyes wide with innocence, Lucy sidled up to Flavia's yellow satin skirts. The woman looked down at the little girl, giving her a false smile. "Why, what a . . . precocious young lady! No, I'm not his mistress, dear. But one never knows what the future might bring. Any woman would be flattered by the attentions of such a handsome specimen as he is."

"I don't think he's handsome. He has a crooked tooth on the bottom, and he scowls all the time." The child's gaze narrowed in the way Ian was coming to dread as she fixed Flavia with a cool stare. "My mama had lovers. Lots of them. She was much prettier than you."

Ian could feel Flavia's hackles rise at the child's well-aimed blow, and he wondered how Lucy had survived to the ripe old age of eight.

He moved in between them, feeling ill equipped to deal with Lucy's latest faux pas. But at that moment the scent of lavender teased his nostrils, a rustle of skirts sounding behind him.

"Your mother must be beautiful, to have a little girl as lovely as you." The voice was soft, musical, shaded with the accent of England.

Ian turned and looked straight into eyes of the most astonishing color he'd ever seen. Deep blue-violet flecked with gold, they were fringed with lashes as dark and rich as the hair that framed the pale cameo of the woman's face.

Her complexion was flawless, rose kissing her sweetly arched cheekbones. A small straight nose was set over lips that were drawn in a perfect Cupid's bow. But it was not an insipid face, nor was it so pure and innocent as to be piously beautiful.

There was just enough strength in her chin to challenge, while the slightest haunted aura about those kissable lips and melting violet eyes made a man's heart squeeze in his chest.

For the first time in Ian's life no flirtatious jest or quick flattery formed with any kind of coherence in his mind.

"Ian, this is Emily Rose d'Autrecourt, just arrived from London," Flavia trilled. "Mrs. d'Autrecourt, this is the most delectable rogue in all the colonies, Mr. Ian Blackheath of Blackheath Hall. I would advise you to take particular care of him, Mrs. d'Autrecourt, for he is the most generous of all men when it comes to his romantic conquests—buys them bonnets, petticoats, whatever their hearts desire. And he has made far more than his share of conquests, let me tell you. If you keep him satisfied, I can assure you your shop will thrive."

Ian groped for words and at length was relieved to find some. "A lady so lovely could hardly help but keep me . . . satisfied."

Currents ran thick and hot beneath his voice—currents no woman had ever misunderstood. He underscored them with a smile that should have melted the knees of a marble statue. But it seemed that Emily d'Autrecourt was made of sterner stuff. No answering heat came into those violet eyes, no blush washed over her cheekbones.

Instead, she leveled him a look filled with quiet censure. "Mr. Blackheath, the only way you could possibly give me satisfaction would be to mind your tongue. I can't think your wife would approve of you behaving this way in front of the child."

"Ian Blackheath with a *wife?*" Flavia dissolved into giggles. "I should like to see the woman who could entrap him!"

Emily d'Autrecourt's eyes grew frigid, her cheeks pinkening just a little. "Then at the very least he should have the decency not to expose his daughter to his affairs."

Ian held up one hand, completely nonplussed. "Madam d'Autrecourt, I'm afraid you misunderstand."

"After overhearing your conversation, Mr. Blackheath, I can assure you that I understand completely."

"No, you don't. Lucy is not my daughter."

"Papa! How can you say that?" Little hands caught at Ian's arm, and he whirled, thunderstruck to see Lucy gazing up at him with soulful eyes. She gave a sorrowful sniff.

"Don't tell me this child is your sideslip!" Flavia gave an

amused laugh. "I'm dying to know which mistress you fathered her on!"

"I didn't! She isn't! She's my sister's child."

"Now, Ian!" Flavia scolded with obvious delight. "In all the years we've been intimate friends, I've never heard you mention a sister!"

"Blast it, Lucy! This isn't funny!" Ian roared, trying to extricate his arm from the child's grasp. "You tell these ladies at once that I am not your father!"

"It's very naughty to lie, Papa!" Lucy said with grave innocence. "I try to be a good girl."

"Dear me, Ian, don't tell me you're all choked up with morals!" Flavia put in. "With the number of women fighting to get into your bed, it's a wonder you haven't sired a dozen little bastards. In fact, even I wouldn't raise much of an objection to thickening with your babe. With you as its sire, it would have to be a pretty little monkey, just like this one."

"That is just about enough!" Emily d'Autrecourt's voice was seared through with outrage as she swept over to Lucy, scooping her into the protective curve of one arm. "I'm afraid I'll have to ask you to leave, Mrs. Varden."

"Leave? A wretched little milliner having the audacity to ask me to leave?"

"I think I've made myself clear."

Flavia bristled. "You can be sure I won't darken your door again! And I shall tell all of my acquaintances how shabbily I was treated!"

"You must do as you think best." The words were quiet, but Ian could sense a certain tension beneath them. "However," Emily d'Autrecourt observed, "considering the fact that you and Mr. Blackheath have already emptied my shop of customers with your disgraceful conversation, I doubt you could do much greater damage."

"Ladies, ladies," Ian interrupted, "I hardly think this is worth daggers drawn."

But it was already too late. Flavia's face turned an unbecoming red as she confronted the seamstress. "Do you think because you are English, you are too good for us colonials? I've heard the gossip about you! A bond servant who sold herself for passage to America. Or are you a convict who should be rotting away in prison?"

"A convict!" Lucy piped up, her face filled with avid curiosity. "Did you shoot somebody dead?"

The seamstress ignored the child, and kept her gaze fixed on Flavia. "My affairs are none of your concern, Mrs. Varden."

"And what will you do if I decide to make them my concern?" Flavia demanded, her painted mouth pursed in threat. "Ian, if I were you, I would take my business elsewhere!" Flavia said, then flounced out of the shop.

Ian raked his hand through his hair. How the hell had things gotten so far out of control? In the space of ten minutes Lucy had not only managed to stir up gossip that she was his illegitimate daughter—a tale Ian was certain would be halfway around Williamsburg in another ten minutes—but had dragged this stubborn, self-righteous seamstress into the mess as well.

"Curse it to hell," Ian muttered. "Maybe I can fix things with Flavia at the fete." But before he could make his generous offer to the woman before him, Emily d'Autrecourt rounded on him, trembling with rage.

"Of all the despicable behavior!" she said. "What kind of a man are you, allowing that woman to say such things to your own child?"

A tear trembled on Lucy's lashes, and trickled down her cheeks with artistic perfection. "My papa doesn't want me! He wouldn't even take my trunks off of the coach that brought me to his house." Her voice quavered. "I don't even have a single dress, and he's been yelling at me all m-morning!"

"For pity's sake, Lucy, haven't you done enough damage?"

"It's not my fault he s-sent away my trunks! But he's mad at me, and he's going to dress me up in ugly clothes to p-punish me!"

Ian gritted his teeth, remembering the spectacle he'd

made when they'd entered the shop. The child had just delivered a masterful sword stroke.

As if to hide her look of triumph, Lucy buried her face in her hands, but Ian could see her peeking out from between her fingers so she could gauge Emily d'Autrecourt's reaction. Lucy could not have been disappointed with what she saw.

Those eyes that had stunned him with their beauty now glared up at him as if he were Attila the Hun just returned from pillaging Europe.

"It *is* true that her trunks were misplaced," Ian said, attempting to explain. "And I did tell her . . . Bloody hell, we'd been through every shop in Williamsburg! Her behavior was abominable!"

"*Her* behavior?"

"All I wanted to do was to buy her some infernal clothes! I can hardly ship her off somewhere with only the dress on her back!"

"You see how hateful he is?" Lucy wailed. "I want my mama! I want my mama!"

A flicker of some stark emotion he couldn't name darkened Emily d'Autrecourt's eyes. Her voice was unsteady as she drew the little girl into her arms. "We shall find her, sweeting. I promise you."

"That's going to be a damn sight difficult," Ian snapped, his temper firing hot. "She's dead."

"My mama's shot dead! All dead and cold and buried in the ground!"

Emily d'Autrecourt looked at him as if she expected to find a smoking pistol in his hand.

"*I* didn't shoot her, for God's sake! It was one of her lovers who—Hellfire and damnation!" Ian banged his fist into a shelf, sending spools of thread scattering. "Just make her some goddamn clothes! I don't care how much they cost. I don't care what bloody color they are! Just rig her out, so I can get the blazes back to Blackheath Hall!"

"There is no reason to bellow at an innocent child."

"*Innocent!*" For the first time since last night, Ian could sympathize with the vicar who had brought Lucy to the plantation. By God, no wonder the man had fled as if the devil's daughter were nipping at his heels.

She had been.

He looked down at Lucy, who was snuggled beneath the swell of Emily d'Autrecourt's breasts. With uncanny stealth, the child stuck out her tongue at him.

She was anticipating an explosion, was glorying in his fury. He could see it. But he'd be damned if he'd give her any further satisfaction at his expense.

He gritted his teeth, his voice like unsheathed steel. "Lucy, you have one hour," he said. "If you are not finished by the time I return, I shall haul you out of here and you can wear the gown you have on until hell freezes over!" His eyes flashed to Emily d'Autrecourt's. "I have only one bit of advice for you, madam. I wouldn't trust her with any sharp objects if I were you." With that he stormed out the door.

Emily stood there, more shaken than she dared admit. The child still clung to her, her little shoulders quivering with what could only have been terror.

How dare the man frighten the little girl that way! she thought furiously. But no one knew better than Emily what a man like Ian Blackheath was capable of—just how far he would go to get his own way.

She had seen such men a hundred times in England—young men like the nobleman who had been her husband. And she had watched in horrified fascination as they sank deeper and deeper into debauchery, not caring who they dragged with them into ruin. They had had the same arrogant cast to their faces, the same appearance of wealth and invincible power as the man who had left Emily's shop moments before.

But she sensed Ian Blackheath was even more dangerous —because of the raw sensuality that rippled off of him in thick, drugging waves.

Those crystal-lake eyes ringed with darker blue beneath thick black lashes had speared awareness into the most secret places of Emily's body. His straight nose had enhanced the hard planes and angles of his cheekbones, the unyielding square of his jaw. But the hard, aristocratic features were softened by lips that were unexpectedly full and looked bone-meltingly soft.

He was an even more potent package of an all too familiar poison. A man who would not hesitate to trample over anyone who dared to interfere with his pleasure, any more than Alexander d'Autrecourt's friends had.

Anyone like a mere wife . . . or a child . . .

A knife blade of pain embedded in Emily's heart twisted afresh. She closed her eyes, fighting back the memories.

"Come, now, little one," she crooned to the child. "We shall teach your papa a lesson at once. He said he would not question the cost of outfitting you. So you may choose anything you want."

"Are—are you certain it's all right?" the little girl asked, gazing up at her with tear-starred eyes. "I want to be a good girl. I don't want to make Papa angry."

"Of course I'm sure. You heard it from his own lips, didn't you?"

The child smiled. It would have been a beautiful smile, Emily was certain, if it had reached the little girl's eyes. "You are a nice lady. I wish that *you* could be my papa's mistress."

Emily's cheeks heated, and she hurried to drag out the most exquisite merchandise her shop had to offer. As the hour flew by, Lucy delved with great relish into planning a wardrobe that could rival the queen's while Emily waged her own battle against the disturbing images the child's words had conjured up in her mind.

Images of Ian Blackheath playing at bed games, his magnificent body reclining like that of some caesar in ancient Rome.

Ian Blackheath, his lips curled in that mocking devil's smile while the bevy of mistresses Flavia Varden had spoken of draped their gauze-covered bodies over his broad chest, hungry for his favors.

Ian Blackheath. The most decadent, dissolute of men. A heart of ice masked by a face that could steal a woman's soul.

Emily felt her heart flutter with apprehension. No! She brought herself up sharply. Ian Blackheath could not hurt her. She was older now, and far wiser than before. She could sense the danger when the shadow of a hawk sailed near her . . . a hawk in the guise of a man.

She had far more dangerous things to worry about than him.

Like the price she had paid for this new beginning. The forfeit she had agreed to in exchange for a chance to start her life anew. If anyone ever discovered . . .

Flavia Varden's threats echoed in Emily's mind.

"Oh, lady!" Lucy's gasp of delight shook Emily from her thoughts as the little girl darted to where a fashion baby was displayed. She scooped up the wooden figure that had been sent from England to exhibit the latest fashions, her fingers trailing with wonder over the tiny burnt-straw hat, the delicate embroidered underpetticoat with its riot of flowers.

Outwardly it seemed no different from a hundred other dolls that ladies used to select the patterns for their gowns and that, once the newness of the fashions on the dolls had dimmed, were handed down to eager little girls at Christmas or on their birthdays. Yet this fashion doll was as different as nightshade from a child's fistful of violets—the secrets beneath its wooden breast as dangerous as the most subtle poison. Just the sight of the doll in Lucy's hands shook Emily so fiercely that she snatched it away.

Lucy's eyes widened in astonishment, then darkened, her mouth setting into an ominous pout. "I want that doll! Give her back to me!"

"I'm sorry, Lucy. This doll is not for sale," Emily said as she crossed to the wooden counter and stepped behind it. "But I'd be happy to part with another. Perhaps the one in the emerald green dress you admired so much."

"I want *that* doll!" she jabbed a finger at the figure Emily was tucking on the counter's lower shelf. "I don't have any doll at all and my mama is dead! I cry every night."

Guilt gnawed inside Emily. The child truly did look distraught.

42

"I'll make you another one even prettier, sweetheart. It will be ready by the time you come to get your new clothes."

"I want the doll in the blue satin! Give her back to me! Now!"

The door opened, and Emily turned to see Ian Blackheath framed in the doorway. There was the slightest hint of smugness about his lips as he surveyed the tangle of cloth and trim and the truculent expression on Lucy's face.

"Having fun, are we?" he asked in dulcet tones.

In a most disturbing turnabout, Lucy flung herself at his legs. "She is being abominable mean! She won't let me have the doll I want! I'd wear this dress forever and ever if I could only have that doll to love!"

Emily winced inwardly, her heart giving an erratic lurch. "Please, Mr. Blackheath. I can explain—"

"I've found that no one can explain anything when Lucy is about," Blackheath said, digging into his waistcoat pocket and withdrawing a leather purse. He flipped it open, withdrawing a handful of gold and silver coins. "Just tell me how much the thing costs, and I'll pay it. It will save us both a world of grief in the long run."

"You don't understand." The heat of a guilty flush washed up Emily's neck and spilled onto her cheeks. "This doll is not for sale."

He chuckled. Those arresting blue eyes flicked in a path to her lips. "It has been my experience that everything has its price, my sweet. And despite all the trouble Lucy has caused, the child *is* far from home. If the doll will bring her comfort—"

"I cannot sell the doll. I'm sorry."

Those ice-blue eyes sharpened, his heavy brows lowering in displeasure and a vague suspicion that made Emily's blood run cold. "Madam d'Autrecourt, don't be absurd. You are new in town, and have only recently opened for business. From what Flavia said, I gathered that you've had a somewhat difficult past. The amount I could pay you for the doll would certainly help. Think of it as a windfall."

"I would prefer to earn my way honestly. And I can hardly expect ladies to order gowns from my shop without having seen the fashions on the dolls first. This particular style has stirred up a good deal of interest already." There was enough suspicion in Ian Blackheath's face to unnerve her. She groped for some way to appease him. "Perhaps if you would give me a few days, I could copy it."

"God's blood, madam, an hour ago you were making me feel like the most despicable villain alive because I was not being sensitive enough to the child's needs to suit you. Now *you* are being unreasonable. I hardly have time to run back and forth to town. I have important matters to attend to. This gown is little different from any other. A bit of ecru chiffon here, a touch of taffeta ruching there. Get a pen and a bit of paper and sketch it."

"Mr. Blackheath, my time would be better spent explaining to you the definition of the word 'no.' Obviously it is beyond your comprehension." Emily looked down at the little girl, whose features were now filled with a most fearsome fury. No hint remained of the angelic innocent who had swept into the shop an hour ago.

"Lucy, I promise that as soon as your clothes are stitched I shall bring the doll out to you. Since your papa is such a busy man, I do not want to inconvenience him with another trip to town." There was a bite to the words. Ian Blackheath's mouth tightened.

"He's *not* my papa!" the child shrilled, her voice breaking. "I don't have a papa. I don't have a mama. I don't have *anybody!*"

With lightning swiftness, the child grasped the edge of the shelf nearest her, shoving it over. Emily heard Ian swear.

Hard hands closed around Emily's waist to drag her out of the way, and she stumbled backward, her legs crashing into the barrel she had been unpacking earlier that morning. She stumbled, Blackheath crashing against her with an oath. For a heartbeat they both struggled for balance. Failed.

The breath whooshed from Emily's lungs as she tumbled to the floor, Blackheath attempting to shield her from the flying materials. His beard-stubbled jaw abraded her cheek, his hips were pressed just off center from the apex of her thighs while his breath, hot and moist, trailed down her throat to pool on the bared swells of her breasts.

He was overwhelming, tall and hard and hot, making her feel suddenly tiny by comparison. Heat seared Emily even through the layers of cloth that separated them—the heat of his anger, the heat of his hard-muscled body, and another heat . . . that dangerous heat she had seen reflected in his eyes.

She would have been far less stunned if the shelf had landed on her head. She started to struggle, but Blackheath was already rolling to one side.

"Blast it, Lucy!" he roared, struggling to clamber upright, his boot soles slipping on the spilled goods.

But in the midst of the confusion, the little girl had disappeared. There was the sound of the door slamming at the rear of the shop.

"Damn that child to hell," Blackheath swore, looking around in a daze. "She has to stop throwing furniture!"

Emily sat up, more shaken than she cared to admit. Thread and ribbons, buttons and trim, were scattered to the corners of the room. The entire display of bonnets had been obliterated, while the expensive French fans that had been Emily's pride were nothing but a mass of broken sticks.

But it wasn't the ruined merchandise that disturbed Emily so deeply. Rather, it was the jagged edge of anguish that she had heard in the little girl's voice.

I don't have anyone.

Oh, God, how many times in the past five years had Emily fought back bitter tears, the same words echoing in her soul? Emptiness. Loneliness. Despair.

She had suppressed her sadness during the day, keeping busy at an almost frenzied pace. But every night when she fell onto her bed in exhaustion, the emptiness had been waiting for her.

She started, jarred from her thoughts as warm, reins-toughened hands closed about hers—Ian Blackheath, pulling her to her feet with astonishing gentleness. Instead of releasing her, he looked down at their joined hands, the corners of his mouth turned down in what Emily sensed was a rare moment of introspection.

"Mrs. d'Autrecourt, I must apologize for my niece's behavior." There was something wrenching in Ian Blackheath's voice. "Lucy is not a . . . lukewarm child, and she's been through a great deal of turmoil lately. I didn't even know she existed until last night, when she was dumped on my doorstep. I'm afraid I behaved rather badly."

"Did you throw the furniture, too?" Emily asked, with a half smile.

"No. I showed admirable restraint in that respect. But you can see that Lucy and I don't suit. I have to get rid of her as quickly as possible."

Emily's heart gave a dull twist at the image of the little girl facing this daunting uncle she had never met. And then being rejected. "I suppose a child would definitely be inappropriate at a Roman fete," she allowed.

"Er, exactly." He cleared his throat. "Of course, I can't ship her off somewhere without clothing her first, so if you could hurry with the stitching, I would make it worth your while. The sooner this is all behind Lucy and me, the better it will be for both of us."

Emily winced, feeling the child's pain as if it were her own. "I'll do my best."

"Of course I'll pay for whatever damage she caused in her little temper fit. Just let me know how much you need when you bring the garments to Blackheath Hall."

Emily looked away, suddenly unable to bear the weight of that steady blue gaze.

"You had best go after Lucy," she said quietly. "She seemed quite upset."

"Yes. Yes, she did. I don't suppose you would reconsider. About the doll, I mean. I know Lucy went about it the wrong way, but she is very much alone."

Emily sucked in a deep breath. Her desire to go out into the streets of Williamsburg herself and lay the plaything in the miserable little girl's arms was almost more than she could resist. But it was impossible.

There were secrets hidden inside the wooden body beneath the tiny gown—secrets that could end the threat of rebellion in the colonies, destroy the enemies of the Crown. Messages from the spies who were the eyes and ears of the English forces.

She stiffened, afraid that far too much had already been revealed in her eyes.

"I'm sorry." She forced the words through taut lips. "I can't give up the doll."

Blackheath started toward the door. He hesitated with a hand curved around the knob and glanced over one broad shoulder. His lips twisted in a smile that could have lured an angel into hell. "If you won't give me the doll, perhaps I should give Lucy to you. What say you, Madam d'Autrecourt? Would you like a little girl?"

The words were a dagger-thrust to Emily's soul. Her throat constricted with memories, with grief. Her mind filled with images of a tiny stone marker among the imposing crypts of the noble family d'Autrecourt.

"Good-bye Mr. Blackheath," she choked out.

The door closed behind him, but Emily barely heard it. Blindly she picked her way across the debris to the door and latched it. She sank to the floor and buried her face in her hands, remembering. . . .

But no matter how hard she tried, she couldn't keep her mind from spiralling back five long, barren years to memories that still haunted her dreams. Emily closed her eyes, surrendering to her own private hell.

3

For a hundred years the brass lion had stood guard at the
ducal seat Avonstea, its fangs bared as it stared out across
the lands that were the d'Autrecourt birthright. How many
times, in summers long ago, had Emily climbed on this very
lion? How many times had she curled up in the lion's
shadow while Alexander d'Autrecourt sang some melody he
had written, the notes in his child-voice pure and haunting
and sweet?

But today she didn't come to this place with the innocent
optimism of a child, her head filled with mythical beasts and
heroes. She came as a woman, pursued by demons far more
terrifying because they were real.

Emily stood in front of the heavy carved door, cold rain
soaking through the layers of her cloak. She was desperate,
frightened. Fragments of prayers formed inside her as she
pulled the bell.

She glanced back at the hired coach. The driver, half
soused on blue ruin, lounged on his perch, his pockmarked
face surly. His pocket was already lined with the last coin
Emily possessed. If she was not allowed entry here, she had
no doubt that the coachman would leave her. But more
terrifying still, he would abandon the coach's other passen-
gers to the relentless elements as well.

A hollow, racking cough sounded from the coach, making panic surge through her once more.

Alexander lay inside the vehicle, wrapped up in a woolen blanket. Emily knew the skin beneath his pale gold curls was blazing with fever. His gentle, haunted eyes were sunken with hopelessness and self-blame. He had tried to drag himself out of the coach, not wanting her to face the ordeal of confronting his family alone. But he hadn't had the strength to raise his head. The defeat in his features had been heartbreaking to see.

Emily's heart lurched, desperation welling up inside her again. She couldn't let him die. This boy who had been her dearest childhood friend, who as a newly grown man had sacrificed himself into marriage with her, though he had not loved her with a husband's passion.

As a child, he had played the knight-errant to her damsel in distress a hundred times in the shadow of this same brass lion, and had often brandished his wooden sword to drive the beast to its knees. But on that fateful day when he had found her sobbing in the meadow, the only weapon he'd had to defend her with was his name.

He'd given it to her gladly, saving her from the marriage her parents had arranged for her to a crude and brutal country squire. But this was not a game of pretend to be ended at nightfall when they had both trailed back to their own separate nurseries. And neither of them had suspected the price Alexander's unselfishness would exact.

Everything.

Everything this grand estate symbolized, everything Alexander had been born to. He had lost it all. It would be too cruel a price if he lost his life as well.

Emily blinked back tears, pulling more insistently on the bell. Oh, God, they had to help him now—his father, the all powerful duke; his mother, one of the greatest ladies in all England. When they saw him—how sick he was, how defeated—surely they would be merciful.

Emily swallowed the lump of desperation clogging her throat. She would throw herself at their feet if she had to, beg them not to let their son be hurled into Newgate for debts he could not pay. She would beg them to save him from the life of genteel poverty he had known since he had shyly slipped his wedding ring on the finger of a girl who was not his social equal.

Alexander, always the dreamer, bewildered now by a reality that could be so brutal, so unforgiving. He lay shivering in the coach, holding the one miracle that remained pure and beautiful and good in this nightmare. Their sleeping golden-haired daughter.

Jenny. Just three years old. Frightened. So frightened.

"Papa's hot, Mama." The child's whimpers echoed in Emily's mind. "Make me a song, Papa. I'm frightened."

Emily choked back her own sob, her tiny daughter's terror magnifying a hundredfold in Emily's own breast. The image of those pleading, innocent eyes turned up to her with such absolute trust was torture beyond imagining when Emily felt so helpless.

She grasped the bellpull again and yanked, but at that moment the door swung open. A servant in white and gold livery stared down his nose at her in regal disdain. "May I help you, miss?" His gaze skimmed with obvious disinterest over her threadbare cloak, her face half hidden by a faded hood.

"Tulbridge?" she queried softly, drawing the hood back from her rain-soaked curls. "It's me. Emily Rose."

Recognition flickered in the man's eyes. Quicksilver flashes of disbelief and sympathy flared in his expression, but he quelled them instantly, schooling his features into the bland expression of a well-trained servant. "I regret to inform you that the duke and duchess are presently engaged in a house party, miss, and are not receiving uninvited guests."

"If you will let me come in and wait in an anteroom, I'll—"

"If you waited a hundred years, they would not receive you, madam," Tulbridge said, the chill in his accents only a little forced. "You are not welcome on these premises."

"Tulbridge, please! It's Lord Alexander. He—"

"Lord Alexander is dead to his family. Good day, madam." He started to close the door, but Emily darted into the opening, blocking it, half afraid the servant would summarily shove her out.

"He's alive and you know it! So does his father. But unless His Grace helps us, his son might be lost to him forever! Tulbridge, have pity, for God's sake. You carried Alexander on your shoulders when he was a boy! You mended his kites and—"

The sound of laughter echoed from deep inside the house. Music from the pianoforte rippled out from a distant room—an indifferent player, savaging the instrument that had been Alexander's most cherished treasure.

Anguish shot through Emily as she remembered Alexander's music filling these halls.

"Miss Emily, you must go," Tulbridge insisted urgently. "If anything, His Grace's heart has grown harder against Lord Alex over the years. The duke is a proud man. An unforgiving one."

"I don't care if he casts my soul into hell! He can't let Alexander die!" Desperate, Emily darted past the butler. She scooped up her threadbare skirts as she ran through the halls she'd traipsed in her childhood, the horrified servant in hot pursuit. But panic made her feet swift. That and the knowledge that the lives of the only two people she had ever loved teetered in the balance.

She barely avoided Tulbridge's hand as she burst through the door to the music room. The melody ended on a discordant note, cries of surprise, gasps of shock and outrage, rose from the guests who were gathered to worship at the feet of the powerful duke of Avonstea.

Emily was almost blinded by the glitter of jewels, the shimmer of candlelight upon oceans of satin. A dozen faces stared at her, their lead-painted skin white like haughty masks. Emily caught a glimpse of the duchess, still beautiful and aloof against the backdrop of other familiar faces from what seemed a lifetime ago. But Emily's gaze locked on the man enthroned upon a velvet chair. A fortune in diamonds shimmered like crystals of ice upon the winter white of his clothes, his eyes glacial above the sneering line of his mouth.

It had been four years since Emily had stood in the presence of the duke of Avonstea, a trembling girl of sixteen with eighteen-year-old Alexander at her side. Oh, God, if she and Alexander had been able to gaze into a magic crystal, to see the future that day, would they have succumbed to the duke's furious demands for an annulment? Would they ever have dared to go to London to seek their fortune?

They had been so innocent then. So naive. But the duke had known. He had known that they were nothing but belligerent children, stumbling into the jaws of a reality far harsher than anything they could have imagined.

How he must have laughed inside when Alexander claimed he would support Emily with his music. That he would be as famous as the prodigy Mozart someday. He was far more suited to being a composer than to playing the role of a nobleman's younger son, doomed to take the army commission that his father intended to buy for him.

Alexander had sounded so brave as he had defied his father that Emily had believed with all her heart, all her soul, that everything would be all right.

"What is the meaning of this?" the duke's sharp demand splintered her memories as he rose to his feet. "How dare you come here!" It was the tone he used to terrorize those of lower standing than himself, the tone that had once made Emily's knees quake. But she had faced things that were far more terrifying than the duke of Avonstea these past four years.

Lifting her chin, she crossed the room to where he stood.

"Your son is sick. He may be dying."

"I have other sons." Avonstea flicked open his snuffbox and held a pinch to one classically shaped nostril. "Tulbridge, you will take this . . . *person* . . . from my presence and fling her into the street where she belongs."

"Listen to me!" Emily turned to plead with the duchess. "You are the woman who bore Alexander, who felt his life in your womb. Can you sit there now and let him die? He is in a coach outside, sick with fever. He needs a doctor. Decent food. He needs a bed to warm him."

"As I remember, he had no need for my support," the duke put in. "The fool was going to provide such necessities by assaulting the ears of unsuspecting idiots with those ridiculous tunes he was constantly scribbling."

"He needs you now, Your Grace. Desperately. He's beyond hope. They will hurl him into Newgate. He'll die there!"

"Ah, I see. And you would prefer that he die *here?* Save yourself the cost of his burial?"

"I say, Avonstea!" the blustering sound of a man Emily recognized as Sir Jedediah Whitley intruded. "That's a bit outrageous even for you! The boy—"

"He's no boy, as he so loftily informed me after he wedded and bedded this ungrateful fortune seeker." Avonstea turned back to Emily, and she could see the pleasure in his eyes, knew that he'd been anticipating this very scene for four long years. He was savoring his triumph even now.

The knowledge drove a hard wedge of anger into Emily's chest. She faced him squarely. "If you leave Alexander to die, his death will be on your soul. You will never be able to cleanse the stain away."

"My soul? You are the one who killed him, madam, the day you entangled him in your web. To think I harbored you upon this estate. The vicar's daughter, a prim, wide-eyed innocent. I can only be grateful that your parents had the wisdom to disown you for the evil you had done."

Emily met the hatred in those cold eyes and saw Avonstea's fiendish pleasure. The duke was hungry for complete victory. If it would save Alexander's life and the life of their daughter, Emily would give it to him.

With a force of will she hadn't known she possessed, she battled back hatred, battled back pride, and crossed to stand before him. Her nails dug deep into her palms as she slowly sank to her knees. "Please, Your Grace. I beg you. Help him. Help our little girl."

A flutter of gasps and murmurs went through the assembled guests. Disapproval was now aimed not at the bedraggled girl who had flung herself into the room but at the cold man standing before her.

"A child?" the duke demanded. "There is a child?"

"Yes, Your Grace. Alexander's daughter. Your granddaughter. She is only three years old. So tiny. So helpless. She has done nothing to deserve your hatred."

"Avonstea, by God, man, how can you cast your own flesh and blood aside like this?" Whitley demanded. "I swear, I can't bear it! Scowl at me if you wish, sir, but I'll not stand by and see a babe cast to the wolves—nay, nor Alexander. He was a good boy, except for wasting himself on this girl. If you'll not live up to your responsibilities—"

"You forget yourself, Whitley." Avonstea's voice slid slivers of ice beneath Emily's skin.

There was a rustle of silk as the duchess rose and glided to her husband's side. If possible, the woman's eyes were filled with even deeper hatred than her husband's as she stared into Emily's face. A hatred caused by the fact that the duchess truly had loved Alexander in her way, and Emily had stolen him from her.

"I'll not have it bruited about England that the d'Autrecourts let those of their own blood die," the duchess said, her nostrils flaring as if Emily were something foul, impure. "Tulbridge, you will escort Lord Alexander upstairs at once. Put him in one of the rear rooms in the old part of the house. And as for the child, put her in the care of one of the housemaids."

Relief and gratitude swept through Emily. Tears welled up in her eyes. "Thank you, Your Grace."

"You may thank me by removing yourself from my presence."

"Of course. I'll help Tulbridge get Alexander settled—"

"You misunderstand me. I will not have it said that the d'Autrecourts allow their blood kin to die. But you are nothing to me. Less than nothing."

Emily struggled to her feet, her whole body trembling. Surely the duchess couldn't mean to separate Emily from the rest of her little family? Any woman who had lain with a man, who had borne a child, could not be so heartless. . . .

"Please, Your Grace. My husband is sick. And my daughter . . . we have never been apart. Have mercy."

Disgust curled that haughty mouth. "I will serve you up the same brand of mercy you showed to me the day you robbed me of my son."

"No! How can I leave them?"

"What can you give them, now, Emily Rose," the woman sneered, "except a pauper's grave? I can only hope that you end in one yourself."

The room blurred before Emily's eyes, the faces distorting into sickening masks around her. The horror and disgust, the anger and righteous indignation, of the crowd were all overset by the repulsive hunger for gossip that Emily had seen so often before in the *haut ton*.

Slowly Emily turned, struggling to keep her knees from buckling as she made her way out of the room. Tulbridge shut the door behind her, and she sagged against it, raising her shaking hands to her face.

"Miss Emily," the butler said hesitantly, "I—"

"You must not tell Lord Alexander," she said in a tremulous voice. "You mustn't tell him that I . . . I have to leave."

"But, Miss—"

"Tulbridge, he'd never stay if he knew the truth," she said fiercely. "And if he doesn't stay, he'll die. Her Grace is right. There is nothing I can give him now. Nothing I can give my daughter."

"But what about you? Where will you go? What will you do?"

"It doesn't matter, Tulbridge. Don't you see?" She swallowed hard. "Come, now. We need to get Alexander warm. And you . . . you need to meet Mistress Jenny."

She murmured words of comfort as Tulbridge lifted Alexander's fever-racked body from the coach. She soothed her little daughter as she cradled Jenny in her arms.

"Mama, I'm frightened," the child snuffled against Emily's breasts. "Don't like this place. Bad lion got teeth. Eat Jenny all up!"

"Sh, moppet. It's only made of brass. Your papa and I used to play on it when we were small." The words raked Emily's throat, leaving it raw. She couldn't start to cry. Couldn't let Jenny see the anguish she felt. Oh, God, how could she leave her?

"I want to go back to *my* house. I want my pretty flowers an' Papa's pianoforte. I want you to sing my Night Song."

It was as if Emily's heart was being ripped from her breast. Every night since Jenny had first been laid in her arms, she had sung for the child the melody that had been Alexander's gift to her. The melody that had always broken Emily's heart with its poignancy and longing. Never once had Alexander played it for anyone else's ears. Never once had it been sung by anyone other than Emily.

Even when things had been darkest, the Night Song had been a haunting treasure.

"You will have to sing it to yourself tonight, my angel," Emily said. "Can you do that for me?"

"No! *You* sing!" Jenny's lower lip quivered.

"I have to go away for a little while, Jenny. Only for a little while. You'll have to sing the night song yourself until I return."

"No!" The little one's voice fractured on a sob. "Stay with me. I'm scared, Mama!"

Emily stroked the child's curls with fierce protectiveness. "Everything will be all right. You are going to stay with your grandmama and grandpapa until Papa gets well."

"No! No! Let me stay with you!"

"But how will Papa get better without your smiles to bring him sunshine?" Emily forced the words through a throat swollen with misery as she carried the little girl up the wide steps to where a housemaid was waiting. The woman's cheeks were tear-streaked, her kind eyes giving Emily some vague comfort.

"Take care of her for me," Emily couldn't stop the sob that rose in her throat. "Oh, God, she's so little . . ."

"I will, ma'am. I've three children of my own, I do. 'Tis a sinful wicked thing the d'Autrecourts be doing to you."

"Jenny, I'll come back for you. When Papa is well, I'll come back." Emily pressed a final desperate kiss against Jenny's cheek, then began the agonizing task of peeling those clinging arms away from her neck.

The child screamed, kicked, her little fingers clawing for purchase about her mother. But the housemaid got hold of her and pulled her away.

"Poor lamb, poor little lamb," she cooed as the child shrieked with terror.

Emily pressed her hand against her mouth and ran down the rain-slicked stairs. Sobbing, she ran past the rickety coach and along the road where she and Alexander had played as children, sobbing, certain that no greater agony could ever befall her.

She had been wrong.

When she had returned to Avonstea two weeks later, it was to find black wreaths of mourning upon those massive doors.

Alexander was dead, his tortured soul at peace. But the fever that had carried him away had been a greedy one.

It had stolen away forever the child who had been Emily's only joy.

4

$\mathcal{E}$mily struggled to draw back from the yawning chasm of her grief and to return her thoughts to the present. She raised her face from her hands, feeling drained, as she always did when the memories came too strong. Her gaze swept over the tiny shop like that of someone freshly wakened from a nightmare. She touched the tumble of ribbons that littered the floor, and traced trembling fingers over the edge of a crushed bonnet as if to assure herself that they were real.

It had been five years since she had last stood at the doorway of the ducal seat of Avonstea. Five years since Tulbridge had taken her out to the d'Autrecourt burial grounds to see the graves of her husband and child.

When he'd finally urged her away, she had wandered blindly, on the very fringes of sanity. She had felt nothing but the tearing jaws of her grief, had struggled merely to exist. She had been lonely. Agonizingly lonely.

"I have no one. . . ."

The words of the child, Lucy, echoed in Emily's head. In the space of an hour the little girl had ripped open the wounds Emily had suffered those many years ago. She had made Emily's own grief pour forth like poison from a festering sore.

Defenses. There were so many defenses wrapped about the little girl. An unbreachable armor of denial. Emily was certain of it. She was a master at building such defenses of her own.

There were times when Emily almost believed that she had tucked away the grief, and all she had left was the dull ache in her chest where Jenny had once been.

She had helped little boys recover the toy boats they'd lost while sailing at Saint James's Park. She had sewn bonnets for little girls and tied the ribbons beneath their chins. She had even managed a stiff smile as she listened to harried mamas complain about the behavior of their children.

But it was all an illusion. She had known it in her heart. That was why she had fled England. To escape.

Yet was it possible to make a new beginning when she was really running away? Was it possible to build a new life when all during the voyage from Bristol she had fingered dried rose blossoms that had been taken not from a homeplace she wanted to remember always but from a tiny grave?

What had she expected to find here in this strange and foreign land that was so raw and so new?

Peace?

The sudden rap upon the door reverberated like cannon fire in the silent room. Emily clambered to her feet and scrubbed at her cheeks with the back of her hand, wiping away the last traces of her tears.

Who in God's name could it be?

She couldn't face anyone right now. She didn't have the fortitude to fend off curious glances or questions designed to determine where her political loyalties lay. She didn't have the energy to explain the total disaster that had befallen her shop.

But what if it was Ian Blackheath, returning after his search for Lucy? What if he hadn't been able to find the child after all?

Emily shook back her hair and stiffened her spine as the knocking grew more insistent. She shifted to peek past a display of bonnets in the window, her eyes fixing on the person standing at the door.

Bright scarlet regimentals were a vivid slash in the tapestry of passersby as the tall dragoon on Emily's doorstep observed the shop with increasing concern.

Emily's heart plunged to her toes. Oh, God, what was he doing here, striding up to her shop in broad daylight with half of Williamsburg watching?

Her fingers shaking, she unlatched the door and swung it open. Plumed hat in hand, Captain Reginald Atwood of His Majesty's dragoons met her with his usual winning smile. But as his gaze locked on her face and then on the chaos of the shop, his features twisted with outrage. He charged past her, surveying the damage with a furious protective light in his eyes.

"My dearest lady! What has happened here?" Atwood demanded, hastily closing the door behind him. "Don't tell me these villainous rebels have discovered your purpose here already? If that bastard Pendragon has dared to attack you—"

"It is nothing like that, Captain Atwood, I assure you."

Atwood's shoulders sagged with relief. "Whatever has happened here, I can only be thankful that the latest missive is not due for another week," he said. "The information it contains is vital."

"The doll dressed in blue satin? A woman delivered it just before the shop closed last evening."

Atwood blanched. "My God, then—"

"Don't fear. It's tucked safe beneath the counter."

"But if no rebel has been searching for the missive, why such mass destruction?" Atwood asked, waving one hand at the damage.

Emily couldn't help the tiny smile that curled her lips. "There was some difficulty with a little girl and she tipped over the shelf."

"A child caused all this? And just where was her mother when she was displaying such an unattractive temper?"

"Her mother is dead. It seems her uncle is to be her guardian, a prospect neither the child nor the man is adapting to very amicably."

"I can't say that I blame the uncle. No sane person would

want to be saddled with a child who would hurl things in a fit of temper. Such passions are very distressing in female children. If the girl were in my care, I would curb such behavior immediately. An acquaintance with a willow switch should suffice."

Emily bristled. "You cannot *curb* a child's grief, Captain. You can only help her to battle through it as best she can."

Atwood flushed at the sudden defensiveness in Emily's voice. "No doubt you are right, my dear," he said. "You must forgive me if I am a bit overzealous. Dealing with soldiers day in and day out, I am particularly sensitive to a lack of discipline."

With some shyness, Atwood reached out, and Emily was surprised to feel his fingers close about her hand. "As to children," he said softly, "I am only an ignorant bachelor, without a woman's wisdom in such matters. But there have been times these past weeks, my dear lady, when I've begun to hope you might teach me." There was something vaguely discordant in the self-deprecating smile he gave her, but his palm was warm, his fingers strong.

It had been such a long time since Emily had been touched by anyone that she couldn't stop herself from savoring the feel of Atwood's hand—until the memory of another man's touch made her flush and draw away. The imprint of Ian Blackheath's hard-muscled body seemed to have branded itself on hers, the feel of those strong hands engulfing hers making her stomach quiver.

More than a little flustered, she drew away from the captain. She stooped to retrieve a length of ribbon and busied herself by winding it around her hand.

"I have been too forward," Atwood said quietly. "I'm sorry."

Emily raised her eyes to his, forcing a half smile. "You've been nothing but kind, Captain Atwood."

"I would be more than kind if you would let me. And I would guard you with my life, but"—his brow creased, and he examined the plume on his tricorne—"sometimes I fear even that might not be enough. Mrs. d'Autrecourt, I admire your courage in aiding the Crown in this way. And I can't tell you how much pleasure your presence has brought to me, personally—a wild English rose in the middle of these colonial thorns. But you must know that it is a dangerous task you've undertaken."

He looked so solemn, an almost boyish sweetness in his features, that she couldn't help but like the man. "Captain, I took the possibility of danger into consideration before I agreed to come to Williamsburg."

"Of course you did. But I want you to be especially careful at present. You see, there was an . . . incident that . . . By God, madam, I'm a soldier, and as such, I should be accustomed to violence. But this goes far beyond any horror I've ever heard of."

"An *incident?*"

"A wigmaker named Lemming Crane was torn from his bed last night under the very noses of my men, I'm ashamed to say. He was abducted by that rebel scoundrel who calls himself Pendragon."

The nape of Emily's neck prickled, ice water seeming to trickle down her spine. Pendragon. The name seemed to be woven of the mysteries of the night—dark, terrifying. She had heard snippets of gossip about the patriot raider, bits of conversations that died whenever she came near—An Englishwoman, an enemy, not to be trusted. "You say Crane was abducted," she prodded. "But why?"

Atwood's eyes clouded with distress. "He was not unlike you, madam," he said hesitantly. "In secret service to the Crown."

Emily's heart gave an odd lurch. "He was . . . like me?"

"Not really! In truth, he was somewhat of a fool. We all laughed at him. But he *was* one of our sources for information."

"I see. What happened to him? You must have some idea."

Atwood's Adam's apple bobbed in his throat. He looked away. "I don't know for certain. There are only rumors."

"Tell me."

"They say that—" Atwood paused for a heartbeat. "They

say that Pendragon and his band buried Lemming Crane—alive."

Emily's stomach churned, and she pressed her fingers to her lips, bile rising in her throat to mingle with the sharp tang of fear. "Merciful heavens!" she gasped, turning horrified eyes up to Atwood. "What kind of a monster would do such a thing?"

"Rebel scum mounting insurrection against his king. A traitor hungry to rape England, steal away her rightful taxes." Atwood's eyes were alive with loathing. "The fools around here see the raider as a hero. But Pendragon is a villain in the common way. A murderer thirsting for blood, taking pleasure in the kill."

"If this Pendragon discovered the truth about Mr. Crane, who is to say he hasn't identified the rest of us as well? If he were to discover that I've been passing along messages—"

"You mustn't even think about such a thing!" Atwood's hands caught hers again. "Crane was a careless fool, while you are a very brave and intelligent woman, far beyond that traitorous villain's touch. And anyway, I am confident Pendragon's reign of terror will soon be over. We are closing in on the rabid cur. In fact, my superiors are hoping that the information contained in the doll that has just been delivered will hold the clues we need to run the bastard to ground."

Remembering Lucy cradling that doll against her little chest, Emily was as stricken as if she had seen the girl cuddling a viper.

Totally unaware of the turmoil inside Emily, the captain continued. "The fact that this doll might hold news of Pendragon is the reason I came today. I wanted to inform you that when the message arrived I would fetch it myself rather than passing it along through the usual channels. My superiors will be overjoyed when I deliver it to them early. The sooner the rebel dog's neck is snapped by a hangman's noose, the better loyal citizens like you will sleep at night."

"Of course," Emily said, hating the gruesome picture Atwood's words invoked—a man dangling from a noose, his eyes bulging, his mouth gasping for air. It was a horrifying vision set in counterpoint to that of another man clawing at the earth from the depths of a grave.

Her fingers shook as she picked at a frayed end of the ribbon in her hand. "I can only wish you godspeed in your mission, Captain. Let me wrap the doll for you at once."

Emily hurried behind the counter where she had placed the doll during the altercation with Lucy. But as her gaze fixed on the ledge under the counter, her chest convulsed with horror.

She grabbed the counter's edge to keep her balance, her hand running with desperation over the neatly folded piles of cloth that were to be made into dresses her customers had ordered.

At last she forced herself to meet Captain Atwood's questioning gaze.

"The—the doll. It's gone."

"What do you mean it's *gone?*" His face turned ice white as Atwood lunged behind the counter to look for himself, clawing through the materials that were stored there. "It couldn't have just walked away!"

"It did. I mean, it didn't." Emily stammered, her fingers knotting in her skirts. "It must have been taken by the little girl I was telling you about earlier. The argument we had was over the doll. She wanted it."

"Do you mean to tell me you allowed a child to walk out of here with vital communication?"

"No! I took the doll away from her and tucked it beneath the counter just as her uncle returned. But she was so upset that she tipped over the shelf and ran out the back through the counting room. She must have taken the doll in the confusion."

Atwood's face turned red with fury. "By God, we shall see if she's quite so brazen when she faces the courts for this! In England we do not tolerate thieves!"

Emily blanched as she recalled her visits to the prisoners at Newgate. The nightmarish images had stalked her ever since. Pinched faces had stared vacantly out from behind iron bars, many of them children who were locked in the jaws of English "justice," where the harshest of penalties were handed down to starving people for the crime of stealing a crust of bread.

The prospect of Lucy at the mercy of such a system was unbearable, and Emily was certain that the child would make things even worse with her ill-guarded tongue.

"You will tell me the name of this hell-spawned brat at once!" Atwood demanded. "I shall teach her what it means to steal from the English Crown!"

Desperate, Emily groped for a way to shield the defiant little girl. "Captain Atwood, the child doesn't know that she's taken anything but a fashion baby. A plaything," she reasoned. "How are you going to explain yourself if you go charging into her house—one of the king's soldiers demanding a doll from a child? What will you say to her uncle?"

Atwood slammed his fist against the counter. "I will have that doll! The information it contains could be vital."

"It *could* be," Emily echoed. "And then again, it might *not*. What if this particular doll doesn't hold the information you need? What if that information is in the next doll to arrive here, or the next? The instant you interfere, people's suspicions will be aroused against me. From what you have said about this raider, Pendragon, I've gathered that he is ruthless and cunning. If he discovers my complicity in these activities, I've no doubt he will crush me as thoroughly as he did Lemming Crane."

Giving voice to those fears made them loom in Emily's consciousness like great chill shadows. "Think, Captain Atwood. If Pendragon were to dispose of me in some equally . . . heinous manner, you would have no way of receiving future messages."

"What would you have me do?" Atwood blustered. "Stand by while that message is lost?"

"No. Let me attempt to retrieve it myself. Lucy's uncle knows about the child's fascination with the doll and about my refusal to sell it. I'm certain I can get it back without jeopardizing my position here."

"Blast it, Mrs. d'Autrecourt. I don't know."

"Please." She looked up at him through the fans of her lashes, using the only weapon she had left—the attraction she had seen in Atwood's eyes minutes earlier. "Trust me, Captain Atwood," she cajoled. "I won't fail you."

He paced the length of the shop, reluctance in every line of his face. "I don't like complications," he muttered. "If the doll is lost, it will look bad on my record."

"There is almost no danger of that happening. And besides, wouldn't it look worse on your record if we were to rush in and reveal that messages are being passed in this shop? Mr. Fraser went to a great deal of trouble to establish me here. I can't imagine he would appreciate having his plan ruined before a month was out, especially since he lost Mr. Crane so recently."

The mention of Stirling Fraser appeared to daunt Atwood somewhat. He tugged at his neckcloth. Emily crossed to where he stood, tipping her face up to his.

"Please, Reginald," she said, calling him by his given name for the first time. "I don't mean to press you, but I know that I'm right in this. The doll is safer with Lucy than if it were locked in the king's own treasury. The child wanted it so desperately that I'm certain she has it tucked away somewhere safe. Besides, it's possible that her uncle has already discovered her mischief. He could be on his way back to return the doll even as we speak."

Atwood stalked across the room, restless with indecision. After a moment he turned with a disgruntled sigh. "I suppose there is little choice except to do as you say."

"I will not fail you," she said quietly, wishing she were as certain as she sounded.

"I'd advise that you don't." Atwood's jaw clenched. "I have a certain affection for you, Mrs. d'Autrecourt, but my superiors have little patience when affairs like this one are bungled. They would not be swayed by your considerable beauty."

It was a warning. Emily heeded it well. "I understand the risk," she said, squaring her shoulders.

"Do you? I sincerely hope so." Atwood grimaced. "However, I do have to set one condition if I am to go along with this mad scheme of yours."

"Condition?" For a moment Emily was haunted by memories of Alexander's friends, who sometimes attempted to maneuver her into sordid affairs. Men demanding the only price that seemed to satisfy their sense of worth, and their lust. Surely Atwood would not be so . . . Emily swallowed hard. What did she really know about the English captain other than the fact that he had been polite when ever they had met and had begged her to give him news of the homeland he obviously missed so much?

"You needn't be frightened of me, Emily," Atwood gave her a wounded look, and she was chagrined to realize that he had read her thoughts in her eyes. "I would never be so ungentlemanly as to demand of a lady anything she would not give freely."

"Of course not. I'm sorry."

"My condition has to do with the doll. You must give me the name of the child and that of her uncle as well. If, God forbid, something should happen to you, I must have some way to trace the message."

Emily hesitated.

"Come, Emily," Atwood murmured. "I am trusting you. It's only fair that you should do the same."

Emily vacillated for a moment more, but in the end she knew she had no choice. "The little girl's name is Lucy," she said at last. "Lucy Dubbonet. She is staying with her uncle, a planter by the name of Ian Blackheath."

"Blackheath!"

If she'd said the child lived with Satan, Atwood couldn't have been any more stunned. "That scoundrel is said to rival Bacchus in his excesses," Atwood roared. "I'll not have a virtuous lady like you plunging into that den of iniquity!"

Emily forced a smile, remembering all too well her own reaction to Flavia Varden's descriptions of Blackheath's outlandish house parties. But Emily didn't dare reveal her sick dread to the man standing, so outraged, before her.

"I'm certain my virtue is quite safe," Emily soothed. "I've

met Mr. Blackheath already and we were not overly impressed by each other."

Emily tried to keep a guilty flush from staining her cheeks as she remembered certain parts of Blackheath's anatomy that had been impressed quite relentlessly against her own.

"Don't be lulled into a false sense of security by the man. It's said he could have seduced the vestal virgins if he'd had a mind to." Atwood stopped, embarrassed. He frowned, suddenly lost in his own thoughts. "And yet," he said at last, "maybe it's not such a bad thing that Blackheath is involved after all. At least we don't have to worry about the message falling into enemy hands. It's well known that Blackheath cares for nothing except his own decadent pleasures. From the gossip bandied about, it's astonishing the man can even raise himself from his bed in the morning, he's so far gone with drink and women."

As if suddenly remembering that he was in the presence of a lady, Atwood flushed. "I'm sorry . . . Emily. I didn't mean to scandalize you with such talk. It's just that I'm a little . . . tense at present."

"I understand."

An earnest light shone in Atwood's eyes. "You will take care?" he said, capturing her hand. "I do not want any harm to befall you."

"I'll be careful."

Atwood chewed meditatively at the corner of his lip. "In the meantime I think it best if you're not alone here any longer, what with that bastard Pendragon on a rampage." He smiled, as if just seizing upon some idea. "I think your shop is becoming so profitable that you have been forced to take on another seamstress. The man who owns your indenture is thrilled, of course."

"Hire someone else?" Emily pulled her hand from Atwood's grip, the thought of some stranger barging into her hard-won sanctuary dismaying her. "No. I don't think—"

"After what happened with Crane, I'm afraid I have to insist. Also, if you're going to travel to the Blackheath plantation, there must be someone else here to receive messages."

"You mean, another . . . spy?" That was an even more disturbing thought. "If loyalists are so plentiful that you can just pluck one from the streets at a moment's notice, why did Mr. Fraser go to such lengths to hire me?"

"This person would not be involved in our . . . business transactions. She would be just what she seems. A helper for you. Someone to sound the alarm if you should be visited by Pendragon. Someone to accept deliveries when you are gone. One of my men has a daughter who would suit well enough. She's very willing, if somewhat dull-witted, and she is tolerably adept with a needle. I shall send her to you tomorrow morning."

"No. I'd so much rather you would not do that."

"This is not something I can leave up to you, Emily. I'm already taking a great risk on your behalf. I can only hope I won't regret it."

Something in his face made Emily fall silent, afraid she might jeopardize the victory she had already won.

Atwood straightened his coat, his mouth suddenly grim. "Of course, things could get very awkward if my superiors somehow receive word that the message arrived early. There is always the chance . . ." Atwood paused. "One week is the most time I can possibly give you to retrieve the doll, Emily. I don't want to frighten you, but you must be aware of the danger you are in. The men who command me are not tolerant of mistakes. And Pendragon has the devil's own insight when it comes to ferreting out secrets like the one you are keeping now. I don't want to find you buried by the brigand in some hellish grave."

Emily fought back a shudder as Atwood raised her hand to his lips and pressed a kiss to her fear-whitened knuckles. "Good-bye, my dear," he said, then turned and left the shop.

Emily locked the door behind him and made her way into her private quarters in the back room, Atwood's warnings ringing in her ears.

Oh, God, what had she done? What had ever made her believe she could come here and play at being a spy? The idea had sounded so simple, so reasonable, when Stirling

Fraser had proposed it to her two months ago. One year of minimal danger in exchange for a new life. One year of service to the Crown while she built up a shop that would be hers to keep when her period of servitude ended.

Fraser had offered her a chance at independence. He had offered her a chance at prosperity—as much as her own wits and ambition could buy her.

In return she merely had to turn a blind eye while his other employees dropped off parcels and message-carrying dolls. She only had to smile across the counter and give those parcels to other couriers who would carry them on their way.

True, in some vague way she had wondered what might happen if some rebel demanded the parcel or uncovered her own part in this plan.

But in the end, she had agreed.

She had wanted so much to believe this was her chance. . . .

She sank onto her bed. How could she have been such a fool?

Now, because of her ineptitude, she had put not only her own life but the life of an innocent child in danger as well. For if Atwood's superiors would be unforgiving to one of their own agents, they would be doubly so when it came to someone who was not in their employ.

Someone like a child who had stumbled onto a deadly secret.

No. Lucy would be fine. She would be safe, Emily vowed to herself fiercely.

Emily had been shunted aside while death had claimed her own daughter. She had felt helpless. Responsible. Certain it was her fault that her child had died, that if she had been with Jenny, she could have held back the hand of death.

She would not be rendered helpless again.

She would not allow another child to suffer because of her mistakes.

Emily stood up and hurried over to a cracked looking glass that hung on the wall. The reflection staring back at her was ravaged by the multitude of emotions that had racked her this day. But the eyes that were ringed with blue smudges of exhaustion stared back at her with hard resolve.

After Ian Blackheath and his niece had left the shop, Emily had wanted nothing more than to block their existence from her mind and heart.

But now . . . now there was no help for it. After straightening the shop, she would hire a horse to take her to Blackheath plantation.

Emily couldn't stop the shimmer of unease that came to her eyes.

She would offer anything, say anything, do anything, to protect Lucy Dubbonet from this danger—even if she had to wade through a hundred of Ian Blackheath's mistresses in the process.

5

*I*an stalked into the dining room at Blackheath Hall, his lips compressed in a white line. His shirt and waistcoat hung open, exposing a generous vee of hair-roughened chest. A fresh gash, an inch long, angled to the left of his chin, and his eyes glittered dangerously beneath heavy dark brows.

Those eyes fixed on Anthony Gray with unholy menace.

"If you laugh, damn your hide, I'll flay you alive!"

Gray contemplated him over the rim of a goblet of wine, his lips quivering with the effort it took to keep them in a solemn line. "My dear Ian, I know we rarely stand on ceremony here, but you might consider covering yourself decently. Buttoning your shirt, for example. Fastening your waistcoat."

"I would be happy to do so if it were not for one small problem," Ian said between gritted teeth. "Tell me, do you *see* any fastenings on my shirt? Look here, at my waistcoat —my *favorite* goddamn waistcoat," Ian snarled, holding the placket of the vest toward his friend. "Do you *see* any buttons?"

Tony's throat worked convulsively as he examined the shredded threads that still clung to the cloth where the elegant rows of buttons should have been. "My dear fellow, they seem to have gone missing," Tony observed. "Don't tell me. You've had a tiff with one of your mistresses and she's gotten revenge."

"My mistresses aren't sly enough for this kind of a coup. No. It was that hell-spawned niece of mine, taking her pound of flesh! Or rather her pound of buttons."

"Lucy?"

"She was vexed with me because she saw some infernal doll at the dressmaker's shop this afternoon and she wanted it."

"I've always taken you for a reasonably intelligent man," Tony interjected. "You should have struck your colors and surrendered the field at once. Bought her the doll and saved yourself a cartload of trouble."

Ian flung himself into a chair. "I tried, by God's blood. But the blasted dressmaker wouldn't sell it! She said the ladies must be able to view the latest fashions," Ian mimicked, "and damn the cost to me! Hell, by the time I was done, I would have traded *you* to get the doll and have Lucy leave me in peace."

"Sounds like a most desperate situation, eh?"

"Let's just say that Lucy totally destroyed the woman's shop in her fury. Then the little wretch ran away. I found her three hours later in Applebea's garden sipping lemonade, cool as you please, while regaling the town's biggest gossip about everything that has happened since she arrived at Blackheath Hall last night—including my more colorful language and the fact that I was roaring drunk."

"Oh, Lord, that . . . that is unfortunate," Tony choked out, his eyes sparkling.

Ian took a gulp of wine from his goblet, as if to sustain himself for the story to come.

"You know I'm a reasonable man, Tony. I tried to remember what you had said about being tolerant with the girl. I tried to soothe her. Cozen her. Bloody *bribe* her, for God's sake. The whole way home I kept telling her it wasn't my fault that I couldn't get her the doll, that I'd get her another one the next time we went to town, but the hell-spawned brat just sat there with *that look* on her face."

"That look?"

"The one that makes me want to check to see if she's set my coattails afire. When we got home, off she went, meek as some little cherub." Ian's jaw knotted. "I should have *known* there would be trouble."

Tony tried manfully to squelch a chuckle. "You perceive me positively agog with curiosity."

"I go into my study to enjoy a little Madeira and read a bit of that John Locke I've been picking at," Ian continued in long-suffering accents. "Then I retire upstairs to prepare for dinner. I'm leaned back in my chair, with Priam shaving me, when *she* comes sashaying in."

"Into your bed chamber?"

"Yes, by God, bold as you please. She told me that before her papa died, she used to watch him shave every morning. It was her favorite time. Well, what the blazes could I say to that? She leaned against my knees, watching for a while. And I must say she looked particularly winning—she's a fetching little thing when she gives you that big-eyed look. I was actually beginning to be amused by her chatter. *Until* she smiled the most poisonous smile I've ever seen and told me that she had taken the 'cunning little scissors' out of Mrs. Willoby's sewing basket and snipped every button off every coat and waistcoat I own. I came out of the chair like cannon shot, causing Priam to lay open my chin. I flung open the clothespress, and sure enough, the little demon had taken every button I owned. She had also shredded my neckcloths and cut the fastenings off my breeches."

"Good God," Tony chortled. "You must have been swearing like a sinner trapped in church."

"The only fastenings she *didn't* cut up," Ian continued, "were the ones on the shirt I loaned her to sleep in last night. And that is only because the little hellion *won't give it back!*"

"How . . . enterprising of her." Twin imps danced in Gray's eyes. "Perhaps you could pay her a ransom for the return of the buttons—say, a fortune in peppermint drops or nonpareils."

"Unless I decide to drown the little wretch, which is not out of the question at the moment. In any event, the buttons are lost for good. You see, she 'adored' listening to the sound they made when they plopped into the well."

"I shall have to try doing that myself sometime. Tell me, is she joining us for dinner so that I can ask her to explain the proper technique?"

"That depends on whether or not she has any instinct for survival. I shan't be surprised if Cook serves her up a hemlock tart."

"Come now! Not only is Mattie the finest cook in Virginia, she also *loves* children! She usually has half a dozen of the little beggars trailing after her."

Ian arched one brow, his mouth grim. "Let's just say that it's hard work ruining someone's entire wardrobe. It made Lucy 'intolerable hungry.' So she slipped down into the pantry for a snack. The apples were all so lovely that she couldn't make up her mind which one to eat. So she took one bite out of every apple in the barrel. Next, she opened a whole shelf full of Mattie's preserves and took a fingerful of each."

Tony gave a snort of laughter. "Ian, don't be absurd! How could such a little thing get those jars open?"

"I don't know!" Ian snarled. "She probably snapped them off with her teeth. All I'm interested in right now is whether or not you've written a letter of introduction for the little hellcat to that school your sister went to."

Tony extended a folded sheet of paper, his seal in wax at the edges. "Here you are, sir. But after hearing about this campaign the child has mounted, I think it would be more useful to nail her into a keg and ship her off to Samuel Adams in Boston. She seems even more adept at fomenting rebellion than he is."

"Ah, yes, this is all incredibly amusing," Ian said caustically. "A revolution would be a relief in comparison to housing that child beneath my roof!"

"Come, now, Ian. It's not like you to preach propriety. Remember when we were at Hargrove's and the Latin master whipped me for neglecting to learn how to conjugate my verbs? As I recall, you filled his shoes up with honey."

"That was different! The bastard deserved it."

"Obviously Lucy thinks you deserve to be tormented, too," Tony reasoned. "It couldn't have been pleasant being greeted the way she was last night."

Ian sputtered a protest, but Gray held up one hand. "I know that you'd had one devil of a night and that you were half drowned in brandy, but that was hardly Lucy's fault. Nor was it Lucy's fault that she was orphaned and dumped on your doorstep. Give the little one a chance to adjust, and I'm sure these childish pranks will stop. You must be patient with the poor little moppet."

"Gray, you don't have the least idea what I am dealing with here!" Ian snapped. "I'm half crazed with wondering what the devil she'll do next—"

Ian's words were cut off by a howl of dismay from the corridor beyond.

He swore. "Unfortunately I think we're about to find out."

At that instant the dining room door slammed open and Lucy raced in, her rose-pink satin somewhat crumpled, her hands hidden suspiciously behind her back.

Three steps behind her was Ian's most trusted groom. Ian had seen the man deal with countless stable yard disasters—stallions gone wild, mares nearly dying while bringing forth their foals. There had even been a stable fire once that old Buckley had single-handedly managed to extinguish while saving every animal in the barn.

But this time the groom looked as if he'd been dragged through a battlefield under the belly of one of his cherished horses. "Oh, sir!" he pleaded brokenly. "Pray, it was not my fault! I do a good job, I do, watching over the darlings. I'd never have allowed her to . . . if I had known. I—"

"Calm yourself, Buckley," Ian commanded. "Lucy, what the blazes have you done now?"

"I used the cunning little scissors again," Lucy said, flouncing over to take a seat beside Tony. "I just couldn't resist—"

"I had given him a share of oats and some water." Buckley was rattling on like a battle-shocked soldier. "I was taking care of him just as I always have. But when I went to get cloths to rub him down, she'd cut off his tail!"

"Oh, Lord, not Ian's stallion!" Tony choked into his wine with horrified amusement.

"No, s-sir!" Buckley stammered. "Not Master Ian's. She . . . she did it to *your* mount!"

The look on Gray's face would have been alarming if Ian had not enjoyed it so much. At that instant Lucy pulled her hands from behind her back, displaying the shiny little scissors and a thick, silky braid of tail hair tied up in strips cut from one of Ian's neckcloths.

"You can have this back now, Mr. Gray," she said sweetly, placing the rope of horsehair on Tony's empty plate. "I'm all done practicing my braiding."

"Have it . . . back . . ." Tony wheezed, staggering to his feet. "By God, I—"

"Whoa, now, Gray," Ian cautioned, holding up one hand. "Remember what you said about childish pranks a few moments ago?"

"My horse! My . . . By God . . ." Tony groped across the table, scooping up the scissors. "I'll teach you a lesson, you little wretch! I'll shear *your* hair and practice tying it about *your neck!*"

With a wail, Lucy raced out the dining room door, upsetting a servant and sending a glass tree of sweetmeats shattering against the wall.

Ian raced after her in hot pursuit, knowing he'd better get ahold of her before Tony made good his threat. The child would have been far wiser to snip off Tony's own locks than to crop those of his cherished stallion.

"Lucy! Lucy, I order you to stop this instant!" Ian bellowed, racing down the hall. She was heading for the front door at full tilt. Christ, he'd spent half the afternoon searching for her in town; he wasn't going to spend the night searching for her on his own lands.

With a cry, she threw open the heavy door and careened out into the darkness. In desperation, Ian hurled himself toward her, catching a handful of her skirts. There was a ripping sound and a cry of a very different sort, as Ian and the child tumbled onto the wide front step. Ian grabbed the child's ankle as she wailed and kicked.

"Ian, quick, take my neckcloth," Tony snarled, shoving the scarf toward him. "Truss her up before she can do any more damage!"

At that instant Ian became aware of the clicking of heels hastening toward them from the carriage circle, a waterfall of pale blue skirts all but engulfing them. "I think that is just about enough, all of you!"

"Shut up and make yourself useful, whoever the hell you are! Grab her arms!" Ian ordered, arching his head back to glare up that fall of skirts. He hadn't expected to see the dark-haired figure who stood glaring down at him with affronted violet eyes.

He groaned inwardly as he looked into the indignant face of Emily d'Autrecourt, illuminated by the flicker of lights on either side of the doorway.

"You should be ashamed of yourselves!" she scolded. "Two grown men picking on a child!"

"That's no child!" Tony blustered. "She—"

In one fluid movement Emily scooped the little girl out of Ian's astonished grasp. Lucy flung her arms around the woman, clinging to her as if she were caught in a raging river and Emily d'Autrecourt was a rope.

"Have a care, madam!" Tony cried out warning. "The little wretch bites!"

"I *don't* bite!" Lucy cried, outraged. "It is very naughty to bite!"

Ian swore under his breath as he levered himself to a sitting position.

Lucy continued with wounded dignity. "I only wanted to practice braiding, and the horse had such lovely long hair! I didn't think the horse would miss it if I took just a little! But *he* started chasing me and said he would take the scissors and cut off *my* hair and—"

Ian got to his feet, feeling surly and defensive and more embarrassed than he'd ever been in his life.

"Mrs. d'Autrecourt, after the way Lucy behaved in your

shop, you above anyone should know what she's capable of!
Now, as you can see, we are rather busy at present, so
just . . . just dump whatever clothes you've brought for her
in the hallway, and we'll settle the bill later."

"I haven't brought any clothing. There is something I
need to discuss with . . ." Those huge violet eyes shifted
from Lucy's tear-streaked face to his furious one, and the
sentence trailed off. Ian couldn't be certain if the woman
had stopped because of the expression in his eyes or in
Lucy's. "Mr. Blackheath, I've come a very long way. If I
could just have a few moments of your time."

"Oh, bloody hell," Ian said, getting to his feet. "Come in,
then. Things can hardly get any worse than they already
are."

Ian grasped Lucy by the shoulders and glared into his
niece's belligerent face. "Lucy, I shall tell Cook to send a
supper tray to your room. If you so much as touch a single
apple, a single jar of preserves, a single horse, or a single
button on these premises, I will personally snip off every
curl on your head. Do we understand each other?"

"You are terrible mean!" the child shrilled, yanking away
from him. "I want to go back to Vicar Clyvedon's!"

"It's too late! I doubt a heavenly mandate could make him
take you back!"

"I don't want to stay with you anymore!"

"Believe me," Ian shouted, "I'm trying to remedy that
situation as quickly as I can! Now, *go.*"

The little girl turned and swept regally into the house.
Silence fell. Even the usually loquacious Tony was at a loss
for words. Probably, Ian thought with grim amusement,
Gray was still in shock from the attack upon his treasured
stallion.

"I suppose introductions are in order," Ian said, feeling
ridiculous. "Mrs. Emily d'Autrecourt, this is Mr. Anthony
Gray. Tony, this is the lady whose shop Lucy destroyed this
morning before she ran away."

Tony gave the woman a look filled with soulful commiseration. "I'm terribly sorry."

But Ian wasn't specifically certain what Tony was expressing his regret over—the ruined shop, the shorn stallion, or ever having set foot on Blackheath land to begin with.

"If you will, madam?" Ian said, gesturing to the open door. A gaggle of servants, who had been watching the tussle with Lucy with great interest, scattered to the corners of the house, only poor Buckley standing there, sniffling into the dirty sleeve of his shirt.

"I didn't know she was a demon! I didn't know. Poor shorn darling. The whole stable yard will be pure laughing at him."

Ian stalked down the hallway and entered his study, the sound of Emily d'Autrecourt's footsteps following him. He didn't turn to look at her; he only went to a wooden stand and poured himself a glass of Madeira.

He heard the woman softly shut the door. "Mr. Blackheath, I'm afraid we have a—a small problem."

"A *small* problem?" Ian echoed with a harsh laugh. "That would be pleasant for a change!"

"Yes. Well, you see, Lucy . . ." the woman seemed to hesitate for a moment. "You remember the doll that Lucy wanted from my shop?"

"Vaguely. Considering that she almost crowned us both with a shelf when she didn't get it."

"Well, you see, I was looking for it just after you left, and . . ."

Ian turned to look at her, a muscle in his jaw throbbing. *"And?"*

Emily d'Autrecourt seemed only to stare at him, a kind of dazed light in her eyes. Her lips parted, her cheeks flushed, and she seemed to forcibly tear her gaze away from him. "And I think that—that she might have . . . have . . ."

"Have what, for God's sake?"

She licked her lips, as if they were suddenly dry, her gaze flitting about the room like a damned butterfly. "The doll . . . I believe that . . . that Lucy . . ."

"Hellfire and damnation, woman! Just look me in the eye and say whatever it is you came to say so I can get you the blazes out of here and deal with Lucy's latest disaster!"

Her face went scarlet, her chin jutting up. "I'm trying to!

But it's difficult to concentrate with you standing there, all bare!"

"Bare?" At that moment Ian became excruciatingly aware of a breeze ruffling his shirt, the coolness of a draft wisping over the heated skin of his chest where his clothes gaped open. He didn't so much as look down, but he was furious with himself for the instinctive urge he felt to grab the edges of his shirt and clutch them together.

Damn the woman! She made him feel as if he were sixteen again, caught swimming at the lake in nothing but his skin.

Disgusted, he scowled. "Mrs. d'Autrecourt, I didn't invite you here, so you can hardly expect to find me dressed for company. And truth to tell, I've had about enough of your holier-than-thou attitude about everything from the way I handle my niece to my choice of attire. If you must know, Lucy cut all the fastenings off my clothes. I suppose I should be glad she didn't carry her vengeance a bit further and snip up all the cloth as well."

"I—I see," she stammered. There was something innocent about the tentative sound of her voice and the becoming blush stealing along those delicate cheekbones. It made Ian feel jaded, wicked, as if he'd set out to make her uncomfortable on purpose.

The sensation made him furious.

He planted his hands on his hips, his eyes lit with a kind of fierce defiance. "Come now, madam. It's not as if you are some prim virgin to be shocked by a glimpse of a man's skin. You're a widowed woman. You've seen a man's chest before, I would imagine. And I'll be damned if I'm going to make a fool of myself by clutching my clothes together like a raw lad."

Emily tried to drag her gaze away, but in all her life, she had never seen a masculine chest like the one displayed so boldly before her.

His posture was rigid, tugging the linen of his shirt even farther apart, the white of the shirt accenting the hard, sun-bronzed plane it revealed. A gilding of crisp, dark hair webbed those sharply delineated muscles, glimmering in the candlelight.

Shadows pooled soft as velvet among the corded muscles of his throat and the dip above his collarbone. A crescent of deep brown nipple was just visible along the edge of white linen, while the vee of tanned flesh arrowing down toward his belly stirred in Emily a horrifying curiosity as to what lay beyond, in that velvety shadow.

"You've seen a man's chest before"—Blackheath's words mocked her.

True, she had caught rare glimpses of Alexander's chest, smooth and pale, without the dark mat of hair that gilded Blackheath's own.

Her husband might have had a fine chest, but it wasn't anything Emily could attest to. For in spite of four years of marriage and the baby that had been born of their union, she had never once seen her husband shirtless. She had only touched him, with almost agonizing shyness, through the fabric of his modest nightshirt.

Emily swallowed hard as she stared at Blackheath's blatantly sensual features, certain that *this* man would not take his wife by lifting only the hem of her night shift. Nor would he lavish apologies on her after he had spent his seed inside her.

No, a man like Ian Blackheath would demand far wilder pleasures. A dark, searing intensity Emily knew she couldn't even hope to guess.

"You were saying something about the doll, Mrs. d'Autrecourt," Blackheath prodded in measured accents.

Emily shook herself inwardly, her mind filling with far more imminent dangers than the power of Ian Blackheath's virility.

"The doll is gone."

"Is that all?" Ian gave a derisive snort. "Considering everything else that has gone on of late, you'll forgive me if I don't go into apoplexy."

Emily felt her cheeks burn. "I'm all but certain that Lucy has . . . taken it."

"You mean the girl stole it? You needn't look so nervous about making an outright accusation. Nothing that child

82

does could surprise me." Blackheath raked his hand back through that thick, dark hair. The contrast between his strong fingers and the silky tresses made Emily's pulse leap. She saw his fingers snag in the black ribbon that held it in a neat queue. With an oath, he yanked the bit of silk free, his hair flowing loose about his neck.

If he had looked like a master seducer moments before, he now looked like some pagan God, the fall of chestnut hair trailing down to his shoulder blades in a glossy mane.

Emily struggled to maintain some sort of hold on her rioting senses. "Mr. Blackheath, I must have that doll."

"Well, I sure as hell don't have it, and knowing Lucy, I assume she tossed it down the well with all my buttons!"

Emily paled at the suggestion that the child might have disposed of it. "No. She wanted that doll to love. She must have hidden it somewhere."

"And just *where* do you suppose she hid it? Under her bonnet? I was with her during the entire drive to the plantation, and I saw absolutely nothing that resembled a doll! Furthermore, if the child *had* brought it here, I imagine she would have wanted to play with it, wouldn't you?"

"I suppose," Emily said, the sick feeling inside her intensifying. "But she would have played secretly, so you wouldn't discover what she'd done and take it away."

"Perhaps." Blackheath seemed to consider that notion. "Still, if Lucy was playing with this doll she supposedly wanted so badly, Mrs. d'Autrecourt, when do you think she would have had time to wreak so much havoc about this house? It takes a great amount of time to do the kind of damage she's done this afternoon and evening."

The logic in his arguments made Emily's knees shake with alarm. She raised one hand to her throat. "That doll has to be here. You don't understand," she said in a quavery voice.

"It's only a doll," Blackheath's voice held a sudden tinge of gentleness. "You have half a dozen others scattered about the shop. I'll be happy to pay for your inconvenience."

Emily knit her fingers together, clenching them hard against the bubble of panic building inside her. She stole a glance at Ian Blackheath's hard-angled face and saw again that vague stirring of confusion in those incredibly blue eyes, felt again the prickle of foreboding.

God in heaven, what could she say? He'd think her mad if she continued to argue about the doll. Worse, he might come to suspect . . . Suspect what? she thought wildly. That the prim little London seamstress was really an English spy?

Still, she had to do something. . . .

She seized upon the only thing she could think of. "Mr. Blackheath, I know you think the doll is of small importance."

"That's true enough, in light of everything else."

"However, I doubt you were amused at what happened to your . . . clothing." Emily cursed her eyes for straying again to that deliciously masculine chest. "Nor," she said with a little croak, "can I imagine that Mr. Gray is particularly pleased about having his horse's tail shorn."

"You're bloody right about that, madam."

"If you want Lucy to stop doing things like this, you are going to have to take the child in hand."

Ian gave an eloquent grimace. "If I remember correctly, I was doing just that when you arrived. You seemed to take exception to it."

Emily's chin tipped up. "I hardly believe giving way to your own temper is going to help Lucy learn to control hers. If I were you, I would make the child accountable for her mischief. If she cuts off the buttons on a waistcoat, make her sit and sew them back on. If she clips the tails of the horses, let her be responsible for some of their care."

"Lucy neck deep in dirty straw? Now that *is* a pleasant thought."

"*And,*" Emily plunged on, "if she takes something that belongs to someone else, make her return it."

"A lovely theory, Madam Philosopher," Blackheath saluted her. "Tell me, just exactly how you propose I do all this? Half of my servants are threatening to quit. The other half are cowering in corners, afraid of drawing Lucy's attention. I ordered one of the housemaids to watch her, and you can see exactly what a wonderful job she did at the task.

Of course, it probably wasn't the poor girl's fault. I assume we'll find her locked up in the icehouse, or somewhere equally appealing, before the night is out. Now, unless *you* are willing to take the child in hand yourself, Mrs. d'Autrecourt, I suggest you mind your own infernal business."

He was flinging out the words as if they were a gauntlet—one he knew she would never pick up. Emily stared into those thunderous blue eyes and felt a hard tug deep inside her, in places she hadn't even known existed.

She was frightened, terribly frightened—by the recklessness in him, the intensity that seemed to pulse like blue flame.

But even more terrifying was that slight edge of weariness in his stunningly blue gaze. The hint of self-blame that clung about those full lips.

Why did she suddenly suspect that Ian Blackheath was every bit as angry and hurt as his niece?

She wanted to run, wanted to flee. Instead she met his gaze with a calm she didn't feel.

"All right, Mr. Blackheath. As long as I can travel to my shop when I need to, and as long as you give me complete control over the child, I'll do it."

If she had poleaxed Ian Blackheath the man couldn't have looked more stunned. "You'll *what?"*

"I'll be Lucy's governess until you can find someone more suitable, or until you send her away to school."

"You can't be serious. I wasn't! I . . ."

"You have a better solution?"

"No!" Blackheath said with almost comical haste. "I just can't believe that—that, knowing Lucy the way you do, you'd be willing to watch her. Flavia mentioned that you were indentured. I'd be happy to buy your papers, whatever the cost. God knows it would be worth it."

The thought of being *owned* by Ian Blackheath stirred up a dizzying torrent of fear and of something deeper. It made Emily's blood heat, her hands tremble with what could only have been dread.

"No, no. That will not be necessary. My employer and I

have a flexible agreement. As long as I keep up with my stitchery here, I'm sure he'll have no objection. I was going to hire another girl, anyway."

"No! I won't have her!" The fierce cry from the other side of the study door made both adults wheel around to see Lucy pushing the panel wide. It was evident from the look on her face that she had heard every word they'd said. "Go away, lady! Go back to your ugly little shop with your ugly little dresses and leave me alone!"

"Blast it, girl," Ian roared, his features white, more agitated than the occasion warranted. "What the devil are you doing?"

"Creeping around," Lucy said. "Listening at doors. It's one of my favorite games, and I'm most accomplished at it! I'm a liar, too! A good one! *She* was stupid enough to believe me."

"Is this what your mother taught you? Listening at doors?" Ian demanded. "Snooping about? Damn you, did no one ever warn you that it's dangerous to pry where you don't belong?"

Emily stared at him, astonished.

"How else can I find out people's secrets and make them do what I want them to?" Lucy flung back.

Something dangerous flashed across Blackheath's face.

"I won't tolerate that kind of behavior here, Lucy. I'm warning you." His voice held a low note of threat that most brave men would have run from.

Lucy Dubbonet only met him glare for glare, her little brows a slash over eyes simmering with challenge. *"I'm* warning *you!"* she said. "I won't have this lady near me! She wants to be mean to me, and you're going to let her!"

"Believe me, at the moment you are far safer with her than with me."

"No! I won't have her! And I won't give her the doll back! Not ever! I don't care what you do to me! I won't!"

Emily felt a swift stab of relief at the knowledge that the child had used the word "won't." She must have the plaything tucked away somewhere. Somewhere safe. Surely Emily could find it.

Even so, her heart went out to the little girl who suddenly appeared so pale and exhausted.

"Lucy, we have plenty of time to discuss the doll later," Emily put in, her voice firm yet soothing. "You've had a very big day."

"Don't pretend to be nice to me! I know what you're thinking! You think I am spoiled! And vexatious! And you want to be sneaky and make me think you like me."

"There are things about you that I admire very much. You are a very brave little girl. And resourceful."

"Stop saying that! You just want me to like you, so you can get me to tell you what you want to know! But then you'll go away, and you won't care about me anymore."

There was enough truth in the child's words to make Emily flinch inside.

"Lucy, we are more alike than you know," Emily said softly.

"We're not at all alike! I'm pretty and you . . . you look all prim and perfect. I'm very, very bad. Nobody likes me because I'm the most irksome child ever born!"

Emily winced, knowing that those were not Lucy's words. They were echoes from someone else, someone who had hurt the child far more deeply than even Lucy knew. Emily looked into the child's eyes, fighting the urge to smooth a hand over her curls, knowing instinctively that the child would reject any show of empathy. "I am certain you have to work very hard to be irksome. It must get very tiring."

Lucy's eyes grew round in astonishment. But the child was not accustomed to anyone slipping past her guard. Emily could see her grope inwardly for yet another verbal weapon.

Lucy turned to Ian, a light far too old for her years shining in her eyes. "You can't fool me, either! *I* know why *you* want her to stay! You'd lock me right up in my room forever and ever and not care about me at all! You just want her here so you can bed her!"

The child's blunt words made Emily's face flame with humiliation, her heart twisting in sympathy for the little girl whose innocence had been stripped away.

"You want to take her to bed with you and make those 'sgusting sounds like my mama's lovers did every night! But *she* won't dress up in Roman gauze and play conqueror the way that other woman in the shop wanted to do. She's a *lady*, all proper and pinch-nosed. She probably never even had a lover before."

"Lucy!" Ian bellowed. "Stop it at once."

"It's true!" the child snapped back at him. *"I* saw the way you were looking at her in that shop! Your eyes were practically popping out of your head."

"You're imagining things!" There was an edge to Blackheath's voice, but as Emily stared at him, she saw a dark flush spread onto those sharply drawn cheekbones, saw his fists clench. Her own cheeks burned.

"I'm not imagining things! I saw hundreds of men— hundreds and hundreds and hundreds—look at my mama like that! They would come with flowers and sweetmeats, and she would laugh at them. I laughed too. I laughed and laughed!" Her voice broke on a sob. "I'll laugh at you, too, when I find out your secrets! I'll tell everyone that you're lying with her! Everyone! And they'll believe me! Because . . . because I'm a . . . a most accomplished liar!" The child turned and ran out the door.

For long minutes Ian and Emily stood in suffocating silence. And Emily was surprised when she saw him pace to the window and stare out into the night, a rare vulnerability shadowing his fallen-angel features.

"Maybe your staying here isn't such an inspired idea after all," Blackheath said quietly. "The child is right about one thing. If she chose to spread gossip regarding the two of us . . . well, let's just say she wouldn't have to work very hard to make people believe that I'd taken you to my bed."

Just those words spoken in that smoky voice were enough to make Emily's hands shake.

He grimaced. "I have the very devil of a reputation."

"I suppose it would be hard not to, when you run about publicizing the fact that you are hosting house parties where the guests run about dressed in nothing but gauze."

There was the slightest ironic curve to the corners of his lips. "People do tend to take offense at my little entertainments."

"Mr. Blackheath, I learned a long time ago that if people choose to talk, you can't stop them. And that they are far more interested in spreading juicy lies than in telling the truth. As for Lucy's assumptions about what our relationship might be, I think it best if you understand something right away: I have absolutely no interest in going to any man's . . . bed. Ever again."

Blackheath's eyes darkened, and he reached out to trail those long fingers down the curve of her cheek. The contact was strangely tender, making little frissons of sensation sizzle beneath Emily's skin. "That would be a tragic waste, Emily Rose," he said softly, his eyes heating up. "Did you love him so much?"

"Him?"

"Your husband."

She couldn't seem to breathe as his gaze traveled to her trembling lips and clung there.

"I could make you forget him."

"I don't want to forget."

"Don't you?" The words were a murmur deep in his chest.

Emily stared into those vivid blue eyes, mesmerized, unable to keep herself from wondering what it would be like if Ian Blackheath drew just a little closer. If he tipped up her chin and touched her lips with that arrogant mouth that had given so many other women pleasure.

Just the thought of his other lovers made her flatten one hand against his chest as if to hold him at bay. But her palm came in contact with hot satin skin, rippling muscle, the prickly silk mat of hair covering Blackheath's bare chest.

"If that is an effort on your part to make me not want you, it was a drastic tactical error, Emily Rose." Something flickered in his eyes, driving the vulnerability from his gaze, replacing it with a wariness and a blatant sensuality that stunned her.

She started to snatch her hand away, but Ian caught her wrist, holding her splayed fingers against the unsteady beat of his heart.

She wanted to run away from this man who so stirred her, away from the child who tore at her heart. But she was helpless. She couldn't leave, dared not leave, for that would mean abandoning both Lucy and herself to the mercy of Atwood's superiors.

"Please, Mr. Blackheath," she said softly, "don't."

"Ian," he urged her in that silky-hot voice. "Call me Ian." His other hand swept up to trace the lower curve of her lip. "I'm a dangerous man, Emily. Dangerous. You would do well to remember that."

He leaned so close to her that his breath heated her tingling lips. "I'll try to keep from acting on my . . . impulses," His voice was low, rough-edged. "It won't be easy, what with those eyes of yours . . . all soft and amethyst. If I were you, I would stay in the nursery, as far away from the east wing of the house as possible."

"The east wing?" Emily asked unsteadily.

"My private domain. Forbidden. I assure you, you would not like what you find there."

Emily swallowed hard, her mind filling with images of the decadent party Flavia Varden had described. But she would not show weakness to this man. She didn't dare.

"You'll find me difficult to shock, Mr. Blackheath," she said.

"Oh, I'd wager I could shock you, Emily Rose, and take great pleasure in doing it." He cupped her chin in his hand, and Emily's breath snagged in her chest as he lowered his mouth to hers. He brushed her lips with a carnal mastery that made Emily weak, left her shaken, wanting. . . .

She gave a whimper of protest, hating herself for not drawing away, hating herself as the hot, wet tip of Ian Blackheath's tongue swept out to probe at the corner of her mouth, to taste her there.

He gave a low groan, his arm curving around her waist,

and for an instant Emily knew a swift stab of compassion for those women who had come before her. Wondered how any woman could deny the wine-dark potency that simmered beneath Ian Blackheath's lips.

She battled to pull away, wondered if she still possessed the will to do so. She never knew.

At that instant a crash upon the ceiling above tore a cry from Emily's throat, making her all but leap from her skin.

As if by instinct Ian shoved her behind him, his hand flashing to his side as if seeking a weapon.

Emily regarded him, stunned, as she heard the muffled sound of Lucy's wailing and some beleaguered servant's pleading as she doubtless tried to calm the child.

Blackheath paled a little as he saw the question in Emily's eyes. "Bloody hell! You must forgive my . . . somewhat alarming reaction. I've never been the same since Isabelle Dentworth's husband attempted to shoot me in a jealous fit. I don't mind a civilized duel, you understand, but when someone sneaks up on a man in his own bedchamber and starts blasting away, a person tends to get skittish."

There was something vaguely disturbing about the way Blackheath flung out the words, as if he wanted to disgust her.

It worked.

Memories of Alexander's supposed friends flooded back to her. Memories of invitations flashed to her from beneath half-closed eyelids after Alexander's death, of lingering touches that hinted at desires that had turned Emily's stomach. Liaisons that would have meant nothing. Less than nothing to the men who had indulged in them.

The thoughts splashed across Emily's consciousness like icy water, obliterating the thrumming heat that had coursed through her at Ian Blackheath's touch.

"The noise. It must be Lucy," she said needlessly. "I'll deal with it."

"I wish you good luck, madam. Somewhere in the hall there is an old suit of armor I brought back from my travels in England. If you'd like to gird yourself for battle . . . ?"

"Battle with whom?" Emily asked, losing herself in those compelling blue eyes.

He smiled, just a little. Not that mocking smile, not the rakehell grin.

It was a sad smile, a disarming one.

"We shall see, Emily Rose," he murmured. "We shall most definitely see."

6

*I*an stared after Emily d'Autrecourt as she left the room, her sky-colored skirts rippling behind her. The gleaming masses of her hair were caught up in a chignon revealing the vulnerable nape of her neck—a soft little hollow that was so inviting with its dusting of fragile curls. Ian would have been tempted to press his lips against it, except that it was set above shoulders stiffened with disapproval and more than a little fear.

She was afraid of him now. Wasn't that what he'd wanted when he'd all but leveled her with his blatantly sexual innuendos? He had wanted this prim little seamstress to taste the danger in him, to feel it, a living thing inside him, consuming . . .

Instinctively Ian had been certain that Emily d'Autrecourt would not be like those other women who were attracted to the dangerous pull he seemed to exude so effortlessly. He had known she would not be drawn to him with the heedlessness of moth to flame, not caring whether she was burned, as long as she sampled his fire.

He had wanted to make certain that she would keep her distance from him in the weeks to come. That she would care for his niece, keeping the blasted little wretch in tow before someone really did decide to string her up from an

93

oak tree, and that she stay as far away as possible from the secrets that lurked in the east wing.

What he had never suspected was what *he* would taste on *her* lips. Something winsome and wooing. Something sweet and all but forgotten.

Yearning.

A hushed, sorrowful questing like a whisper in the wind, touching him in places he didn't want to be touched, awakening needs he didn't want to feel.

He understood lust. God knew he'd drunk his fill of it often enough. He was a man of passionate appetites, and he had the face and body to ensure that he would not often be denied. Quick, feral hungers, wild, primitive thirsts—he'd had his share of both.

This was a far different emotion he felt now.

In the bedchamber he had experienced the expertise of women so skilled they could bring a man to climax with the merest brush of their fingers.

He'd taken women with seething passion, and so languorously that it was akin to torture. And when the sex was done, he'd forgotten them.

But somehow he knew that he would remember forever the sound of Emily d'Autrecourt's gasp the moment his lips first touched hers. He'd remember the astonishment in those eyes, as if she'd awakened for the very first time. And he knew he would never forget the way he had felt as something stirred to life inside him, way down deep.

No, Ian thought grimly. It had to be lust. Pure and simple. He was just aroused because, no matter how much Emily Rose d'Autrecourt might have loved her dead husband, Ian was certain that there were sensual rivers inside her that the man had never coursed. There were secret places, hidden places on that delicate ivory-blushed body that d'Autrecourt had never inflamed.

And a man would have to be dead between his thighs not to be intrigued by the thought of bringing a woman as beautiful as Emily to her first pleasures.

Ian's lips gave a wry twist. Few men realized that the loss

of virginity was not merely the tearing of a lover's maidenhead but was rather a woman's slow initiation into the mystical rites of her own body. But Ian did.

"Don't be a fool, Blackheath!" Ian upbraided himself. "You should be trying to drive her away from you, not tempting yourself beyond reason."

But the damage was done, he admitted with a grimace. He *was* aching, in that old familiar way that was suddenly excruciatingly intense, incredibly new.

"Is she gone yet?" Tony Gray peeked around the corner as if expecting to be hit by flying bric-a-brac.

Ian shook away his sensual thoughts and managed a smile at his friend, hoping his attraction to the seamstress wasn't as evident in his eyes as it was in the pulsing center of what made him a man. "Lucy? Yes, she's off terrorizing the upstairs maids for a change."

Gray looked like the very devil. His hair stuck up in spikes, doubtless from raking his fingers through it in distress. His eyes were still a trifle wild, and a muscle in his jaw twitched ominously. "Tell me right now, Ian. What do you plan to do about that wretched child? By God, she should be cast afloat on a nail keg for what she did to my Zeus!"

"That poor abused child? That wayward little moppet I was to lavish with understanding?"

"Don't you dare mock me, Ian! You have no idea the state of mind I'm in! I've been to the stable with Buckley, and I've never seen such a tragic sight!"

"For God's sake, Tony, the stallion's tail *will* grow back. It's not as if she cut off more . . . er, irreplaceable parts."

"She might as well have!" Gray flung out. "Zeus was supposed to stand stud to Vickersby's mare—that fine leggy filly out of Explycit. How can he face her looking like that?"

Ian laughed, the tide of his desire for Emily d'Autrecourt ebbing a little in the wake of Tony's theatrics.

"Aren't you being a trifle overdramatic?" Ian asked. "I vow, you and Lucy should tour on the stage together! I've never yet seen a breeding in which the mare examined the stud's tail. Zeus is quite a superior male specimen. If he finds the lady attractive, I doubt she'll be able to resist his charms. He'll be a proud papa once again before you know it."

"This is not amusing, Blackheath. I want to know what you propose to do about that girl!"

"Lucy?" With a sigh of consummate satisfaction, Ian sank down in a chair, and stretched his legs out before him. "You will be relieved to hear that I have at last found a solution to the problem of my wayward niece."

"You drowned her? Well done, Ian!"

"Anthony, Anthony, your lack of sensitivity appalls me! No. I did my familial duty by Lucy quite admirably, for once. You recall the lady I introduced to you a little while ago?"

Tony gave him a blank stare. "The seamstress?"

"Yes. For some reason only God himself can fathom, she has agreed to take hold of Lucy's reins."

"What?" Gray's jaw dropped.

"It's true." Ian shook his head with a grin. "The woman must be insane."

"There is a God in heaven," Tony said, sinking into a chair with a sigh of patent relief. "I shall take myself off to church this very Sunday and fill up the vicar's coffers with every shilling I won at hazard last night. Tell me, is that sainted woman upstairs packing the child's trunk this minute?"

"Trunk? What trunk?"

"Why, Lucy's trunk, of course. So that Mrs. d'Autrecourt can carry her off to her new domicile. No, I'd forgotten. The child didn't have a trunk. Well, then, let's hurry out to wave farewell to her from the doorstep."

"So that's what you're thinking. No, Tony. You mistake me. Lucy isn't going away. Mrs. d'Autrecourt is coming to live *here.*"

"Here?" Tony gasped. "At *Blackheath Hall?"*

"Since we are sitting in Blackheath Hall this very instant, that would seem self-evident."

"Ian, you must be mad!" Tony bounded from his chair,

his face red with anger and disbelief. "What the devil have you done?"

"I've found a governess for Lucy. Managed the whole affair quite nicely, if I do say so myself. We couldn't risk allowing the chit to run about loose, especially with her penchant for listening at doors and spreading the latest gossip. And you seem to have an aversion to my throwing the child out into the streets."

"I've changed my mind," Gray hissed between gritted teeth.

"This way," Ian continued as if Tony hadn't spoken, "Mrs. d'Autrecourt can keep Lucy out of mischief, and you and I can turn our attention to more important things—like the shipment of brown Besses and black powder that are to be channeled through here a few days from now."

Ian let his eyes drift shut and gave a contented sigh. "Come, Tony, I await your congratulations."

"Congratulations?"

Ian's eyes flew open at that thrumming of fury in Tony's voice.

"Before Lucy arrived, you were flaying me alive, railing on and on about how I was betraying the cause by getting engaged to Nora. And now here you are, housing a child who runs about listening at doors, and an Englishwoman fresh from the ship!"

"I didn't choose to be saddled with Lucy," Ian said, indignant. "You can hardly hold me responsible."

"You invited that seamstress into your home! She's English, Ian! Just where do you think her loyalties lie? Do you think she understands about the rights we seek? The anger we feel here in the colonies?" Tony broke off in disgust. "It was only a day ago that we dealt with Crane, for God's sake! Have you forgotten how precarious our position can be?"

"Ah, yes. Crane. He is probably hanging his head over the rail of one of my ships right now, retching into the sea on his way to the Gold Coast."

"Had the hand been played out just a little differently, he'd be spending the blood money he received for our capture, and our friend Atwood would be fitting ropes about our necks for a hanging. Crane came damned close to discovering the truth about all of us," Tony said. "If he'd been able to pass along the information he had found—"

"He did not. He cannot. And he will not," Ian brushed Tony's concerns aside.

"That doesn't mean someone else won't."

"Someone like our little seamstress?" Ian asked, with a cynical smile. "But of course! Doubtless she has been caught up in this ring of spies to take Crane's place. She's been sent by Atwood to seduce me. To pry free my dastardly secret. By God, it would be pleasant letting her try."

Tony flushed. "Don't be ridiculous! I didn't say she was a spy! But if she ever discovers the nest of treason she's come to roost in, I doubt she'll agonize very long about whether she should go to the authorities."

Ian's mouth twisted in an arrogant grin. "I think the east wing is safe enough from her prying. I made it clear that I was not terribly set against social clichés. I would be more than happy to have an affair with the family governess."

"You did what?"

"I offered to indulge in an amorous relationship with her—any sacrifice in the name of the cause, you know." Ian grinned. "Of course I had to demonstrate to her the fact that I was quite in earnest."

Tony leaped to his feet, jabbing an accusatory finger at Ian. "Wonderful! Perfect! I know that look in your eye." Tony swore. "Not only are you harboring an Englishwoman in your very house, but you're also plotting ways to get her into your *bed!*"

"I have it on highest authority that Emily d'Autrecourt isn't interested in any such liaisons. A pity. And yet"—Ian gave a shrug—"I have never been able to resist that sort of a challenge."

Ian stiffened at the feel of Tony's fingers biting into his shoulder, hard. There was fury and desperation in Gray's face. "Damn it, Ian, I have a feeling about this. A bad one. You have to get rid of her. Now."

Sparks kindled in Ian's eyes. He gripped Tony's wrist, and

yanked it away from his shoulder. "You forget yourself, Tony. No man tells me what to do. Not even you."

The words were ice-cold.

"Oh, no. *No* one tells you what to do, Ian!" Gray roared in disgust. "But you feel free to order everyone else about! You run around using your body as a goddamn shield for the rest of us, clearly hoping to take a pistol ball or a sword thrust. You expect people who care about you to watch you ride straight over the edge of a damned cliff, if you want to, just so you can feel the cursed thrill of it!"

"Tony . . ." The word was a warning.

"No, I won't be quiet. Not this time. Tell me the truth for once in your benighted life, Ian. Is that why you've brought an Englishwoman into your home? So you can walk on that blade edge of danger you love, even here at Blackheath Hall? Is this just another part of the infernal game you are playing with your life?"

"Tony, no more."

"Why? Because it might be the truth?" Gray's hazel eyes were filled with torment, boiling with frustration.

"You want the child out of here?" Ian challenged. "Then use your family connections to get her into school at once. You want Emily d'Autrecourt away from Blackheath Hall? Then find me some other woman with the nerve to take Lucy on. Hellfire and damnation, the child has kept all twenty of my servants running around as if they were dancing on live coals ever since she's been here."

"I'm doing the best I can, damn it!" Tony raged. "I wrote the blasted letter and had Polly write one, too. I—"

"Let me know when you have a reply. Until then kindly stop annoying me with your complaints."

Tony slammed his fist on a table, making the prisms on the candlestick dance wildly. "You don't even hear what I'm saying, do you, Ian? You never bloody listen! Fine, then. Drown yourself in insane risks. Court your own doom, if you want to. I'm sure Dame Death is like any other woman and won't be able to resist making you her own. Maybe you've found your way into her arms at last, Ian—through a winsome pair of violet blue eyes."

With a curse, Tony turned and stalked from the room. Ian listened to the hoofbeats of Gray's much abused stallion as it thundered from the yard.

Restless, Ian paced to the window, staring out into the darkness. Thunder rolled in the distance, whispering of wild winds and jagged lightning, a coming storm.

A storm that now moved over Virginia as inexorably as the rumblings of revolution that were engulfing the colonies.

Could it be that Tony was right this time? Ian wondered vaguely. Did it matter if he was?

Ian straightened his back, feeling the familiar thrumming in his veins that could not be denied.

The hunger was inside him again. Deeper, stronger, since his encounter with the beautiful Englishwoman whose taste still lingered on his lips.

With an oath he turned and strode out of the house. The wind raked through his hair and tugged at the open edges of his shirt, caressing his heated skin like the fingers of a lover.

Ian's mouth curled into that devil-smile as a jagged flash of lightning split the sky.

The rogue Pendragon had to be one with the night.

7

The storm was over. It had raged for hours, a torrent of rain, howling wind, and crashing thunder outside the bedchamber window.

A flood of fury and pain and helplessness inside the room.

Emily sat on the side of the huge bed amid the ruin that had once been Lucy's chamber, watching the little girl sleep. She hadn't even attempted to pick up the countless objects the child had thrown to underscore her shrieks that she didn't need a governess, didn't need anybody. Emily hadn't attempted to right tables, straighten coverlets, or even brush back the waves of her own hair that had tumbled from its pins in the fracas.

She hadn't moved even once from the child's side since the moment the exhausted little girl had surrendered to sleep.

Tears had dried in salty tracks on Lucy's cheeks; her golden curls lay snarled across the pillow. The shirt she wore as a night shift was twisted and crumpled; Lucy's fingers were tangled in the lace at the throat, as if she feared that in the night someone would try to take it from her.

Take it as death had taken her mother. Her father. Take it as Emily would take the doll if she ever found it.

The reality was agonizing but inevitable. The knowledge

that she would have to betray the child was almost unbearable. But what choice did she have when the child's need for the plaything was compared to the danger of leaving brave little Lucy to the mercy of the ruthless men Captain Atwood had hinted at?

It was a choice that was no choice. One Emily had made even before she had come to Blackheath Hall.

But when she made that decision, she'd only seen hints of Lucy Dubbonet's inner torment. Now she felt as if the child's pain had crawled inside her own skin, embedded itself in Emily's own heart.

Never had she witnessed such an enormous well of wrath in such a small child. A hurt too big to hold.

Now, with Lucy asleep, Emily dared to smooth a hand over that round cheek. Her heart wrenched at the occasional catch in Lucy's breath as if, even in sleep, the child's soul was still crying.

There was something so pathetic about defiant little Lucy sleeping in the huge masculine shirt that Emily knew could only belong to Ian Blackheath.

Not just some plain linen garment—heaven knew, even a man like Blackheath must have *some* clothes that didn't cost a fortune—but a shirt with lace as costly as jewels dripping from the collar and cuffs.

A shirt that would delight the heart of a beauty-loving little baggage like Lucy Dubbonet.

It would have been touching to think that Ian Blackheath had wanted to please the little girl by such a gift, but Emily knew better. He had probably just stalked to his own clothespress and ripped out the first garment he grabbed, hurling it at her in impatience.

This was no tender man with an understanding of fragile child-hearts. This was not Alexander, who had always seemed to know how to delight a little girl.

Emily swallowed hard, remembering that even when there had been little money for coal, and chilblains had nipped at Jenny's hands, the child's face had lit up with smiles when Alexander arrived home.

Jenny would run to him on her sturdy little legs, her hair

ribbons flying as she flung her arms about his legs in an ecstatic hug. Then she would drag him off to the pianoforte with demands for nursery songs and little tunes that they made up together.

There was something so infinitely precious about a man who could be led about quite willingly by a little girl's hand.

But Emily sensed that Ian Blackheath was not the type of man to form that kind of an attachment with anyone, most especially a child like the headstrong Lucy. He had made it perfectly clear that she was to go off to school as quickly as possible. And the look of relief on his face when Emily had agreed to take charge of the child had been almost comical.

No, if Lucy was searching for someone to hold on to as tightly as she was clinging to the tangle of her shirt, she would have to look for someone besides her rakehell uncle.

But who would it be? Emily thought sadly.

The headmistress of some school where the child would just be one of countless girls? Lucy was such a unique child, so different from the common way of things. She was strong, yes. But she would never belong in a passel of girls like those she would find at school—girls with adoring parents. Pampered little misses who had everything Lucy did not have, would never have. She would always be excluded, outside the charmed circle of giggles after midnight and whispered stories in the garden. She would always be without the warm hugs of a mama and papa, the holiday visits, the presents on birthdays and Christmas.

She'd never let on that it hurt her. Oh, no. She would only act even more imperious, as if it were all far beneath her notice.

But as Emily looked down at Lucy's face, unguarded in sleep, she was certain that the pain Lucy felt would cut even deeper, scar her even more terribly . . . perhaps for the rest of her life.

If it had not already done so.

Emily smoothed a curl from Lucy's brow. "Oh, Lucy, Lucy," she whispered to the little girl, "who did this to you? Who hurt you so badly that now you hurt others so swiftly, so completely, that they can never ever touch you?"

Emily's own eyes stung as she thought about the missing doll. Lucy had wanted the doll to love. Not to play with. Not to make believe or rig out in scraps of ribbon and lace. But to love.

A little wood-carved lady with horsehair fastened to the top of her head, and flat, painted eyes, and a smile that never changed. She wanted to love something safe. That could never deal her the pain of rejection.

But the doll would never love Lucy back.

"I'll make it up to you, Lucy. When I have to take the doll, I'll find you something else to love. I'll give you a puppy that will lick your face or a kitten you can trail ribbons to play with."

No, even that seemed a pale offering at best. A puppy didn't have arms to hold you when you cried. It couldn't whisper that it loved you, or kiss away the tears when you were hurt or lost or frightened.

A soft, muffled sound caught at Emily's ears, and she looked down to see Lucy stirring restlessly against the coverlets.

"Hush, little one. Hush. You're safe, Lucy." Emily crooned the words, almost as if to comfort herself.

But Lucy would not be comforted. Tears squeezed again from the corners of her eyelids, the sounds becoming soft little gasps.

She was humming to herself in her sleep. Snippets of some tune so badly fragmented it was unrecognizable. Emily strained to hear it, hoping it was some bit of a lullaby. For it would soothe her own spirit to know that someone had once comforted the child in that method that was as old as time.

But abruptly the murmuring stopped, Lucy's face seeming to relax as some of the tension seeped out of her limbs.

Emily leaned over and slipped her fingers around Lucy's limp ones. Oh, God, she didn't want to feel like this. Ache like this. Ache because of this unwanted child who reminded her so fiercely of how much she wanted her own little girl. Ache with forgotten longings because of the man who had pulled her into his arms and kissed her with such consummate skill she'd barely been able to stand.

She had wanted to flee Blackheath Hall and not stop to count the cost. Had thought of racing off someplace where Atwood would never find her. But she had told Atwood Lucy's name and would leave her at risk.

Risk . . .

Why did the danger threatened by Atwood and his superiors seem to pale when compared to the danger she had sensed in Ian Blackheath's arms? In those eyes that were so reckless, so bewitching?

Heat spread under her skin at the memory of the things he had said to her in that hot, husky voice, the way he had touched her, as if he knew her body far better than she did and could wring from her any response he chose.

And he could have, Emily realized with a jolt. It had been so long since she'd been touched by anyone, it had been so long since she'd been held in the circle of someone's arms.

There had been times as a girl when she'd had dreams—fairy tales and legends that had captured her imagination. Even though she was a humble vicar's daughter and her romantic prospects were modest at best, she had read tales of knights in armor and princes disguised as beggar lads.

But there had been no room for dreams in Emily's life after her father had announced her betrothal to Squire Toombs. There had been no dreams when Alexander had insisted on becoming her husband.

"I can't let you sacrifice yourself," she'd said. "You don't love me, Alexander. Not that way . . ."

"You're the finest girl I've ever known, Emmy. My best friend. I'm sure we'll learn to . . . to rub along all right with each other in that other way, with time. And even if we don't, Emmy, it won't matter."

But it had mattered. In ways they had never been able to speak about. It had mattered in the darkness on the narrow bed that they shared. It had mattered at those rare times when Alexander had reached for her, his head a little muddled with drink, his hands sweating and awkward, his gentle eyes filled with shame. She had never refused him, but they had known each other for too long, understood each other too well, for him not to know that there was no real passion in her touch, none of the sense of urgency she felt in him.

There had been such a lost look in his eyes. She could still see him as he had been the night he'd taken ill. Rain soaking him to his skin, those hands that could weave such sweet music shaking as he whispered, "I'm sorry, Emmy. I'm so sorry."

Had he been sorry because he'd lost their last money in a game of faro, condemning them to the horror of debtors' prison? Or had he been sorry for other things, the wounds they'd dealt each other while trying so hard not to. Or had Alexander been sorry he'd ever married her at all?

Her throat constricted. How many times had she wondered if Alexander would have been able to fight the world and his illness if they had been able to love each other in the way of a man and a woman, a husband and a wife. If she had reached deeper into herself and given him more . . .

No, Emily chided herself firmly. There was no point in tearing herself apart with guilt, no point in wondering what might have been. Such feelings were every bit as futile as the emotions that were stirring inside her toward the little girl who lay curled up in the bed before her.

They could only leave her feeling even more empty than she had before.

With a parting caress to that stubborn little jaw, Emily drew away, a tiny thread of unease teasing her.

It was time. Time to leave Lucy to whatever dreams had given her that tranquil expression. Time for Emily to take care of the task that had brought her to Blackheath Hall.

It was time to try to find the doll.

Find it and leave this child who wrenched at her heart, this man who aroused such conflicting emotions in her.

Find it so that she could run back to the safety of her little shop and busy herself with problems that were no more demanding than whether to stitch a blue plume or a red one into the brim of a hat.

But where could she even begin her search? Emily chewed at her lower lip, glancing about the room. Quickly, quietly, she made a thorough examination of the tall clothespress and felt with her hand beneath the bed. But every drawer, every nook and cranny, was empty, a poignant reminder that Lucy Dubbonet had brought nothing with her when she came to Blackheath Hall, except the pain that lurked in her eyes.

Fidgeting with an end of ribbon on her sleeve, Emily racked her brain, thinking. Where could the doll be? Was it possible that it wasn't here at all? That it was hidden somewhere in town, beneath a garden hedge? Under a keg?

No. In spite of Ian's assurances that he had seen nothing resembling a doll on their trip home from town, Emily was certain it had to be somewhere nearby, where Lucy could steal off to cuddle it.

But where?

Knowing Lucy, Emily was certain that the doll would be in the most astonishing place imaginable.

Emily went to the bedside table, her fingers closing about the pewter candleholder. If she could just become familiar with the layout of the house she might get some idea where to begin.

Her eyes strayed to the closed door, her heart beating faster. Swallowing the lump of nervousness in her throat, she slipped out into the corridor.

Pools of light wavered in the darkness where occasional candles had been left burning. A clock in the hallway gave off the only sound, a hushed ticking that seemed to emphasize the quiet rather than break it.

The big house was silent, holding the same brooding quality Emily had seen beneath the thick lashes of Ian Blackheath's eyes. The empty doorways seemed to stare out at Emily, watching her.

Her fingers tightened on the candlestick as she hesitated on the threshold.

God above, what was she doing prowling around the house of a man like Ian Blackheath in the middle of the night?

What if Blackheath was lurking in one of these rooms

right now, trying out his centurion style on one of the housemaids? What if he and Flavia Varden had begun their own Roman conquest early?

Her cheeks grew hot at the memory of the bed games Flavia Varden had hinted at in the shop that morning. But the thoughts were even more alarming now, because as she pictured Ian Blackheath taking part in those hedonistic pleasures it was not the lust-hungry Flavia who arched back her neck to seek his fierce kiss. It was Emily herself, a tangle of gauze dripping about her shoulders, Blackheath's sure, seductive hands peeling the gossamer layer away.

She clutched the candleholder more tightly, trying to stop their trembling. She was being ridiculous. What was she afraid of? That he would throw her down on the floor and force himself on her? No, a man like Blackheath would never use so crude a manner. He wouldn't have to.

And yet, what *could* Emily say if she stumbled across him?

Excuse me, Mr. Blackheath, but I couldn't sleep and decided to come downstairs to look for a good book? Something intellectually edifying?

She had been excruciatingly embarrassed once, when one of Alexander's friends had produced some shockingly erotic sketches he'd bought from a sea captain who had sailed to Cathay. Would Blackheath hand her something like that and tell her to have sweet dreams?

Her stomach rumbled, the startling sound making her all but drop the candle.

That was it!

The excuse she needed for wandering the house.

She'd had nothing to eat since breakfast, and none of the servants had dared to come into Lucy's room during their battle. Emily couldn't stifle a twinge of amusement. The whole staff had probably been cowering as far away from Lucy's temper as possible. If she stumbled upon anyone, she would merely ask them to direct her to the kitchen and ask where she was expected to sleep tonight.

It was a perfect excuse, one that nobody would question. Feeling a little better, she continued along the hall, then slipped stealthily down the grand staircase that was all too easy to picture filled with beautiful, immoral women busily displaying their charms to the wildest and most dashing men Virginia had to offer.

The first door on the right was ajar, and Emily eased her way through the opening, turning to look at the room beyond. Nothing would have surprised her—except what she saw there. Row upon row of books lined the walls, their bindings having a well-fingered look. A portrait of the cavalier King Charles II fleeing from Worcester in disguise graced one wall, while the other displayed a beautiful image of stallions fighting with majestic savagery over an elegant mare.

Surely even Lucy could not have had the temerity to enter this room. But Emily couldn't stop herself from pacing over to where a massive desk abutted one wall. The surface was clear of the usual mess of papers to be found on such a desk. Three volumes lay open on the gleaming wood. Emily fingered the bindings, and held the candle closer to them, her lips parting in astonishment.

John Locke. Rousseau. Voltaire.

Radical philosophers whose dangerous thoughts had put frightening ideas into the minds of men. Ideas that were already shaking the foundations of monarchies and making men question the divine right of kings.

She tried to picture Ian Blackheath leaning intently over these books, attempting to stretch his consciousness and see the world that these men saw. But it was impossible to imagine Blackheath bothering with any thoughts more serious than what color gauze to dress his mistresses in or which card to play at the gaming table.

No, most likely he was browsing through the volumes to find things he could mock to his friends. Jokes that he could fling out to his neighbors who had caught the fever of rebellion. Yes, that she could imagine: Ian taking the greatest of pleasure in treating such serious-minded rabble to the sharp edge of his tongue.

She started to turn away, but the candle flame glimmered

on something shiny, there atop the desk. Her fingers stole out, touching the object that was every bit as surprising as the books themselves had been.

It was a paperweight. One far too whimsical to belong to a man as cynical as Ian Blackheath. A milky chunk of stone about the size of Emily's fist was crowned by a miniature silver anvil. Thrust through it, and deep into the stone itself, was an intricate golden sword.

The craftsmanship was remarkable, every detail perfection. Emily couldn't stop herself from running her fingertips over the sword's miniature hilt. The single sheet of foolscap it sat atop held a cryptic note: "Beautiful Bessie arrived safely. Meet her at the Red Dragon."

Bessie? The confusion she'd felt about Ian faded, and she grimaced. No doubt Bessie was some mistress who was waiting for Blackheath with eager hands and hungry lips. Some woman as skilled in love-play as Ian himself obviously was.

Here Emily had been creeping around the house, scared half out of her wits while Blackheath was wrapped up in the arms of some temptress miles away at an inn!

She shook her head in disgust, her hand closing on the handle of a desk drawer when suddenly the sound of a door crashing open made her heart fall to her toes.

Panicking, she reached for the candlewick, meaning to extinguish the flame with her fingers, but it was too late. The ring of telltale light spilled out into the corridor like a pool of blood, the heavy, measured tread of boot soles drawing relentlessly closer.

Panic constricted Emily's throat, her hand shaking where it held the flickering candle.

Sweet God in Heaven, Ian Blackheath had come home.

8

Never in her life had Emily been skilled at subterfuge. But in that frozen moment she knew her life, and perhaps Lucy Dubbonet's life as well, depended on her ability to fool Ian Blackheath with the flimsiest of lies, for if he suspected that she was prying through his things, she was certain he would fling her out of his house. And then whatever forces Atwood held at bay would be set loose upon them all.

She could only pray that the darkness would hide the guilt she was certain was stamped so plainly on her face.

Rubbing at her eyes in a great show of exhaustion, she stepped out of the room and all but bumped into Ian Blackheath's tall frame.

"What the devil?" Blackheath growled.

Emily didn't have to act when she jumped at the quick, savage anger in his voice.

He was every bit as intimidating as she'd feared he would be. The sight of him, still half hidden in shadows, made her pulse trip. A scarlet cloak was flung over his shoulders, sweeping down his back like the wings of a fallen angel. His shirt still hung open, the glistening bronze plane of his chest temptation garbed in shadow, beautiful, so beautiful.

The scent of wind and rain and leather filled Emily's nostrils, so alluring she could almost taste it on her tongue.

"For God's sake, I took you for a housebreaker!" Blackheath snarled. "I could have skewered you where you stand! What the hell are you doing wandering about the house at this ungodly hour?"

"I'm looking for a . . . bed to sleep in," Emily said, with a huge feigned yawn. "I'm exhausted, and no one remembered to tell me where I am to . . . go."

She stole a peek at Ian from beneath her lashes and saw that she had caught him totally off guard with her words. The wrath drained out of him in a rush, leaving in its place a very real chagrin.

"No . . . bed? The servants didn't get you settled in?"

"Let's just say I'm amazed they didn't nail the door to Lucy's room shut and be done with it. I think they stayed as far away from the mayhem as possible."

His manner changed abruptly, one corner of his mouth curving into that lazy smile. "You mean to tell me that they left you stranded without a bed to sleep in?" Blackheath's voice was teasing now, silky. "It's insufferable. Criminal. Fortunately I am a most generous fellow. I shall be happy to offer you half of mine."

Emily's mouth went dry as pictures of Ian danced in her head, his sun-bronzed body naked against the startling white of love-tumbled sheets, his dark mane tousled across the pillow. Temptation incarnate. But then, the devil's own angel would have to be beautiful on the outside to lure the unwary into hell. She had to remember the emotional shallowness that lurked beneath that seductive smile.

She struggled to swallow. "You, sir, have a most abominable reputation. I am quite certain that you would attempt to swindle me out of my portion of the bed if I were to accept your offer."

"How can you know me so quickly, Emily Rose? I am an incorrigible cheat at everything but gambling and horse races. And yet, think of the offer as a challenge, my sweet. You could prove to the world, and to yourself, that you are able to resist my charms."

"You are the most arrogant, most . . ." Emily looked into those teasing blue eyes and couldn't stop the laugh that rose to her lips. He was trying to be outrageous and was enjoying it far too much, judging from the beguiling curl at the corner of his lips and the twinkle of his eye, just visible in the shadows.

"I would hate to damage your high opinion of yourself by rejecting you, Mr. Blackheath," Emily said, running her fingers back through her hair until the last of the pins tugged free. "So if you will kindly tell me where I can find a bed of my own, I'll spare your vanity such a fatal wound."

He favored her with a courtly bow. "Ah, my lady of mercy, my angel of understanding. Such a rare jewel . . ."

But his teasing banter was lost in Emily's gasp as the candlelight flowed over him and a cold droplet of water splashed Emily's bare forearm. He straightened up at the sound of her distress, and she held the candle closer to him, unable to stifle the quick twist of panic in her stomach as her gaze locked on his face.

It gleamed with a sheen of moisture, his hair clinging in dark wet strands to his neck. The fine linen of his shirt stuck to his skin, the front of the garment still hanging wide open, baring his hair-roughened chest.

The breeches that fit him like a second skin were soaked, outlining every curve and ridge of his muscular thighs, while water dripped from his hair, running down the corded muscles in his neck to pool in the hollow above his collarbone.

"Emily?" His fingers curved around her cheek, and raw terror knifed through Emily as she felt the chill of his skin.

"You're soaked!" Emily cried.

In the shadows she could see the white flash of Ian's grin. "I've ridden through storms before and been so drunk I slept in the wet clothes. Believe me, I barely noticed—"

"Have you never heard of lung fever, you great fool?"

"I'm fine. I promise you." But at that moment a shiver worked through him, as if to belie his words.

"To your room. Now," she said, tugging him out of the room and toward the stairs. "Hurry. You don't know how quickly the fever can settle in your lungs. How swiftly it can sicken you."

"I'm disgustingly healthy. Always have been. I—"

"Do you think that matters?" Emily cried in alarm. "It only takes one bout of illness to send a man to his grave. We need to get you out of these clothes at once, dry you—"

"Getting me out of my clothes is a wonderful idea," he said, following her up the staircase. "That is, as long as you follow suit. After all, turnabout is fair play."

"This isn't a jest!" There was real desperation in her voice. "Please! Do as you're told."

With a quizzical look at her, he struggled with the clinging fabric of his wet shirt. She reached out with her free hand to help him, her fingers skimming the cold material away from his broad shoulders and heavily muscled arms, as they hurried up the stairs.

She peeled the fabric down his back with fingers that shook, barely aware of the hardness of his flesh or the firm, sleek silk of his skin. Tossing the garment on the floor of the upstairs corridor, she hurried into the room he indicated, pressing the taper she held into his hand.

As Ian lit a branch of candles, Emily rummaged through the ornate washstand, shoving aside a bone-handled razor and soap, a china shaving bowl, and a bottle of Hungary water, the scent shoved so far back it was obviously rarely used. On the bottom shelf she found what she was looking for. She grabbed up the toweling. Then she hurried to pull a wingback chair closer to the crackling fire and guided Ian to it.

He sat watching her from beneath brows lowered in puzzlement as she rushed over and began rubbing the rough, warm linen across his chilled body.

She leaned close against him to reach the dark, damp cap of his hair, blotting up most of the moisture that ran from the soaked locks onto his skin. She sponged away the droplets that clung to his cheeks, his jaw, and smoothed the cloth down his neck. Her fingers brushed his skin as she applied the towel to the curve of his arm, the muscled ridges of his chest.

His head arched back against the chair, his eyes squeezed closed. Emily glimpsed his mouth compressing in a tight line and was certain that, despite his protest that he was fine, he was now feeling the aftereffects of that mad race through the rain.

With renewed haste she moved to dry him lower down, the slight curve beneath his nipple, the flat disk hardened in its silk-spun web of dark gold. Her little finger grazed the point, and his muscles jumped beneath her hand, a sharp hiss coming from between his teeth.

"I'm sorry," she said, hurrying to dry the other side, then moving down the ridges of his flat stomach. "You're so cold."

She knelt down to reach the area near his navel, her hair, falling in a cascade against his chilled skin as she skimmed her cloth over the waistband of his breeches. Her forearm brushed the thick bulge beneath the breech flap. Her cheeks burned, but she was too desperate to worry.

Her mind was filled with memories of Alexander. He had endured her ministrations in the same, searing quiet. His flesh had been less heavily muscled, less taut and sleek, but every bit as clammy-cold as the skin beneath Emily's fingers now.

She tugged off boots sodden with water, then closed her palms over the tops of Ian's mud-spattered stockings and rolled them down rock-hard calves that were dusted with prickly dark hair.

Her own fingers were chilled now, that sick lump of dread feeling like a stone in her stomach as she worked the buckles that fastened his breeches at the knee.

"You have to take them off," she warned, instinctively reaching for the waistband of the garment.

"Whoa, now, Emily Rose." He caught both of her hands in his to stop her, his eyes staring down into hers with an unreadable expression.

She knelt before him, her hair a stream of midnight over the flat plane of his stomach, her breasts pressed against the corded muscles of his calves. Her heartbeat thudded where she touched him.

The smile he gave her was more than a little strained, the sudden sulky heat about his mouth making her pulse flutter beneath his fingertips. "If I had known that this was part of a governess's service, I would have hired one for myself long ago." He was attempting to tease her, but the words were frayed with just the slightest rough edging of something Emily couldn't name.

"You can't sit around in wet breeches," she said, a trifle breathless. "You'll take a chill and—"

"I am quite warm now, I assure you." He gave a hoarse chuckle. "And as for removing my breeches, let's just say that after the attentions you've given me, I'm not about to display how . . . er, revived certain parts of my anatomy are behind this doeskin," he brushed his breeches with long fingers.

"Don't you understand? It's dangerous!" She tried to pull away, but he held her firm.

"I can assure you I know just how . . . dangerous the feelings I'm having at the moment are."

"Please." Her voice quavered. "You must not treat this so lightly—"

"Why not, Emily Rose?" The teasing in his features eased. His voice was soft, his face wearing a solemn expression at odds with the rakehell facade she'd seen so many times before. "Why *this?*" He smoothed his thumb over her cheek.

"Why what?" Impatience edged her voice.

"Fear."

She stared at him, taken aback by that single, insightful word. She could see her reflection in his eyes—her wariness, the soft grief in the exhaustion-rimmed amethyst of her own eyes. The hand that had been applying the towel dropped limply onto his knee.

"My husband died of lung fever. He was walking home in the rain one night. He was never the most robust of men. He took a chill. Began to cough. These horrible racking coughs." Her voice dropped low. "Three weeks later he was dead."

Blackheath peered down at her, his eyes darkening with compassion and a tenderness Emily had not suspected him capable of. "It must have been very hard for you."

Emily drew in a shaky breath and looked away from the compelling softness in his eyes. "Alexander was a very good man. Gentle and sensitive." Her voice broke. "Kind."

"Everything I am not." There was a faint thread of regret in his voice. "You see how unjust the world is, Emily Rose? That good, kind man you loved died by merely walking in the rain. I am not a good man. No woman waits for me. Loves me. But no matter what I do, the devil will not take me."

He was quiet for a moment, one hand reaching out to stroke a mahogany tendril of her hair. "You deserve someone to be kind to you," he said.

She gave an unsteady laugh. "How can you know that? You don't know anything about me."

"I've seen the way you are with Lucy. I see a goodness along with the sorrow in your eyes. But I would know more." His callused fingertips feathered across the sensitive skin behind her ear, tenderly, so tenderly. "Who are you, Emily Rose?" he queried softly. "And what on God's earth could make a lone woman leave everything she's ever known to come to a place she's never seen before? A woman of obviously gentle birth? A lady?"

It was a question more dangerous that Ian Blackheath could ever imagine. Emily stared down at her hands, afraid that her eyes would betray her.

"There was nothing left for me in England," she said. "Except memories."

"Of your husband?"

"Yes." Emily hesitated for a heartbeat before adding in whisper, "My husband and . . . and my daughter." Never could she remember willingly speaking of her child to another person. Her grief over Jenny was too precious, too devastating, to share. She was stunned as her words seemed to hang in the air like mist between her and this man who was all but a stranger . . . this man with a thousand mysteries in his eyes.

"A child?" Blackheath prodded, that sensual mouth seeming to soften with an echo of her pain.

"She died five years ago, swept away by the same fever that took Alexander," Emily confided. "She was only three. So small. If she had lived, she would have been about Lucy's age. She would have been wearing long dresses and curling up her hair. She would be stitching at her samplers and helping me with my tasks. And chattering on and on and on . . ."

The words trailed off. Her gaze dropped to her hands.

"Eight years ago," Ian said, stroking back her tumbled curls. "You must have been little more than a child yourself."

Emily gave a strained laugh. "Seventeen is hardly considered a child in these times. Some women are mothers three times over by then."

"But you . . . Forgive me, but you're so small, your face so sweet. I can't imagine the agony you must have suffered."

"Bearing a child was the most wonderful thing that ever happened to me. I loved her . . . so much." Emily's voice trembled. "I still wonder what she would have been like if she had lived. Her papa was musical, and she loved to listen to him play. She would dance about with her little arms in the air. She would laugh and laugh."

Silence fell. A tear trembled at the ends of her lashes and then trickled free. Emily looked into Ian Blackheath's eyes, and she was astonished to see within them a vivid reflection of a tiny golden-curled moppet, whirling about gaily in a dance that was all her own. The arrogant planes of his face were touched by her own sorrow.

"You say that this tragedy befell you five years ago," he urged gently. "Why did you wait so long to make a new start? Why come to the colonies now?"

Emily looked away, pleating a damp fold of her gown between fingers suddenly unsteady. "Does it really matter?"

"I think it does."

"Mr. Blackheath," she started to protest, "I—"

"Ian. Call me Ian." There was a poignant urgency in his voice that she had never heard before. She'd had no idea how wrenchingly tender that whiskey-warm voice could be.

"Ian," she repeated, softly.

He reached out to cup her hand in his large one and held it as if it were something precious.

"Emily, I want to know. I want to understand. Tell me."

Never in her life had she spoken about the aftermath of Jenny's death. Not even with the Quakeress who had taken her in, like a wounded bird. Allowed her to heal, and then, in spite of her reluctance, forced her to fly.

But as Emily felt herself drawn deeper into the shimmering blue of Ian Blackheath's eyes, the soft compassion that clung about his mouth, she found herself speaking in halting phrases.

"We were barely scraping by on what Alexander could earn giving music lessons. He had a half dozen students—most of them abysmally tone-deaf. But one of them showed enough promise to make up for all the rest. There was never money for extra things, but we managed. Especially since the boy's parents, were most generous. Then one day the child just refused to play another note. Ever. Alexander was never the same after. And financially it was impossible for us to afford even the most basic things . . . things like doctors. It wasn't long afterward that Alexander got sick. I was desperate. I took him back to his parents and begged them to help him."

She paused a minute. "Alexander was the younger son of a duke. His parents were furious about our marriage. While they felt duty bound to take in Alexander and our daughter, I was not welcome."

"Heartless bastards!" Ian bit out with some savagery, his fingers tightening protectively about hers. "Your husband should have told them to go to bloody hell."

"I forbade anyone to tell him that I . . . was made to leave. He was so sick by then that I can only hope he never knew."

"But your daughter? Your little girl—"

"They took her in, too. When I left her she was—was crying. Clinging to me. But she was healthy. I swear to God she was. Her cheeks all rosy, her eyes bright. So bright. They used to sparkle like a handful of stars. I never saw such life in anyone's eyes."

Rough, callused fingers stroked her hand with fierce tenderness, but he said nothing, just waited. After a moment Emily went on.

"I was crazed with grief when I found out she was gone. I didn't want to live. I wandered down to the river. Stepped into the water. I can still remember how cold it was about my legs. I can still remember the feel of my skirts swirling in the currents."

She turned her face away, watching the gold and crimson tongues of flame on the hearth lick at the darkness. "I just had to keep walking," she whispered, "deeper, deeper, and I knew the current would sweep me away. I would be with my baby then. I didn't want her to be alone, even with angels to tend her."

Silence. The pain pulsed inside her, deep, so deep.

"A Quakeress found me and drew me back out of the water. She put me to work helping others. Sewing things for the inmates of Newgate, brewing stew to take to the sick. I could work until I fell into bed. Exhausted, past seeing, past feeling."

"Did the pain ease?" The words were a gentle probing. He leaned toward her, and she could feel the warmth in him, the caring. Strange, to feel such caring . . .

"I didn't feel anything at all," she said softly. "I deadened myself. It was the only way I could bear the pain."

"What happened to awaken you?"

"One day we were stitching in the garden at sunset, and the Quaker woman took my hand. She told me I was still standing in the river. That it was time for me to decide whether to walk deeper into the water or turn around and take my first steps back into life."

Her hair was a curtain about her face, dark and rich. Ian stroked it back. His finger curved beneath her chin, tipping up so he could look into her face. "And what did you do, Emily Rose?"

"I knew she was right. I could never make a life in England. The hatred I felt for Alexander's parents was too deep, even after his father died. So I decided to come to the colonies."

"Somewhere new. Unsullied by men like the bastard duke who turned you out onto the streets."

Unsullied. It was an odd word to use, hinting that somewhere in those reckless eyes Ian Blackheath saw something beautiful in this raw new land, something he kept hidden inside him.

Emily sucked in a deep breath. "I gained passage the only way I could, by indenturing myself. I would have done anything to get away. But for once it seemed the fates were with me. One of the people I had brought soup to was an old woman, wealthy but without friends. She knew of an English gentleman who had outfitted a milliner's shop for his wayward cousin in the colonies. Fortunately for me, the cousin preferred the attentions of an amorous blacksmith. On the day she was to be sent overseas, she announced to her family that she and her blacksmith had been secretly married and that she was carrying his child."

Blackheath's mouth curved in a hint of his accustomed ironic grin. "I'd wager your English gentleman was not amused."

"I suppose not." Emily shrugged. "He had wanted to set his cousin up in style, and so he had already invested a fair amount of money in the shop. After her announcement, he had only two choices. To take his losses and forget the whole affair or attempt to recoup his funds. To do that, he needed someone to run the shop in his cousin's place."

"Why didn't he just sell it? That would have been the most logical path to take."

"I don't know. Maybe Miss Higgins talked him out of it by pleading my cause. Or perhaps he wanted to do someone else a kindness. In the end, we met, and he bought my indenture. I was given passage to Virginia and told that when my time of service was through, he would give me the shop."

"Damned generous of him. You'd think that even a rich gentleman would demand some price." There was a shadow of suspicion in Ian's tone.

Emily drew away, not wanting him to see the flicker of unease in her face as she thought of the secret payment the man had demanded. She groped for a way to calm Ian's suspicions, an explanation that a man like Blackheath would understand. She felt a jab of embarrassment, but lifted her chin to meet his gaze. "If you are thinking he demanded a physical price, you are wrong," she said.

Ian's cheekbones darkened in a guilty flush. "I'm sorry. I didn't mean to offend you."

"You didn't. Not really." Emily favored him with a soft smile. "It's just . . . I know it's hard to believe. But the whole proposition was such a miracle for a woman like me that I didn't question it, Ian. I just took it and was grateful."

"So you took up your miracle and packed your ribbons and bonnets and buttons and boarded a ship and sailed to the colonies." Ian's eyes shone with respect. "You are a very brave lady, Emily Rose."

"No. Not brave." She shook her head wistfully. "You cannot call someone brave when she is running away."

Unease flickered across Ian's face, as if her words had touched something raw inside him.

He bent close to her, his gaze touching her features as gently as his hands had moments before.

"Poor lost angel, wandering alone," he murmured without a hint of mockery. "Are you waiting for someone to find you?" His fingertips were warm as they curved about her cheek.

There was something like yearning in the hard angles of his face, something she didn't understand. She saw his throat work, his eyes hidden beneath a thick fall of lashes that only made the masculine lines of his face all the more appealing.

His lips parted, as if they hungered to taste something sweet, something forever beyond his reach. She sensed him drawing back from that gentle hunger, and knew a fleeting sense of regret.

He sighed, his lashes drooping over the misty blue depths of his eyes.

"You should get some rest, Emily Rose," he said after a moment, his thumb tracing a delicate path along the bruised shadows beneath her eyes. "I have a feeling tomorrow is going to be a very long day."

Emily climbed wearily to her feet, feeling somehow bereft. "I suppose it couldn't be any longer than today was." She felt the aching stiffness in her muscles and wondered how long they had been sitting there together, speaking of things she'd never spoken of, revealing things she'd kept hidden for so long.

It seemed as though an eternity had passed since she had followed Ian Blackheath into this room. It seemed as if eternity had suddenly become too short a time.

She was shaken from her thoughts by Ian's voice as he rose to stand beside her, towering over her, his dark hair a tumbled mane about his face.

"I won't offend you by offering half of my bed to you again. Instead I'll just tell you to take whatever room you want for your own. Both of the chambers next door to Lucy are available, as are the ones across the hall."

There was something sad about this man offering her any room in his vast house. Beautiful empty spaces with no one to love them. She started at the echo of Lucy's words, and was surprised at the fleeting vulnerability that ghosted across the sensual curve of Ian Blackheath's mouth—this Ian Blackheath who somehow seemed more frightening than the rakehell she had known before, because of the haunting quality in his eyes.

Catching her lower lip between her teeth, Emily laid the towel she had dried him with on the foot of his bed, then turned toward the door.

"Good night, Emily Rose."

She stole a glance at him and knew she would never forget how he appeared, his body gleaming all gold and tan and velvet-dark shadows in the candlelight.

"Thank you," he said huskily, "for . . . warming me."

"You're welcome." She gave him an uncertain smile and took a candle from a sconce. Quietly she slipped through the door.

"Emily?"

There was something in his voice, almost an urgency, as he called her back, and she turned, hesitating there in the doorway.

"What was her name?"

Her brow creased in confusion. "Whose name?"

That fallen-angel face was wreathed with a solemn light, reluctance darting in his eyes, as if he didn't want to ask but couldn't help himself. "Your daughter's," he said at last. "What was your little girl's name?"

Emily's throat constricted, her fingers tightening on the candlestick. "Her name was Jenny."

"Jenny." He repeated it, soft, like an echo.

She turned away, walking down the corridor.

This time he let her go.

9

*I*an lay stretched out naked on the rumpled sheets of his bed, the breeze from the open window feathering over his bare chest, his thighs, the curve of his arm that lay crooked above his head. A thin sheen of sweat clung to every sinew, as if he'd just finished with passionate love-play, but his muscles were as taut as iron bands, his limbs restless as he stared at the dark canopy above him.

How long had he lain here listening to the night sounds and the unsteady beat of his own heart? How many hours had he attempted to steel himself against a hundred sensations that would give him no peace?

Emily Rose . . .

Even her name was like a prayer, soft, sweet. Far beyond his touch.

But she had touched him . . . with those desperation-tinged hands as she peeled away his sodden clothing. She had touched him with the haunting sorrow in those wide violet eyes as she whispered to him of tragedies so crushing he was stunned by her courage in the face of such pain.

Every place her fingers had brushed against his skin, it was as if she had pressed the feel of her into his flesh, as if she had stripped away things far more dangerous than the wet linen that had covered him.

She had peeled away his protective layer of cynicism, the biting edge of humor he'd used for so long to keep people at a distance. She'd stripped away the image of the arrogant, selfish bastard who cared for nothing, no one. She had made him say things he knew he shouldn't say, ask things he knew he shouldn't ask.

And when she had answered—sweet God, when she had answered him in that halting angel's voice, trusting him with secrets he sensed she'd confided to almost no one before—Ian had felt more exposed than he'd ever been in his life. Vulnerable to a woman with eyes like a wounded Madonna, bewitched by hands as soft as gardenias, enchanted by a smile so lovely, so fragile, it had pierced his heart.

Ian tossed his head against the pillow and flung his arm over his eyes as he remembered what she had said about the husband she had buried in England years ago.

He was a good man. Gentle. Sensitive. Kind.

Why had those words twisted inside Ian, forming a hard knot of pain? He had never wanted to be any of those things. He had fought to crush those traits in himself since he was fifteen, a boy on the brink of manhood, who had watched his father destroy his mother and watched his mother willingly sacrifice herself to his father's appetites.

From that time on, Ian had wanted to be the kind of man who inspired only lust in women's hearts, fleeting rushes of pleasure with no chains of responsibility, no duties or obligations, no hideous swelling of their stomachs with his seed, to be followed by hours of screaming and agony giving birth.

It had sickened Ian to watch his father sob time after time as the echoes of his wife's travail battered at him from the bedchamber above. It had infuriated Ian to see him kneeling at his wife's bedside time after time, swearing he would never put her through such torture again.

But his father had been a *good* man. He had *loved* his wife. And he was far too *sensitive* and *kind* to commit adultery against her.

No. Ian had made certain he was not a man like his father.

But now the true extent of Ian's own debauchery was being revealed.

He wanted Emily d'Autrecourt.

He felt the primal pull to mate with her as certainly as did his stallion when he scented an exquisite mare. The urges were just as primitive. And there could be little doubt that once the coupling was over, Ian would forget about her just as quickly as Mordred forgot the filly who had caught his fancy for such a wildly passionate moment.

Ian had sampled more women than he could count. Enjoyed their beauty, their wit, their bodies. Then he had left them. It was a game. They had all understood that before they began.

Why should he be stricken with this damned inconvenient case of scruples now?

It was not as if he would ruin the violet-eyed governess with his attentions. Emily d'Autrecourt was no naive virgin guarding her maidenhead. She had shared a man's bed before. Then why should his feelings toward her be any different from his feelings toward the other experienced women who had caught his eye? Why did these new, uncomfortable emotions chafe at him, make him feel somehow unclean? Unworthy?

Ian grimaced. That was what came of not downing enough claret with dinner. He was being absurd.

What kind of madness had he been afflicted with in that hour when he had stared down into Emily d'Autrecourt's delicate face? Why did he suddenly feel as if the fates had decreed that he make amends for his degenerate past? Go off like some knight of old in quest of the Holy Grail? And bathe in a blessed waterfall to cleanse himself of sin? Embark on some pilgrimage so he could be worthy to offer himself in humble devotion to a princess in a tower?

No, it was too late for that. He was far beyond redemption, already the devil's own. He could only hope to take as many of his fellow damned souls down to hell's gates along with him as possible.

And tomorrow at dawn he would put the devil's calling cards into the hands of hard-eyed men who knew how to use them. Weapons. Nearly a hundred of them were hidden in lethal perfection at Pendragon's lair. In the morning he would sort through them and ready them for shipment north. North, to belligerent Boston, where pugnacious colonials had been thumbing their noses at English authority for so long. Boston, that bed of hot coals that King George's soldiers had been dancing upon.

What better way to forget a heart-shaped face blushed with the most subtle rose? What better way to forget the shivers of sensation that had jolted through him at a touch so innocent, so potently stirring, it seemed to thrum through him still? What better way to remember the very things he had said to Tony on the night Lucy had arrived, bringing a whirlwind of chaos with her?

Ian froze, suddenly struck with the memory of his argument with Tony the night they had abducted Lemming Crane. The echoes of his words haunted him.

What if Atwood and his dogs captured someone you loved? Ian remembered demanding of his friend. What would you sacrifice to save her? How far would you go . . . ?

With an oath Ian levered himself upright in bed. By God, this torment he was feeling was ridiculous. He hadn't even known the Englishwoman for an entire day, and as for Lucy, he had not even known of her existence before last night. Why the devil was he feeling so damned raw? Why did his own words seem to mock him?

Ian flung his legs over the edge of the bed, stood up, and paced to the window. Cooled by the storm, the breeze caressed his face like the touch of a familiar lover.

But even the night, with its dark promise, couldn't banish the taste of Emily d'Autrecourt's kiss from his lips. Even the night couldn't drive the pulsing emptiness from the core of Ian's soul.

The afternoon sun was coasting down the sky, trailing ribbons of mauve and gold behind it, like bonnet strings in the wind. Ian tossed the reins of his stallion to the young groom standing at the foot of the steps and strode up to Blackheath Hall.

Triumph surged inside him, filling him with hope. The Bostonians' patriotic fervor alone would have been more than enough payment for the weapons he had sold them. The words they had carried from the radical Samuel Adams, and his more sedate cousin, lawyer John Adams, had fed the hunger for freedom in Ian's own soul.

By God, it was going to happen. The dream. The miracle. Revolution and ultimately independence would be here in time. The knowledge was a gift beyond price. A fearsome, festive feeling raced through Ian as he burst through the door.

"Priam!" He greeted the youth enthusiastically. "I can only hope that your day was as enjoyable as mine."

"It was quiet. *Very* quiet." The youth looked both relieved and a little dazed, totally unaffected by Ian's own mood. Ian's brow creased in puzzlement over the absence of Priam's usual guarded questions about his patriot missions.

"Quiet?" Ian echoed.

"Yes, sir. There was not a peep all day from the little missy. Cook, she's wondering if Miss Lucy has murdered the poor lady, or the other way around."

"You mean to tell me you didn't check to see?"

Priam bristled, drawing himself up with the hauteur of a house servant asked to do some menial chore. "It's not *my* business to go poking around after children—not even demon children like that one! I've more important things to do."

"Coward." Ian grinned as the servant's dark eyebrows lowered into a scowl.

"I don't see you chasing off after the child, either, Mr. Ian." Priam crossed his arms over his narrow chest. "No, better not to know what mischief she's about, that one."

"Possibly." Ian chuckled. "Unfortunately I've always been plagued by an overabundance of curiosity. Perhaps I shall head up to the nursery myself."

"They're not in the nursery," Hettie, a wide-eyed house-maid lisped, peeking shyly from behind the silver urn she was polishing.

"Is that so?" Ian asked.

"Yes, sir. Cook said so. She took some biscuits and cream out to the garden for Miss Lucy and Mrs. d'Autrecourt two hours ago. We've not heard a word since. Cook, she says Mrs. d'Autrecourt casted a spell on that child. She be in a trance."

"Of all the ridiculous— Tell Cook to quit spreading such nonsense before I cast a spell on *her!*" Ian tossed his riding cape to Priam. "I believe I'll go out into the garden and see for myself what Lucy and Emily Rose are about."

"You'd best have a care, sir," Priam warned. "Just because that child's quiet don't mean you should trust her! I've heard tell alligators are quiet, too, when they slipping up on their prey. Next you know, you got a bite right out of your hinderparts."

Ian laughed and headed for the rear of the house, then out the door to the walled-in garden.

It was huge and pretentious and perfectly tended. And it was as foreign to Ian as the garden of a stranger. Only rarely had he come here during the day, and at those times he had either been on his way out the back gate to the stable or had been attempting to get Tony off somewhere free of eavesdroppers so they could discuss secret business.

He spent undistracted time here only when he was hosting fetes and musicales, balls and entertainments. Then night had spread its dusky wings over the garden. Lantern lights had picked out winding paths, illuminating the way for lovers who were stealing away to their trysting places. Of course Ian hadn't given much scrutiny to the vegetation during those times, for one never knew which guests one would see bedded down among the hollyhocks, their clothes in disarray as they stole sips of honeyed pleasure.

But today as he walked the paths, Ian was vaguely surprised to see how pretty the garden was. Cascades of purple and pink, scarlet and primrose yellow, were splashed across a canvas of green. Precisely trimmed hedges formed intricate designs, while stone paths wound like silver ribbons through lush grass. On either side of the garden, and along its rear wall, lovely arches of beech trees had been trained to weave together like an upturned basket, making

cool tunnels in which to spend stifling hot summer after-
noons.

But as Ian rounded a copse of yews, he saw something far
more breathtakingly beautiful, far more inviting. Something
that made him hesitate, his fingers clenching, as he held
himself back, just out of sight.

Emily sat on a curved stone bench in a new gown she
seemed to have pulled from thin air. Cascades of apple-
green satin trimmed with snowy chiffon flowed around her.
A silver galloon stomacher pushed her breasts high, making
them swell just a few delicious inches above the ruffled edge
of her bodice. A bonnet of yellow straw crowned her dark
curls, the ribbon tied to one side of her chin, accenting her
soft smile as she leaned close to the little girl who sat beside
her.

It was Lucy, all but unrecognizable in a froth of white
muslin, her waist tied up in a wide pink sash. Her head was
bent over something she held in her hands, every line of her
body a study in concentration.

"There you are! You are becoming better at it all the
time!" Emily's praise drifted to where Ian stood. "This is
beautiful work, Lucy."

Something about the scene pained Ian, the little girl
without her mother, pressing so close against Emily. Emily,
whose arms still ached for the child she had lost, bending so
near to the lonely little girl.

Ian felt unwilling to disturb that charmed circle from
which he was so obviously excluded. That circle that held so
much attraction and yet so much danger for him. Danger in
the form of these stealthy emotions that seemed to be
seeping beneath his hardened armor, leaving him with this
unwelcome sense of confusion.

He started to slip away, but his boot heel snapped a twig,
and a glad cry ripped through the silence.

"Uncle Ian! Uncle Ian!" Lucy bounced to her feet and
raced over to him in a flurry of white skirts, her eyes shining.
"I have been waiting for you *forever*, but you did not come!
You will never guess what the lady did for me today."

Nonplussed, Ian stared down at the winning little creature. "You mean what Mrs. d'Autrecourt did? You must be polite and call her by name."

"It's a terrible waste of time learning governesses' names," Lucy said with a breezy wave of her hand. "I'm so bad they never stay very long. They go away, and then I have to remember another one. I gave up trying . . . oh, years ago, when I was six."

"I see." Ian tried to suppress a smile, his imagination filling with visions of Lucy enthroned in a nursery somewhere, a line of governesses entering the front door and then fleeing through the back way as quickly as they were able.

But that amusing image was banished when Lucy cried insistently, "You must come! Look!" The child caught at his hand. Ian stared at her, stunned, then let his long fingers close about her small ones, surprised at how little her hand felt, how warm and soft and fragile.

He let himself be led to where Emily sat, her cheeks the color of the most delicate roses, her lips trembling just a bit, as if she felt ill at ease. Shyness stole across features that were as dainty as a cameo's, and Ian was struck by the memory of the night before. The way her hands had stripped away his clothes and her eyes had skimmed over the skin she had bared.

Was she remembering how her attentions had affected him in the most physical way possible?

Did she have any idea what a tempest of desire she had stirred in him? Could she know how damned hard it was for him to keep it at bay?

What the devil was the matter with him? Ian wondered. He had been naked with women before, but never once had he felt such irritating embarrassment afterward. Never once had he been at a loss for words the next time he met a woman.

He tried to think of something light, something easy to break the tension. But before he could, Emily gave him the tiniest smile, her cheeks darkening, her eyes hidden beneath thick lashes.

"Her Royal Highness here has been a very busy young

lady, sir," she said. "We've been discussing at length the virtue of patience."

"Patience! Bah!" Lucy protested. "I hate patience! It makes my head ache and my nerves get all jiggly. Uncle Ian, we got up very early and you were gone, and the lady made Joab drive us to her shop so that she could get her clothes and things and hire a new seamstress to keep the shop open while the lady takes care of me, and I got to pick out anything I wanted." Lucy barely stopped to draw breath. "You know, you were very boring before, but now you'll be quite handsome, even if your bottom tooth is crooked. She fixed me up my very own basket because she doesn't think little girls are clumsy. And you'll never believe the best thing of all!"

The swirling undercurrents between Ian and Emily ebbed in the wake of the child's chatter, and Ian grinned at the little girl, totally enchanted and thoroughly confused.

"What won't I believe, Lucy?"

"*I* have my *own* cunning little scissors now!" the child announced, beaming. "*She* gave them to me!" Lucy scooped up a small split-oak basket and thrust it hard against Ian's midsection. He looked down to see an array of sewing utensils, most prominent among them a pair of scissors in the shape of a golden heron.

"My dear Mrs. d'Autrecourt, do you mean to tell me that you have willfully armed this child with scissors?" Ian held up his hands as if to ward off the evil eye.

"I did," Emily attested, the nervous light in her eye fading, leaving tenderness and satisfaction. "I gave her quite a lot of other sharp instruments, too, so you'd best be warned. I would be careful if I were you."

Lucy gave a snort of disgust. "I'm not cutting things up anymore, Uncle Ian. That was very wicked of me. And besides, it takes a long time to sew them back on."

"Sew what back on?"

"Don't be stupid. The buttons, of course." Lucy dived for the basket at Emily's feet and dredged out one of the waistcoats the child had savaged the day before.

Where the tasteful matching buttons had been sewn on the cream-colored brocade there was now a row of blue velvet buttons, set just a trifle unevenly. Ian took the garment from Lucy's hands and stared down at it. He frowned at the workmanship, then raised his eyes to Lucy's expectant face.

"Do you mean to tell me that you did this yourself, young lady?" he demanded in ominous tones.

"Yes!" Lucy said, not at all intimidated. "And I only stuck my finger and bled on it once. Lady said you wouldn't mind."

Ian broke into a wide smile. "How could I mind when you've improved the waistcoat a hundredfold? I am vastly in your debt." He sketched the delighted child a bow.

"No, I'm in *her* debt. I'm stitching seams to earn back all the buttons I threw away. It takes a very lot of seams to earn all these buttons, Uncle Ian."

"You're . . . what?" Ian glanced from Lucy to Emily. "You mean you are making the child work to replace the buttons? I'm a wealthy man, Mrs. d'Autrecourt, and can stand the loss of a few buttons, I assure you. It is hardly necessary for Lucy to replace them."

"No! Don't say that!" Lucy protested vehemently. "You'll ruin everything! I want to do it! I always wanted to sew, but my mama said that sewing wasn't for clumsy little girls who get jam all over the pretty things and can't get their stitches straight."

She grabbed up her sewing basket again, cradling it against her like a treasure. "Of course I never understood how I would get my stitches straight if I never got to try it. Lady says it doesn't matter if my stitches are awkward at first. She says that all little girls and little boys should learn how to sew—even big men like you! Then someday, if your buttons get cut off, you can fix them up yourself. Isn't that right, lady?"

"Yes, it is." Emily smiled and revealed a small dimple, and Ian felt a tug down deep in his chest.

He fought back the memory of her fingertips upon him, the hundreds of little flames that licked at his skin where he had felt her touch. He battled the memory of the way her eyes had looked, half hidden by her lashes as she spoke. Spoke with those lips that had been so yielding against his own, so filled with sweet promise.

Oh, God, Ian thought, a little desperately, how could she sit there and smile at him? She was so damned beautiful. Like a flower tucked away in the garden behind the stone walls that would keep her safe. Safe from devils like him.

"Do you know how to sew, Uncle Ian?"

Lucy's demand made him stiffen and force a smile to his lips. "No. I can't say that I do."

Eagerness twinkled in Lucy's eyes. "That is the most wonderful news! I've been wanting and wanting to teach someone since the lady showed me. I'll show you how. It's easy."

Totally off-balance, Ian held up one hand. "Lucy, I don't think . . . I mean, I—"

"Here. First you must sit down." It was not a command. It was a royal decree. But there was something totally captivating about this benevolent golden-haired tyrant. And Ian didn't want to be the one to bring the darkness back into the little girl's eyes.

Heat stole into Ian's cheeks, but he allowed himself to be tugged down onto the stone bench. Lucy thrust the piece she was working on onto his lap.

"I only have one more button to go. They were terrible hard to get on," the child explained, "but when they're finished, you'll just sparkle and sparkle. Everyone will look at you!"

He glanced down at the garment, and his eyes widened as he saw his best black breeches. They were all but unrecognizable because of the decorations stitched to the rich cloth. True, most of the buttons had been replaced, but not with the discreet black buttons that had been there before.

No. Each of the buttons stitched so carefully onto the rich fabric held a chunk of crystal as big as a shilling. The glittering facets caught the sunlight and fractured it, sending rainbows of colored light scattering across the garden.

Hellfire, Ian thought, unamused. The child might as well

have stuck beacons on his breeches and been done with it! By God, Lucy was right about one thing. Whenever he wore these things, everyone he met would gape at him!

"Lucy insisted on picking out most of the buttons herself," Emily's voice intruded softly. "It seemed to mean so much to her. I assure you that most of your other garments are not quite so . . . unique."

"Unique?" He looked up at her, fully intending to explain quite logically why the buttons would have to be replaced. But at that instant he caught a glimpse of Lucy's upturned face. Her eyes were brimming with pride. The mouth that had been pursed up with fury or frustration or stubbornness ever since she'd arrived at Blackheath Hall was curved into a beatific smile.

"He likes it! See? I told you he would!"

Ian glanced at Emily and sensed that she was waiting, holding her breath. He grimaced inwardly. What the hell could he say when they were both looking at him like that, all big eyes and smiles?

"They are . . . quite the most remarkable buttons I have ever seen," Ian said with heartfelt honesty. "I'm certain no other man in Virginia has any like them."

Gratitude shone in Emily's eyes, washing over him in a warm violet tide that made his mouth go dry. The corners of her lips curved in a smile that warmed parts of him he'd never allowed any woman to touch.

The wariness that had been so obvious in her face vanished, and he knew she was trying to hide the laughter that sparkled in her delicate features. Ian found himself allowing his own amusement to dance in his eyes. If Emily d'Autrecourt had pressed her hand against his heart, he could have felt her touch no more deeply.

"So, madam"—he forced a teasing note into his voice— "you believe that men should know how to wield a needle. Is that so?"

"Indubitably," she said, her own fingers flying as she basted silver lace on a petticoat for Lucy. "Unfortunately, not many men are equal to the challenge of such a demanding task."

"Wielding a needle can't be so much different from using a sword," Ian said with a shrug. "Both implements are made of steel, both have sharp points, and both make holes in clothes when used with any skill. Of course, these garments don't have your enemy's body beneath them, so stitchery is a good deal less messy, I suppose."

Lucy laughed uproariously at his grisly humor.

"Lucy, you must help me show the lady just how skilled this particular gentleman can be," Ian said.

"Thread a needle for him, lady!" Lucy commanded.

Emily let the silver lace fall into a pool upon her apple-green petticoats and took up a shiny bit of steel and a length of thread.

It was such a simple, common thing, this rite of feminine sewing. But Ian watched, transfixed, as Emily slipped the end of the thread between those tantalizingly full lips to moisten it. His own imagination stirred with images of dampening her lips with his own kisses.

Her hands were deft as she eased the thread through the eye of the needle, and Ian shivered inwardly as he imagined them at other tasks—loosening the ribbon that bound the queue at the nape of his neck, slipping her fingers through his hair.

She had the hands of an angel—hands that should not have had any task heavier than lifting a teacup to her lips or tracing maddening patterns on some besotted man's burning flesh. But as she put the needle in his hand, Ian felt the small calluses on her fingertips and saw tiny cuts where needles had pricked and shears had nipped and thread had bitten deep.

And he had to stifle the urge to lift those fingers to his lips and smooth soft kisses across the evidence of the harshness life had dealt her.

"You don't hold a needle like that, Uncle Ian!"

Relief raced through him at the distraction of Lucy's disgusted cry.

"Here! You must take it and—"

The bit of steel slipped as she attempted to maneuver it in his hand, the point sticking his finger. Ian focused on the tiny, stinging pain, driving away his thoughts of Emily by force of will.

Lucy pulled his hand into the light, examining the drop of blood with great interest. "I didn't mean to do it on purpose," she informed him gravely. "I would have told you if I did."

Ian managed a crooked smile. "I am certain you would, and with great relish. That is one thing I admire about you, Miss Lucy Dubbonet. You are totally open about your skulduggery."

Lucy preened at the compliment, then hustled him about his business with a brisk command. "Here, now. Take the needle. And the button . . ."

Minutes passed as Ian propped the breeches against his leg and labored to attach the button. But it was difficult to concentrate, between Lucy's somewhat muddled directions and the distraction of feeling Emily's eyes on him time and time again.

After a long struggle, in which he swallowed more swearwords than could be heard on a fleet in a week's worth of gales, he tied off the thread in a knot, and snipped it free.

"There," he said, shooting her a grin laced with relief. "Are you satisfied now, Madam Emily Rose?"

"Not completely." She caught at the corner of her lip as if attempting to stifle another of those heart-wrenching smiles. "But I will be when you stand up."

"Stand up?" He set the needle aside and grabbed the breeches with his other hand, starting to stand and put the garment back in the basket. But the breeches wouldn't budge from where they lay against his thigh. They were stitched to the leg of the breeches he was wearing.

He swore as he yanked at the cloth, feeling like a perfect ass, as Lucy dissolved into apoplexies of laughter.

"I'll help you, Uncle Ian," she said at last through her giggles. "I'll take my cunning little scissors and—"

"Oh, no, you won't, you little wretch!" Ian said, with very real alarm. "I'm not letting you anywhere in *that* vicinity with a sharp object!"

"Coward!" Emily's laughter joined theirs, and Ian was

stunned by the music in it, dulcet tones that he had never heard before, sounds that he sensed were precious, and far too rare.

"Ho, madam," Ian said, giving her a mocking glare from beneath his thick, straight brows. "I have no intention of being shorn in the way of Tony's poor stallion. Now hand over those scissors at once!"

He clipped the threads with the greatest care, then solemnly handed both breeches and button to Lucy. "I bow to your expertise, Mademoiselle Dubbonet."

Lucy glowed. "Sewing is not so very hard. Really."

Ian couldn't resist reaching out to smooth his hand over that mop of glossy curls.

The touch made Lucy stiffen, and she seemed to catch herself, distrustful of her own enthusiasm. "Of course, I am only doing this because *I* want to," she said. "If I didn't want to, nobody could make me."

"Are you sure you wouldn't rather take a bit of a rest and go for a run through the garden?" Emily asked her. "You've been working very hard."

"No! I want to sew." Lucy's chin set at a stubborn angle, and Ian could see a wary light in her eyes. "But you can go away walking. You've been here for a very long time." Lucy shifted that dismissive gaze to Ian. "Why don't you take him with you. I like to be by myself." With that, the child turned away from both of them, shutting them out as effectively as if she had drawn an invisible curtain around herself.

Ian's brow furrowed, and he looked into the equally concerned features of Emily d'Autrecourt. There was an aching understanding in her face as she regarded the child, the emotion overlaid with nervousness, as Emily stole a glance at Ian.

If he'd had any doubts that her memories of last night were as clear as his were, they were quelled in that instant as he saw her moisten her lips, her fingers chafing the silver lace she'd been working with.

"You needn't trouble yourself to keep me company," she protested faintly. "I know you are a very busy man."

Busy? By God, he'd like to be busy right now. Snarling his

fingers in the fastenings of her gown, sliding the stomacher aside to reveal the ivory treasures that lay beneath . . .

Ian couldn't stop himself from remembering the heated trysts for which this garden had been the setting in times past. He'd never been quite as zealous in his romantic pursuits as some of his guests had been. Though he was more than willing to kindle passionate fires in the garden, he'd preferred bringing them to conflagration in the more civilized softness of a bed. Ian couldn't suppress an inward grin, remembering the raging case of insect bites Tony had gotten when he and Flavia had christened the Pennington azalea border. Ian had laughed uproariously at Tony's misery, telling him it was no more than he deserved for showing such a lack of finesse.

But as Ian looked at Emily, the thought of tumbling her back into soft pillows of blossoms was far too appealing for comfort.

Ian knew that he should excuse himself and go back into the house. Barricade himself in the sanctuary of his study or ride off to Pennington to see if Tony's temper had cooled.

But he had never been able to nobly resist temptation. And he had never seen a more exquisite temptation than Emily Rose d'Autrecourt dressed in apple-green satin.

"There is nothing I would like better than to stroll with you in the garden," Ian said. "Especially since if I stay here and continue with the sewing lesson, I will probably stitch so many things to my clothing I'll look like a washerwoman's basket. You must be merciful, Emily Rose. Save me from myself." The words were meant to be teasing. He'd had no idea how they would affect him, a strange sensation stealing over him, as if he'd asked for so much more.

"I . . . If Lucy is sure she doesn't need me . . ." Emily hedged, looking as if she very much hoped the child did.

"I told you to go away already," Lucy said somewhat petulantly.

Ian could see that Emily was wavering, most likely trying to think of some way to escape his company. He reached out and took her hand, unwilling to allow her retreat.

"The sunshine will do you good," he insisted, helping her to her feet and drawing her hand through his arm.

Surrendering, Emily set aside the petticoat she'd been stitching. "We won't be very long, Lucy. If you need anything, just call."

She fell into step beside Ian, and he was aware of each brush of her skirts against his thigh as he guided her among the tall hedges of yew. He heard the subtle swishing sound of satin against doeskin and was enchanted by the contrast of her small white hand resting lightly on his hard-muscled forearm.

They walked down the winding path in silence, going deeper and deeper into the flower-spangled reaches of the garden. And Ian found himself savoring her presence far too much to bother with conversation.

"The flowers are so beautiful," she said at last. "It's astonishing they weren't more bruised by the storm." She lowered her face, shielding it with the brim of the bonnet. "I trust you have . . . have weathered the storm as well. That you haven't developed a cough after your soaking last night?"

Ian recalled the night he'd spent tossing in bed, thinking of her, dreaming of her and of the storm they could create together.

He looked away, not wanting her to suspect what he was thinking, certain it would frighten her if she knew. "The truth is that after last night I have decided to pray for rain and to ride in it with great regularity. The aftermath was so pleasant. You warmed me so quickly and so thoroughly that I am still . . . affected by your ministrations."

"I—I would rather not discuss . . . I mean, last night was . . ."

"Was what, Emily Rose?"

"It was a curiosity to me. I don't usually allow myself to become so overwrought." She brushed her fingertips across a tiny blossom, her voice hushed. "You must have thought me quite mad."

"I thought you were quite the most beautiful angel of

mercy I have ever known," he said honestly. "You have wondrously healing hands, Emily Rose."

She reacted by attempting to tug her hand away from him. Ian trapped it with his other fingers. "Look what you've done, not only for me but for Lucy as well," he insisted. "By God, if someone had told me a child could be so changed in just one day, I would have called him a fool."

"It's far too early to hand out congratulations," she warned. "I hope I have helped her, but the hurt runs so deep."

"And you would know all about such pain, wouldn't you? You'd know about such grief?"

He could feel her muscles tense just a whisper where he touched her. "I should have said nothing about my past," she said. "It wasn't a fitting conversation to have with . . . with . . ."

"With Virginia's most infamous rakehell?"

"With any man," she corrected hastily. "I am not comfortable revealing such personal matters."

Ian couldn't suppress the teasing note that entered his voice. "Considering what *I* was exposing at the time, madam, I would say we are even."

He heard her catch her breath, her gaze sweeping unwillingly across his chest. He knew she was remembering how he had looked, half naked in the candlelight. Maybe she was remembering how he'd felt. Had his body pleased her? Tempted her? In spite of her pain, had she wanted him even half as much as he had desired her? The possibility was the headiest aphrodisiac Ian had ever known.

"Mr. Blackheath, I hardly think it was appropriate for me to be in your bedchamber to begin with. It's even less so for us to discuss it now. Please, let us speak of Lucy or of—of the beauty all around us here in the garden."

"Beauty? God, yes, there is beauty here," Ian murmured, glancing at the scenery around him, the hedges and copses that shielded them from view, the flowers lifting their bright faces to the sun, filling the air with their drugging perfume. "But that beauty has nothing to do with roses and foxglove,"

Ian breathed. "Nothing to do with the sunshine or the scent of the blossoms in the air."

He couldn't resist reaching up to trail his finger down the blush-heated curve of her cheek.

"Please," she pleaded, turning her face away from him. "Don't."

Ian's gaze skimmed over the brim of Emily d'Autrecourt's bonnet. The yellow straw now obscured her features from his view, and he felt a compelling need to see the heart-shaped perfection of her face, the sweetness that clung about her lips, the emotions that darted like quicksilver in her eyes.

"You told me to speak of beauty, Emily Rose," he said in a devastatingly reasonable voice, thrumming with desire. "I am only granting you your wish."

"You are trying to . . . entice me. With your words. Words that mean nothing. I'm not a complete innocent. Alexander's friends attempted it often enough. It seemed to amuse them, to try to seduce a vicar's daughter."

"Is that what I'm trying to do? Seduce you?"

Her shoulders stiffened. "Yes."

"Then you are making it infernally difficult, with your face turned toward the flower beds."

Unable to stop himself he took the brim of her bonnet between his fingers, those silken dark curls sliding against his knuckles as he eased the hat down until it dangled by its crisp ribbon ties down her back.

She lifted her chin, and he was struck again by how much she resembled an angel, all sweetness and innocence, courage and a very real fire that burned in those exquisite eyes.

"If I gave you the wrong idea last night when I came to your room, I am sorry," she said. "But I—"

"I know," Ian interrupted. "You are not accustomed to exposing your pain to a man like me. What would you say, Emily Rose, if I told you that this man is not . . . accustomed to what happened last night, either? I am not much given to having a beautiful woman in my bedchamber, having her touch me, run her fingertips over my skin, and then . . . letting her escape without so much as tasting her lips."

"You kissed me when I first came here." Those lips were trembling now, berry sweet, inviting. "You tried very hard to make me think you were wicked. But after watching you with Lucy, I don't believe it."

Ian's breath snagged in his throat. "That could be a fatal error in judgment," he said in a husky voice. "You are a very lovely woman, Emily. An angel who should be far beyond the touch of a sinner like me." The rough-edged tones softened, dropped to a whisper. "Why is it, then, that I cannot seem to keep myself from *this.*"

It was madness, but Ian couldn't stop himself from cupping her cheeks in his palms and lowering his mouth until it was a breath away from hers. "This is a mistake, Emily," he murmured. "But then, I've made mistakes before."

"No!" she protested. "Lucy—"

"Lucy can't see us now. No one can. What are you afraid of? Are you afraid of me, Emily Rose? Or are you afraid of what I make you feel? What I make you dream of? Are you afraid of what I make you see inside yourself?"

He could see the alarm in her eyes, but before she could pull away, he surrendered to impulse and let his lips melt against the mind-numbing sweetness of hers. He felt her gasp of surprise and drank in the soft sound of denial and of pleasure.

He'd learned to kiss a woman with the same skill he used to wield a sword, and with as devastating an effect. His mouth could be ruthless, demanding responses a lady like Emily could not even imagine. It could plunge a woman into rivers of passion so swift and overwhelming she would forever hunger for its power.

But as his mouth moved over Emily's now there were no demands, only a slow immersion in enchantment. His lips brushed over the full, moist curves, the warmth of her kiss insinuating itself deep into the core of him.

His hands slid down the swanlike curve of her neck to cup the bare flesh of her shoulders, his thumbs testing the soft hollow at the base of her throat. Her pulse beat against him there, a frantic racing, as if a trapped dove were trying to battle its way to freedom. A freedom Ian knew he could give to her, if he could only lay her down among the blossoms and do with her the things his body was clamoring to do, show her the things his body was hungering to show her.

Her head fell back as he trailed kisses down her throat, down to the swell of her breasts, and he could feel her shudder with the pleasure she was trying to suppress.

Now he was the one who groaned as he breathed in the faint scent of gardenias on her skin and felt the hot satin of that fragile forbidden place against the beard-stubbled roughness of his jaw.

He let his lips part, tasting the valley where her breasts began. It was flavored with desire and the erratic beat of her heart.

"Ian . . ." It was only his name, whispered in a passion-hazed voice that was laced with surprise and a very real dread.

He gathered her into his arms, and this time his mouth found hers with a hunger he didn't bother to conceal, a raging desire he could no longer temper.

But this was not the familiar hunger of his body. Rather it was a hunger of the soul he'd thought dead long ago.

It stirred to life, agonizingly raw, terrifying.

And in that moment he didn't want her to be afraid of him, didn't want her to see him for what he was—the wicked rakehell, the hardened cynic. Ian Blackheath, Satan's son.

He didn't want her to taste in him the obsession, the bitterness, the legacy that had borne fruit in Pendragon.

Pendragon . . .

Awareness slammed into Ian with the force of a mace.

He tore himself away from her, feeling shattered as he stared into those misty amethyst eyes, those lips red with his kisses, her throat, still blushed from the brush of his jaw and the hunger in his mouth.

Sweet Christ, what had he almost done?

Desperate, he groped for harsh words, brutal words, any

words that would crush the light that shone in her eyes, the light that awakened in him a yearning that was past bearing.

It took every bit of will he possessed to speak in the arrogant, detached voice that had become such a part of him.

"If all governesses are such a temptation, I understand why they lure so many men down the path to perdition. You make me consider paying off my current mistress and taking you in her place."

She blanched as if he had struck her, but he gritted his teeth and went on.

"Come, now, Emily Rose. Let us make a game of it, shall we? I shall douse myself with water, and you may strip my clothes away."

Stricken. She looked so stricken. Ian's gut clenched.

"You are a bastard," she said quietly, so quietly.

"Yes, I am. But you cannot say I didn't warn you from the first. Now, I've amused myself quite enough here in the garden. I do believe it's getting chill."

With that he turned and strode down the path, hating himself for the hurt in her eyes.

10

*E*mily pressed shaking palms to her mouth, feeling sickened by the fever that Ian Blackheath had spread to her with his kiss. A fever of dark, swirling needs, needs she had never acknowledged. A soul-searing weakness that had made her want to thread her fingers through the dark strands of his hair, to draw his mouth tighter, deeper against hers, to taste the enigma that lay beyond that bedeviling smile.

Oh, God, hadn't she learned anything in the years she had spent fending off the advances of Alexander's supposed friends? Had she truly been so foolish as to . . . as to what? Be enchanted by the sight of Ian Blackheath allowing Lucy to teach him to sew? Had she been so foolish as to forget the danger that lurked in Blackheath's insatiable appetites, the shallow selfishness she had witnessed in men like him so many times before?

God, yes, they could be charming. They could fairly reek with understanding and compassion while they were trying to get beneath the lacings of a woman's bodice. Any woman's bodice. But most especially that of a woman who dared to challenge them with her virtue.

Hadn't she seen a hundred times that the only woman a man like Ian Blackheath wanted in his bed was the woman he had not yet sampled? Hadn't she watched starry-eyed brides in Alexander's circle succumb to a pair of soulful eyes and skintight breeches and fall into a torrid affair, only to find that the moment they had surrendered to their own feminine passions, the man who had pursued them so relentlessly raced off to lay siege to an even more unattainable beauty?

Hadn't she seen the devastation and the crushing scandal that followed in the affair's wake?

"Let us make a game of it," he had said. "I shall douse myself with water, and you may strip my clothes away."

A game.

That was what such affairs were to men of that kind. A game that was rigged so there could be only one possible winner. The man, and his selfish lust.

And it was evident from Ian Blackheath's words, and from the fever of desire in those sinfully skillful lips, that he had chosen her hands and body and mouth as the prizes he wanted at present. The diversion of the moment, to be plucked and savored. The conquest to be boasted of over Madeira with all of his fine rakehell friends.

She had suspected from the beginning the kind of man that Ian Blackheath was. And he had taken an almost unholy satisfaction in confirming her suspicions at every opportunity. But never had she suspected the traitorous feelings that were buried in her own breast. She hadn't realized that beneath the heart of the proper vicar's daughter and Lord Alexander d'Autrecourt's child bride there was a woman hungry for the fire in Ian Blackheath's hands and the unquenchable thirst that had been in his lips when he kissed her.

Never had she suspected that she would want him.

She shivered, agonizingly aware of her own response to the beauty of that virile masculine body she had stripped the clothes from the night before.

Despite her own inner pain, she could still remember the hard musculature beneath her hands, could feel his skin slipping like hot satin beneath her palms. She could see in her mind's eye the curve and ripple of sun-darkened flesh that spanned his chest, the flat plane of his stomach, the fine-spun web of dark golden hair that had accented the magnificence of his seminude body.

Her cheeks flamed at the memory of how her hands had flown from the knee buckles of his breeches to the flap of doeskin shielding his final mysteries from her gaze.

He had smiled that dazzling smile, full of suppressed pleasure, amusement, and a beguiling touch of what was almost embarrassment as he had hinted at the evidence his body was already revealing. She had moved him. Stirred him. Made him want her.

What was it he had said on that first night? That he was not used to self-denial?

Emily had had much more practice in that virtue. She had denied herself so many things, so many feelings, so many dreams, that it was little wonder the attentions of a charming rogue with sea-blue eyes had been able to lead her into this foolishness here in a sunlit garden.

But there must be no more missteps in this dangerous dance she was trapped in. There must be no more moments of weakness, when the sensual adventures that beckoned her from Blackheath's eyes lured her away from her own well-developed sense of caution.

"This is a mistake," Blackheath had murmured, every sinew of his body straining toward her, heating her blood until it raced through her veins.

Emily caught her lower lip between her teeth, remembering his brief hesitation, the wariness that had stolen across those features that were as strong and compelling as those of a warring king.

A mistake . . .

Merciful God, hadn't she made enough of those already? And endured the consequences of her folly? Was she foolish enough to have her head turned by a handsome man who flustered her with his attentiveness, unnerved her with the secrets hidden in the exquisite blue of his eyes?

His eyes . . .

Emily wrapped her arms about her ribs as if to shield herself from the memory of those incredible eyes. So blue she could drown in them, so filled with sensual promise she could feel it to the feminine center of her that still throbbed with wanting him.

But the thing that disturbed her most was the other, more fleeting emotions she had seen in his gaze . . . a kind of bewilderment where there should have been only diamond-hard cynicism. A hesitation, as if he were teetering upon the brink of something he didn't understand. And a kind of quiet longing that had softened the arrogant planes of his face, leaving him even more beautiful than before.

The night before, during the storm, Ian had gotten her to reveal things she'd rarely spoken of, and never to a man who was a virtual stranger.

Her memories of Jenny had been treasures far too precious to share with anyone. Her memories of Alexander were laced with guilt and shame and regret.

But Ian had revealed nothing of himself. He had given her no hint of what lay beyond his rapier-sharp wit and his debauched ways. Only rarely in the past two days had she caught glimpses beyond that hardened shell of his and seen genuine warmth in his smile as he looked at Lucy. Only rarely had Emily sensed his delight in the little girl's blunt manner, sensing that he felt a certain kinship of spirit with Lucy when the child was most unruly and most intrepid.

And last night, when Emily left his bedchamber, Ian had called her back, his voice tender, aching.

"What was your little girl's name?" he had asked.

Oh, God, that he should want to know Jenny's name.

She closed her eyes, remembering the look on his face. Haunted. Compassionate. As if he understood . . .

Emily crossed shakily to a statue of Cupid and Psyche and leaned against the exquisite carving.

Who was he, this man who had barreled into her life in Lucy Dubbonet's wake? This man who could at once seem so reckless, so wild, and yet so . . . lonely?

Lonely in spite of his rakehell friends, his wealth, his power.

Lonely in spite of the sensual response he seemed able to coax out of any woman with the merest wave of one long-fingered hand.

Who was he?

No. She didn't want to know. More than that, she didn't want to understand.

She only wanted to find what she had come for. The doll. The hidden message.

Then she wanted to leave this house with its lovely gardens and its huge empty rooms. She wanted to leave this man with his empty heart, and the little girl with her too wise eyes and her wary smiles.

In the short time she'd been at Blackheath Hall, Emily had learned only one thing for certain.

Ian Blackheath was not what he seemed.

Secrets were hidden beneath that mocking grin. Loyalties warred inside that broad chest. She could sense them, feel them.

Tonight she would take the risk and search through the house again, no matter what the danger. She would find the doll and run back to the safety of her solitary life in the shop.

Away from Lucy. Away from Ian Blackheath. She'd hurry back to her tiny shop and stitch ribbons and laces, and argue with portly dames about what color plumes to affix to their bonnets.

She would forget Ian Blackheath and the rebellious little girl working so industriously over her buttons.

She would find a way to stop feeling the pain, the confusion, the aching sense of coming to life that Blackheath had awakened in her blood . . .

"Lady?"

Emily started at the sound of Lucy's voice from some distance away, indignant, almost tearful.

She hurried down the path toward the girl, her unsteady fingers fumbling with her bonnet. She pulled it up to shield her face, hoping it would conceal her distress from this little girl who was far too old and jaded for her years.

"What is it, Lucy?" she asked as she caught sight of the little girl. Lucy stood a few steps away from the stone bench, clutching at one elbow beneath the edge of her muslin ruffle.

"It hurt me. A bee," the child said, displaying a reddening

sting. "But I hurt him back." Tears trembled on her lashes, but she was trying valiantly to be brave. "I swatted him away, and when he fell on the path I smashed him flat."

"You must've looked so sweet sitting there that the bee thought you were a flower," Emily said.

"Then it must've been a very stupid bee." Lucy's lips pressed in a thin line. "I am not sweet at all."

There was something vulnerable in that small, belligerent face. And as Emily busied herself removing the tiny stinger from Lucy's rosy elbow, she was astonished to hear her own voice continuing gently.

"I had a little girl once," she said, "years ago. I would have loved it if she had been just like you."

"You had a girl? What did you do with her? Give her away because she was noisy and cried and wanted to be hugged when you were all dressed up for company?"

"Of course I didn't give her away!" Emily gasped, horrified at what she saw in the child's face.

"Then what did you do with her?"

"I . . . She got sick one day when I was . . . was gone. She died."

Lucy tilted her head to one side, just a little subdued. "She must not have liked it that you were gone," the child said after a moment. "Did your lover take you to Paris, or were you on a trip to see fashions?"

"No." Emily struggled to block out the vivid memory of Jenny's arms clinging to her, Jenny's shrieks deafening her. She looked away from the child before her and said quietly, "It's very hard to explain."

"My mama was gone . . . oh, all the time. I would have been very angry if she left me and I died. I would have come back and haunted her. I would have rattled chains and . . ." Lucy stopped, seemed to consider. "My mama doesn't haunt me. I think she is very glad to be far away in heaven. I think when I get dead, she will lock up the door and not let me in."

Emily was sickened by the child's words and the rejection they revealed.

"But then," Lucy said with a shrug, "everyone is quite certain that I will go straight down to hell, anyhow."

"No, Lucy. You most certainly will not."

The child gave a wave of her hand, as if flitting off to a far more interesting subject. "Lady?" the child asked, tilting her head questioningly. "Does your little girl haunt you?"

"Yes. Yes, she does. And I'm glad. I miss her very much." Emily felt tears stinging the corners of her eyes.

"You miss her?" Lucy stared, fascinated, as Emily nodded. Her little finger stole out to catch one of the crystal droplets trickling down Emily's cheek. "Your face is getting all red. It is not at all pretty. My mama always looked pretty when she cried so that people gave her everything she wanted."

Emily couldn't stop from taking Lucy's hand, squeezing it.

"Lady, what did you do when your little girl got mistaken for a flower?" Lucy asked.

Emily stared at the child, confused for a moment. Then she glimpsed the reddening sting on the little girl's arm.

"I kissed it and made it better," Emily said softly.

"Kissed it? I thought only mistresses and their lovers did kissing things."

Emily's lips tingled at the memory of how thoroughly Ian Blackheath had done the "kissing thing" to her minutes ago in the hidden nook of the garden. But she shoved the disturbing thought away. "A kiss can just be a way of showing that you care about someone. Of making you feel good inside."

"Show me." The child ordered, her face as hard and demanding as that of a general sending his troops to battle. She thrust her elbow out, her muscles stiff as if she expected to be dealt more pain.

Emily cupped Lucy's round little arm in her hand and bent over it, touching the irritated skin softly with her lips. She closed her eyes, a fist seeming to squeeze her heart at the familiar ritual she had performed so many times with her own child, soothing the countless scrapes and cuts of the adventuresome toddler who had been hers for such a brief and precious time.

"That was ... funny." Lucy's puzzled voice broke through Emily's thoughts. "It felt a little wet and kind of warm. It shouldn't make my elbow feel any better at all." Those dark brows knitted together over her pugnacious upturned nose. After a moment she added softly. "But it did."

"I'm glad, sweeting." Emily's voice trembled, but she smiled.

"You are a very nice lady when you kiss things better and give me buttons to sew," Lucy said. "I might decide to keep you."

Emily felt a lump rise again in her throat, knowing that this was one battle Lucy would not be able to win by throwing one of her tantrums. No matter how much Emily might want to stay and to get this child to open up and trust people, there would be no room for Lucy Dubbonet's slow blossoming in Ian Blackheath's garden.

There would be no space in his life for a wayward little girl or for the love she would need to flourish.

And what of her own betrayal? The blow that Emily herself would deal the child when she found the doll that Lucy Dubbonet had taken to love?

Oh, God, there had to be something she could do, some way to spare the child that crushing loss.

Perhaps she could take the message out of the doll and repair the plaything so that Lucy would never know the difference.

But she could hear Stirling Fraser's warning: "Under no circumstances are you ever to tamper with the enclosures. This is for your own protection, my dear Emily, to keep you from becoming a pawn in some rebel scheme. To keep you out of danger."

But that was a danger she was willing to face if it meant that she could spare the child one final shattering betrayal. This was the one gift she could give to this child's battered, lonely heart.

Something to love.

Yet as Emily stared into Lucy's face and felt the need in the child, the loneliness, she knew that she had to move quickly to find the lost fashion doll.

If she did not, Emily d'Autrecourt might face a far more terrifying risk.

A risk greater than any punishment a patriot villain might devise. A risk even greater than the silken seduction in Ian Blackheath's mouth.

A risk so terrifying it made Emily's hands shake and her heart twist in her breast.

If she stayed here much longer she might make the most tragic mistake of all.

She might dare to love Lucy Dubbonet.

11

Lantern light spilled across the rough-hewn beams of Pendragon's lair, the sounds of restive horses in the hidden stable beneath the plank floor seeming to deepen the restlessness in Ian's own spirit.

Except for Ian and Anthony Gray, the building hidden deep in the Virginia woods had been deserted by the men who had filled it hours earlier, readying their weapons, saddling their horses, and drawing on masks in preparation for the mission to come.

A mission that was supposed to be simple, so simple. Far less dangerous than their usual sorties.

But it had been no simpler than the demons Emily d'Autrecourt had released in Ian. It had been no simpler than the fury that seethed between Ian and the man who was even now sloshing water into a cracked basin.

Tony. He looked as if he hadn't slept since he'd left Blackheath Hall. As if he'd spent the whole time since then pacing like some caged beast, most probably attempting to figure out new and creative ways to wring Ian's neck.

And it was doubtful the events of the past three hours had done anything to calm him.

With barely suppressed savagery, Gray stomped across

the room and thunked the basin down on the table, crushing Pendragon's discarded mask.

"Blast it, watch out!" Ian snapped, drinking the dregs from the flask of brandy he'd kept tucked beneath his frock coat. "You're getting my mask all wet!"

"I'm getting your mask wet?" Tony sneered. "Oh, forgive me, mighty and great Pendragon! Please pardon your humble servant! Of course, you got a bloody hole in it yourself, by God's feet! But that doesn't matter a damn! Oh, no. Who the devil cares if—"

"It's an insignificant hole at best, though I do think it was rude of Atwood to deface such a cunning disguise. It's not as if I can run down to the milliner and have her stitch up another." Noting the flash of disapproval on Tony's face as he glared at the liquor, Ian saluted his friend with the flask before he stowed it away. His only regret was that he hadn't brought a keg of the stuff with him tonight.

"Ah, but wait! I had forgotten!" Ian infused his voice with teeth-grinding enthusiasm. "I have a seamstress living under my very own roof! And quite a winning little sweetmeat at that—delicate-boned, full-breasted. Tonight when everyone is sleeping I shall steal into her bedchamber and humbly ask her to stitch me another."

"Son of a bitch, Ian! Don't bait me! You won't like the consequences! I'm sick to death of your damned heedlessness!" Gray grabbed up the cloth floating in the water. Curving his hand under Ian's jaw, he jerked it none too gently until Ian's face was held into the light.

Ian saw Gray pale a little as those hazel eyes skimmed the three-inch gash at Ian's left temple, a deadly kiss from the mouth of one of Atwood's pistols.

"You're crazed to keep that Englishwoman in your house," Tony raged on, swabbing at the gash. "Crazed to keep racing blindly into disaster after disaster as if you want to— Damn you, hold still!" Tony snapped the command. The wound burned, and Ian gritted his teeth against the stinging pain.

"Have done, for the love of Satan! The wound is hardly mortal!"

"It's a bloody miracle it isn't! A fraction to the right, and we'd be writing your epitaph. What the hell were you attempting to do out there tonight, Ian?"

"If I remember correctly, we were helping Nate Hardy move his printing press out of the reach of Atwood's soldiers so that Hardy could continue printing up those delightfully seditious pamphlets he is so good at. However, our beloved Captain Atwood took exception to our interference. Perhaps he didn't think the caricature Hardy printed of him last week was flattering enough."

"Blast it, you *wanted* to engage Atwood!" Tony exploded. "You went out of your way to clash with him when we could easily have avoided it! We've got a horse injured, your head half blown off—"

"Son of Satan, I *hate* it when you pick at minor details."

"Minor!" Tony swore. "We're lucky no one was killed, and that you were the only one wounded! And you wouldn't have gotten hurt, either, if you had followed the goddamn rules and stayed with the rest of the band." Tony swiped again at the three-inch gash with far more energy than necessary.

"Damn it, Tony, that hurts! If you're itching for a fight, tell me, and I'll be more than happy to cross swords with you. But I'm not going to sit here unarmed while you grind that accursed cloth of yours into my skull! The raid is over, and it was a roaring success. Hardy's printing press is safe. Atwood has once again been made to look a fool. The brief acquaintance I had with that pistol ball was well worth the entertainment of watching him squirm."

"Was it, Ian?" Tony's face was hard. "I'm not sure the rest of the band considered it so."

Ian stilled, his eyes narrowing dangerously. "I wasn't aware I had asked their opinion."

"Well, maybe you should have," Tony said, meeting his glare. "There are those who think that you go too far."

"Jesus God, are we back to that again?" Ian shook his head in disgust. "My own men are wary of me? They're whispering of insubordination? If the damned varlets want to slink back to their firesides and drink hot toddies instead of riding the highroads with Pendragon, then we're well rid of them. We can hardly keep King George's soldiers off-balance by playing pat-a-cake with them. We must seem fearless, invincible!"

"It's rather hard to seem invincible when your mask is covered with blood," Tony said. "And placing your neck in a noose for the thrill in it is not fearlessness, Ian. It's pure stupidity, and you damn well know it."

Ian's muscles tensed with fury, and he hated the truth in Tony's words. "Maybe I should have let Atwood shoot me square between the eyes. It would have saved me the irritation of listening to you."

"Blast it, Ian, if you want to get yourself killed, it's your life. But there are other men who have reasons to live. Men who are willing to shed their blood in the cause of freedom, but who are not willing to spill it for no other reason than to feed into your mad sense of adventure."

"Men like you, Tony? Now that you're besotted with the lovely Nora?" Ian heard the bitterness in his voice but knew that it no longer arose from his scorn for such relationships. Now it was heated with the hot ember of despair that had been planted in his chest when he lost himself in Emily d'Autrecourt's violet eyes. "There is the door, my friend," he bit out harshly. "Feel free to shut it on your way out."

"Damn you to hell!" Tony grabbed up the basin and threw it, shattering it against the wall. The alarmed whinnies of the horses rose through the floorboards like echoes of the two men's fury. "The men who ride with you don't deserve your contempt, and neither do I. After what you did last night, riding out alone, robbing the colonel in the middle of an accursed musicale—"

"It was an act of mercy. I ask you, Tony, what would you have done if you'd been riding along and heard that pompous oaf annihilating a piece by Bach on the pianoforte? The doors of the music room were open wide, and he was disturbing not only his unfortunate guests but helpless woodland creatures and passersby as well. I could hardly allow the torment to continue. And considering the way he assaulted my ears, I felt justified in assaulting his purse strings."

"I'm sure it was incredibly amusing, Ian," Tony snarled. "It was also incredibly stupid. If they had captured you—"

"They did not capture me. The ladies swooned over this dashing rogue, the colonel quaked in his boots, and the instrument was silent, thank the saints."

"You made a foolish choice, Ian, a dangerous one, last night, and then again tonight, when we moved Hardy's printing press. Even I am beginning to doubt you can be trusted to make decisions for the rest of us."

Ian's mouth thinned. "Are you saying I'm no longer fit to lead?"

Tony turned away, raking his fingers through his hair. "There is not a man alive I would rather have fighting at my side than you, Ian—when you are whole, when you are not fighting these demons that possess you. Damn it, man, I love you like a brother. But I don't know if I can watch you destroy yourself any longer."

Ian took up the torn mask, his fingers crushing it in an iron-hard fist. "Then do me the courtesy of averting your eyes."

Tony stalked toward the door, but Ian couldn't resist calling to him. "Tony, you'll be relieved to know that you might not have to worry about me leading the raiders much longer anyway. I received a bit of information when we were with the soldiers tonight that was quite . . . intriguing. A private said that my reign of terror is nearly over. It is rumored that some information is loose that will destroy me. Courtesy of our friend Mr. Lemming Crane."

Tony went white, but he said nothing.

"There is one saving grace, however. It seems the stupid asses have misplaced this damning bit of information. Can you imagine? Of course, at any time, at any moment, they might find it."

"I'm sure it will be a relief to you when they do, Ian." Tony said quietly. "But I don't suppose you've stopped to think how that will affect the people you leave behind."

"What *people?* Even you will doubtless be glad to be rid of me. I seem to have been destined from birth to be a burden to those foolhardy enough to harbor affection for me. No one will shed more than a few misguided tears over my grave. And I will not regret leaving anyone behind."

He turned his gaze to the table, thinking of Emily d'Autrecourt, the way her gasp of pleasure and surprise had tasted on his lips, the way her hair had glistened in the sunlight as she smiled up at him from beneath the brim of her straw bonnet. An angel, far too good for a devil like him.

"What about that little girl, Ian? Your niece?"

"And here I thought you and Lucy were at daggers drawn. When last we spoke, you were congratulating me for having drowned the poor little waif."

"Listen to me, you arrogant bastard. You are the only person in the world that little girl has to care for her! You may not be much, especially when you're drowning in self-pity, but you are the only relative Lucy has."

Ian stiffened as he thought of the intrepid little girl who had infuriated him, amused him, and somehow . . . yes, damn it, touched him with her acid tongue and wary eyes.

"Lucy is none of your concern."

"Perhaps not, but she is yours. What do you think will happen to her if you die? Especially if you are judged a traitor? Everything you own will be confiscated by the Crown. She'll be left penniless. But what the hell?" Tony gave a bitter shrug. "You didn't ask for the responsibility. You didn't want her. And you never do a damned thing you don't want to do."

Ian scowled. "I have enough wealth tucked away out of the country to support her like a princess. She'll be taken care of."

"By *whom?*" Tony demanded. "A jack-a-dumpling like that idiot Clyvedon? Who would know how to reach that money? Whom could you trust not to swindle the child out of it?"

Ian met Tony's gaze squarely. "You."

"No, Ian. If you are shot down on the highroad, my

friend, I shall fall with you. Let that rest on your thrice-cursed conscience."

Ian shrugged. "It's your choice to make. I've never hidden my certainty that I'm bound straight for hell. But I never asked for your company on the trip."

"No. You never asked for anything. Never needed anything. Or anyone. Why do you suppose that is, Ian?"

"You are the man who fancies himself a philosopher, Tony. I'm certain you're aching to tell me."

"Because you're afraid," Tony accused. "You need someone so much that it terrifies you, Ian. You're scared as hell you'll be like your father and need a woman so deeply you'll destroy her."

The acid-hot words seared Ian. "Go to hell, Tony."

"Do you know what is wrong with you, Ian? You've been working so hard at playing the role of bastard all these years that you've finally convinced yourself that you are one." With those words, Tony turned and walked out the door.

Ian sat there a long time, staring at the walls he had built with such care, remembering how he and Tony had laughed, here in this hideaway, half drunk the night they had created the legend that was to become Pendragon.

Why did that suddenly seem so long ago?

Why was he suddenly so damned tired?

Tired of the rage inside him, tired of the places in his heart he'd battled to keep empty so long? Tired of the things people expected of him, the things he expected of himself?

He felt like one of the Four Horsemen of the Apocalypse riding straight into perdition.

Because if he didn't keep riding, he wouldn't feel alive.

But he had felt alive when he brushed back Emily Rose d'Autrecourt's bonnet and tasted her lips in the garden, Ian thought with a coiling sensation of something like fear. He had felt a shuddering sense of rebirth, as if he had taken some indefinable step that could never be reclaimed.

A bone-deep feeling of rightness had shaken him, even though there could be nothing between him and the beautiful Englishwoman who had known so much tragedy.

There had been a racing in his blood to rival any wild,

careening surge of power he'd known while riding behind Pendragon's mask.

But he was no man for a woman like Emily d'Autrecourt. He was no man for any woman to truly love. He was a bastard, hard, cold, ruthless. There was nothing of goodness left inside him.

He closed his eyes, hearing in his memory the sound of Lucy's laughter when he'd stitched the breeches to his clothes. He heard her voice calling out to him in that delighted way.

Uncle Ian.

Sweet God, he hadn't even known the child had existed a week ago. Why should that simple word, "uncle," sound so infernally sweet to his ears? Why did he catch himself smiling throughout the day whenever his mind wandered to Lucy's mischief?

He didn't even like normal children, let alone a disaster in hair ribbons like Lucy. And when it came to vicars' daughters, he had avoided entanglements with them as if *they* were the ones who might carry the French pox.

Why was it, then, that for the first time he could remember, he was tempted not to spend his nights drinking and gambling at some jaded party but rather to sit at his own hearthside, curious to see what kind of mischief Lucy had been up to, hungry to see Emily's face, search for an excuse to touch Emily's hand?

No. This was madness. They would be gone soon, the woman and the little girl. And these new emotions he felt were far too hazardous for even Pendragon to allow.

He had to keep Lucy out of his thoughts, keep Emily from beneath his hands.

He had to ride farther, court danger more fiercely, so that it could drown out these new, unwelcome needs inside him. He had to forget the sadness in Lucy's face, forget how small her hand had felt when she had slipped it confidingly into his. He had to let his obsession with danger wash away the taste of Emily's lips, the goodness, the strength, the loneliness, that he had found there.

Danger.

That was what he wanted. What he needed. That was the path he had chosen, and it was far too late to turn back now.

With everything in him, he had worked to become the devil's own—rakehell, wastrel, gambler—a dissolute bastard whom no woman would ever look at with trust in her eyes, let alone with love . . . the way his mother had looked at his father.

Yes, Ian told himself fiercely. Danger was what he wanted.

Endless night-dark highways with pistols firing and branches ripping at his cape as he spurred his stallion into the wind. No one waiting for him, watching for him, welcoming him.

This was what he had always wanted.

He lowered his face into his hands.

Sweet Jesus, why did he suddenly feel so alone?

Emily paced the green salon, her fingers trembling as she sipped at tea that had grown cold long ago. She had retired here after Lucy drifted to sleep, seeking the soothing quiet of this room to get control of her own shaken emotions. The child's curiosity about how Emily had treated her own little girl had been insatiable in the hours since they had left the garden. Lucy had asked question after question. What color ribbons looked prettiest in Jenny's hair? Did Jenny like blancmange or syllabub best? Was Jenny noisy or quiet? And had she ever committed the heinous sin of getting jam prints on her mother's dress just as company came calling?

It had been painful at first, those first halting steps as Emily had spoken of all the tiny things that had made up her daughter. How Jenny had loved sparkly things and bright colors. How Jenny had hated syllabub and adored the sweets her papa sometimes kept for her in his pockets.

Lucy had shared memories of her own sea-captain father. A man with a booming voice who had tossed her high in the air and let her climb on the rigging of his ship.

Emily had heard genuine affection in the little girl's voice when she spoke of the man, and she wished that the captain had been spared a watery grave so he could have tended to his little girl.

Only at bedtime had Lucy's inquiries grown painful again, twisting deep into wounds that Emily sensed would never heal.

"When I went to bed," Lucy had confided, "my last lady put out the light and made the room dark, and she laughed and told me that the devil was going to come and get me because I was bad. I told her if he did, I'd make the devil sorry! I wager you didn't make the room all dark for your girl and talk about devils."

"No." Emily had turned away from Lucy, not wanting the child to see the pain in her eyes, but her throat was thick with grief. "Before I put Jenny to bed, I would dress her in her night shift—her favorite one, with the sky-blue ribbons—and I would carry her to the window. She liked to—to say good night to the stars."

"The stars don't have ears. They can't hear you."

"I know it sounds silly, but I loved to hear her saying 'Go to bed now, little twinklies. Go to bed.' And then she'd wrap her arms around my neck, and I would . . . sing to her."

"Sing?" Lucy had piped up, her eyes sparking with interest. "Are you an accomplished singer or a very bad one? Bad singing makes my ears hurt."

"I'm not accomplished, but I sing well enough."

"Show me. I will say good night to the stars, and then you will sing to me. But I haven't got a night shift at all, only Uncle Ian's shirt that I am never ever giving back to him. Perhaps you could stitch me a shift while I'm sleeping, though, and put ribbons on it, and then I could wear it tomorrow."

"If you'd like."

Emily had smiled secretly as Lucy bade the stars a very embarrassed, incredibly gruff good-night, and then had tucked the child in bed.

"Now you must sing for me," the girl had demanded. "Like for Jenny. But if your voice is very detestable, I shall have to tell you."

Emily had stroked the curls back from Lucy's furrowed brow. She'd swallowed hard, looking down at those resolutely closed eyes. For a heartbeat, just a heartbeat, she had clung to the notes of that very special song, those exquisite tones filled with longing and love and sorrow and hope that Alexander had created for Jenny on the day she was born.

But the notes snagged on the ragged edges of Emily's heart, tangling there, Jenny's Night Song evoking too deep an anguish, too wrenching a heartache, to share.

Instead, Emily had sung a little French melody that she'd taught Jenny one winter night. When it was done, Lucy's eyes popped open, and she regarded Emily critically.

"I imagine you are quite a tolerable singer, lady, when your voice doesn't get all choky. You may sing to me tomorrow."

The royal seal of approval, so precious when delivered in that haughty little voice.

"I like the kissing thing, too." There was just a hint of wistfulness in Lucy's tone.

Emily bent down and pressed a kiss to Lucy's forehead. She was just starting to slip out the door when Lucy's voice called her back.

"Lady? What was your little girl's favorite thing to play with?"

"She loved to play on her papa's pianoforte. She would sit on the bench for hours, just pressing down the keys, making up little songs. She said it sounded like angels."

"My mama had a pianoforte. I played and played and played on it all the time. But she didn't like it very much."

Emily felt certain that Celestia Dubbonet was not the sort of mother to listen indulgently while a child picked out her first awkward melodies. "Everyone needs time to learn, Lucy. I'm certain with practice you could be . . . tolerable." She smiled teasingly, using Lucy's word.

"Oh, I wasn't tolerable. I was much better than Mama was. I never hurt the music's soul by banging and crashing like she did. One of Mama's gentlemen liked for me to play for him. Mama got very angry. She pinched me and told me never to touch the pianoforte again. She locked up the room, and I never ever got to make music again. Sometimes I pressed my ear against the door, and I could hear the pianoforte crying."

Emily looked down into the little girl's face and saw her lower lip quiver. There was a vulnerability in her eyes that she knew Lucy worked hard to keep hidden.

"I don't have a pianoforte to love anymore. Now I have . . . I have . . . something else. I won't let anyone take it away from . . . me. Don't want to . . . hear her . . . crying . . ." The words drifted off on a sleepy sigh, Lucy curling up in her accustomed ball, her fingers tangled in the lace of Ian Blackheath's shirt.

Emily's fists had knotted, her nails digging deep into her palms. The doll. Lucy hadn't said the word, but Emily was certain she'd been speaking of the fashion doll.

Heartsick, she had gathered up her stitching and taken up her vigil in the salon. She had tried to look as if she'd settled down for an evening of sewing, but she was really watching the servants as they finished their work and then began drifting off to their own beds.

Ian had been gone ever since he had left her in the garden. And though Emily certainly had no wish to see him, she didn't dare begin her search until Blackheath was safe in his own bed. For even a man like Blackheath might grow suspicious of a governess caught roaming through his house twice.

She couldn't risk confronting the man again in a darkened corridor . . . not after what had happened in the garden.

And yet the waiting was driving her mad. The tightening band of desperation about her chest made her want to scream, to break the unnatural silence that hung over the huge, mysterious house.

She paced back to her abandoned sewing, grinding her teeth in frustration as she began to tear out a lopsided seam she had stitched in the night shift that Lucy had asked her to sew. But she had barely taken out a dozen ill-set stitches when she heard the sounds of someone's arrival.

Scraps of conversation were audible from the hallway, and Emily could hear Priam and Ian conversing as Blackheath disposed of his cloak and hat.

The tromp of boot soles neared the salon, and Emily all

but skewered her right thumb on the needle in her effort to appear engrossed in her task.

She heard Ian stop and glanced over, her eyes widening in surprise. His dark mane rippled loose about the planes of his face, and his eyes seethed with clashing emotions—a dangerous restlessness, a stark despair, and a wild, bounding anger. On his temple she saw a nasty gash.

She felt a quick surge of alarm as she rose and hurried to him.

"Ian, you've hurt yourself!" She stood on tiptoe, reaching up to comb back the waves of his hair with her fingers so she could see the extent of the wound, but he pulled away as if her touch had burned him.

"It is less than nothing. The merest scratch."

"I beg to differ, sir. It needs to be cleansed and—"

"Tony scrubbed the blue blazes out of it already, I assure you," His mouth was a bitter line of amusement. "I don't need you fussing over me as well."

"But you should have sticking plaster to cover an open wound. I'm certain we can find some."

"Blast it, I said to stop this infernal hovering!" he bellowed. "It's nothing! I merely . . ." He seemed to think for a moment. Then the light in his eyes grew even harder, more than a little frightening. "I had an argument with another gentleman as to which Grecian slave I would claim at the Roman fete next week."

Emily took a step back, her stomach lurching at his cavalier attitude toward something so perverted and debauched. But as she stared into Ian Blackheath's face, she suddenly wondered if he was lying. Was it possible that a man who could smile so beguilingly at a child, and comfort a woman with so much tenderness while she spoke of her own private pain, could have lost his way so completely, so thoroughly, and been left to wander the dark paths Ian Blackheath had chosen.

What could have driven him to the cutting cynicism beneath his ready wit? The contempt that seemed to be aimed most often at himself?

His frown darkened as he met her gaze.

"So," he demanded, "is the girl asleep, or has she decided to break up all the table legs so she can get a cunning little hammer to pound with tomorrow?"

Emily winced just a little at his harsh tone. "She is asleep." Even in Emily's haste to get rid of him, she couldn't resist saying, "Lucy confided something astonishing to me tonight."

"Lucy lives to astonish people. I can't even begin to guess what she said."

"Did you know that Lucy plays the pianoforte? From what she said, I gather she is quite gifted. In fact, she is so skillful that her mother objected to the attention the child was getting and prohibited her from playing."

"That sounds like the Celestia I always knew. She could never stand for anyone else to display talent greater than hers, beauty more dazzling, wit more entertaining."

"I was wondering . . ." Emily searched for the right words. "There was so much longing in Lucy's face when she spoke of her music. There was a . . . an openness—"

"That should hardly be surprising. Lucy has never been shy about expressing her personal views."

"She wasn't flinging out her opinion this time, nor was she attempting to shock me or to get her own way. This time there was something about her that was . . . fragile, Ian. So . . . fragile. It was as if I could peel away the mask she's developed through the years because of her mother's cruelty. It was as if I could see the Lucy who might have been, if life had been kinder to her."

Ian dragged a hand wearily over his face. "I am very sorry for the tragedies that have befallen the girl, if that is what you are asking. And I am certain Celestia's motherly instincts leaned toward eating her own young if the child dared to upstage her. But I can do nothing to change what has happened to Lucy. There is absolutely nothing—"

"I think there is," Emily broke in softly. "You could buy her a pianoforte."

"For the love of Saint Michael." Ian gave a bark of astounded laughter. "The girl is only going to be here until I can pack her off to school. Three months at best. It would be absurd to buy a pianoforte and have it moved in here for such a short time. It would be an inexcusable waste to—"

"You told me you were a wealthy man. If you intend to pack Lucy off, don't you think you at least owe her a little happiness before she leaves? If you would let her have her music, you might be able to reach her in ways that are impossible now."

"You don't know what you're asking. I made it a point *not* to have any instruments about. They ruin every entertainment. At every ball, every fete, every goddamn house party, the ladies feel obliged to scoop the instruments up and torment people's ears with their half-honed musical skills, and I vow, if I see one more chit simpering over the keys, I'll go stark raving mad!"

"We can allow Lucy to play only when you are gone," Emily cajoled. "I'll set rules for the child."

Ian gave an ironic laugh. "If you tell Lucy not to play when I'm present, the moment I walk in the door, the child will bang on the keys so loud the blacksmith in Williamsburg will be able to hear her!"

"No. Lucy said she never bangs. She says it hurts the pianoforte's spirit."

Ian frowned and then swore as the skin near his injury pulled tight. He raised one long-fingered hand to touch the reddened gash. "The instrument's spirit?"

"That is what she said."

"I see. A pianoforte has a spirit, but obviously my waistcoats do not."

Emily stared at him, feeling wounded herself. What had she really expected? That just because this man had been so good with Lucy about the buttons, he would care about what lay in the little girl's heart?

"Maybe pianofortes and waistcoats don't have spirits," she said, "but little girls do. Spirits that can be battered. Broken. Judging from the things Lucy has said, I consider it a miracle she has any spirit left at all. If you could just trouble yourself to take a few moments away from playing centurion, and help her."

Blackheath grimaced, then crossed to where a decanter of

Madeira stood on a polished stand. He poured himself a goblet of the wine and took a long swallow. "But it is so amusing playing centurion. You should try it sometime, my sweet. Perhaps I shall invite you to my next orgy—in the *chambre d'amour,* five o'clock. Refreshments served. Clothing optional."

Emily felt as if he had struck her. "Why? Why do you do this?"

"Do what?"

"Try to act as if you don't care about anything or anyone? I saw you with Lucy. You were—"

"Christ, I'd pay attention to a performing monkey if it amused me! That wouldn't mean I had developed any abiding affection for it! Believe me, madam, the honey that lured me into the garden this afternoon was most certainly *not* the child."

His lips curled with such mocking sensuality that Emily's heart tripped. She wanted to scoop up her sewing and leave the room, but she didn't dare. It was too important for her to finish her business in this house and leave it forever.

Leave the child who could never be hers. Leave this man whose eyes brimmed with a thousand contradictions—anger and hunger, heated desire and a hidden, anguished yearning. This man who could be such a bastard but who made her want to look beyond what he had said, to find the meanings she sensed were hidden beneath that mocking smile.

Mustering all her will, Emily turned away from him and went to the settee, taking up her stitchery. She bent over it, replacing the stitches she had ripped out with even clumsier ones.

"What?" Blackheath demanded. "You have nothing to say about the fact that I find you beautiful, Emily Rose? You have nothing to say about the fact that I want you? Want you in the way a man wants a woman—naked, needing . . ."

"I believe that you are the one who is needing, Mr. Blackheath. But I don't think you know what it is that you need so badly."

He paced toward her, an almost feral look in his face—

wild, pagan. "Shall I show you what I need, Emily Rose? Shall I?" He towered over, his hand curving under her chin. His callused palm was hot, so hot, the scent of liquor clinging to his breath.

"Give me your mouth, Emily. Those lips that are so damned soft. Open them under mine and let me taste you with my tongue. Let my hands skim away the lacings of your bodice."

She stared back at him, knowing how a soldier in deadly combat must feel. She didn't dare show him how his touch was affecting her . . . that tingling, hateful need his rough-edged words were starting in her most secret places.

"I am no different from any other woman to you," she said.

"Aren't you?" Raw emotion flickered across those devastatingly handsome features. His laugh was almost tortured. "By God, I wish I could believe that. But then I look into your eyes, taste your lips, and I know that there has never been another woman like you. No, never, since the dawn of time."

For a heartbeat, Emily feared that he would take her as he'd threatened to do. Kiss her . . . and far more.

And if he did, she feared what her own response to his demands might be. But at that instant Blackheath swore, yanking his fingers away from her.

"Don't look at me like that!" he roared. "It's too late, damn you! Can't you see, it's too late!"

With a sound that was stark despair, Ian wheeled around and stalked from the room.

12

It's too late. . . ."

Emily sank back against the settee, those tortured words roiling inside her. The look on Ian's face had been that of a damned soul peering through the gates into heaven, locked out, the way Lucy had described, banished . . . abandoned.

But Ian had not been abandoned by someone else, like his little niece. The tragedy of Ian Blackheath, Emily knew with a sudden certainty, was that he had abandoned himself.

Somewhere he had made a conscious choice, taken roads that would lead him here—to this empty house filled only with a glittering throng of acquaintances with artifical smiles, all of them attempting to outdo one another in their depravity.

He had hidden his feelings beneath his arrogance, giving the impression that he didn't give a damn about anything, anyone—especially himself.

But none of these debauched friends had come to linger around Blackheath's forbidden east wing since Emily had arrived here. No one but Tony Gray had been here—and there was an inherent goodness about Gray's face that made it impossible for Emily to imagine the man strutting about in a toga while lewd women fawned over him.

Of course, Flavia Varden had made no secret that she was anticipating the fete with great relish. Then why was it that Emily couldn't imagine Ian in that passion-greedy woman's arms? Why couldn't she imagine a woman of Flavia's kind delving past the sheen of roguery in Ian's eyes to touch what lay beneath?

Secrets. So many secrets . . .

Secrets that Emily sensed because she had so many of her own.

Secrets, like the reason she had come to this room that first night.

The thought drove back the unwelcome tide of empathy she felt for the dark-haired rakehell who had stared at her with such hopeless longing and kissed her with such untamable fire.

And she knew that her instincts had been right. She must finish what she had come here for and leave because the Ian Blackheath who had come to her tonight was far more dangerous than the debauched satyr who had tried to frighten her before.

This Ian, who revealed those startling glimpses of vulnerability and loneliness, was far too enticing, too compelling.

Save me from myself . . .

She was certain he had whispered those words in the garden to tease her. But they had been colored with an emotion that was far from lightsome.

To save a rakehell from himself. To calm a maelstrom of pain and guide a man like Ian away from the path to destruction. It was a scene all too tempting to picture. One Emily had seen countless women embark upon in England. But in the end their dreams had been trampled beneath a rogue's impulses. Reckless impulses that were far too strong for mere love to conquer.

Love?

Emily stiffened. Where had that word come from? She would never trust a man like Ian with that sort of emotion. No doubt it would repel him and send him racing to a woman like Flavia at breakneck speed. Because a woman like Flavia would not expect him to give her anything except the use of his powerful body and the skill in those sun-darkened hands.

Flavia would not expect him to reveal any of the secrets locked inside him. She would not want to heal him.

Sweet God, not that! Emily brought herself up ruthlessly. She must never, *never* think that she could somehow reach Ian Blackheath, somehow help him.

She couldn't even help herself.

She stood, restless, and paced to the window where the Virginia countryside was spread out like a velvet blanket beneath the night.

In the darkness the numerous outbuildings of the plantation slept—the stables, the kitchen, the dovecote that was tucked beneath a spreading oak.

There were countless places on Blackheath land where Lucy could have hidden the doll, Emily thought a little desperately. And yet there had to be some way to reason out where the child had hidden it. If she were Lucy, where would she tuck away something treasured, something she wanted no one to find?

A place where few people would go. Somewhere . . . forbidden.

Forbidden.

Emily froze for a heartbeat, unable to breathe. Of course. Of all the places on this vast plantation, Lucy would doubtless take the doll to the one place she was forbidden to enter. The place everyone was forbidden to enter.

The east wing.

Emily's heart thudded against her rib cage as she remembered Ian's warning: "If I were you, I would stay as far away from the East Wing of the house as possible. You would not like what you find there."

What could there be? Something so sordid she could not even imagine? Or was he lying about what lurked there, as certainly as he was about his own soul? Blackening it in her eyes so that she wouldn't suspect the truth.

She took up a brass candleholder and touched the wick of the candle to one of the others that illuminated the room. But as she started for the door, she was disturbed by memories of Ian stumbling across her last night while she searched.

What if she encountered him again?

No. He had looked exhausted when he left the green salon a while ago. Between the throbbing pain he must have been feeling from the gash in his head, and the effects of the liquor she had smelled on his breath, he was probably in his own room by now, sprawled out across his own bed.

She quickly crushed the vivid vision she had of him there, tossing fitfully on the coverlets as he fought the secret pain that lurked in the hidden depths of his eyes.

"There has never been another woman like you." He had rasped the words in the Green Salon, unable to keep the raw longing from his voice.

"It's too late. . . ."

Emily caught her lip between her teeth. It was too late. For him. For her. For Lucy. Too late . . .

Quietly she slipped out of the room, into the hall. There would be no chance meetings in Ian's private wing. No danger of running afoul of stray servants. She could go about her search, and then . . . then go upstairs and peek into Lucy's bedroom, tuck her little feet beneath the coverlets just as she had Jenny's every night in their rooms in London.

She could stand, looking at Lucy's face, angelic in sleep. Serene in a way it would never be when the child was awake and waging battle against the world.

Her hand would be clutched in the lace that iced the shirt. If only Ian could see it, he might smile again and . . .

Stop this! Emily raged inwardly. Hurry!

She wound her way through corridors that were wide and airy to allow in the cooling flow of summer's breeze. Then she came to a pair of intricately carved doors. She hesitated for a moment, astonished by their beauty. Carved into the doors was a scene from an ancient myth. Man's awkward attempt to explain the inexplicable, to reason out how life's horrors had been poured out over the world. A lovely Pandora held a box in her hands, the lid open wide, while plagues and hunger, death and demons, swirled around her.

It was a warning.

Emily felt herself shiver. But she was not like Pandora, compelled to uncover the forbidden only because of her own curiosity. There was far too much at stake here to turn back now.

Glancing over her shoulder to make certain she was alone, Emily reached for the doorknob and was relieved to feel it turn easily in her hand. She slipped through the doors and shut them behind her.

Her single candle did little to drive back the darkness. The corridor flowed out before her as dark as the river Styx, as mysterious as the man who called this wing his own.

But as she glimpsed beautiful pictures and lovely statuary in the corridor leading east, she felt slightly more at ease. It seemed little different from the rest of Blackheath Hall. At the end of the hallway was a half-open door. Emily was drawn toward it as if it possessed some secret current, some magical spell.

Her fingers trembled on the candlestick, the light reflecting off the walls writhing in ghostly patterns, as if even the flame were frightened.

She sucked in a deep breath as she neared the door, swallowed hard as she pushed it open.

The chamber was so vast that the candlelight did nothing to chase the shadows away from the far corners of the room. Emily glanced at the area caught in the web of the candle's glow, a gasp of astonishment breaching her lips.

If ever the Lord of Darkness had wished to tempt angels away from heaven, he would have chosen this site for their seduction.

It was a room fashioned for pleasures of the flesh— unashamedly lush, sensual—and as Emily's eyes scanned the chamber, she felt a swift stab of pain as she wondered how many women Ian Blackheath had escorted down that long, forbidden hallway and into this, his private domain.

An exquisite bed was enthroned on a dais in the center of the room. A volume of love sonnets lay open upon a bedside table, twin goblets in readiness beside an elegant decanter of wine. Imported sweetmeats waited on a silver tray to tempt tongues heated by kisses, tangling in passion.

In one corner stood the oddest-shaped piece of furniture Emily had ever seen. It looked almost like a two-tiered divan covered in damask with curled bits of ornamental ironwork in the shape of vestal virgins protruding at strange angles.

Emily ran her fingers over it, totally nonplussed. What was it? A place for two people to lounge, one above the other? A convenience for a room in which there was not enough space for more pieces of furniture?

But that made no sense at all. This room was gigantic.

She raised her gaze again to look around, her eyes now focusing on the walls.

A hot flush stained her cheeks at what she saw, but there was such amazing beauty that she couldn't tear her gaze away.

Black velvet was looped back to reveal stunningly beautiful murals that covered the walls from the floor to the soaring ceilings. Figures that Emily recognized as the most famed lovers of myth succumbed to passion there upon the walls, feeding the flames of their desire.

Orpheus reveled in Eurydice's arms, Jason arched his muscular body against the lush breasts of Medea. Persephone, willing and wanton, forgot her anguished separation from her mother in the heated embrace of Hades, the illicit pleasures he schooled her in darker and more forbidden than his mythical domain.

While above the strange piece of furniture, Cupid, perfection in masculine face and form, adored Psyche with his hands and mouth. The likeness was a study in exquisite line and shadow, portraying the darkness in which the two loved, so that the mortal Psyche could not look upon the face of the god who was her husband.

Emily stepped nearer the image of the Roman god of erotic love, transfixed as she tried to make out the features the artist had painted veiled in shadow. There was something vaguely familiar about the angle of jaw, the thick, rippling darkness of his hair, the straight, aristocratic nose, the mouth, full and soft and sensual.

The image seemed so real that Emily almost reached out to touch it. But as she stared into Cupid's heavy-lidded eyes her breath caught at the fierce yearning in eyes of night-shadowed blue.

"Sweet heaven, it . . . it's Ian."

"Very perceptive."

The hard voice made Emily wheel around, a scream caught in her throat as candlelight groped with tentative fingers beneath a midnight velvet curtain that shielded a window seat.

In a heartbeat the sight imprinted itself in her mind forever. Gold ribbons of light tangled in glossy dark hair and flowed over features so unyielding that Emily could scarce draw breath.

Ian.

He lounged against a scarlet cushion, every bit as sensual and as threatening as the image of the Roman gods all around her. Black breeches were molded tight against the long thighs stretched out before him. His shirt was open, those strong tanned fingers curved around the stem of a goblet half full of something intoxicating.

Dear God, what had he been doing here? she thought a little wildly. Sitting in the darkness, like Hades, alone?

The candlelight writhed drunkenly in her shaking hand, as she watched him uncoil himself from the seat with the grace of a stalking panther. He drained the goblet, then paced toward her, slowly, deliberately, his upper lip curled in a snarl that was terrifying.

But even though his eyes were filled with anger and dark desire, Emily could see in them the yearning that the artist had captured in the mural. And she felt as if she could touch the pain that seemed to vibrate from every pore of his body.

He was dangerous. Yes. In the same way an animal was, caught in some snare he alone could see. Yet never had she felt such an urgent need to reach out and release him.

He took the candle from her hand, then turned to touch its flame to the cascade of tapers in a silver branch on the table beside the odd-looking settee. The room was washed in light.

If it had been sinfully beautiful before, now it was even more stunning, more imposing. . . .

Not with the lewdness that some of Alexander's friends had displayed on occasion. Rather, the mythical men, locked in passion with their lovers, were strangely tender despite their hot desire, and their women were both ardent and adoring.

Passion. Never had Emily seen the secrets between a man and a woman so vividly displayed. Never had she guessed that the awkward fumblings she and Alexander had experienced beneath the sheets of their bridal bed could be spun out into a primal dance that was at once awesomely beautiful and wildly sensual.

Never had she been able to envision quite so clearly what the heat in Ian Blackheath's hands had promised her.

But her woman's body had known. It had shuddered and tingled and burned. Her mouth had known when it opened beneath his kiss, allowing him entry.

He turned away from the candles, his eyes finding hers again, harsh, compelling. "The artist thought that it might be amusing for me to pose for one of the murals. I was happy to oblige him, although it was difficult to pose with such a beautiful lady in my arms for so many hours, feel her skin beneath me, her feminine charm, and not act on my baser impulses. Of course, any sacrifice in the name of art."

Emily stared at him, all words trapped in her throat as certainly as she was trapped in this room, her escape cut off by this hard-eyed man with the mouth of a fallen angel.

"What are you doing here, Emily Rose? Searching for a bed?" his words were a trifle slurred with drink, his laugh a trifle ugly. "By God, my little beauty, this time you've assuredly found one."

"I came to search for the doll Lucy took from my shop," Emily flung back, resolved not to show him how terrified she was. "I thought . . . thought she might have hidden it here."

"The doll?" His eyes narrowed. He took a step closer. The aura of sensuality about him was so thick Emily could scarce draw breath. "Do you mean to tell me that you sat with the child all day, that you listened to her, heard her pain, and you would still take the doll away from her? What was the sewing basket, Emily Rose? And all those lovely smiles you gave to Lucy? Were they bribes to get what you wanted?"

"I just—just need to see the pattern of the gown. I already have orders—"

"Tell the women who made them to go to the devil. You don't need their coin anymore. I'm certain you have other talents besides stitchery. You are far too beautiful to be wasted as a milliner, to spend your life bending over your needlework until these lovely shoulders grow stooped, those eyes of yours, so damn wide and wondering and filled with promise becoming squinty from plying your needle in the dimness."

His hand reached out, tangling in a silken skein of her hair. "No, Emily, you were fashioned for far different pursuits. To open yourself to a man, to take his passion. To feel it break over you, so wild you go mad with the power of it."

"I've already been a man's wife," she said in a shaky voice.

"Ah," Ian said with a nasty smile. "But have you ever been a man's *lover?* Tell me, Emily Rose, did your husband know how to seduce you? Entice you? Did he know how to draw out the ribbon of your pleasure until it was so taut you were crying out for release?"

Emily's whole body quivered at his words. It was as if she were some instrument he was stroking with the fingers of a master. She battled to keep her voice steady. "I've heard enough," she managed. "You're drunk, Ian, and—"

"Not nearly drunk enough." Ian gave a harsh laugh. "If I were drunk enough, I wouldn't ache for you like this. If I were drunk enough, I could pretend I didn't want you. If I were drunk enough, I could satisfy myself with some other woman, Emily. I could close my eyes and imagine she was you."

A sound caught in her throat, and she started to dart past him.

His arm shot out, a steely length of muscle blocking her way. "Tell me, Emily, did Alexander d'Autrecourt ever strip away your clothes and leave the candles lit so that he could just look at you? I would, by God. I would spread you out across the coverlets like some pagan goddess, and I would taste you. Everywhere. Anywhere."

"What happened between my husband and me is none of your concern. Now, move your arm and let me leave at once."

"Oh, yes, I remember now," Ian sneered. "Your husband was a *good* man. *Sensitive. Kind.* I wager he barely raised up the edge of your nightgown when he bedded you and apologized afterward for the hunger he had for your beautiful body."

The words were so close to the truth that they lashed Emily like a whipcord. She spun away from him, but her vision filled with the image of Cupid seducing his wife. The wife who would destroy their love because she refused to trust him.

Emily looked at the eyes that had been captured by the artist. She saw the secrets he had stroked into that fathomless blue. And she sensed that every word Ian Blackheath had just spoken was like the brushstrokes of that artist, carried out with consummate skill, for the most devastating effect.

To keep her away from him. To keep everyone away.

She met his gaze with her own unwavering one. "I won't be intimidated, Ian," she said. "I know exactly what kind of man you are."

One satanically dark brow arched, the corner of his mouth ticking up in a tigerish smile that sizzled with sexuality. "How refreshing." He closed the space between them. "We can dispense with the tedious preliminaries and get on to more important matters."

"Important matters?" Emily took a step back, and bumped against the strange piece of furniture, its elegant gilt and damask bulk blocking all escape.

"Yes." The affirmation was a throaty growl. Something frightening shivered to life in those eyes—eyes of blue fire.

"Important matters such as whether you prefer diamonds or emeralds to adorn you, though I think I would prefer amethysts to be pillowed upon your breasts. Such pretty white breasts, soft as the petals of a rose."

Hot fire spilled onto Emily's cheeks, but she met his gaze without flinching. "Do you know what I think, Ian?"

"I've just asked for your opinion, haven't I? Purchasing gifts for mistresses and finding they don't suit can be so annoying."

"I think you are a fraud."

There was the slightest whitening about his lips, and something unreadable stole into his eyes. "What in the devil's name do you mean by that?"

"You are not what you seem. A master of disguise."

For a heartbeat she was frightened by what she saw in his face.

"I see. And how did you come to this conclusion? By searching through my house in the dark of night?"

"I didn't have to look into anything but your eyes. I didn't have to see anything except the way you behaved with Lucy yesterday. The way you were so gentle with me the night the storm came. And tonight . . . when you came into the salon—"

"I was a perfect bastard when I came into the salon." He seemed almost affronted.

"Yes, you were," she flung back at him. "Perfect. Far too perfect for a man with eyes that were so beautiful, so . . . so filled with . . ."

"With what, pray tell?"

"With pain," she said softly. "With loneliness."

His eyes widened, his sneer faltering. "I fear you've given way to wild romantic fancies, Emily Rose. I'm no lost hero, I assure you."

"For a while you nearly had me convinced that you were all the things you wanted me to believe, but now I realize that you are every bit as accomplished a liar as Lucy is."

"I'm burning to hear how you came to that conclusion."

"It was simple enough. I realized that any man who was really as wicked as you say you are wouldn't have to spend so much time and effort trying to convince people that it was so. Any man as depraved as you say you are . . ."

Her words were like acid on old wounds. She could see it in the way his whole body stiffened, as if she'd touched places inside him that were raw, so raw.

"My debauchery should be easy enough to convince you of, at least." Velvet-soft menace laced his voice. "Tell me, Emily Rose, do you know what you are leaning against?"

Emily's brow creased in confusion. "A settee of some sort."

He laughed. "It would be an interesting tea party that you served upon this *settee*. No, it is fitted for a feast of a far different kind than mere tea cakes, though one three times as sweet."

He ran one hand caressingly over the rich damask. "This is called a *siège d'amour*—a chair designed for lovemaking." He drew out the words in a way that made Emily's softest places tingle.

She swallowed hard, attempting to hide her reaction. "It looks patently uncomfortable to me."

"Au contraire. Not for particular purposes. It is designed so that one gentleman can . . . entertain several ladies at once. In the most elemental way possible."

Emily couldn't help stealing a glance at the piece of furniture. "I don't believe a word of it. It would be—be anatomically impossible."

"That would depend on the attributes of a person's anatomy, wouldn't it?" She flinched as those big hands shot out to span her waist, her blood racing in her veins beneath the heat of his fingers. "Here, my sweet, my angel love. Let me demonstrate."

She stifled a cry as he swept her up and placed her on the top tier of the *siège*.

It was astonishingly soft, like a mattress. But then, if what Ian claimed was true, wouldn't it need to be? She felt a sharp sting of something like jealousy as she imagined him here with other women, playing the irredeemable sinner with mistresses who didn't bother to look beneath the hooded expression in his eyes, didn't feel in him the almost desperate self-loathing, the sense that he deserved to be abandoned, held in contempt.

Why? Who had made him feel this way? Who had put those shadows into his eyes? Shadows that were as cunningly hidden as those in his little niece's face?

"No, Ian. You're not going to frighten me," she said steadily. "No matter what you do."

"Frighten you? Ah, no, my sweet. I'm not trying to frighten you. I'm anticipating touching all those soft, hidden places I've been dreaming of since the first time I saw you. I'm thinking of unlocking secrets for you, so many secrets."

His eyes were on fire as he stood on the lower tier, cascades of apple-green satin and ruffled petticoat swallowing the long-muscled hardness of his legs. Emily had to force herself to breathe as he leaned over her, overpowering her with just the breadth of his shoulders, the glitter in his eyes.

He was large, so large, so strong. She knew in that instant that he could do anything to her he wished, that she could do nothing to stop him. And yet, a part of her was certain he would never hurt her, no matter how much he might want her to believe he would.

He forced her to recline on the sloping damask. One hand manacled her two wrists, stretching them above her head, until she felt as if she were laid out before him like some sensual banquet before a heathen king.

He eased his body atop hers, his weight a heady wonder, his iron-honed muscles imprinting themselves in her flesh even through the layers of her clothing. She could feel his chest crushing her breasts, his legs tangling with her own. She could feel the steely hard lance that made him a man pressing insistently against her thigh.

And his mouth . . . it started at the gentle curve of her collarbone, spreading tiny nipping kisses up the sensitive cords of her throat. Emily felt as if she were slowly melting, sinking deeper and deeper into the silk damask of the *siège,* sinking deeper and deeper into the sensations of Ian's velvety lips toying with her, treasuring her.

With a subtle circling movement of his hips he made her excruciatingly aware of the effect this game was having on him, made her feel the power of him, the length of him. "Do you know how deep inside you I want to bury myself, Emily? Can you even guess where I want to kiss you? Taste you?"

Emily knew that she should struggle, but she felt hypnotized by his touch. By the whisperings of pain in his eyes.

"Sweet Jesus, you're beautiful. You're so . . . beautiful," he groaned. "Ah, Emily Rose, you should never have come here. Angels should never stray this close to hell. The devil will drag you in."

His fingers tightened around her wrists, his other hand grasping her chin, raising her mouth to his. His lips were hot and wild, capturing her with ferocious passion, devouring the fragile curves of her soft lips, taking them with such savagery that they burned.

Emily's lips parted on a tiny cry, and he ground his mouth down tighter on hers, sealing the kiss more ruthlessly, as his tongue swept out, plunged deep. It was a kiss of absolute domination. A kiss designed to show her exactly how powerless she was against him, not because he held her pinned beneath him but because he had made her a slave to the almost drunken pleasure of being in Ian Blackheath's arms.

Emily stirred against him, and Ian deepened the kiss, the kiss that had already pierced so far into the core of her that she knew she would never be free of it. When she was an old woman she would remember the devastation and the glittering wonder that had been left in its wake.

Ian's tongue, hot and sweet and flavored with wine, delved into her mouth, sweeping it with heady fervor, skimming the fragile skin, the ridges of her teeth, tangling with her own tongue in a primal rhythm that matched the slow, sensual circling of his hips against her soft belly.

It was as if he were mating with her, here in this outlandish room, separated by layers of clothing. As if in this kiss, he was already immersing himself in her body in a way that Alexander never had, despite the intimate meeting of their flesh in their marriage bed.

"Do you like this, sweeting?" he growled against her

mouth. "Open wider, Emily. Let me take your mouth the way I will soon take your lovely body."

He caught her lower lip between his teeth, tugged at it ardently, then kissed her again, with almost savage passion.

He brushed his lips down her throat, and Emily ached to feel them skim her breasts, the vulnerable flesh seeming to sizzle with some unseen current of desire that the man in him sensed without words. With unerring skill, Ian pressed his moist, hungry lips against each simmering point, setting it ablaze. He nipped and soothed with his tongue, sucked gently at the pale white skin, then blew against it, deepening the wild sensations that centered in the dusky-soft down between her thighs.

He was kissing her as if she were a whore—hotly, with no hint of tenderness. Demandingly, with no sign of gentleness. Yet somehow, as his lips pillaged Emily's, she imagined what it would be like if Ian Blackheath took her mouth with love.

His hand slid up to claim her breast, tantalizing her hardened nipple through the cloth. She felt him shudder against her at her response, felt his hot flood of passion.

"You shouldn't have come here, Emily," he ground out. "You shouldn't have come here."

She didn't know what he expected from her, but as he broke the kiss, intending to strip her bodice away, Emily raised her hand to that savagely carnal face. Ever so gently she trailed the tips of her fingers against that rigid jaw and down to those half-bruised lips that had been devouring her own.

"Ian, who did this to you?" she asked in a voice that was soft, aching.

"Did what?"

"Who made you hurt so much that you can almost convince yourself that you want to hurt me." Her lips were throbbing, and she lifted her fingertips to touch them.

"I don't—"

"Oh, Ian." She raised her head, and with agonizing tenderness smoothed her own kiss over the hard line of his mouth.

If she had taken a dagger and driven it into his chest he could have seemed no more stunned. And Emily's heart twisted as she remembered Lucy's face when the bee sting had been healed with a kiss.

Tenderness . . .

Had he ever known what it was? Or did it mystify him just as certainly as it had the little girl?

She cupped her palms over the hard square of his jaw, stroking him gently with her thumbs.

"Stop it, damn it!" Ian groaned. "Don't look at me like that! Son of a bitch, I just kissed you as if you were a harlot, all but bruised your lips, and still you look at me with those damned angel eyes, touch me with those hands. Sweet God, Emily Rose, can't you see I'm trying to save you!"

She tipped her face up to his once more, kissing the tiny cut on his chin as she had Lucy's sting, wishing she could heal him as easily.

With an oath, he flung himself off the *siège* and grasped her arm, hauling her with him. He led her out of the east wing, his face dark, immovable. Outside the door he turned to lock it. But as Emily stared at the image of Pandora's box, she knew that it had already been opened.

She and Ian Blackheath had released something that, like Pandora's demons, could not be called back.

And she was certain the stormy-eyed man knew that truth, too, as he stalked away from her as if hell itself were at his heels.

13

The green salon was washed in sunshine, the windows that had been dark two nights before were now glistening with late afternoon sun. For two days Emily had managed to avoid Ian altogether—a task that had proved surprisingly easy, since Ian had only rarely darkened the door of Blackheath Hall.

From servants' gossip, she had learned that business kept him away from the plantation most of the day, and during those rare times when he was about, she had allowed Lucy to go see him but had kept herself as far away as possible, retreating either to the gardens or to this room she had grown familiar with on the night she had wandered into Ian's private domain.

She had filled up the days exploring the plantation grounds with Lucy, the child having no idea that Emily was really searching for the doll. But in spite of all of her efforts, she hadn't found so much as a clue to where the plaything and its precious contents might be.

She wanted more than anything to escape Ian, escape Lucy, escape the feelings that were warring inside herself. She wanted to find the message so that the man and the child she had grown to care for would be safe.

But even her fear on their behalf and her desperate search

for the doll couldn't drive the unwelcome feelings away from her mind, from her heart.

And today even the chatter of the loquacious Lucy, who had exchanged stitching buttons for sketching, couldn't seem to drive the shadows of Ian from the room.

Emily shivered. Even though she had not seen Ian for two days, he had been with her. A presence so strong that Emily almost felt as if she could touch him, feel him haunting her. Every time she drew pen across paper, it was his face she saw, and while she struggled to produce her own drawing— one that Queen Lucy had commanded her to create— Emily's thoughts kept wandering to the man who had tried so hard to drive her away from him, yet had succeeded only in making her more enchanted than ever by the fires in his hands, the secrets in his eyes, and that hopeless longing that had been on his lips when they took hers.

Savaged hers, he would have claimed. But beneath the harshness of his kiss she had sensed emotions that Ian couldn't hide. Beneath the rough passion in his callused hands she had felt hints of a love so potent that she had lain awake all night, remembering.

Remembering the painting that graced the walls of the *chambre d'amour.* Remembering Ian making love to *her* with that look of almost anguished devotion in his eyes.

"You are not drawing again, lady." Lucy's voice made Emily start, and her cheeks flamed as if the child could see the most ungovernesslike thoughts that filled Emily's mind.

"I . . . I'm sorry. I was a bit distracted."

"Everybody is distracted today. Cook was distracted when I went to the kitchen. You are distracted. But Uncle Ian is the very most distracted of all, I think."

Emily looked away, wishing to high heaven the child hadn't begun chattering about Ian. "If your uncle snapped at you, I'm sure he didn't mean it. He is a—a very busy man. I'm sure he has a good deal of business to attend to."

Lucy licked the point of her charcoal pencil and stared meditatively at her composition. "Oh, he wasn't thinking about any business. I'm sure of that. He was thinking about other things. I saw him early this morning when I was sliding down that wonderful curvy rail on the stairway. He had that look on his face, so I knew."

The child was making no sense at all, or was it that any time Ian Blackheath's name was mentioned, Emily's own senses became addled? "That's nice," she said, attempting to guide the child away from the unnerving subject of her uncle. "Are you able to slide down the banister very fast?"

"Uh-huh. 'Specially after I put butter on it." Lucy looked up from her work and eyed Emily with frank appraisal. "You know, I lied when I said you weren't pretty. You make me think about a flower in a garden. My mama was pretty, too. But she made me think of a flower with a bee inside waiting to sting me."

Emily felt that familiar tug of empathy for the intrepid little girl. She smoothed her hand over Lucy's curls. "Thank you for the compliment, your ladyship."

"I am not going to be a ladyship when I grow up. I am going to be a pirate. But I'm not going to use cannons to take other ships. I am going to play on my pianoforte, and all the sailors will listen like 'Dysseus listened to the sirens, and when they're all staring in a trance, my men will board their ships and make them walk the plank if they don't say it's the most wonderfulest music they ever heard."

"I am certain you will be quite notorious. There will have been no other pirate like you."

"You may come with me if you like," Lucy offered with regal grace. "Of course"—her eyes narrowed again—"maybe you would rather stay here and be Uncle Ian's mistress."

"Lucy!" Emily gasped out, with a nervous laugh. "You are the most incorrigible little wretch! You may put such thoughts out of your mind at once, child. Neither your uncle nor I have any intention of—of forming such an attachment."

"I think he has attachments with you already. And I think you just don't know how to begin making him desotted with you. I could tell you how to act, though. I know just exactly what you must do to make it happen."

"Lucy, I—"

"You must wear your bodices cut much lower, and you must touch him whenever you can and tell him he is the most 'stonishingly brilliant man you ever saw, even when he is being the veriest blockhead." Lucy seemed to consider. "Although Uncle Ian doesn't act like a blockhead as often as the other men I know."

"Lucy, I'm not about to discuss this with you a moment longer!"

The child sighed. "I 'spose I can't make you act all silly around him if you don't want to. But I think it would be fun to watch you get all pink in the face, and see him bring you presents. But since you are being detestable stubborn, you must look at my sketchbook and tell me it is lovely."

Emily snatched the child's drawing as if to use it as a shield from the feelings Lucy's words had set loose in her. But the picture the child had drawn only tightened her nerves further still.

It was no child sketch of a house or a bowl of fruit. No bed of flowers or even a pirate ship. There on the page was an image that was strangely frightening—a menacing figure of a man astride a rearing horse, a cape fluttering in the breeze, a mask covering his features. He held a sword that had enough blood dripping from its point to satisfy even Lucy's ghoulish little heart.

"Lucy, what is this?" Emily asked a little faintly.

"It's a picture of Pendragon," Lucy volunteered. "He has just killed some very bad English people. He likes to do that very much."

Emily shivered. "Where did you hear of such a thing?"

"The first night I came here, the housekeeper tried to scare me by telling me that Pendragon would come and fetch me away to the devil. But I think he is too busy fighting bad soldiers to bother with me. I heard Priam and the kitchen maid talking about him, and they said Pendragon was very good. He gives people money for new roofs so the rain can't come and make their children sick. Sometimes he kills those English soldiers dead with his sword. But when he catches a spy, he doesn't even bother to get his sword bloody 'cause they're so despicable. He just throws them in caves and buries them right alive."

Emily felt icy fingers trailing down her spine. "I hardly think someone who would do something so terrible is a hero, Lucy."

"But the spies and soldiers did a terribler thing, Lady." The child's sense of justice only deepened Emily's unease. "I think they deserved to be stuck with his sword. I wish I could see him stick them! I'd dance around and—"

Emily felt the color drain from her face. "Lucy, enough!"

The child looked genuinely stunned. "I was wrong before," she said slowly. "You are much more distracted than Uncle Ian."

"What ho?" The sound of a masculine voice from the doorway made them both turn to see Ian standing there. "Defaming my character again, moppet?"

Emily's heart slammed against her ribs, and she prayed that he would attribute her discomfort to the happenings of two nights before rather than to Lucy's heedless babble about Pendragon and English spies.

She tried to think of something to say, to make his thoughts veer away from the topic of conversation, but her mouth was so dry from taking in the sight of him that she couldn't have strung three words together to save her own life.

His unruly mane was tied back in a neat queue, royal blue breeches clinging to his thighs. He'd abandoned his frock coat somewhere, leaving him garbed in nothing but a snowy white shirt and an open waistcoat of blue and scarlet ribbed silk.

Yet the most beautiful thing of all was his face, that arrogant face now shadowed with just a hint of reticence, the accustomed boldness of his gaze tempered with just a whisper of bewilderment. In a heartbeat, Emily knew his nights had been as restless as her own and that he was struggling to keep that knowledge from her with his jaunty manner.

"Good afternoon, ladies," he said, sweeping them a bow.

"I have been somewhat . . . *distracted* by business the past few days, and I would like you to come and survey my work."

"I have been very busy, too," Lucy piped up. "I have been trying to teach the lady how to be your mistress."

Ian made a sound as if he were strangling on his own neckcloth as Lucy continued.

"I am quite certain that you would like her to be your mistress, but she will not cooperate in the least. So I drew a picture of Pendragon instead."

"Pendragon?" Ian echoed in a strange tone.

"He is a raider who skewers bad English people, but the lady doesn't like him at all."

"I just . . ." Emily put in hastily. "People who commit cold-blooded murder are not . . . not good examples for children, Lucy. I—"

"You are very wise to warn her away from such a devil. I am certain that the lady is right, Lucy. Pendragon is beneath contempt."

What was it about Ian's face that was so disturbing? His features were so tight that Emily couldn't help but wonder whether or not Ian himself had had some sort of confrontation with the seditious revolutionary.

But almost at once, Ian's mouth curved back into that taut grin, though Emily disliked the glint in his eye. "Lucy, I am certain that you won't have to concern yourself with the rogue much longer," Ian said. "A man like Pendragon was born to hang. Doubtless someone will soon be happy to oblige him by providing a rope."

"I always wanted to see a hanging," Lucy said, glancing down at her sketch. "But I don't think I would want to see that one."

"Well, perhaps you would prefer another sort of entertainment. If you will allow me?" Ian gestured to the door. Lucy got up from her chair, seeming to shake away the almost pensive expression that had come onto her face.

"You, too, Emily Rose."

He extended his hand and took hers, drawing it through

the crook of his arm. With the other hand he caught Lucy's fingers.

Emily was struck by the unconscious gesture. There was a certain possessiveness in his touch, as if she and Lucy belonged to him. And in that instant Emily was certain that the child wished that were true as much as Emily herself did.

Ian escorted them through the corridors to the closed doorway that led into the most sunshiny room of the house—a formal blue and gold withdrawing room that the maids had loftily informed Emily was reserved for only the most important guests.

Ian let go of Lucy's hand, his fingers closing on the latch. "Lucy, this is to be your room for the duration of your stay here. And whenever you come to visit at holidays after . . . after you have gone off to school."

"I'm not going off to school," Lucy said breezily. "I've decided."

"I . . . see." Ian seemed to want to contradict the child, then thought better of it. "We'll talk about that later. Right now I think there is something else you would much rather do."

With that he swept open the door.

Lucy gave a choked gasp, Emily's own throat constricting as she looked into the exquisitely decorated room. Gilt dripped from every available surface, crystal prisms glinting from the chandelier that crowned the ornate ceiling. It was a room fit for a princess, especially one like the haughty little baggage who stood poised on the threshold of her very own wonderland.

For in the center of the room, like a glossy-polished shrine, was the most beautiful pianoforte that Emily had ever seen.

With a half sob of joy, Lucy took a few stumbling steps forward, then stopped and gave Ian a look of almost anguished ecstasy mingled with disbelief. "For me? You . . . you said it is for me?"

"Absolutely, Lucy love." His voice was gravelly-rough. Emily loved him for it.

With a cry, the child raced over to the instrument, caressing it with such rapture that Emily thought her heart would break.

But when the little girl slid onto the bench and began to strike the keys, the ache inside Emily's breast intensified until she felt as if she were slowly shattering into a hundred tiny pieces. Pieces that could only be made whole by the child who sat coaxing mystical, magical music out of the pianoforte, and by the man who stood beside Emily, more uneasy than she had ever seen him.

She turned to Ian, letting her heart show in her eyes. "You are the most wonderful man," she managed, her voice shaking. "Wherever did you find it?"

Ian shrugged, his cheekbones darkening. "It was no great feat. I heard that Colonel Glendenning had a bit of a conflict with Pendragon the other evening. It seems the brigand has an ear for fine music and took exception to the way that Glendenning was playing a piece by Bach. Pendragon forbade the man ever to play again."

"A rebel thief ordering about an officer of the king? I can hardly believe it's possible! And the colonel yielded to his wishes?"

"Er, yes. This particular rebel thief has that effect on people. At any rate, I rode to Glendenning's yesterday morning to inquire about his health, after his humiliating confrontation with the rebel scum. And as an afterthought I inquired after his pianoforte as well. Glendenning was more than happy to part with it. Of course, it took a bit of doing to transport it here in one piece."

At that moment, Lucy turned to Ian, and her eyes were shimmering with tears. "I shall keep the windows of my room open, and I shall play Bach every night for Pendragon. And he will wear his mask and his cape and listen. And he will like it very much because music is the one thing I am most accomplished at that isn't very naughty."

Lucy scooted to the end of the bench, her lower lip trembling. "Do you . . . do you think he would like that, Uncle Ian?"

"You shouldn't waste your music on a scoundrel like Pendragon, moppet. It's far too beautiful."

"I like scoundrels," Lucy said stoutly. "That is why I like you."

With that, Lucy sidled up to him, a shy light in her eyes. "Uncle Ian?"

"What, sweeting?"

"The lady showed me something yesterday that I never knew before. Do you know about the kissing thing?"

"The kissing thing?"

"That it's not just only for mistresses and their lovers and such. That you can kiss people to make them feel better. Or to show 'ffection for them. *She* says it's all right."

"Yes, Lucy," Ian said, looking endearingly ill at ease. "I've heard about the kissing thing."

"I've never ever done it to anyone," Lucy confided, her eyes round and serious. "But I'd like to . . . to try it now. If you wouldn't object terrible much."

Emily's eyes stung as Ian Blackheath knelt down to the level of his little niece, his own voice a trifle unsteady.

"No, Lucy," he said softly. "I wouldn't object at all."

The child hesitated a heartbeat longer, then went to Ian and awkwardly kissed his cheek.

"You are much pricklier than when the lady kissed me," Lucy said as she drew away. "But that's all right. It's not your fault that you have whiskers."

With a groan, Ian gathered the little girl in his arms, holding her tight, so tight.

Emily could barely stifle the sob that rose in her own throat as she saw those strong arms encircling the child, Ian's dark head contrasting with Lucy's golden curls as he buried his face against her.

Those dauntingly masculine shoulders quaked just a whisper beneath the shield of his waistcoat, and Emily could feel the white-hot searing of Ian Blackheath's barely suppressed tears.

Moonlight was sifting through the trees that lined the drive to Blackheath plantation. Emily walked along the dusk-shrouded ribbon of road, listening to the night sounds and trying to drive back the shards of pain inside her.

Ian was still in the blue drawing room, listening in enchantment as Lucy Dubbonet spun out music so sweet that Emily was certain the angels had stopped singing and were bending down from their clouds to listen.

Was Jenny listening, too? Emily wondered as she looked up at the sky. Was she clapping her chubby little hands and cooing with delight? Was she crying out in that happy eager voice, as she had in the tiny rooms in London, *"More pretty! More"*?

The child had been insatiable, forever singing or playing her papa's instrument. Her eyes had always shone most brightly when Alexander played for her.

Whenever she played her little compositions for him, he had puffed up with pride and said she showed great promise.

Jenny. Forever three years old. Like the most fragile bud on a broken rose tree, filled with the promise of beauty, but never, never to blossom.

Would Jenny have been very like Lucy? Her fingers touched with that heavenly fire that made them able to transfer every emotion—joy, heartache, frustration, anger, and, sweetest of all, love—into musical notes that could insinuate themselves into other people's souls forever?

Would Jenny have been as brave as the little girl even now sitting on the bench in the drawing room? Would she have been as delightfully amusing, as incredibly resourceful? Would she have been exasperating and adorable all at once?

No, Jenny would have been far different if the fever hadn't stolen her away. She would always have known that her mother loved her. She would always have known "the kissing thing" and how it felt to be tucked into bed with a lullaby. Her own Night Song.

Emily paused beneath the shadowy trunk of a tree and leaned against it.

Oh, God, what had she done? She had fallen in love with Ian—excruciatingly, totally in love. She had given her heart to Lucy, that most astonishing and wonderful of children. She had opened herself to pain beyond imagining.

Pain so great that she hadn't been able to stay in the room with them for another moment, knowing that neither the child nor the man could ever be hers. She had come out into the darkness to endure the familiar ache of her old grief.

Lucy and Ian were a part of her now, as irrevocably as Jenny was. Something precious, painful. Eternal.

The sound of hoofbeats coming up the road made Emily stiffen, and she all but ducked behind the tree, wanting to avoid whoever was approaching. But she hastily wiped the traces of tears from her eyes and attempted to compose herself.

She glimpsed the rider and recognized Tony Gray. And she could almost laugh when she saw that Ian's friend had bound up his horse's tail in such a complex a latticework of ribbons that it would have taken Lucy and her cunning little scissors an aeon to snip them free.

She prayed that she would escape his notice or that, at the very most, he would tip his hat and ride past her. Instead, Gray reined his mount to a stop a short distance from where she stood.

"Mrs. d'Autrecourt," he said a little stiffly. "Good evening. I hope that you are . . ." The words trailed off, and Emily was suddenly, sickeningly aware that the filtering of moonlight had betrayed her.

Gray swung down with great haste, ground-tying his horse, and came to her, his face a study in concern.

"Is something amiss? By damn, if Ian has taken his temper out on you—"

"No! It's nothing with Ian. He's in the house, listening to Lucy play the pianoforte."

"Ian doesn't have a pianoforte!" Gray objected, totally taken aback.

"He does now. He brought it here for Lucy, as a surprise. A Colonel Glendenning didn't want it any longer. And Lucy adores music."

"He bought a pianoforte for the child?" Tony stared, amazed. "By God's feet, I can scarce believe it!"

"She's been playing it for hours," Emily said, "and he's been listening."

"Is she so terrible, then, that you had to flee the house?"

"No. She is so wonderful it breaks my heart." There was something so kind about the blond Tony Gray, something so comforting in the way he took her hand and patted it.

"I don't understand," he said softly.

"It's a very long, very sad story," Emily murmured, looking away. "Suffice it to say that I had a child once, a little daughter who loved to play the pianoforte. She was lost to me when a fever struck."

Gray cleared his throat. He squeezed her fingers in comfort. "I'm sorry."

"I thought that by coming here I could forget. But everywhere I look, I remember. I watch Lucy, and I imagine my little girl. And Ian . . ."

"What about Ian?"

"He is hurting so badly himself, but he won't let me help him."

"You love him." The words were filled with concern but also with a very real joy.

"I can't. I don't want to. He's made it quite clear that—"

"So *that* is why he's been acting like a wolf with his tail caught between two stones! No wonder!"

"I beg your pardon?"

"It all makes perfect sense!" Gray said with almost frenetic enthusiasm. "The man is crazed in love with you, by God, and he's having to eat his own damned words! I wager he's not liking the taste of 'em!" There was consummate satisfaction in Tony's voice. "By God, vengeance *is* every bit as sweet as the philosophers claim it is!"

"Mr.—Mr. Gray," Emily stammered, "I don't understand!"

Tony grinned. "I fell in love myself recently, and Ian was a trifle . . . It's impossible to explain. Just let me say that I am elated for you! And I'll make him see reason if I have to knock him over the head with an anvil."

"No! Please, no!" Emily cried in alarm. "His head already has a gash—"

"Well, I suppose getting his skull blasted apart would have been less discomfiting to him than facing me after what's happened. I . . ." Gray suddenly sobered, as if realizing he'd said too much.

"Mrs. d'Autrecourt . . . Emily," he said quietly. "May I call you Emily?"

She nodded her assent.

"This falling in love will not be easy for Ian. He'll drive you past bearing—God knows he's made me want to murder him this past week. But once he admits that he loves you, you'll never have to doubt him. Despite his reputation and all the gossip you might hear, there is no finer man in Christendom. If he could only be brought to believe it himself." Gray stared down into her face, and in the moonlight she could see his eyes glowing. "Maybe you can convince him of that. Heaven knows I've tried often enough."

Tony looked away, his voice softening. "Ian is the best friend a man could have. He will fight for anyone who is weaker than he. He's the only planter I know who does not use slave labor to work his fields. He buy slaves at the market, but then he sets them free, offers them employment, a plot of their own land, tells them to stay or go as they please. No man has the right to hold others in bondage."

Tony paused for a moment, then gave a crooked smile. "He is the first with a jest when you are disconsolate, and the last to lay blame when someone has failed."

"Because he so often blames himself?"

"You do know him, by God. Yes. He blames himself. The one thing he has the most difficulty believing is that he is worthwhile, that there is something inside him of value."

"Why, Tony?" she asked, praying that this man might be able to give her answers that Ian never would. "What has made him this way? A woman?"

"I wish it were that simple. But it began long before Ian's first affair of the heart." Tony sighed. "He . . . was estranged from his father as a boy, and swore never to be like him."

"Was his father a cruel man?"

"In his way. Ian's mother died because his father forced his, er, marital attentions on her even after the doctor forbade it, saying she would die if she bore another child."

Tony hesitated a moment. "In the end she did die. Why Ian blames himself for that, I can't even guess. And I'm certain he'd never share his thoughts with me. But maybe he could tell you, Emily. Maybe you could help him understand that what happened between his parents was not his fault. Maybe he would let himself love you if you reached out to him. If you made him see himself the way we see him. Through your eyes."

Emily turned away. "I'd like to do that, Tony, but I don't think . . . There are so many things about me that Ian doesn't know. I have my own pain, my own ghosts."

"Then you and Ian must lay your ghosts to rest together."

Tony gave her a gentle hug. "I'm going to pay a call on Ian now. I want to see if that blow he took to the head straightened out his wits or if I need to adjust them some more for the wretch."

With that, Tony swung astride his horse and tipped his tricorne in farewell, then spurred his stallion exuberantly toward the house.

Emily stood there a long time, Tony's words echoing in her head: "If you made Ian see himself . . . through your eyes. . . . You and Ian must lay your ghosts to rest together. . . . If you reached out. . . ."

Reach out . . .

Emily felt a shiver of apprehension shimmer through her, her mind filling with images of stormy blue eyes and a face filled with savage beauty. A face she had seen touched with far different emotions—confusion, almost shyness, and the first fragile stirrings of tenderness.

She remembered the girl she had been, quaking before her parents on the night her betrothal to the squire was announced. She remembered how devastated she had been, yet not strong enough to defy them until Alexander came to stand beside her. And in so doing ruined his life.

She remembered how desperate she had been on the steps of the ducal seat of Avonstea, how she had allowed the d'Autrecourts to take her child from her arms and deprive Alexander of the care of his wife.

She was not that frightened girl any longer. She was far

stronger now. Strong enough to reach out, even when she was afraid.

To take her own life in her hands. To walk, as the gentle Quakeress had said, out of the water.

Emily straightened her back, shifting her eyes to the house, where Ian Blackheath had been alone for so long.

"If you reached out to him," Tony had begged her. "If you made him see himself the way we see him."

Goodness. Strength. That wonderful humor that crept into his crystal blue eyes. The gentleness in his touch when she told him about Jenny. The almost shy delight with which he had presented Lucy with the pianoforte, the treasure ensconced in the most Lucyesque room in the entire house.

"Oh, Ian," she whispered to the night. "There is so little time before I have to leave to deal with Atwood, to finish this disaster I embarked upon from England. But before I go, I will show you. I shall make you see, just this once, what you are in my eyes. A knight-errant, Ian. Battered but more beautiful than any pristine Galahad. A tattered hero with magic in your eyes."

Her voice shook as she whispered, "The only man I have ever loved."

"Damn it, Tony, I'll brook no more of your interference," Ian raged, stalking the length of the *chambre d'amour*. "You have enough problems to deal with in your own romance without trying to foist one off on me."

Tony lounged against the damask *siège* with that unflappable expression that most infuriated Ian. Gray's face was so beatific and filled with commiseration that Ian was hard-pressed not to break a fire iron over the wretch's head. Gray had been in this blissful state of empathy ever since he had interrupted Lucy's concert and all but dragged Ian to this meeting.

A meeting in a room that now held a score of agonizing memories for Ian. Not memories of the almost fiendish amusement Ian and Tony had taken in designing this chamber of pure lechery to shock all those who entered but rather memories of a woman so generous with her hands, her lips, her heart, that Ian had almost been selfish enough, greedy enough, to take what she had offered him with those eyes that were so wide and wondering, with those hands that could soothe away the fiercest pain.

Ian had stalked into the chamber with Tony, hoping to God there was some disaster with the English soldiery to deal with or, better still, that revolution itself had broken out across the land. That way he could escape the tempest Emily d'Autrecourt had unleashed in him by flinging himself into the raging fury of battle.

But when Gray began his infernal prattling, and Ian realized that it was not some dire disaster or political trauma that had brought Tony here but rather an inquiry after Ian's wound and an urge to meddle in Ian's affairs, Ian felt as if Tony Gray had tossed a burning candle into a powder keg.

"Ian, don't you see?" Ian heard Gray's reasonable voice through the red haze of his own fury. "It is all right for you to love Emily."

"You are the one who was railing about the fact that I was fitting my neck for a noose just by having her here until Lucy could be parceled out!" Ian roared. "I remember precisely how you stomped about and—"

Gray gave a shrug, totally unaffected by Ian's rage. "She's an Englishwoman. I admit it made me a trifle jittery on your behalf. But I just saw her walking among the oaks. I saw her face and listened to her speak of you, and—"

"You accosted her on the drive?" Ian rounded on Tony with savage fury, unable to tolerate the knowing grin creasing his friend's face. "By God, if you filled her full of any of your crackbrained theories about the state of my emotions, I *will* kill you and be damned! I can't have her, blast it! Don't you see that?"

"No, I don't see," Tony said in that infernally calm tone. "Why can't you have her?"

Ian slammed his fist against the wall, glad of the pain, as he battled to obliterate the utterly beguiling, utterly impossible visions Tony's words were creating in his mind.

"Because of who I am, damn it! Because of *what* I am! It's too dangerous."

"Don't you think that is for Emily to decide?"

"No! No, I don't! I—"

"What the devil do you think we are fighting for, Ian, when we take to the highroads and ride?" Tony demanded, pacing toward him. "Do you think we are fighting for theories? Cold words printed upon a page by some idealist with his head in the clouds? We're fighting for a place where our children can grow up, free from all the restrictions of the old order. Free, in a new world, Ian. One we can build ourselves. *That* is something worth dying for, my friend."

Ian hated Gray for being right, hated him for the goodness that still wreathed his face. A wholeness of spirit that Ian had never known. He crushed the emotion, struggling to be happy for his friend when his own world was crumbling at his feet.

"There can be a new world for you, Tony," Ian said at last. "And, yes, blast it, one with Nora in it. You're not like me, Gray. You never have been."

"How are you so different?"

"No one knows better than you," Ian said. "You're not tainted, as I am. What kind of husband would I make for her? A man with my past? A man who courts death as if it were a lover."

"Ian, that's not—"

"Those are *your* words, Tony! Not mine!"

Gray's hand closed about Ian's shoulder. "If you had Emily's arms to hold you, Ian, you'd want to live."

"It's too late for me, Tony." Ian ripped away from that steadying hand, needing to feel alone. Alone as he'd always been. He saw a flash of hurt cross Tony's features, along with stubborn determination.

"Maybe Emily doesn't think it is too late, any more than I do. Maybe Lucy doesn't think so."

The words were a jagged blade carving Ian's soul. "They don't even know me! What they see is a mirage, Tony, a facade. Ian Blackheath, planter, rakehell. My reality is on the highroads, wearing the mask of Pendragon."

"Then tell Emily the truth! If she loves you it won't matter."

"Emily has already given me her opinion of the rebel raider Pendragon," Ian said with a bitter laugh. "She told Lucy that he is a rebel thief, a criminal. Lucy actually had the poor judgment to admire the patriot raider, but Emily corrected that notion at once. It seems people who commit cold-blooded murder are not good examples for children."

"Emily just arrived here from England a little while ago. How could she be expected to understand? You have to talk to her, show her what you believe in. By God, you've probably made certain she thinks that the only virtue you prize is the rapidity with which you can untie a woman's garters."

"No." Ian's voice dropped low. His laugh was mirthless, filled with longing. "I am not as good at subterfuge as I was once thought to be, my friend. Emily already knows . . ." He gestured to the room all around him. "She knows that this is all a lie."

"But that can't matter, Tony. I can't let it." Ian paced to where Cupid lay in Psyche's arms, and his fingers traced the glorious midnight waves of Psyche's hair. "I cannot let Emily look upon my true face any more than this poor god could allow it of his lady, Tony. For if Emily does, she will find the same thing as tragical Psyche did."

Ian turned away, his eyes desolate.

"She will find her ruination."

14

*E*mily pulled her comb through hair that rippled like a silken river down her back, as delicately beautiful as the night shift that draped her body. The scent of roses clung to her skin in a gossamer veil, the blossoms having been plucked from the garden and steeped in the hot water of her bath an hour before.

As she gazed at her reflection in the mirror, the woman who stared back at her seemed like a stranger. Her eyes were large and soft and just a little wary. Her cheeks were brushed with the delicate pink of the underside of a seashell cupped in a child's palm. Her lips were reddened from the countless times she had nervously caught at them with her teeth as she imagined the night that was to come.

This that could be the most magical night of her life—or the most humiliating, if Ian should send her away.

Emily brushed back one of the damp curls that clung to her brow and wondered what Ian would think when she entered his room. The bedchamber where she had told him her deepest secrets . . . the chamber where she now hoped he would reveal secrets of a far more dizzying kind to her.

She closed her eyes, little frissons of sensation sizzling through her body, as she remembered the caresses Ian had trailed over her skin, the kisses he had pressed, hot and moist, against her racing pulsebeats.

She could remember every groan of surrender, every laugh, every smile. She could remember how indignant he had been when Lucy claimed he was her papa, and how demonically pleased he'd been when he returned to the shop to see that Lucy had been treating Emily to a taste of equally exasperating mischief.

She could remember his dry humor when it came to Lucy's buttons. She could remember that hot, tempestuous look on his face when he had come to her in the *chambre d'amour,* the magnificent weight of him against her upon the damask *siège.*

But most of all, she could remember how he had cradled Lucy in his arms just a few hours ago, as if he had been entrusted with a most unlikely angel and was not quite certain what to do with her.

Lucy . . .

Emily had tried to stem her own restlessness as she'd tucked the child in bed tonight, singing her asleep with the little French song and doing "the kissing thing," which Lucy pronounced very nice. The child had clamored for her uncle to come as well and sing for her, but Ian had been off with Tony somewhere, talking. And at last Emily had persuaded the little girl to try to sleep.

Emily couldn't help but smile. The child had *tried* for nearly two hours, a fact that Lucy had announced in long-suffering accents at five-minute intervals throughout.

Only for the past half hour had there been a blessed silence. One that Emily was grateful for as she readied herself to become Ian Blackheath's lover.

His lover.

Even the words seemed to hold mysteries as dark as midnight, a sweet promise as hot as berries picked in the blazing sun, bursting on lips that were hungry for the sweetness they offered.

Her pulse skittered, and she turned away from the mirror, setting down the battered comb that was one of the few things she had kept from that other life—the life of the shy vicar's daughter who had been so wide-eyed and innocent when she wandered out through the parsonage gates and into the real world.

This would be a journey every bit as enlightening.

She smiled just a little. She had been a wife for four years. She had shared a man's bed. Comforted his pain. Borne him a child.

But tonight she felt more skittish than she had the night she became Alexander d'Autrecourt's bride.

For a heartbeat she hesitated at the door of her bedchamber, feeling as if she were teetering on the brink of something wonderful, something frightening.

Then she slipped through the corridor to the room where she had taken Ian to warm himself when he'd been soaked by the storm.

She caught her lower lip with her teeth, and raised her hand as if to knock on the door, but then she stopped. A nervous bubble of laughter rose in her throat. Was it proper etiquette for a man's mistress to knock on the door? Or was that definitely *de trop*, drawing the attention of servants and houseguests upon the indiscretion?

In the end she pressed her hand against the door and pushed it open just a crack. She hated the quaver in her voice as she called softly. "Ian. It's me. Emily. May I come in?"

"Emily." Her name was a rasped groan on his lips, and she pushed the door wider, alarm streaking through her.

He sat in a Chippendale chair facing an open window. His shirt lay rumpled over his shoulders; his face was buried in one strong hand. Stifling a cry, Emily shut the door behind her and hurried toward him, then stopped behind the chair, uncertain what to say, what to do.

He seemed devastated. Destroyed. His shoulders sagged, his breathing was ragged.

Any thoughts of seduction vanished in the wake of a fierce need to ease whatever was causing him such pain.

"Oh, Ian, what is distressing you so?" she asked softly. "Did you and Tony argue again?"

"Tony? Bloody bastard. As if he wasn't bad enough. But then to have *her* come here. To find *this* waiting . . ."

Emily took a step toward him. "Who came here, Ian? What did you find waiting?"

"Lucy. She . . . she left this inside the door."

Emily closed the space between them and stared down at what lay pillowed on Ian's lap. Her breath snagged in her throat, elation warring with raw terror.

There in stark relief against Ian's breeches lay the small wooden figure of the fashion doll Lucy had stolen from the shop that first day she had barreled into Emily's life.

For long seconds Emily didn't know what to say. She swallowed hard, groping for words. Sweet heaven, was it possible that Ian knew about her deceit? Was it possible that Lucy had found the message inside the plaything?

What an idiotic question, Emily thought a little wildly. With Lucy *anything* was possible.

Was this despair she saw in Ian because of her? Because he suspected . . . what? That she was an English spy? Could that matter so much to him? A man totally alienated from the patriot cause?

A man who read John Locke? Voltaire?

"Ian, I . . . the doll . . ." She started to stammer. But at that moment he shoved a piece of paper into Emily's hand. On one side was Lucy's drawing of Pendragon. On the other were words penned in a child's awkward hand.

Emily read them, her own heart breaking:

Dear Uncle Ian,
Here is the lady's doll that I stole away from her shop and hid under my dress to bring back here. I was very naughty to take it and keep it in the apple barrel. But sometimes I cannot help being detestable bad.
I just wanted the doll so I could have something to love.
But I have decided to love you and the lady instead.
Your affectionate niece,
Lucy Dubbonet

Tears streamed down Emily's face as she slipped around the chair and sank down on the floor before Ian. She looked up into that face, half covered by his splayed hand, but if he'd had a shield of iron before him, he could not have hidden how deeply the letter had moved him or how much he loved the little girl who had sent it.

Then why the despair? The agony? Why did he look as if he had just lost all of his dreams, instead of having gained Lucy's love?

And Emily's own.

He had to know that, had to sense it.

Or was that only another burden added onto Ian's pain?

"Ian." She said his name softly, reaching up to thread her fingers back through the waves of his hair, skimming over the rugged square of his jaw, those high-slashed, arrogant cheekbones that were damp. And when he turned his face to look at her, what she saw there was both more frightening and more awe-inspiring than anything she'd beheld in her life.

Love.

Such stark love that it savaged her heart just as fiercely as it had obviously savaged his.

"Emily, you have to listen to me. You have to understand, in a way that—that I can never make Lucy comprehend. All my life I've battled to make certain no one would love me. I'm not worth the—"

"Let us decide that for ourselves, Ian. Your own value is something that you can't measure."

"Don't you see? I'm so hungry for you that if I let myself touch you, take you, I could never have enough. I would be like *he* was. My father. I'd be drunk on the taste of the woman I love, unable to keep from hurting her."

"How would you hurt me, Ian?"

"By loving you. Don't you understand?" He levered himself to his feet, pillowing the doll on the chair. Then he stalked the length of the room, restless, edgy.

"No. I don't understand, Ian. Tell me."

"My father was a good, decent man. Everyone said so. He was faithful to his wife—a benighted saint in some circles. I don't doubt that he loved my mother in his way, but he had this—this insatiable hunger."

"For what, Ian?"

"Sons." Ian gave a caustic laugh. "My mother was constantly either with child or recovering from the birth of yet another frail and sickly babe. I'd watch her grow paler and thinner, watch the life die in her eyes a little more with each tiny grave in the family crypt. She would look so agonizingly tired. And sad. So sad."

Emily thought of Jenny's lone grave and the anguish it symbolized, and she tried to imagine that pain magnified time and again with each one of the Blackheath infants.

"Celestia was the eldest, and beneath my father's notice because she was a girl. I was two years younger. The son. The heir. Only I was a rebellious wretch even then. Not at all the upstanding specimen that my father had his heart set on. So he continued to . . . press my mother into her wifely duty. And every time—*every time*—she gave birth to a child, I sat with him in the drawing room while her screams rang out in the bedchamber above us. And I hated him, Emily. I hated him."

"What happened to your mother wasn't your fault, Ian. You can't blame yourself. Whatever was between your parents was their own doing, not yours. You were a child. Just a boy, as full of life as Lucy is. That didn't make you responsible for your father's sins or your mother's inability to tell him no."

"When I was fourteen the doctor told my father that he was killing her. If she attempted one more time to bear him a child, she would die. She was so weak then that her veins seemed to course just below the surface of her skin, blue ribbons that I could touch. I used to come upstairs and read to her from the Bible. She didn't want the comforting parts. No, it was hellfire and damnation, duty in the face of any price. That was what she wanted to hear, but I . . . hated it."

Emily tried to imagine Ian as a boy—with the same flash of temper, the same restless spirit—entombed with his ailing mother in a sickroom, resenting his father for putting her there, hating himself for not being good enough, strong enough, to satisfy the man who had sired him.

"When I was fifteen," he said, his voice heavy with regret, "I saw the signs again. I knew them all by then. The sickness in the morning, that pale, wan expression. The way her hand—such a birdlike little hand—would cup her stomach. She was frightened, Emily. With all those hounds of hell upon her heels, in her mind, a hundred sins. What sins, by God, could such a gentle woman have committed to damn her to hellfire?"

His voice tore on a ragged groan. "I demanded the truth, and she gave it to me. That I was to have a little brother come May. A little brother who would live like all the others had not. One who would wear all the tiny clothes she stitched so faithfully, as if she truly believed the babe would use them. I went to my father, half crazed. He cried. Damn his soul to hell. He cried and told me it was a woman's lot to bring forth children. It was God's will that they bear their babies in travail, for the sin they had committed in the Garden of Eden."

Ian wheeled around, fury pulsing in his voice. "My mother never committed any goddamn sin to suffer so greatly! Why the hell didn't Adam pay the price for eating the apple as well? Why only the woman . . . helpless . . . so damned helpless?"

He fell silent for a moment, raising a shaking hand to his face. "I told my father that if he ever touched her again that way, I would kill him. In May I sat again listening to my mother's screams. Listening to them grow weaker and weaker, until they stopped altogether. My father was at her side, sobbing piteously into her coverlets, telling her he loved her."

Emily sat in tortured silence, seeing so clearly the boy Ian had been, seeing how deeply he'd been scarred by his mother's agony and death. And always gnawing inside him was the knowledge that he was not the son his father had wanted, not the boy that Maitland Blackheath had desired so badly that he was willing to put his wife through torture, and ultimately sacrifice her to death to achieve his goal.

"My sister, Celestia, was so horrified that she went to an Indian woman the day she turned sixteen and had the witch deaden her womb."

"But Lucy—"

"I don't know how Lucy came to be. Maybe the Indian woman's physicking didn't work or . . . I don't know. I only know that Celestia and I embarked from our childhood onto separate paths, both of which led straight to hell.

"My *father*"—there was such loathing in the word—"didn't take well to his only son holding him accountable for what he'd done. He sent me away to school where I summarily determined to take the only vengeance in my power—to excel at being a rakehell, a scoundrel, a villain. A perfect villain who would shame him, leaving him with no son at all."

"A perfect villain," she repeated, her voice choked at the thought of how desperately the boy Ian must have worked to achieve that end, how he must have pushed people away, courted their scorn, as his penance for what he saw as his own sins.

"That is what love is to me, Emily Rose. A fever, a sickness that renders a man helpless, a hunger that makes him hurt the one he loves. When I was a boy, I vowed that I would not be like him, could never be like him. But when I look into your eyes, all soft and melting violet, and touch your mouth, I know that I am exactly as he was." Ian's voice was rough-edged with hopelessness. "I can never get enough of you, Emily," he breathed. "Never. And that is the one risk I am not willing to take."

Slowly Emily got up and walked to where he stood, alone, so alone. "I bore the child of a man I didn't love . . . not in the way I love you. I lost that child. I've never wanted another babe, Ian. It would leave me too vulnerable, too open to pain. What if the child was hurt? What if she took a chill, and fever swept her away from me as it did my little Jenny? I blamed myself for Jenny's death, just as you blamed yourself for your mother's. But when I look into your face, I know that you would never hurt me as your father hurt your mother. And I know that if there was a child . . ."

An anguished sound ripped from his throat.

"If there was a child with your crystal blue eyes and your smile, Ian, sweet God, even though I'm more afraid than I've ever been in my life, I would want to reach out and touch that baby. Hold it. Love it. As much as I love you."

"Emily, for God's sake, have mercy—"

"I can't, Ian. This is too important. You were right about how things were between Alexander and me. I didn't love him the way a wife should. I couldn't seem to give him what he needed of me. I was his wife, but never his lover. And when he touched me I could feel my own failure and his guilt. I've spent years believing that if I had only been able to love him as a woman loves a man, he would have been able to fight through his illness and the financial adversity he was facing. That he would still be alive."

"It's not your fault that he wasn't strong," Ian defended her. "You're the bravest, most beautiful, most generous woman I've ever known. You make me ache for you, Emily Rose. Burn for you. As a man burns for a woman."

"Ian, please. Just this one time I want to know what it is like to be a man's lover. To be *your* lover. I want to know what it's like to feel a man I truly love touch me, kiss me."

"You don't love me, Emily. You don't even know me."

"I know you better than you know yourself, Ian. I'm sure of it. Please. I'm not asking you to stay with me forever. I'm not even asking you to love me back. I just want one night."

She went to where he stood, rigid as a carved stone statue, taut with pain and longing and the battle he was waging inside himself.

"You don't know what you're asking," he rasped, his voice raw. "I've done so many things I'm not proud of. But this . . ." His face contorted. "Making love to you would be the most villainous of all."

There was so much pain in him, so much yearning. His eyes were hot and aching and filled with an agonized reverence as they skimmed over her face.

"No, Ian. What I experienced in Alexander's bed was hurtful. We were husband and wife under law, but not in our hearts." She drew in a breath that made her chest ache. "Ian, to feel what we feel, to love as we love, and never to touch, to take. That would be wicked, Ian. I know it in my heart."

He said nothing, just looked at her in silent torment, a fallen angel reaching through the gates of heaven. If only he would allow her to let him in.

"I couldn't bear to hurt you, Emily Rose. I couldn't stand the pain of knowing what I'd done to you."

"Done to me?" Emily echoed softly.

"Defiling you. In ways you could never even fathom. Because you cannot even imagine how empty I am. Sweet God, Emily Rose, don't make me blacken my soul even further by tainting you."

"Defiling? Tainting? Ian, I'm asking you to make love to me. I know there have been other women. I accept that. But they never loved you as I love you. And you . . ." Her voice faltered for a heartbeat. "You never loved them the way you love me."

He closed his eyes, arched his head back as if she had twisted a knife inside him. "Emily . . ."

"Ian, those women are nothing between us, because they never touched you . . . here"—she pressed her hand against his heart—"any more than Alexander touched me."

She cupped her palms against his jaw and stood on tiptoe, silencing him with delicate, melting kisses that did little to soften the harsh line of his mouth. Dissatisfied, she drew away and feathered her fingertips over those full, sensual lips, parting them just a little. Then she pressed her lips again to that moist, beckoning heat, her cheeks tingling with embarrassment as she let her tongue make a hesitant foray into Ian's mouth to touch the tip of his.

His hands were clenched at his sides, but as Emily mated her mouth with his, making love to it the way Ian had taught her, she could feel the tremors begin in those steely muscles. The knowledge that she was the one who was making this man—so strong, so cynical, so hardened and arrogant—

tremble beneath her hands was the most intoxicating feeling she had ever experienced.

"Ian," she breathed against his lips, "oh, Ian . . ." She let her tongue steal out to trace the corner of his lips, then taste the firm upper lip that could curl with such mocking hauteur, such savage fury, such beguiling amusement. She skimmed down to savor the sulky curve of his lower lip, the soft, wine-sweet place that had made her think of fallen angels and wild, honeyed obsessions.

The trembling in him was fiercer now, his breath rasping like a dying man's, but in anguish, so much anguish.

She couldn't bear it, couldn't stand seeing the agony in those beloved features, couldn't bear the knowledge that she was the one bringing him so much pain.

She couldn't stand to see him suffer so, even for one night in his arms to remember forever.

Without a word she kissed him, soft on the corner of his mouth. Then she turned away and drifted quietly to the door.

Her fingertips had barely brushed the doorknob when a sudden harsh cry rang out behind her.

"Emily!" Just her name, but so much more. It seemed to echo through every fiber of her body. She turned slowly toward him, her gaze taking in the tortured planes of his face, the almost feverish light in his eyes.

"Emily," he whispered, "don't . . . leave me."

"No, Ian. I won't leave you."

There was no slow toppling of walls, no crumbling of resolve. The bastions inside Ian Blackheath seemed to crash in thunderous fury around them.

A wild animal groan started at the back of Ian's chest and tore free as he lifted her off her feet and into the savage heat of his kiss.

Emily cried out at the fire in it, blue flames that hurtled through her veins with a swiftness that terrified her, mesmerized her. His mouth was devouring hers, hungry, so hungry, as if he were dying of thirst and she were some magical wellspring of life.

She tangled her hands in the dark waves of his hair,

delving into the silky mysteries there, mysteries she was already unlocking beneath the undeniable pressure of Ian's body against hers, Ian's hands, urging her tighter, tighter against him, as if he were melting the boundaries of their two bodies and melding them into something wondrously new, magical.

Making them one.

She had heard the wedding vows solemnized between her and Alexander, the holy man who had joined them in marriage saying just such words. But when Alexander had touched her, it had pushed their spirits farther apart, not made their souls embrace each other, as if they had been searching for their second half for all eternity.

Ian's mouth on hers was hot, wet magic. It was desperation. It was surrender. He scooped her up into his arms, as if she were as light as the clouds that dappled the night sky beyond the open window.

He laid her on the softness of his bed and followed her down onto the feather tick, his hands stroking her, stoking the fires he'd ignited, his eyes anguished and ecstatic.

"I want you, Emily," he moaned into her mouth as his fingers ripped at the ribbons that tied her night shift at the hollow between her breasts. "Sweet Jesus, I want you."

His hands were rough, eager. There was no tentative groping, no heat of shame, in their touch as he stripped the gossamer garment over her head and threw it aside.

His breath caught, ragged, his lips parting in wonder as he laid her back on the rumpled sheets. Shadows clung about the bed, and Emily caught her lip between her teeth as Ian took a flickering candle from the bedside table and held it above her, bathing her naked body in golden light.

He didn't touch her with anything but the reverence in his gaze, the worship and the wonder. "You're more beautiful than I could ever have dreamed, Emily Rose. Sweet God, I don't deserve you."

Terror that he would leave her rippled through Emily. "Oh, Ian." She caught his wrist in the circle of her fingers and felt the pulse of his lifeblood throbbing there, deep and strong like the passions he had unleashed in her. "What a sad thing it would be if we got only what we think we deserve."

He set the candle down, his wrist still in her grasp. She tugged him toward her, her mouth seeking his with feathery light kisses, her hands framing Ian's jaw, drawing him deeper against her mouth. Her fingers slid down the cords of his neck to the open collar of his shirt. Her left hand eased through the slit in the material to find the mat of silky-rough hair that webbed in delicious contrast over the steely curves and hollows of his chest.

Hardly believing her own daring, Emily pushed his shirt open. His chest was magnificent, a glistening masterpiece of bone and muscle that caught the light and shadow and captured her gaze.

He was beautiful.

She told him so in a way that was foreign to her, that was so new, but felt so right.

She trailed kisses down the flesh she had exposed and let her fingertips learn every dip, every curve gilded in rough, intriguing hair. He was scalding hot where she tasted him, the scent of recklessness mingling on his skin with the subtle musk of arousal.

When she reached the flat, dark disk of his nipple, lost in intriguing whorls of hair, she let her tongue slip out to touch its pebble-hard tip.

"Sweet Jesus," Ian rasped, seeming to burst into flames beneath her touch. He pressed her down on the bed, his mouth capturing hers with a furious beauty. Wild open-mouthed kisses tore all sense of reason away from Emily as Ian ripped off his breeches.

He was naked against her, one long thigh flung over her restless legs, pulling her hard against the crags and valleys of his body. His palm swept up to cup her breast as if it were the most precious of treasures, and she felt the bud stiffen against his callused hand, felt a dark, bewitching need spiral from that aching crest to the hidden place between her thighs. A place already anticipating possession by the daunting length of his sex that was pressed against the soft curve of her belly.

Velvet . . . His shaft felt like velvet-sheathed steel against her, rigid and demanding, as he pulled her tight against him, giving neither of them a chance to deny how savagely he wanted her, in that most primal way.

Emily arched her head back, as Ian took drugging nips at the vulnerable curve of her jaw, her neck, then soothed them with the moist abrasion of his tongue. She whimpered as he coasted those kisses down the curve of her breast to play about that moon-pale mound with his mouth and the stubble-roughened satin of his cheeks, his jaw.

He murmured words against her skin, whispers she couldn't understand with her mind. She listened to them with her heart.

His mouth left her breast, and hovered for what seemed an eternity over her throbbing nipple. His breath washed over it, a sweet, moist heat.

Emily couldn't breathe, waiting, waiting. She tangled her hands in that thick rosewood-colored hair and arched her back to thrust the hardened rosette against his lips. They parted, closed, sucked. A wet seduction that pushed her past endurance, a hungry caress that left her quivering.

Never had she suspected how a man's mouth could feel there, drawing sustenance from her, giving it back again.

He groaned her name against her fevered flesh, catching the bud in his teeth and tugging gently, so gently, before he released it.

His hands were everywhere, on her breasts, on her hip, smoothing over the round curve of her buttocks. Hands that were shaking with wonder, hands that were building tiny fires all over her body, then returning to feed the flames.

Hands that were treasuring her, worshiping her. Loving her, in a way that made what had happened in her marriage bed seem pale and sad and more than a little tragic.

She returned his caresses, learning the essence of Ian Blackheath. The powerful breadth of shoulders, the narrow hips, the steely curves of his buttocks. She kissed a scar that stood out, white beneath the curve of his arm, she kissed his mouth, his eyelids, his temple, where the half-healed gash still whispered of the danger in him.

When his fingers trailed a path of molten sensation down her belly, she flushed, then caught her lip between her teeth. She was no virgin. She knew what he was searching for. Yet there was the most unbearable melting sensation centered there between her thighs. A dampness that she had never known before.

"No," she whispered, tightening her legs against him. "Ian, don't."

"That is how it's done when you love someone, Emily. I touch you there, stroke you there, dip into the place where I want to bury myself."

"No. It's—it's moist. I don't know why. I . . ."

A half-laugh, half-groan tore from Ian's throat. "Ah, lady, are you trying to drive me mad with wanting you?"

"Don't laugh at me."

"I'm not laughing, Emily Rose. Your dampness means that you want me. That your passage is ready to receive me, to glove me tight inside you. Do you mean you never had that happen before?"

"No. I . . . of course not," she said a little indignantly, "or I would not be making such a fool of myself right now."

"That selfish bastard," Ian bit out. "The lovemaking must have hurt you, then, with your husband."

"It was . . . uncomfortable. But I thought . . . It seemed . . . Well, I'm certain Alexander didn't know it was supposed to be that way, either."

"He could've bloody asked someone or gone to a whore to learn how not to hurt you! For God's sake, it's not as if this were some bloody state secret."

He was spoiling the magic with the anger in his eyes, but then his face softened. His hand splayed, heavy and warm on the delicate skin of her belly. "Let me show you, Emily, how much your body wants me." He moved his hand down to the nest of dark curls, his fingers stroking that thatch of silky hair with such skill her thighs began to tremble.

"Open for me, Emily. Let me inside."

She let her thighs fall apart a little ways, but Ian wasn't satisfied. His big hands curved beneath the slender columns, pulling her legs farther apart, exposing that part of her body that no man had ever seen. His eyes darkened, a tempest raging in their depths as he looked at her, then slid his fingers down to touch the dewy petals below.

Emily stiffened, all but jerking straight up at the excruciatingly intimate contact of that rough fingertip against that dainty pink flesh.

"How does this make you feel, Emily?" Ian was whispering, as he watched the long brown length of his finger move against her. "Does it feel half as good to you as it does to me?"

He was waiting for an answer—impossible man. She was long past speaking.

His fingers dipped inside her, where the moisture seemed to center, then slid up to find a place Emily had not known existed.

If Ian had taken a red-hot brand and pressed it against her, she could have felt no more fire. The flames surged inside of her, wild and wanton and wonderful, as he circled and teased that hidden place, bringing her closer to something she couldn't imagine . . . a place she had seen whenever she had looked into Ian's passion-dark eyes.

She arched against him, unable to stop the moans that rose in her throat. And then suddenly his touch was gone, and he was kissing her, the tiny indentation of her navel, the silky dark curls, the inside of her thigh. His hair brushed against that fragile skin, the tresses so soft, his hands roving over her flesh, heating her, tormenting her.

She stroked his shoulders, his arms, deliciously confused, unbearably eager for whatever new secret he would reveal to her.

But when he lowered that dark head and touched the pulsing center of her with indescribable delicacy with the hot, rough point of his tongue, she gave a low, rasping cry that seemed to echo in the tremor that went through his body.

What was he doing to her? Emily thought wildly, tossing her head as he savored her, seduced her. Oh, God, this must be wicked.

But not to have known this, never to have known . . .

The embers he had set to burning pulsed and glowed, burst and simmered, centering there, where Ian Blackheath was worshiping her with his devastatingly intimate kiss.

And suddenly she couldn't bear another moment, couldn't wait . . .

"Ian!" she cried out his name, and he knew what she wanted, what she needed of him. He raised his head, and what he saw stole his very soul.

A passion-tossed angel, a violet-eyed goddess, alive with love for him, hunger for him.

He kissed the soft petals one last time, then rose above her, bracing his arms on either side of her, his hands lost in cascades of her midnight-dark hair.

"My God, Emily, look at you . . . look at you," he rasped, hardly daring to move as that small, loving hand curled about his white-hot, aching flesh, stroking it with such tenderness, such longing.

And when she guided him to the sweet, fragile opening, he felt his chest tighten, felt his heart ache . . . and slowly, by precious inches, he buried himself inside her.

He groaned in raw pleasure as her wet heat gloved his sex, tight, so tight. He wanted nothing more than to give way to his own mind-shattering urges, to take her, swift, hard, spill his seed deep inside her.

But thoughts of what she must have endured before this loving reined in those primal urges. He was not a gentle man, but he found gentleness inside himself for her. He was not a man given to tenderness, but as he held Emily in his arms, he was more tender than he'd ever been in his life. He subjugated his own needs, in a quest to satisfy hers. Urges he knew Emily didn't even suspect she had.

A primal thrill of possession shot through him, the knowledge that this was a gift that he could give to Emily Rose. The skill he had gained on his path to ruin, the ability to pleasure a woman's body until she sobbed with ecstasy.

His brow furrowed in concentration, his hips settling even deeper into the cradle of her thighs. Then he withdrew the heated core of him and sank time and time again into her waiting sheath.

He could feel Emily grow restless beneath him, her hands on his back, the nails biting just a little with an innocent eroticism that all but unmanned him.

"Ian, I . . . oh, I . . ."

"You're perfect, angel . . . so perfect . . ." He nuzzled his face against her breasts as he stroked deep inside her, his tongue tasting her as he rained kisses up her throat, against her cheeks.

She was quickening around him, he could feel it, feel her getting wilder, hotter in his arms, feel her slipping over the brink.

He wanted to hold her, wanted to help her hurl herself off into madness. His fingers stole down between their bodies, found the pulsing nub that he sensed was screaming for release. He circled it, smoothed it with the tip of his finger as he thrust harder against her, deeper, burying himself to the hilt time and again.

He gritted his teeth as he felt the feathering of his own culmination start at the base of his spine. He battled to keep it at bay, withhold it. Just as he knew the battle was lost, a cry tore from Emily's throat, and she tightened around his throbbing length in shattering contractions that made Ian drive himself with all his strength into her welcoming wetness, as her sweet climax sent him careening over the edge in a flood of heat and passion and soul-deep love.

He fell against her breasts, burying his face in the waves of her hair, unable to speak, unable to breathe. His whole body trembled as the sensations still rocketed through him, echoing in places that were buried deep in his soul.

Oh, God . . . how could he have imagined what it would be like? How could he have known that this time with Emily would make the touch of every other woman seem like callow playacting on a barren stage?

How could he have known that her love would break away all the bitterness inside him and leave him with something so fragile, so unexpected, that he was almost afraid to put a name to it?

Hope.

For the first time since the death of his mother—for perhaps the first time in his life—Ian felt the darkness drain away from his spirit, felt it flowing out of his soul.

He felt clean and whole and so much in love that he thought he might die of it.

Tears burned at the backs of his eyelids as he raised his face from Emily's hair. He traced the backs of his knuckles across the cameolike perfection of her cheek.

Her eyes were shining. Her kiss-reddened lips were parted in a smile that was at once enchanting and amusing, as if she had discovered some delicious secret she wasn't about to share.

And as Ian stared down into those violet depths, he wondered what she would say if he told her his own secrets. Would that smile fade? Would those eyes cloud with blame and confusion?

"Tell her the truth," Tony had urged him. "If she loves you it won't matter."

But it would matter. Oh, God, how it would matter. How could he tell her of the danger he wore like a mantle, when he rode as Pendragon? How could he tell her that she would be the loved one of the rebel thief, the cold-blooded killer she scorned?

How could he subject her to nights pacing the floors of Blackheath Hall, waiting for him, knowing all the while that a stray pistol ball or a sword thrust might already have left him on the road somewhere, spilling his lifeblood into the dirt?

On the night of his last confrontation with the English he'd learned that Atwood was already preparing to tighten the noose around his neck.

How could he condemn Emily to that kind of suffering after what she had already endured?

His chest ached as he looked into that face that was still aglow in the aftermath of his loving.

A sweet, wild enchantress, as irresistible as the song of any Siren, and as dangerous.

But his body was already stirring against her. His hands were already itching to coast over the delicious peaks and valleys that she had surrendered to him minutes before.

"I love you, Emily Rose," he said hoarsely. "By God, I'd give my life, and gladly, if I could be a different man for you . . . one washed clean of all that I have done."

"But then I wouldn't love you, Ian," she said softly, turning her head to press a kiss against his palm. "Every choice you made before I came into your life shaped you into the man you are today. The man I fell in love with. I want to spend a lifetime learning everything about you. A lifetime of having you kiss me and touch me, of watching you smile."

A strangled sound caught in Ian's throat. "There are so many things you don't know about me. So many mistakes I've made, paths I've taken that—"

She stopped his words, pressing her fingertips against his lips. "I know everything that matters, Ian," she said in a voice like an angel's. "We'll find the way together."

He turned his head away from her, his eyes snagging on Lucy's doll, pillowed there upon the chair. The child's words seemed prophetic, terrifying: "I just wanted the doll so I could have something to love. But I have decided to love you and the lady instead."

They were words Ian himself might have said to the child, words he would have died for the pleasure of whispering.

But wasn't love impossible after the roads that he had taken? Night-dark roads stained with blood and reckless courage. Secret bargains in which Ian Blackheath had bartered away his soul.

Gladly, damn it. He'd been glad to give it. Because he'd never known what a price he would have to pay in the end. He'd never suspected that angels with violet eyes came to save sinners, or that little girls could steal away not only a doll but a man's empty heart as well.

He'd never thought that he would want to take a lady of

his own. Pendragon's lady, heiress to the darkness that consumed him.

He closed his eyes so that Emily couldn't see his anguish.

There is no way out of my hell, Emily Rose, he wanted to say. No gilded path you can guide me along as Orpheus did his Eurydice. There is nothing but this space in time. This loving. To last us both for all eternity.

15

*I*an lay upon the tangled white sheets, his thick, dark lashes pillowed on his arrogant cheekbones, the harsh planes of his face softened in sleep. His hand was still curled in the fall of her hair. His arms had held her against him, tightly through the night, cherishing her, in a way that still made Emily's throat feel raw, her fingers tremble.

Ian Blackheath. Rakehell. Scoundrel.

The perfect villain.

The perfect lover.

A man far more gentle in his passion than Alexander had ever been. A man far more good-hearted than her vicar father. A man who refused to enslave another human being. Who had taken a little girl into his heart, reluctantly, but completely. A man who seemed embarrassed by the very fact that there was goodness inside him.

Emily gently slipped from his grasp and propped herself on one elbow to peer down into that beguiling face. She smoothed a tendril of dark hair back from that stone-carved jaw.

She would show him . . . show him the wonder she had found in his wry sense of humor, his gruff tenderness, his bedazzling smiles. She would show him that no secret he had could come between them, any more than she would let her own secrets keep them apart any longer.

She lightly kissed curve of his lip, savoring the warmth in him, the strength. Then she slipped from the bed where he had bound her to him in a way far deeper than vows or promises or rings of gold could ever hope to.

Bare feet padding on the floor, she crossed the room and picked up Lucy's doll.

Atwood. Doubtless things might get a little difficult with the English soldier and his superiors when she told them of her decision to stop being in their service. But she was certain she could make them understand.

She loved Ian, loved Lucy. And though there had been no promises between them, Emily was certain that with time, Ian would come to realize what she already knew. That they had been destined to find each other. That they belonged together, forever.

"It will be over soon, Ian," she whispered to him. "I'll tell them that I love you. I'll make them see . . ."

She slipped from the room into the silent halls. Before a quarter hour had passed, she had donned a simple skirt and jacket, and gone to the stables, where a sleepy-eyed groom saddled a dainty mare for her.

"Where be ye goin' so early, Ma'am?" he asked, looking more than a little worried.

"I have some things to pick up at my shop before the rest of the house is awake. I'll be back this afternoon."

"Perhaps I should come along with you. Master Ian isn't going to like it if I let you run off on your own."

"No!" she said far too quickly. Then desperately attempted to think of some excuse for this solitary ride. "You go along and get some sleep. You look exhausted."

"Master's mare dropped a colt out of Bacchus last night. A fine boy, his is, just like his papa."

Emily closed her eyes, her mind filling with wondrous, hazy images of her arms filled with a wriggling bundle with crystal-blue eyes and the devil's own charm. She could see Ian, reaching out to let his son's tiny, questing hand curl about one long, bronzed finger. A fine boy, she would murmur as he reached down to kiss her. Just like his papa . . .

She flushed, suddenly aware of the vacant smile she must have on her lips, and shook herself inwardly, tightening her grip on the basket in which she had hidden the doll. With the briefest goodbye, she swung up into the saddle and started the mare across Blackheath lands at a gentle canter.

The wind tugged at her bonnet and kissed her cheeks, reminding her of Ian's lips, his touch, so vital, so gentle, so alive.

There are so many things you don't know about me . . .

He had said the words, edged with despair.

Emily's lips curved in a soft smile.

As soon as she finished this last bit of business with Captain Atwood, she would discover Ian Blackheath's secrets for herself.

Captain Reginald Atwood stood before his superior in the tiny, secluded cottage that was Stirling Fraser's headquarters, rivers of sweat trickling from beneath the soldier's wig to soak the collar of his shirt. Never in his illustrious military career had Atwood felt his own mortality so keenly—not even when he'd felt a spanish-steel sword lancing through his side in battle.

"Mr. Fraser, if you would let me explain—"

"That is exactly why I summoned you here, my good Captain," Fraser purred. "You can imagine my distress when I received word that this doll we have been so anxiously awaiting was delivered to the millinery shop days ago—*before* you were sent to speak to Emily d'Autrecourt about its importance. It was most disappointing to realize that something had gone awry. And that you and Mrs. d'Autrecourt, who are supposedly trusted allies, must be aware of the fact. I am not accustomed to being kept unenlightened when difficulties arise."

"I understand that, sir. But this was just a—an unfortunate mishap that the lady was attempting to make right. The message itself was in no real danger. It was just a matter of retrieving it."

"The message was in no danger? How can you be so certain? What do you know of Ian Blackheath, except that the man is a greedy bastard who would sell his own father to turn a profit? A man who deals in weapons and sells them to those mad Bostonians who are itching to bury an ounce of lead in every English breast in the colonies! How dare you take it upon yourself to make such a decision regarding a vital bit of communication? How dare you deceive me."

"It was not my intention to deceive you sir!" Atwood's gloves were fused to his hands with sweat. He swallowed, but couldn't get the lump of fear past his neck cloth. "The lady . . . I thought that she—"

"It is not your position to *think*, Atwood. If you did it more often we would be in even more peril than we are now. I suppose you were thinking with what's enclosed in your breeches, sir. Emily d'Autrecourt is a lovely woman, if I remember. But one of impeccable virtue. Or at least she was before she embroiled herself in Blackheath's household."

"I told her I must have the doll before a week had passed, that otherwise you and I would have to become involved in the matter."

"I shall call in reinforcements at once. It seems that taking a doll away from a little girl would be a task far too arduous for you."

"I promise you, it will all come right," Atwood protested. "I stake my life on it."

Fraser raised one bushy brow with such eloquence Atwood was hard pressed to keep his knees from knocking together. He stole a glance behind him, half expecting some sinister form in black to be preparing to slip a stiletto between his ribs.

"Mr. Fraser, I . . ."

But his words were cut off by a wave of Fraser's hand, as the big man rose from his chair and went to the window.

Hoofbeats. How had the wily old bastard heard them, long seconds before Atwood had picked up the sound? Both men stared out the window, Atwood's hand curved on the dragoon pistol shoved into his belt.

But when the rider broke through the trees, Atwood all

but cried out in relief, even Fraser giving a grunt that was both surprise and satisfaction.

Emily d'Autrecourt looked like the embodiment of spring, a flowing green cloak rippling back from her shoulders, a white mare beneath her. Glimpses of primrose colored petticoats were visible in the gap of the cloak, while her arm was crooked in the handle of a split-oak basket. Some mysterious bundle lay inside it, wrapped in a pale blue cloth.

"How the devil did she know to find me here?" Atwood muttered.

"She wasn't looking for you," Fraser snapped. "She was looking for me. The girl is disgustingly honest and well bred—I have it on the highest authority from someone who was acquainted with her in the days before her disgrace. Had she not been such a dependable sort, I would have hardly put myself through the trouble of dredging her out of the rabble in London. She is probably coming to confess the whole disaster very prettily, and save your worthless hide."

A discreet knock on the door made Atwood lunge toward it, but Fraser held up a warning hand, and called out. "Come in."

The girl opened the door, and stepped inside, just a little hesitantly, her cheeks pink, her eyes just a trifle nervous.

"My dearest Emily," Fraser said, "don't hover in the door, child."

She slipped through the opening and closed the panel softly behind her.

"What a happy coincidence," Fraser observed with that hearty chuckle Atwood had learned to mistrust. "The good Captain and I were just talking about you."

Those purple-blue eyes flashed to where Atwood stood, and he saw her blush prettily, and step forward, one hand outstretched.

"Mr. Fraser, you must have been speaking of the . . . difficulty I had. I want to assure you that it was not the Captain's fault. I was totally to blame for the loss of the doll, and the somewhat unorthodox way that we dealt with the problem."

"It was a very messy business, I'm sorry to say, and I quite detest such entanglements. You must understand, that in our line of service, they can be quite costly."

Her knuckles whitened on the handle of the basket. "Of course." She lifted one hand to the edge of her hood, lowering it from her dark curls. Fraser took unholy pleasure in the fact that her fingers trembled, and felt a reluctant sense of respect as he saw her forcibly still them.

"You must have heard by now that we have been searching for an outlaw by the name of Pendragon. Quite a troublesome scoundrel, eluding us these many months. Taunting the soldiery and harassing his majesty's tax collectors, while courting the loyalty of the rabble by flinging coin their way."

"I have heard something of Pendragon since I arrived here," the girl said slowly.

"Well, then, you can imagine our outrage. Some poverty stricken widow suddenly has funds for a new cow, some chicks for the yard. We know she hasn't any coin, but she insists the money fell like manna from heaven. A farmer who has had an accident and cannot even get out of bed suddenly has the money to pay his majesty's taxes, but we know he has already spent his savings merely attempting to feed his children. A family with a rebel son spouting treason finds a way to send him off to Barbados or France just before he is to be made accountable for his transgressions." Fraser's lips pursed, as if attempting to stop himself from listing more of Pendragon's sins.

"Yes, my dear child, it is most aggravating to be made to look like a fool in the eyes of those you are trying to subdue. And these colonials take the greatest of pleasure in watching Atwood's soldiers run about like school boys whose breech-legs have been stitched together, falling all over each other in their quest to bring Pendragon to justice."

There was an uncertain light in the girl's eyes, as if the incidents he'd recounted had stunned her, troubled her. But not in the way Fraser had intended. "I am certain that you will discover his identity," she said, with a touch of reluctance.

"In good time, no doubt. In good time."

Suddenly she seemed very eager to finish her business. She set the basket on the table before him. "I have brought the lost doll." There was such an innocent distress in her eyes, that Fraser was reminded of lambs being led to the pens where knifes waited to slit their throats. "It took a little while to find it, but nothing has been harmed." She took the bundle from the basket, unwrapping it. Fraser's hands closed upon it, so tightly one of the wooden arms snapped.

The girl winced, as if the doll were alive, but Fraser only held it tighter, savoring the anticipation of splitting it open and taking out the message inside.

"I thank you for your good service, Emily. Your benefactor was right. You are a most resourceful young lady."

"Benefactor? I have no benefactor."

"Yes, you do, my dear. And a very powerful one. I am vastly in his debt for having brought you to my attention. Now, is there anything that I can do to repay you for your tenacity in recovering this important bit of communication?"

"No. I mean, yes. Yes there is." Her fingers knitted together, and she looked at him earnestly. "Mr. Fraser, I am afraid that I can no longer be in your employ."

"What?" Fraser exclaimed, taken aback.

"I cannot be in your employ any longer. I can pass no more messages, nor be responsible for them."

"But my dear," Fraser objected, "you were so eager to have your own millinery shop when first I proposed this arrangement. You wanted to be independent. A woman of substance."

"I know. But the things that I want are different now." Her cheeks were scarlet, her voice low. "I have fallen in love, sir."

"In *love?*" Atwood's gruff scorn made Emily turn her gaze again to the room's floor.

"In the time I was at Blackheath Hall, I came to know its master. I came to love him."

Atwood's face washed dull red. "You're not saying

Blackheath has promised you marriage?" the captain blustered. "By God, madam, you can't believe him."

"He has offered me nothing. Not in so many words. But still, I am certain of the feelings we have for each other."

"So the legendary satyr of Blackheath Hall has enslaved yet another woman," Atwood spat out.

"Apparently so," Fraser said. "You must tell me how he does that sometime, dear. It could prove quite useful in convincing people to part with information."

The girl grew paler, more stiff. "I only wanted to return the doll," she said, "and tell you that I'll no longer be working with you. Ian once said he would buy out my indenture papers from my owner, so if you will figure out how much is owed you—"

"Did you truly believe that you could just come here today, and bid all this farewell?" Fraser chuckled, incredulous. "No one is able to just quit this type of calling, my dear. It is possible for you to take a brief respite. But I think you could be very useful to us if you were Ian Blackheath's wife. He has a most eccentric circle of friends."

Fraser took the doll in one hand, a penknife in the other, his eagerness to get to the message making him pry at the wooden peg that concealed the hidden compartment. "It is possible that through Blackheath's friends you might find out something useful, Emily. After all, once Pendragon is hanged, we will have to busy ourselves with other pursuits."

"Mr. Fraser, you don't understand. I cannot—will not—be a party to this anymore."

At that moment the peg in the doll pulled free, Fraser's fingers dipping in to slip out the message, unfold it. He read the missive, his eyes widening with triumph.

"What does it say?" Atwood clamored, straining to see over Fraser's shoulder. The Englishman hid the message against his waistcoat, his mouth splitting into a smile as terrifying as that of a crocodile with a child's leg dangling over its mouth.

At that moment, it was as if Emily could feel those cruel jaws close around her.

"My dearest Emily, I fear that I shall have to detain you, for a little while," Fraser said.

"Detain me?" Foreboding crushed her throat. "I don't understand."

"It seems I suddenly have the most urgent need for you at the moment. You see, you are going to be the bait that lures our most estimable enemy, Pendragon, to his death."

"You're mad! Pendragon has nothing to do with me!"

"I'm afraid he does." Fraser's voice was poisoned silk. "You see, my dear, he was to have been your lover. Unfortunately he will have to face a traitor's death instead."

"Ian? Pendragon?" Her mind whirled, the image of the paperweight on Ian's desk at its center—a miniature sword in a stone, the heart of the Arthurian legend. Pendragon. The once and future king . . .

Horror raced through Emily, her numb hand clutching at the table to steady herself. "That's insane! Ian would never . . . could never . . ."

"Ah, but that is where you are wrong, my sweet. It was the most diabolically clever disguise ever invented. There is a touch of evil genius in it. Enough that we might never have discovered the truth. Fortunately, my dear, we had you to destroy him."

"No," Emily breathed, feeling as if she were going to retch. Of course Pendragon was Ian. She should have guessed, should have known. A man who would not hold slaves would not allow others to be enslaved, even by their king. A man who would give a child a pianoforte would scarcely stand by and watch a widow-woman's children starve, or an injured farmer lose his land. Those long, late nights, his solitary rides, the gash on his forehead, even the outrageous entertainments that he'd boasted about had all been his effort to hide his heroism.

And now, because of her, he was to die.

"You are wrong, Mr. Fraser," Emily lied desperately. "Ian Blackheath is no patriot. Much as I love him, he is exactly what he seems. A scoundrel who would never sacrifice himself. Not even for me."

Fraser smiled that cunning smile. "By your own words

you give me the power to condemn him. If he is indeed the kind of rogue you claim, he will abandon you, my poor lamb. But if he is Pendragon, he will ride like the wind to rescue you, his lady love."

Fraser's words scraped like a dull blade against her nerves, spilling terror in their wake. For Ian would come, heedless of his own safety, wanting only to free her. And when he did, he would meet his own Armageddon.

No.

Emily spun toward the door, intending to run, to warn him.

But at that moment Atwood lunged for her, manacling her wrists with hands hard as iron.

"It was very unwise to allow us to see how much this rogue means to you, my dear child," Fraser tsked.

"No!" Emily cried. "I won't let you hurt him!"

"We'll do worlds more than hurt him, my dear. Because of you, we will not only capture Pendragon. We will drag from his very mouth the name of every man who serves under him."

"Ian would never betray them!"

An evil smile creased Fraser's face. "True. Nobility of spirit can be such an inconvenient obstacle at times. But there are ways to break even the most honorable of men. Ways to make them beg."

"Ian would die before he'd let you break him."

"Undoubtedly. But tell me, Emily Rose, how long do you think Blackheath could endure watching *you* suffer in his place?"

"Just a minute, Fraser," Atwood blustered. "Mrs. d'Autrecourt is innocent of any wrongdoing in this. She could not have known that Blackheath was a traitor to the crown!"

"Twice now Emily has shown a distressing lack of common sense in her romantic entanglements. Unfortunately for her, I predict that this episode will have consequences that are every bit as tragic as those from her liaison with Alexander d'Autrecourt."

Emily gaped at Fraser. "How—how do you know about Alexander?"

"I am a master at discovering people's secrets. Solving puzzles. I anticipate with great relish solving the riddle of how much pressure I'll have to apply on Ian Blackheath before he tells me everything I wish to know. How many lashes do you think he could watch Atwood deal you? Splitting that velvety skin upon your back? How long do you think Blackheath can stay silent as he listens to your screams?"

Bile rose in Emily's throat, but she lifted her chin in defiance. "You can't make me scream."

"Don't make vows that you shall tempt me to challenge, Emily. It is a very dangerous game. But even if you were to remain . . . resolute in the matter, there are other ways to make a man like Blackheath shatter. Other methods far more devastating to a man than the bite of the lash."

Emily shuddered inwardly, struggling to keep from showing her terror.

"Fraser, damn it, enough!" Atwood burst out. "I protest this."

"Ah, yes, I'd forgotten that you hold a *tendre* for the lady," Fraser continued. "Perhaps we should press it to our best advantage, Captain. I wonder what Blackheath would do if he were compelled to watch while his woman was forced to receive another man between her thighs?"

Horror. Stark. Relentless. It ravaged Emily's soul as her mind filled with images of the torture Fraser had planned—a torture more hellish than anything Emily could imagine.

"I'm a soldier, curse you, not a rapist!" Atwood shouted. "I'll be damned if I'll be party to such savagery!"

"You'll be damned if you refuse me, sir. Your position is already tenuous at best after your part in this debacle. Tell me, Atwood, what would your esteemed father say if he found out about your distressing lack of loyalty? Especially after he purchased you this commission to keep you from being hurled into gaol for the unfortunate death of that young man in the tavern brawl at Brighton?"

Atwood paled and Emily could feel the blade-edge of Fraser's evil as if it were pressed against both of their throats.

Oh, God, how could she have been so blind when Fraser had come to her with his offer? How could she have believed him for a moment?

It is perfectly safe, my dear, he had said in that grandfatherly voice. *You cannot think I would endanger such a lovely young lady as yourself, one battered by misfortune . . .*

He had been as shrewd as a snake poised to strike, just waiting for the moment when he would fill her with his venom.

There was such consummate satisfaction on his face, such scorn. The same scorn Emily had seen on the Duke of Avonstea's face the day he had taken her daughter from her.

No. She was not that frightened girl any longer. She would not allow anyone to manipulate her that way again, or hurt someone she loved.

Out of the corner of her eye she glimpsed the penknife Fraser had abandoned. Far better to take it and plunge it into her own heart, than allow such a monster to use her as a weapon to rob Ian, not only of his life, but of his very soul.

For that is what Fraser would do if Ian suffered the fate planned for him.

Ian, that tattered knight errant, that bold, generous, most loving of men, would never be able to watch her be raped. He would never be able to keep silent, no matter what the cost.

The cost . . . oh, sweet Jesus, the cost . . .

Emily felt Atwood's hands loosen on her in his own sick horror.

Desperate, she slammed her elbow back into Atwood's ribs, ripping free, but just as her fingers reached the knife, Fraser snatched it away, the blade slicing Emily's finger.

In a heartbeat, she was staring down the barrel of a pistol in Fraser's other hand. She started to fling herself toward him, wanting nothing more than to feel the hot piercing of lead through flesh, to be certain she could no longer be used to destroy the man she loved.

But that instant, Atwood recovered himself, grabbing her arms.

"No! For God's sake, he'll kill you," the Captain warned, his fingers tightening around her until they crushed, bruised.

"He doesn't understand, does he, Emily Rose?" Fraser purred, those opaque eyes assessing her with a sly amusement that terrified her. "You'd like nothing more than to have me pull the trigger. Destroy you, before you can be made a part of Blackheath's destruction. But it's too late. You have already sealed his fate, my dear. His torture and death, will be on your conscience, regardless of what happens now."

Fraser lay the pistol upon the table, smiling with unholy glee. "For the instant I send a note to Blackheath Hall regarding your tragic plight, I am dead certain Pendragon will dash here at the speed of lightning, rushing to your defense. And when he does, my dearest Emily . . . when he does . . . we will be here. Waiting."

16

The late morning sun gilded the meadow with the pastoral loveliness of a Gainsborough landscape. Ian leaned against the pasture fence beside the unusually quiet Tony, drinking in the beauty of the scene so that he could remember it forever.

Lucy was knee-deep in flowers, her rose-pink dress making her look like a blossom herself, her curls glistening like sunshine as she attempted to feed blades of grass to the wobbly newborn colt.

Ian sighed, remembering how unsettled he'd been when he'd awakened alone, how he had gone to search for Emily and ended up seeking her in the stable.

When Buckley explained that Emily had ridden into Williamsburg on some errand, Ian had been unable to suppress a stinging sense of concern, but he had quelled it. It was not as if she had to ask his permission to go on a simple errand. It was not as if he had any real hold on her.

The thought had been troubling, bringing with it the wistful yearnings he had felt as he'd fallen asleep last night with her in his arms. The feeling that things were impossible between them. That they could never be.

He had attempted to drown the emotions by focusing on something tangible—the long-anticipated arrival of

Mordred's colt. Ian grinned, remembering how he and Tony had pulled off the incredible deception at Pendragon's lair. Even Ian's head groom still believed that the colt was spawned not from the loins of Ian Blackheath's stallion when in reality the foal had been the issue of the mount ridden by Pendragon.

Ian had hoped that the foal would inherit his sire's beauty and spirit. He had expected the little one to be a jewel. What he had not expected was to find Lucy perched on an overturned box in the stall.

He had been terrified for a heartbeat, knowing how protective a mare could be, knowing what deadly damage those sharp hooves could wreak.

But the colt's mama had apparently not heard the story of Lucy shearing Tony's stallion, because the high-strung mare seemed every bit as entranced by the little girl as Lucy was with the wobbly colt.

Lucy had been scratching delicately behind the colt's ears, her voice gentle. "You are a very bobbly little horse, I think. But as soon as you can stand up and not wiggle so much, I shall teach you how to be very naughty."

Ian's mouth had quirked in a grin. "How, now, Mistress Lucy. And just what devilment are you up to with my new colt?"

"He is not yours. He's mine," she informed Ian, loftily. "He told me so. His name is Cristofori, and he loves me . . . oh, very much."

"I can see that." Ian had grinned as the colt nudged Lucy's cheek with his velvety nose, apparently affronted that she was paying attention to someone else. "But Cristofori seems a powerfully large name for such a little fellow."

"It's the name of the man who made the first pianoforte. And when Cristofori is not quite so wobbly, I am going to bring him into my blue drawing room and play songs for him."

"Are you, now? I am certain the downstairs maids will be thrilled to hear it." Ian opened the stall door and started inside, but the mare pranced toward him, her eyes menacing, her ears flattened in warning.

"Hush, now, Mama," Lucy said, skittering off of the box and going to the mare's head. "He won't hurt your baby."

"Lucy, it's dangerous to . . ."

But astonishingly the mare seemed to settle down beneath Lucy's small hand, merely satisfying her equine sense of maternal protectiveness by tossing her head in Ian's direction one last time and watching him with liquid brown eyes.

"This mama loves her baby very much," Lucy said softly. "When Cristofori fell down, she came and licked him and made soft sounds. She was telling him that he was the best baby horse in the world and that she would never ever leave him alone."

The wistfulness in the little girl's voice had made Ian's heart ache.

"Cristofori's mama would never, ever hurt him. She would do the kissing thing and not care if he played the pianoforte better than she did. I think that Cristofori's mama is like the lady."

She reached up to stroke the mare's rippling mane. "But then, I s'pose that Cristofori is a very good baby horse while I am a very fractious girl and not easy to have affection for."

"Lucy, I wouldn't trade your mischief for all the angelic little misses in Christendom. Who would play on the pianoforte for me? And who would snip off my buttons and put on such stunning new ones? And who would . . . who would give me kisses on the cheek and assure me that my whiskers were not my fault?"

"If I give you a kiss now, Uncle Ian, would you let me take Cristofori out into the pasture to play? I want to show him the sunshine."

The soft sound of Tony saying his name brought Ian back to the present, and he turned to regard his friend.

"You've done wonders, Ian. Pure wonders," Tony said quietly, his eyes on the child and the foal separated from them by a sweep of green pasture. "My God, when I think what the little termagant was like when she arrived here, I can scarce believe it has been so short a time. And"—Tony smiled—"when I think what you were like before, I swear I could kiss the hem of Emily's petticoat in adulation."

"Touch one thread on her gown, Gray, and I'll have you at sword point," Ian said with a kind of possessiveness.

Tony's eyes grew bright, assessing. "My, but we seem to have had a change of . . . attitude since I almost wrung your neck last night. What did Emily do to unleash this uncharacteristic show of good sense in you? Clobber you with an anvil?"

"No. She . . ." Ian looked away, his eyes burning, his voice threaded through with awe. "She came to me, Tony, and—" A tiny sound tore from Ian's throat. "My God, Tony, what am I going to do with her?"

"Love her, Ian."

"Love her? How can I? How can I expect *her* to love *me* after I tell her the truth? I've been lying to her from the beginning, Tony. A woman like Emily would never understand that kind of deceit."

Tony's mouth curved in a warm smile. "With the kind of love that was shining in your lady's eyes when I saw her last night, Ian, I am certain she would forgive you almost anything. Trust me in this, as one who has already suffered through the first agonies of giving his heart. There is no help for it, my friend. Just hurl yourself off the cliff and savor the fall."

Ian winced at how beautiful that sounded, how enticing. "I can't ask her to share the kind of life I live."

"You're not asking her, Ian," Tony interjected. "She came to you freely. That was her gift to you. And as for the kind of life you live . . ." A wide grin split Tony's face. "With Emily and Lucy running amok in Blackheath Hall, I'm certain it will never be quite the same again, thank God. I think you might begin the transformation by canceling the Roman fete in favor of a betrothal party."

"The fete? Son of a bitch!" Ian exploded. "I'd forgotten. I'll have Priam see to it at once. All I need is for the house to be flooded with togas and gauze. Lucy would kick up so much mischief she'd make the burning of Rome seem like a musicale!"

"True. And your lady would definitely take exception to your . . . adoring throng. Nora would unman me forever if she were ever confronted with my sordid past in such a fashion."

"Emily said my past didn't matter," Ian said softly. "That it had made me the man I am. She loves me, Tony, and would change nothing."

"Well, I wouldn't go so far as to nominate you for sainthood, old friend. There are still some things about you I'd like to alter—your infernal stubbornness for example."

But Tony's teasing faded into an indistinguishable murmur as Ian's eyes alighted again upon Lucy.

The child knelt beside the colt, her hands on Cristofori's knobby knees. As if she felt Ian's gaze upon her, Lucy turned and called out, "My baby horse is much less wobbly now, Uncle Ian! Tomorrow I shall ride him!"

"Not for two years, sweeting. It would hurt his tiny legs if you tried it now."

Lucy's face fell as she regarded the colt, but when she turned back, she called out, "It will be detestable hard to be patient, but I would never, ever hurt him." With that she wrapped her arms about the animal's silky neck.

"My God, Tony, I can't wait until Emily sees that," Ian said, raking his hand back through his hair. "I wish to hell she'd return from . . ."

At that moment there was a muffled sound of hoofbeats approaching, and both men wheeled around, expecting to see Emily's dark hair. Ian's whole body stiffened in shock and unease as his gaze locked upon something far different—a young private in bright regimentals, guiding his horse along the drive.

"What the devil?" Ian gritted out, then schooled his face into the expression of lazy arrogance that was the mask of Ian Blackheath.

"What a delightful surprise, Private," he said, bowing amicably as the young man drew rein. "What business brings you so far afield this fine day? Some patriot rumblings? An escaped criminal, perhaps?"

"I am to deliver a message to you, sir," the boy said, looking incredibly uncomfortable. He extended a note sealed with a glob of wax as red as blood.

"For me? How intriguing. Perhaps a letter from Captain Atwood requesting an invitation to my Roman fete. It has been canceled, however, so you may give the good captain my most humble regrets."

"I'm not privy to what's in the note, sir."

"Would you care to wait for a reply? I can order up some refreshment after your long ride."

"No, thank you, sir. I was instructed to go straight back to the guardhouse. No reply is expected."

"I . . . see." Ian's brow furrowed as he fingered the edge of the note. "Then I'll thank you and bid you godspeed."

The boy wheeled his mount around and cantered down the drive as if he feared some malaise infecting Blackheath land would poison him.

Ian frowned, looking at the note, a chill of wariness trailing up his spine. He broke the seal, unfolding the message.

His eyes scanned the painfully precise lines of script, and the blood drained from Ian's face. He grabbed the fence rail, so stricken his knees nearly buckled.

"My God, Ian, what is it?" Tony gasped, grabbing Ian's arm to steady him.

"It's Emily," Ian rasped. "The bastards have her."

"What bastards? Who the blazes—"

"Someone who is threatening to kill her, Tony, unless Pendragon surrenders himself at Harrelson's deserted cottage within the hour."

Tony snatched the note from Ian's numb fingers. "The missive is directed to you. That means . . . Judas Priest, it means . . . What the devil are you going to do?"

Ian's jaw knotted. "Exactly what they commanded me to do. I will not gamble with Emily's life."

"For God's sake, you can't just ride out alone!" Tony cried. "It would be suicide! I'll round up the men. We'll find some way to—"

"There's no time. Damn it, they said to come alone. In an hour, by God! Tony, don't you understand? They'll kill her! Because of me. To get to me . . ." A tortured sound snagged

246

in Ian's throat, dizzying guilt, raw terror all but driving him to his knees.

Oh, God, what had he done, dragging Emily into the morass that was his life? Shattering her quiet, gentle world with the swirling darkness that was his own.

It was his fault, all of it. If she was sacrificed, it would be upon his soul.

"I will not allow you to do this!" Tony raged, grabbing Ian's arm. "Use your head, blast you! Emily wouldn't want you to take such an insane risk."

Ian ripped his arm from Tony's grasp with savage fury. "Emily isn't here! If I don't help her, she'll die!"

"You'll die if you go charging in there half crazed!" Tony said. "Ian, we have to stop, think! Why do you think we've been so damned successful in our raids? Because with your daring and my strategies, the English haven't got a chance. These bastards who hold Emily captive can't be certain you are Pendragon. There must be some way to deceive them instead of racing straight into enemy hands."

"There's no time for plotting, Tony. No time to argue! No time!" Hating himself, Ian did the only thing he could to silence his friend and stop him from following. With a savage uppercut, he connected with Tony's jaw.

Ian heard Lucy scream as Gray slammed backward, thudding to the ground. Then she was running toward them across the broad expanse of meadow, flinging herself through the fence.

"Don't—don't hit anymore! You're scaring Cristofori!" she wailed, when in truth it was her own small face that was streaked with fear.

Regret sliced through Ian as he looked from the child to Tony's still face.

"Lucy, I had to do it," Ian said, catching the child by her trembling shoulders. "Something has happened, and I have to leave."

"No! Don't go 'way!" The child sobbed, clinging to his neck. "Tony said it was sooeyside! I heard him! You'll get killed all dead like my mama, and—"

"The lady is in danger, Lucy! I have to go."

The child released him, skittering back in raw terror. Tears flowed in crystal rivers down her cheeks. "I'm frightened, Uncle Ian. I'm frightened."

Ian caught the little girl in his arms, hugged her fiercely. "I'm frightened too. Stay with Tony, sweeting. And pray, angel. Pray hard."

"I don't want to be alone anymore!" Lucy sobbed. "I'll be in-intolerable angry if you get dead!"

Ian could hear her choking words as he raced away.

Ian leaned low over the neck of his stallion, urging the animal to a pace so wild, so reckless, it seemed as if they danced in death's own palm. The Virginia countryside was a blur around him, the wind whipping his cape and tearing at his hair, the sound of the birds raking across Ian's nerves like a woman's screams.

He had ridden the highroads a hundred times. He had savored the blade-edge of danger.

But now the thundering sound of the horse's hoofbeats pulsed with a peril far too brutal to be exhilarating, a menace that brought not the addictive rush of anticipation or the surging sensation of power but rather a fear that crushed Ian's chest in a vise of terror and ravaged his soul with the most devastating guilt.

Emily. Her name was a ragged plea on lips that had long ago forgotten how to pray.

She was captive somewhere in the pools of shadow. Afraid.

From the moment the young private had pressed the message into Ian's hand, he had felt Emily's terror inside his own skin, felt her confusion, her pain.

No! He would not let them hurt her! Would not let her die! Since the first day he had donned the mask of Pendragon he had triumphed over the English. He had to focus on the single purpose of snatching Emily from whatever heinous trap she'd stumbled into. He had to stay alert and draw on his strength, his own cunning.

But he couldn't free his mind of the torturous images of

Emily, captured, terrified. Emily, an innocent angel with no knowledge of the dark world Ian was embroiled in. Emily, swept from the shores of her safe existence, into the swirling poison that was Ian's own.

He tried to grasp that steely courage that had ever been inside him, that strength that Tony had so often called cold-blooded. An almost superhuman confidence in his own ability to triumph—to triumph or to taste of the grand adventure that was death, not much caring which way the fate's ax fell.

But Ian's own words, flung out the night Crane was entombed echoed back to him, hideous now, laid bare of their dark despair, their withering cynicism.

The man who had uttered those words so heedlessly no longer existed. The man who had been willing—no, *anxious*—to hurl away his life, to be done with the pain of it all, had been changed forever by a little girl's antics and by a woman's loving hands.

Emily had told him he had aspired to be a perfect villain. Hadn't he triumphed in that at last? Could there be any crime more reprehensible, more unforgivable, than the one he was guilty of now?

There could be no fate more horrible than this bone-deep terror, this grinding sense of self-blame. Knowing that he was responsible for placing the woman he loved, the woman who trusted him, in deadly jeopardy.

Ian drove his heels into the stallion's sides, urging the beast to race like the very wind, wishing the raking branches could scour away his sick sense of foreboding.

"Emily, I love you . . ." The words echoed in his head. "Emily, please God, be alive. . . ."

But there were fates far worse than death, Ian knew. And his lady now lay in the hands of men who were no doubt well acquainted with those more ghoulish pleasures.

Men who would not be opposed to using those skills in order to win the prize they desired.

The life of Pendragon.

It was a forfeit Ian would pay gladly—one night of heaven in Emily's arms in exchange for his own worthless hide.

Yet he doubted it would be that simple. No matter what they promised, the men who held Emily would never free her. Not even after they had him in chains. They would want no loose ends to trouble them later. No one to spread the tale of the capture of a patriot raider, the death of a political martyr who might incite even more Virginians to rebellion.

No, it would be far neater if Emily d'Autrecourt, recently arrived from England, just disappeared. Vanished. No one cared enough to discover what fate had befallen her.

No one except the terrified child he had left in the flower-starred meadow. Pain twisted in Ian's chest at the memory of Lucy's tear-streaked face as he had raced away.

What would happen to the little girl if neither Ian nor Emily ever returned?

Who would she order around in that imperious little voice? Whose buttons would she snip off and then sew on again with such delight?

Would she be shunted off to someone who would attempt to mold her into some proper little miss and shatter forever the tenuous glimmer of trust that had appeared in those child eyes—the trust that Emily had nurtured in the child and that had spilled over onto him?

The trust that he had repaid with lie upon lie.

Was this to be the final vengeance for his myriad sins? That he had been able to touch a future he'd never dreamed possible for just one dream-kissed night, only to have it snatched away?

Damn Emily d'Autrecourt! Damn Lucy! Damn them both for forcing him to open places he'd kept locked for so long. Damn them for making him feel, making him hope. Damn them for giving him a glimpse of the beauty that might have been his. If they hadn't battered through those walls inside him, he would be the same as he'd been on those nights he had ridden before.

Possessed by an almost savage vigilance. A vigilance that might save Emily's life.

A vine slashed at Ian's face as he rode past a copse of trees, and he was grateful for the sting.

Oh, God, what had she thought? His Emily Rose? What had raced through her mind when his true identity was exposed to her?

He winced at the memory of how she had recoiled at the mention of Pendragon. She had shuddered as if she considered the patriot raider a monster.

And maybe he had been.

A wolf, stalking, hungry, ruthless.

It had been easier that way. Far less painful to rove the night like a beast hunting its prey than as a man whose mortality seemed to jeer at him from every shadow, mocking him with his own helplessness and with the fragility of the life of the woman he loved.

Ian reined Mordred in at the brink of a hill where a winding, overgrown path ribboned down to a cottage nestled in the crook of a stream—the meeting place Emily's captors had specified in the letter.

A dozen sentries were visible, scattered about at different posts, more terrified of Pendragon's legend than alert at their duties. They were Atwood's men—bumbling fools Ian and his band had outwitted and outfought a score of times.

Yet when they matched swords before, Tony had been riding at Ian's side, along with numerous other brave men. This time Ian was alone.

His eyes scanned the area, his jaw hardening.

How many other soldiers lurked about, waiting? Ian wondered. There was no way to tell. Instead, he surveyed the structure where Emily was being held prisoner.

The building was small but defensible if Ian was foolhardy to enter the place intending to draw blood. The mare Emily had ridden from the stables was tethered to a hitching post outside. Ian could only hope they were still holding her somewhere inside.

That she was in the cottage, waiting for him, praying.

Jesus, God, how terrified she must be.

Instinctively Ian checked his pistol and the sword at his belt, then let his hand stray down to where a dagger was concealed in his Russian leather boot.

He had been instructed to walk to the front of the cottage

and surrender his weapons. But once his enemies had him unarmed, he had little doubt about the fate he and Emily would meet.

There had been a time when Ian would have been eager for this battle. He would have been irritated that the rescue would not be even more challenging, with more swords to avoid, more pistol balls flying.

But as he swung down from his mount and tied the stallion to a low-hanging branch, he was only relieved that the odds were not even more heavily weighted against him.

Of course, Ian thought grimly, there was always the chance that an even bigger army of men waited for him inside the cottage, their pistols cocked, their swords drawn.

Tugging his cape tighter around his shoulders, Ian stealthily slipped past the guards and made his way down to where a set of shutters were closed tight over the back window of the cottage, only a small crack allowing him a glimpse of the room beyond.

He could make out some sort of table, a few chairs.

But the sight that made his heart lurch was that of flowing mahogany curls and the soft folds of a primrose-hued petticoat. He searched for a better vantage point and found an empty knothole in one of the shutters. When he peered through it, what he saw only tightened the noose of fury about his throat, deepening the hideous sense of imbalance that seemed to rock inside him.

Those violet eyes had been brimming with wild, sweet passion the night before; now they were huge in Emily's face, filled with so much terror, so much pain, that Ian felt himself sinking into those same emotions until he could hardly draw breath.

Those slender hands that had comforted little Lucy with such tenderness and explored his body with such fervor, were bound in front of Emily, rendering her helpless.

No, Emily was far worse than helpless. Five soldiers stood guard at different points in the room while a jowl-faced bulldog of a man lounged with his back against the thick stone wall, a pistol pointed with studied negligence against Emily's back.

The sly bastard was far enough away from any window so that he could pull the trigger before Ian could reach him. And those eyes, those soulless eyes lost in pockets of flesh, were fixed on the only door.

It was a perfect trap unless . . . Could he set up a diversion? Set the building aflame? Oh, God, he had to get her out of there. . . .

The metallic click of a pistol being cocked shattered Ian's thoughts, and he froze, feeling the nub of cold steel jab against the back of his head.

Out of the corner of his eye he caught a glimpse of Reginald Atwood's face. The captain's features were contorted with anger and unease, a far cry from the expected reaction of triumph.

"You've made your first mistake, rebel scum, disobeying the orders given you!" Atwood hissed. "For your lady's sake I hope it is your last."

17

Fury and disgust ripped through Ian. By God's wounds, how could he have been so reckless, so heedless? How could he have failed to hear Atwood's approach? The man was a bumbling ass at best. He'd been made to look the fool a dozen times in comparison to Pendragon.

But this time Ian had been the fool. His mind had not been emptied of all but his own keen awareness. He lacked that single-minded focus that shut out everything except his mission.

This time his mind had been filled to bursting with the terror in Emily's wide violet eyes and the pistol's kiss of death pressed against her slender back. His mind had been distracted by the self-blame that had savaged him from the moment he opened the ominous message.

"You've made your first mistake," Atwood had said. And the Englishman was right.

But this mistake—the first of its kind he'd ever made—might well be his last. His stomach clenched. He might have just cost Emily her life.

"Fraser is waiting for you, and getting damned impatient," Atwood snarled. "If you've brought anyone with you, you'd best tell me now, or it will be death to—"

"I am alone." Ian interrupted firmly, suddenly struck by

how strange that felt, how oddly fitting. If he was to die, it would be better that it happen without his men around him, without a blaze of patriotic glory. No, far more fitting that Ian Blackheath should die alone.

If only he could save Emily first.

Atwood's gaze slashed through the underbrush to where the nearest sentries were just visible. "I have Blackheath at the point of my pistol, you dolts," Atwood shouted. "Be alert, damn you, in case he has brought any of his men."

"We saw nothing!" A youth of about nineteen cried twenty yards to the north. "By God, how could he have gotten through?"

"Black magic," Ian said, forcing a sneer to his lips. "Everyone knows that I am the devil's own."

"Enough, damn you," Atwood snapped, nudging him none too gently with the pistol.

Ian dredged up Pendragon's usual scathing sarcasm. "You'd be advised not get too energetic with that weapon, Captain. It might go off and kill me, and then what would you do for amusement?"

"Rebel scum!" Atwood bit out. "You'd best leash your tongue before you meet with Mr. Fraser, or the fate that will befall Emily . . . My God, man, what he has planned . . ."

Was there the slightest hint in Atwood's voice that he was sickened? The tiniest quaver of disgust.

Sweet Jesus, Ian thought, if even Atwood was horrified, their plans must be beyond heinous. Beyond imagining. Panic twisted in Ian's belly. What kind of monstrous evil had he unloosed upon the woman he loved?

"Your sword, your pistol—leave them both out here," Atwood said. "Make one false move, and I'll kill you."

Carefully, so carefully, Ian divested himself of sword and pistol, praying that Atwood would not see the dagger in his boot, not know it was there.

The captain gave a grunt of satisfaction as the weapons clunked to the ground. Then his eyes narrowed. "What's that in your boot, Blackheath? The dagger I've heard you carry sheathed there?" With fury, Ian withdrew the slender blade, his fist clenching and unclenching on the hilt before he let it clatter against his other weapons. Now nothing stood between Emily and death save Ian's own wits.

"Get moving," Atwood commanded, shoving him toward the cottage door. "And if you love Emily d'Autrecourt at all, damn your eyes, you'll do exactly as Fraser tells you."

"Let me guess," Ian said dryly. "Then your friend Fraser will kill us *mercifully* as opposed to . . . more *creatively?*"

"No! He'll release her. He would have to. She's loyal to the Crown. She's done nothing to warrant death."

"You really believe he'll let her live?" Ian hissed. "My God, Atwood, you are a fool. He'll kill her, just as he'll have me killed. I might suggest that you watch your back as well, Captain. If things get messy, men of his kind are always compelled to tidy things up. Permanently."

"Don't be absurd, you traitorous dog! Fraser will not—" Atwood stopped abruptly, as if realizing the precarious conversation he was holding with his captive. "Her life is in God's hands," he said tightly.

"No." Ian glanced down at his own fingers, empty of weapons. "Her life is in the devil's hands."

With a measured stride, Ian moved toward the cottage, his eyes covertly taking in his surroundings. Seven horses besides Emily's were tied to the hitching post, in addition to those of the soldiers Ian had taken note of before. Even more riders could be concealed among the trees, though his stallion's whickering would most likely have raised an answering whinny from their mounts by now.

Was it possible there were so few men here? Not even enough to match Pendragon's raiders in number? Whoever this Fraser was, God curse his soul, he was either a brave man or a fool.

Or was Fraser so damned certain of himself that he had taken too few precautions? Was it possible that what Ian had just said to Atwood was true—that Fraser intended for things to get very untidy indeed?

"Open the door and enter."

For an instant Ian considered wheeling around, grabbing Atwood's pistol, counting on surprise to get to Fraser in time. But the other soldiers were still in the room, and the gun was still pointed at Emily.

Ian had rescued people before, under far worse conditions. He had moved swiftly, ruthlessly, and most times he had been rewarded by success.

But could he risk this being the one time that he failed?

Could he risk Fraser's bullet slamming into Emily's spine?

The image was so vivid Ian's stomach churned. He opened the door.

Atwood's hand slammed against Ian's back, sending him stumbling into the room. The soldiers leaped as if Atwood had just pushed forth Lucifer himself, Emily crying out in horror.

Her sob lanced through him. "Oh, sweet God, Ian, you shouldn't have come!"

His throat constricted at the torment in her face, but he glanced around at the soldiers stationed about the room, their faces devoid of any emotion save that almost satanic terror the legend of Pendragon always spawned.

His eyes returned to Emily, her face so filled with anguish. His voice was soft, loving. "Of course I came, Emily Rose," he said. "How could I have abandoned my lady?"

Even the threat of the pistol couldn't hold her as she wrenched away from Fraser's grasp. She flung herself against Ian. His arms closed around her, and he felt the warmth in her, that agonizingly fragile pulse of life. Her bound hands reached up to touch his face, her eyes stark and filled with self-loathing.

"Ian, I'm so—so sorry," she choked out.

Oh, Christ, that she should feel guilty. Guilty because they had used her to bring him here!

It was pain beyond bearing.

He caught her trembling fingers in his. "Sh, love. Don't even think it! It was my doing. All of it."

"No, Ian. You don't understand. It was mine!"

His gaze locked on her swollen fingers, the circulation all but cut off in her hands. Ian wheeled on Fraser. "Do you have to keep her tied so tightly? What, are you afraid a lone woman could escape you?"

"Oh, your lady is going nowhere, Blackheath. Of that I am certain. Perhaps we could strike a compromise. Captain Atwood, take the ropes from Mrs. d'Autrecourt's hands and place them on our most recently arrived guest. You will understand, Blackheath, that I couldn't stand to see a good length of rope left to languish in a corner when it could be so much more divertingly applied about someone's wrists."

Fraser jerked his head toward Atwood. "Bind him to that chair over there, so that he may be quite comfortable. I wouldn't want to be considered an ill-mannered host."

Atwood shoved his pistol into the waistband at the back of his breeches—a ploy Ian recognized as an effort to keep it out of a prisoner's reach.

Ian's fists knotted. He had to make his move now, do something before they immobilized him. He had to find some way . . . His muscles tensed, poised, ready, but Fraser chuckled with mocking evil.

"I know exactly what you are thinking, Blackheath—how desperate you are as you plot to keep your hands free. But you will be the most docile of captives. Not only because the rest of these soldiers have their weapons at the ready but also because, if you prove difficult, I will be forced to bury a most unsightly pistol ball . . . where? Oh, say, between your woman's breasts."

Gently but firmly, Ian attempted to put Emily away from him, but she clung to him, glaring at Fraser. "No! I won't let you do this. I don't care if you pull that trigger!"

"This mutual adoration between you and Blackheath is becoming tiresome, Mrs. d'Autrecourt. Perhaps you would be more amenable if I explained to you that I will disable your lover either with ropes or with a creatively placed bullet."

"Do as he says, love," Ian tried to keep his voice soothing, tried to convey all he felt for her in his heart—a lifetime of love that they had possessed so briefly. One that they might never live to share.

Fraser pulled back the hammer on the pistol. Emily gave a tiny cry and stepped away.

"You're making a big mistake, Fraser," Ian said as

Atwood fumbled with the bindings about Emily's wrists. "I'm one of the most powerful planters in all Virginia, with business interests all over the world. You're going to live to regret this."

The rope fell free, and Atwood grabbed a wooden chair, dragging it across the floor to where Ian stood.

"Do you think any of your fine connections will step forward to defend you when I prove that you are Pendragon?" Fraser jeered. "A rebel cur who will meet a traitor's death?"

Atwood gave Ian a shove, forcing him to sit, then looped the thick cords roughly about his wrists.

Ian caught one of the loops in his palm, desperately attempting to employ a trick he'd once learned, but the rope tangled about his thumb. Atwood tightened the bindings so brutally that Ian wondered if he'd further disabled his hands and failed Emily yet again.

"You're insane, Fraser," Ian spat. "I don't give a damn about political drivel. Everyone knows that."

"Oh, yes, you've announced it to countless audiences. You've all but taken out an advertisement in the London *Times.* But the game is up this time, and you have come out the loser."

"Prove your accusations, you bastard! I dare you to—"

"I fully intend to. With the lovely Emily d'Autrecourt's help."

"No, Ian!" Emily flung herself against him, as if to shield him with her own slender body, her fingers knotting in his shirt. "You cannot listen to him. You must not betray—"

"Name your price, Fraser. For her life." Ian said the words, knowing already that if he could give Fraser the world in ransom for Emily, it would make no difference. The cold glimmer in the man's eyes was a precursor to dealing death. A glimmer that Ian had seen far too often. One that, on occasion, had shown in his own eyes.

Fraser's lips split in a diabolical smile. "I prefer to set forth my terms in private. Captain Atwood, you may dismiss your soldiers. Send them outside to guard against any intrusions by Pendragon's men."

"I told you. I have no connection to the rebel raider," Ian asserted as the soldiers filed out. "I have no men. I am nothing but what you see—a dissolute bastard, a—"

"Yes. A dissolute bastard who has ridden to his own death because a woman was in danger. A rakehell and a scoundrel, a man who cares for no one, but who is apparently willing to sacrifice himself in an uncharacteristically noble fashion. Spare me your protestations of innocence, Blackheath. You and I are men of business. Let us begin our bartering for the woman's life, now that only Atwood is present to overhear us."

Fraser's eyes seethed with triumph. "I have a desire to host a somewhat elaborate entertainment," Fraser purred. "And since you are so adept at organizing such debauchery, I want you to provide me with a . . . guest list of sorts."

"A guest list?"

Fraser's gaze sharpened. "I want to hang your friends, to show those foolhardy enough to espouse the rebel cause that they are courting death, disaster. But a single hanging, with a single martyr for them to rally around, would do more harm than good. You and I are both students of human nature, Pendragon. You know what an annoying rallying point a martyr can be. Therefore, as I see it, I must discourage people from clinging to your ghostly cape by horrifying them so deeply that they would never dare take action of their own."

Ian cringed inwardly. So close to his own words. Spoken the night he had clashed with Lemming Crane. Had he ever suspected how bitter they would sound when turned against him?

"I want a full confession from you, Blackheath. And I want the names of your men, in exchange for your woman's life."

Ian's blood froze.

Sweet God, that it should come to this—his most horrifying nightmare. Real now. So hellishly real.

Faces flashed before his eyes—Tony, furious that night at Brigand's Cave, and later as he tried to explain his love for his Nora. Talbot and Taylor, Dettmer and Benetton. And the others . . . so many others . . .

"You're hallucinating, Fraser." Ian forced the words from between stiff lips. He closed his eyes, and even Tony Gray's face blurred beneath the burning vision of Emily . . . sweet, innocent Emily. "I'm no rebel raider."

"Then why do you look as if I'd just twisted a knife in your gut?" Fraser gloated.

"Maybe because it turns my stomach to see a bastard like you terrorizing a woman."

"So you do love her." There was a sadistic satisfaction in Fraser's purr. "Ah, my friend, have you not read enough heroic tales to learn that a woman is the most certain path to destruction?"

"I've done well enough in traveling that path on my own. I would not stoop to blaming an innocent woman."

"Of course you must save the tragic innocent, protect her at all costs." Fraser gave an ugly laugh. "You know, I have been waiting a very long time to entertain you, Pendragon. You have proved a most elusive enigma to solve. Of course, it is unfortunate that your lady had to become entangled. But such things are a regrettable necessity at times."

Fraser smiled. "I shall be open with you, Blackheath. Honest. We can accomplish the task before us in two ways, as I am certain you have already surmised. You can tell me now the things I need to know. And then—a swift bullet through the skull. Or you can decide to be . . . difficult. And I will have to punish Mrs. d'Autrecourt for your stubbornness."

"She's innocent, damn you! Even Atwood—"

"Atwood has also been much smitten with Emily's charms, it seems. A fact that I find most advantageous at present. You see, it seems the captain has been craving the bounty between Emily d'Autrecourt's thighs. I mean to give it to him, in plenty, unless my own desires are satisfied."

Ian glared at Atwood. "You would savage Emily?" he demanded. "Rape her? By God, you know she's done nothing."

Atwood's face was ice-white. "I am a soldier."

"A soldier," Ian spat. "Is that what English soldiers do in the name of their king now? Rape defenseless women?"

"Damn you, Blackheath, what is worse? My . . . touch, or a bullet through her flesh! For God's sake, man, what would you have me do?"

"Atwood, take her," Fraser commanded.

Ian caught the slightest hesitation in the soldier, before Atwood grabbed Emily's shoulders, hauled her away from Ian.

She cried out, stumbled back.

Ian strained against the ropes on his wrists, but Fraser's voice cut in.

"Her thigh, Blackheath. Perhaps I'll shatter her thigh. How many times have you imagined those thighs, Blackheath, silky smooth, wrapped around your hips, urging you deeper, harder—"

"No, Ian, don't—" Emily was crying out.

"That way," Fraser continued, "you will be properly chastised, but she will still be useful to—"

"Stop it, you bastard! I'll kill you, I swear—"

"That might be difficult, considering the fact that you are tied up and I am holding a loaded gun. Of course, you are welcome to try it, if you'd like to endanger the woman's life."

Fraser was enjoying this, damn him, with the sick pleasure, of a fallen preacher titillating himself with the confession of a whore.

Atwood's hands were on Emily, her skin starkly pale against the captain's regimentals, the scarlet surrounding her like a pool of blood.

"Her bodice, Atwood. Perhaps you would like to begin unlacing it."

Emily was shaking, her hair tumbling down in a cascade of mahogany curls, clinging about her white face. Fraser laughed at her terror, caressing the barrel of his pistol. "My dear captain, when you seduce a beautiful lady on your own, I would hope you would be more ardent."

"Don't mock me, Fraser!" Atwood raged. "Do what you

will to Blackheath, but I won't be a party to hurting this woman, damn your eyes!"

"You won't be a party to this? And who is giving the orders here? You'd best not forget."

"The king himself could order me to rape a defenseless woman and I would tell him to go to perdition."

"Would you? And what would you say if I put a pistol ball through your groin so that you would never again have to worry about such carnal urges?"

Atwood's lips thinned. "Just because I oppose this rebel scum doesn't mean I am willing to taste his blood by harming innocents."

"Then perhaps I shall dally with the lady myself. But not in the way I suggested to you. No, I prefer applying the bite of a knife to someone's flesh rather than answering the clamoring in my loins. What think you, Blackheath? Perhaps if I were to carve the name of Pendragon on her cheek, you would be ready to confess your villainy? If I were to slice that satiny smooth skin until it lies in bloody ribbons . . ."

Impotent rage thundered through Ian's veins, a helplessness such as he'd never known before. Desperately he tore at his bindings, his wrists growing slick with sweat and blood as he struggled to free himself, his eyes searching for a weapon, something, anything, he could use to defend her.

His gaze skimmed Emily's face, and it was as if a blade had carved out his heart. Those beautiful features were wild, stark, her face like that of a damned soul slipping inexorably into hell while Fraser watched her—Lucifer incarnate, greedily feasting on her pain.

"Would you like me to entertain your woman, Pendragon? It is your choice."

And in that paralyzing instant Ian knew that he would say anything, do anything, to keep Emily from suffering. Desperately he groped for something to deflect Fraser's fury from the trembling woman in Atwood's arms. Anything, except the one price Fraser demanded—the death of the men who had served so bravely under Pendragon's command.

Oh, God, if he could only face Fraser alone, the English

scum could do his worst—unleash whatever savagery lurked in the bastard's soul. Ian had reconciled himself to death long ago. He knew he possessed the courage to endure whatever brutal payment Fraser demanded for Pendragon's sins.

But to watch Emily pay in his place . . .

"You have me, Fraser," Ian said through gritted teeth. "I don't give a damn if you make an example out of me before the whole of Virginia. Flay my bloody flesh away an inch at a time, and I vow I'll not so much as turn a damned eyelash, if you'll just let her go."

"You'll sign a full confession?"

"No, Ian," Emily cried, "I can't let you—"

"I'll confess to being bloody King George himself if you'll release her."

"That would be highly amusing, but unfortunately one corpse would not be quite as impressive as, say, twenty would be. You know my price, Pendragon."

"Damn you, even if I were Pendragon, how could I condemn my own men to death?" He gave one more savage, futile tug on his bindings, knew it was hopeless to think he could get free. His gaze slashed to Emily, sick with defeat. "Oh, God, Emily Rose, how can I let them hurt you?"

She ripped free of Atwood's grasp, stumbled toward Ian. And it was as if she were shattering, a strange, fierce light in her eyes. "No! Ian, you must listen to me. I'm not worthy of your protection. I—I am the one who brought you to this pass."

"It's hardly your fault they captured you, lady. Forced you to—"

"I came here of my own free will." Her words slashed through him like a Saracen's blade. "I brought Fraser the evidence that condemned you."

"You mean that you—" Ian stared at her, a ravaged angel in her flowing gown, her lips trembling. And he felt as if he were being swept away by a nightmarish sea, drowning in a haze of disbelief. "No. It can't be. You would not have—"

"You said once you thought it generous that my benefactor gave me title to my shop," she cut in, her eyes meeting his, level, steady. "The price he demanded was that I pass information to the English troops."

"You're trying to convince me that you were some kind of English spy? Emily, don't be absurd! It's impossible."

"Secret messages were hidden inside fashion dolls." Emily had stretched out the hand that he had begun to hope could heal him, and had dealt him a wound so jagged that he knew he would never be whole again. She gestured to a table. "Dolls exactly like the one that Lucy stole from my shop."

Ian's gaze locked on the wooden lady sprawled like a half-torn corpse on the scarred oak surface. The doll Lucy had left for him last night, along with the letter in which she confided her love. The doll that had been abandoned when he made love to Emily.

He swayed against the chair, hating himself for his own gullibility, trying to grasp something too ghastly to comprehend. Suddenly the pieces of a hideous puzzle locked into focus with mind-shattering clarity.

He staggered beneath memories of Emily demanding the doll, Emily wandering about Blackheath Hall, searching . . . For a bed, she had said one night, and on another night she had admitted she was searching for the doll in the *chambre d'amour.*

But never had he suspected the reason she was so desperately searching. Never had he realized that the mysterious secret that had eluded Atwood was hidden away in Ian Blackheath's own house.

A part of him died as he looked into that treacherously lovely face. "That is why you came to Blackheath Hall. That's why you feigned concern for Lucy, *love* for the child. You were all sweet smiles and cloying understanding—only because you wanted the doll."

"What did you think, Blackheath? That she was a gift from God?" Fraser sneered. "Didn't it ever seem a trifle *too* convenient that you had a child dropped upon your doorstep one night, and a governess the next?"

The words were brutal, ripping away the veil of mystery

from so many things, baring ugliness, deception, in place of what Ian had so briefly believed was his own special miracle.

"Did you really believe that a woman like this one would want anything to do with a depraved fellow like you? A worthless, debauched animal with a reputation so foul that people can smell the stench of you clear to Boston? You fool, you witless fool! Did you truly believe she could *love* you?"

"Love me?" Ian ground out, his gaze flashing to Emily's. "No. In truth I never believed that was possible. Never."

Emily raised her chin, her voice only a little unsteady. "I would have done anything to get the doll back, Ian. Anything."

Why was there such pain lurking along the edges of those soft, kissable lips? Why could he now see a shadow of deception in those amethyst eyes? Sweet God, why hadn't he seen it before?

"You would have done anything?" His heart was an open wound. "You would even have suffered coming to my bed."

She paled, and Ian hated her for the way she seemed to waver for a moment, looking fragile, bruised. He cursed himself for his own weakness. "Yes. Even coming to your bed."

"Perhaps"—Fraser's malevolent chuckle raked across Ian's nerves—"it is a mercy that we must kill her. Most likely she's been infected with French pox by such a notorious whore-chaser as you, Blackheath."

"Kill her?" Atwood cut in. "No! Curse you, Fraser, I—"

Fraser cast a scorn-filled glance from Atwood to Ian, laughing, laughing. "What asinine fools the pair of you are! You, Atwood, for believing I would let the woman live after all she's seen, and you, Blackheath for believing that a woman of quality such as Emily d'Autrecourt would stoop to bed you."

Ian said nothing, wished to God that he could feel nothing.

"However," Fraser continued, "while this distressing if belated honesty on Mrs. d'Autrecourt's part does nothing to change my plans for her, it might change your reaction to them, Blackheath. Perhaps you will savor watching her scream beneath my knife, since you know that she prostituted herself in your bed."

Fraser paced toward him, that greedy light in his soulless eyes. "What are you doing, even now, Blackheath? Remembering her shrill cries of pleasure, her faithless words of love? Are you remembering the hunger you believed you felt in her hands? Lies! All lies! While she suffered you to touch her, she was filled with revulsion."

Ian felt himself teeter on the blade edge of sanity, felt the waves of darkness ooze inside him, thick, unyielding, plunging him into a hopelessness so complete the suffocating blackness obliterated everything in its path, crushed the flicker of hope Emily had stirred in him when she became his ladylove.

His love?

No. His betrayer. The woman who had finally destroyed Pendragon, all but brought him to his knees.

Sweat beaded on Ian's brow. One more glimpse of Atwood's hands on her or Fraser's threats and she might have been woman who had broken him, made him turn Judas.

No. Surely even the poisonous love he'd felt for her would not have brought him so low.

"You traitorous bitch." The words were deadly. Quiet. His mouth curled in hatred.

She pulled away from Atwood, her fingers clutching at the delicate silver lace gilding the front her jacket, her hands shaking as she paced over to the table, braced herself against it. "Yes, Ian. That is exactly what I am."

"And now, that you've been caught in the jaws of your own trap, what do you expect me to do? Sacrifice a score of brave men in your place just because you are a woman? Go to hell, Emily Rose. You're about as helpless as an adder and thrice as dangerous."

Fraser chuckled. "Then you should rejoice when you see her writhing, hear her screaming, shouldn't you? I wonder. Are you man enough to listen? Even after all she has done, do you have the stomach to stand here and watch her with me?"

Ian despised himself for the surge of bile that rose in his throat, the fierce protectiveness he couldn't deny.

Damn her, he hated her. Liar. Spy. Tory. He hated her. Didn't he?

"Blackheath, for God's sake," Atwood pleaded. "Whatever happened between you, don't let him do this to her. Tell him—"

"I would rather watch her suffer than watch a score of brave men die." It was a lie. He hated the fact that he was still held in thrall by those eyes. Those lovely, treacherous eyes.

Hemp sawed deep into his wrists, shards of pain shooting up his arms as he twisted his hands against the ropes. "She made her choice long before I laid eyes on her."

Ian detected the slightest scraping sound on the table, saw Emily turn, one hand concealed in the folds of her satin skirts. "You're right, Ian," she said softly, walking behind him. "I have made my choice."

Sharp, slicing pain ripped into his hand as she passed, and Ian steeled himself not to cry out, not to betray her as he felt something sharp jammed between the ropes and his hand.

He grasped what she had wedged there . . . a knife. Small, by the feel of it, but a weapon nonetheless.

Stunned, Ian grasped the hilt in one hand, worked to saw at the bindings.

Sweet God, why had she done that? Given him the weapon when she was the one in deadly peril? Because she cared for him?

No, Ian thought savagely. Because he was able to take on both Fraser and Atwood far better than she was.

Even a stalking tigress would want to save her own skin.

"Mr. Fraser, you can see that now he cares nothing for me." She was pleading, in a broken angel's voice. "I—I did exactly as you ordered. I passed the messages. I was loyal."

"Yes. You've given ample evidences of where your loyalties lie," Fraser snickered as if at a jest only he understood.

"I don't deserve to be savaged for my service to the

Crown." Emily wrung her hands as she moved nearer Fraser. "When I sought out this opportunity to come to the colonies, I—"

"When *you* sought the opportunity?" Fraser sneered. "Still the naive little vicar's daughter, are you? I sought you out specifically to ensnare you into my service. A dangerous business in which I could use you as long as it amused me and then dispose of you."

Emily looked stunned, faltered for a moment. "I don't understand. Why . . ."

"I did it as a favor to a longtime acquaintance. His Grace, the duke of Avonstea. It was the duke's final wish that you be eliminated in a way commensurate with the amount of pain you had heaped upon his family."

"That makes no sense! Alexander has been dead for five years! Why would the duke wait so long to take action against me? What possible reason could he—"

"It seems that one Jedediah Whitley had discovered some distressing information that he planned to convey to you. Avonstea was eager to make certain it could never reach you."

At that second, Ian gave a savage tug on the knife, his ropes snapping free. The knife skidded from his grasp, slickened with his own blood, the sound charging the room into chaos as he launched himself to his feet, grabbed the chair, and sent it flying at the stunned Atwood. The captain gave a hoarse cry as he fell, his head cracking with a sickening sound against the floor.

Ian wheeled toward Fraser, expecting to feel the burning impact of a bullet, but the man's bulky body was obscured by a blur that was Emily, hurling herself against Fraser's arm.

Fraser gave a cry of rage as the pistol flew from his hand.

Before the man could right himself, Ian slammed his shoulder into Fraser's midsection. Knotting his fist, Ian slammed it into the man again and again, but Fraser was deceptively agile and well schooled in combat.

With brutal power, Fraser drove his fist into Ian's jaw. Ian sprawled backward, struggling to roll over, regain his feet, but before he could, Fraser landed on one knee with killing force upon Ian's stomach. There was a sickening sound of ribs cracking. Ian's chest felt as if it had caved in. But he gritted his teeth against the blinding pain, bringing his own knee up, hard, into Fraser's groin.

The man howled, doubling over, and Ian shoved Fraser off of him and rolled atop the big man. In a flash Ian grabbed up the knife and pressed the point against Fraser's throat.

Ian caught a glimpse of Emily, Fraser's pistol looking ludicrous in her shaking hand as she held the moaning Atwood at bay. Then Ian turned to Fraser. The man stared back with soulless eyes, and Ian could see the reflection of what he himself might have become.

"Well carried out, milord Pendragon," Fraser purred. "But how do you expect to escape the men still on alert outside?"

"You can watch me escape them while you're on your way to hell."

Fraser smiled that evil smile. "Ah, I see. You have it all planned out. All you have to do is kill me. There is only one problem, Blackheath. If you do, the woman will never know."

"Know what?" Ian snapped. "Damn your eyes, tell me—"

"It doesn't matter!" Emily's hands were shaking even worse. She sounded sick, exhausted, hopeless. "Ian, just . . . just finish it. Nothing matters anymore."

"Not even were I to tell you about your daughter?" Fraser chuckled malevolently.

"My . . . daughter?" Emily echoed faintly.

"He's stalling, Emily," Ian snapped. "This is just a ploy to unnerve you."

"Is it?" Fraser demanded. "Are you willing to risk that it is not, Emily? Let me tell you what I know about Jenny d'Autrecourt. Her gravestone is Italian marble with roses climbing over it. Roses like the ones you kept on your windowsill in London before your husband died. There is an angel carved on the stone you commissioned with what money you earned working for a Quakeress. And you would visit the grave as often as you could, to tend the roses, and you would sing to the child. A melody—"

"J-Jenny's Night Song." There was a stark, broken sound to Emily's voice. Ian didn't want to feel it wrench inside him, but it did.

"Damn it, Emily, don't listen to him!" He couldn't help but shift his gaze to her for a heartbeat. That was all Fraser needed.

With lightning swiftness he hurled Ian off of him, the back of Ian's head connecting with the edge of the table. Red haze engulfed Ian, his stomach heaving at the pain. He heard the deadly swish of steel against scabbard as Fraser unsheathed his sword.

But before that gleaming arc of steel could find flesh, an explosion shattered the room. Fraser flew back against the wall, crimson blossoming on his chest as he fell.

Ian surged to his feet, stunned to see Emily standing an arm's length away, Fraser's smoking pistol in her hand, her face so pale he feared she would collapse.

"Now you'll never know the truth . . ." Fraser sneered, even as the death rattle sounded in his throat. "The duke would think that a fitting . . . hell."

Thick eyelids fluttered as his head fell back. His eyes stared sightlessly at the ceiling, the room still echoing with the sound of his fiendish mockery.

Ian stood up, turning away from Fraser's body and grabbing up the Englishman's sword. At any second he expected Fraser's soldiers to charge through the door. "Get behind me, Emily," Ian snapped. "The bastards will be coming—"

But at that instant, Ian's gaze fell upon Emily, her image branding itself forever in his mind. Her face was as pale as a shade, something ethereal, fragile, seeming to wisp about her until it seemed as if the merest touch would make her crumble. A thousand nightmares haunted her violet eyes. Fraser's death added yet another one.

Ian tore his gaze away from her, unable to bear the pain of

seeing her face, so beautiful, so treacherous. And he knew in that moment that a pistol ball through his heart would have been far more merciful than enduring this moment.

"It may mean my own life," Atwood's voice. Quiet. So quiet as he struggled to his feet, still disoriented by the blow of the chair. "But by God, I'm glad you killed him. I'm glad that Fraser is dead. The soldiers outside are my men, Blackheath," the captain said. "They're loyal to me. Use me as a hostage to get Emily the blazes out of here."

"What the devil—"

"There is no other choice, man. Do what you have to do. Having seen what His Majesty's minions are capable of, I've little stomach for returning to the ranks."

Atwood's words died in the sound of a rush of hoofbeats. Ian swore, grabbing Atwood.

"The sword, damn it," Atwood urged. "Put the damned thing to use instead of waving it in the bloody air!" For the first time in his life, Ian hated the feel of the weapon in his hand, knew he had no choice but to make it seem that Atwood was in deadly peril.

Fury, confusion, and a sick despair warred inside Ian as he pressed the blade to Atwood's throat and burst out through the doorway, into the sunlight.

But the moment his eyes fixed upon the scene in the yard, Ian froze, stunned. Two groups of guards had been trussed together like a child's posy, gags stuffed into their mouths, their eyes wide with terror. And in the distance Ian could see other, similar clusters of men in scarlet regimentals.

A jolt of gratitude, of pride, ripped through Ian as a dozen horsemen seemed to melt out of the woods to join those finishing their task of binding up the soldiers.

Pendragon's raiders. Their capes streamed out behind them, their masks glowing in the fading light.

Ian had seen them in battle scores of times, had felt that sharp surge of satisfaction at what he and Tony had built together. A fighting force so swift, so daring, that none could defeat them.

But now, as Ian stared at the mass of prancing horses, saw the glint of the men's swords, the flash of courage in their bearing, his mind filled with other images he knew he would never forget.

A gallows with a row of ropes shining golden in the sun. Bodies of the men who had served Pendragon and the patriot cause so loyally, dangling, lifeless, a result of Ian's own betrayal.

A part of him died inside, because he knew in that instant that he would never ride among those men again, never lead them through the night to avenge wrongs done the innocent, never fuel the flames of that wondrous, astonishing new ideal that had grown here in this wild new land of freedom, of new beginnings. . . .

Maybe it was better that way.

Hadn't Emily d'Autrecourt taught him that there could be no new beginnings for a man like him? He would only sully that precious, fragile dream.

Ian's eyes blurred. Then he stiffened, stunned, for at that moment, from the midst of those men, Mordred burst through, and the figure astride the stallion's back drove the breath from Ian's lungs.

He stared at his own reflection—Pendragon—the flowing cape exactly like the one about Ian's shoulders, the mask hiding a face that could only be Tony Gray's.

Tony, attempting to be as menacing as possible—and, by God, almost succeeding.

He bore down on Ian, the stallion racing, a pistol in his hand. Atwood gave a cry of disbelief as the soldier gaped at the figure before them.

"Atwood," Tony's voice was gravelly, threatening. "As usual, your men have proven little challenge to defeat. But I much doubt that you will be around when it comes time to release them. I full intend to shoot you where you stand for the insult you have done me!"

"The . . . insult?"

"Believing for even a moment that this arrogant popinjay, this womanizer and gambler, could be Pendragon! *Pendragon!*" Tony tightened his knees about Mordred, the stallion rearing, pawing the air like the hell-spawned mount he was supposed to be.

"We . . . we received a communication from . . . from Lemming Crane, assuring us that this man was . . . was you."

"Crane? That bumbling idiot! The man has as much wit as that stone there. It's a wonder he could find the hem of his mistress's petticoats when he wanted to bed her, let alone discover the identity of Pendragon! I am far taller than Blackheath, and my shoulders are twice as wide! How could that hell-raking cur ever hope to cut the dash that *I* do?" Tony thumped his chest with his fist.

"I . . . can see that now." Atwood's voice was quiet, low. "Blackheath is nothing like Pendragon."

"A tardy bit of insight, I'm afraid. Perhaps this time I should kill you, Atwood. Before, you were merely annoying, a trifle, like a bee buzzing in my ear. But to spread such slander as this, to announce to the world that Ian Blackheath is the patriot raider—*that* is beyond forgiving!"

"No one was privy to the information but Fraser and me," Atwood said. "And Fraser is dead."

There was grim satisfaction in the captain's voice, despite his obvious peril. Tony seemed taken aback.

"That may well be," Tony said, "but you still must have been distressing this lovely lady. The new milliner in town, are you not? A . . . Mrs. d'Autrecourt?"

"Y-yes. I—"

"I have some mending I might like to have done. There is a hole in my mask."

"Pendragon," Ian broke in, unable to bear Tony even speaking to the woman who, but for God's grace, might have caused Gray's death. "As astonishing as it seems, the truth is that the captain was *reluctant* to distress the lady. In fact it was his reluctance that turned the odds in our favor," Ian said, attempting to communicate his wishes to his friend.

A flicker of amazement brightened Tony's eyes. "Are you saying that I should spare Atwood's life?"

"Yes." Ian cleared his throat. "Considering Atwood's actions in the cottage, a permanent solution to the problem would be excessive. Just before you arrived, the captain was telling me that he was uncertain where his loyalties lay after all that happened here. I have a frigate sailing upon the next tide. If Captain Atwood were kept aboard it for a time, he might consider career options other than the king's service."

Atwood gaped at Ian. "A ship? You would . . . spare my life?"

Ian met the man's gaze levelly. "I have the feeling that in the end you would have done all in your power to spare mine. And the lady's."

Tony jerked his head at the two raiders nearest him. "Lancelot and Dinadan, if you could see to binding our friend, and delivering him aboard the *Bon Chance?*"

The men hastened to do just that. Ian watched in silence as they cantered away with Atwood, grateful to the captain who had been his enemy for so long.

"Mr. Blackheath." Tony's voice made Ian turn to face him. "It seems you have handled this situation with aplomb. Perhaps we should recruit you into our number."

"No, my lord Pendragon," Ian said, looking into the eyes of his friend. "Never have I seen the mask of Pendragon worn so bravely. Things are as they should be now. I shall never be fit to ride with a worthy leader like you."

"I think you deceive yourself." Tony's frown showed beneath the mask. "After all, you managed to rescue your ladylove even without our aid."

Ian turned his gaze to where Emily stood, her hair a tumble about her features, her eyes still, pulsing with pain and horror and a soul-deep weariness that made Ian knot his hands into fists to keep from going to her.

"She is not my lady." He forced himself to turn away from her. "Everyone knows that a man like me would never be so foolish as to fall in love."

18

The child sat on the bed, her eyes solemn, her face pale. In her arms was a pillow, a meager replacement for the doll she had so briefly been allowed to love. The doll that had shattered Emily's world, and Ian's. That had destroyed the fragile dream that Emily was certain the child had begun to cherish.

Emily forced herself to keep her face cheerful as possible, to hide from the little girl the agony that sliced through her veins far more savagely than Fraser's blade ever could have. "We both knew from the beginning that I would only stay for a little while," Emily said. "Now you will stay with your uncle Ian, who loves you very much."

"But I had decided to keep you," Lucy protested, her voice fogged with tears. "Both you and Uncle Ian. I never wanted to keep anybody else in my whole life."

"I know, sweeting. But we cannot keep everything we want. Sometimes, no matter how hard it is, Lucy love, we have to let go."

Emily swallowed the knot of grief in her throat and smoothed her hand over the little girl's silken curls, memorizing the feel of them, so soft, beneath her hand. She didn't need to memorize Lucy's little face, for it was already imprinted forever in Emily's heart, captured like a twin miniature next to the image of Emily's own little daughter.

"I think Uncle Ian is very mean to make you go away!" Lucy cried, a catch in her defiant little voice.

"No, no, you mustn't think that. Your uncle is very brave, Lucy. And good." Emily thought of Ian's face, so tortured as he battled to save her.

"I think the note the soldier brought made him very angry," Lucy said. "He hit Mr. Gray, and then he rode away so I had to dump water on Mr. Gray and make him get up and stop Uncle Ian from committing sooeyside. My . . . my baby horse was very frightened."

"I'm sorry Cristofori was frightened. You were a very good girl to send Mr. Gray to help."

"Mr. Gray liked it very much that I got him all wet. I pinched him, too, and I was going to bite his finger next of all, if he didn't open his eyes up."

"You are a most resourceful little girl, Lucy. I'm very proud of you."

"It's very hard to understand how not to be naughty. Usually when I throw water, people get very angry. And once I bit my mama when she took away a puppy I had found, and she filled up my mouth with soap. I was very, very sick. But this time I didn't care if I had to eat soap. I didn't care if I got locked in a clothespress that was all dark for hours and hours and hours. You were in trouble, Uncle Ian said, and he was, too, and I . . ." She flushed. "I tried to get up on the mama horse to go find you, too. But she was very high. I scraped my elbow and cried."

Emily thought of Lucy struggling to ride to the rescue, and a swift wave of gratitude worked its way through her. She felt grateful not only that the child had not been hurt but also that she had opened her heart enough to love someone, to care enough about someone to take such a risk.

"Lady," the child said tentatively, "maybe if you 'pologized for what happened, Uncle Ian could forgive you like he forgave me when I cut off his buttons."

"There are some things that grown-ups can't forgive, Lucy."

"Oh." Lucy looked at her, subdued. "Did you take another lover? My mama did that sometimes, but then she cried copious tears all over the angry gentlemen, and they always took her upstairs to her bedroom. Maybe if you cried . . ."

Emily thought of the tears she had shed on the long ride from Fraser's cottage back to Blackheath Hall—silent tears that slid like slivers of glass down her cheeks as she rode her mare beside Tony Gray. She had told him everything, confided all that had happened.

Gray had been stone silent, then had said softly, "I'm sorry, Emily. I can't imagine the depth of pain that would drive a woman like you into the hands of a man like Fraser. And I can't imagine Ian ever being able to forget what has happened. It was so difficult for him to believe that you loved him. And now it will be impossible."

Impossible.

She had known that already. Known it from the instant she looked into Ian's eyes. Those crystal blue depths that had so beguiled her were flat, dead. The love, the hope, that had shone in them when Atwood brought him through the door had been killed, by Emily's own hand.

But she didn't regret having denied her love for him. No. She couldn't regret that, for it had kept Ian from betraying his men for her sake. It had saved him from making the one mistake for which he would never have forgiven himself.

"Lucy, I love your uncle very much, but I hurt him in ways that will never heal. You must understand that this was my fault, little one. Mine. He'll need you so much, Lucy, when I am gone."

Lucy's face clouded. "Maybe I will be very naughty, and he'll get angry with me and send me away, too."

"No, angel. Oh, no." Emily crossed to the bed, scooping the little girl into her arms. Lucy felt warm and precious and so very small. "Nothing you could do would make your uncle love you any less. You two will have wonderful times together. You'll forget all about me in time."

"I didn't forget about my papa. He was a sea captain, and he wanted me very much. He told me that the angels dropped me right into his hands." Lucy nibbled at her lower lip. "I try very hard to forget my mama, lady. Someday I won't even remember that she didn't love me at all. But, lady . . . I know I'll never ever forget you."

"Oh, Lucy." Emily choked back tears, holding the child tight, burying her face in Lucy's fragrant curls. She loved the child. Oh, God, the pain of it, the joy. She loved Lucy as much as she had loved her own little daughter. She adored the stubborn, belligerent, wonderful little girl in her arms.

And she was losing Lucy, just as she had lost her own little girl. Because of her own weakness. Her own stupidity. Because she deserved to lose Lucy for what she had done.

Her lips formed the words against the child's cheek, but she said nothing. How could she tell the child she loved her and then turn and walk away, leaving the child even more hurt and bewildered than she was already.

No. Better that Lucy and Ian be left to strengthen the bond that they had. Better that they find comfort in each other. While Emily went on alone.

After a moment the child pressed a kiss on Emily's cheek, her voice a tiny whisper in Emily's ear. "I love you, lady," Lucy said in a choked voice. "G'bye," she whispered, then she scrambled out of Emily's arms and ran from the room.

Ian sat in his study, all light shut out by the window hangings, only the fire flickering in the grate. He leaned his face in his hand, listening to the silence, the loneliness seeming to suffocate him. The confrontation at the cottage still played in vivid images in his mind. He shuddered to think of what had almost happened, of how close, how agonizingly close, he had come to selling his own soul and the souls of all the men he led, in order to save Emily d'Autrecourt's life.

The life of a faithless bitch who had lied to him. Deceived him from the first day she had stood on his doorstep, her eyes filled with righteous indignation over his treatment of Lucy. Deceived him even earlier, in the milliner's shop, when he had thought her an angel, far above his touch.

If only he had known they were two of a kind, he and this

woman. Dark souls that had crushed what was good inside them. Dangerous liars, selfishly seeing to their own needs. Both ruthless in their own ways, desperate to reach their own ends.

"I would have done anything to get the doll back," she had said. "Even come to your bed."

His bed.

Ian fought back the wave of agony that ripped through him, and tried to kill the images of Emily beneath his hands, beneath his mouth, as he released that part of him no woman had ever touched, the place in his soul he had guarded for so long.

The place he should have kept locked away forever.

He'd been a fool to think that anything good could touch his life and change it forever.

No. His life had been changed forever. Bitterness gave way to an aching wonder at the memory of Lucy when she had raced out to meet him hours before, when they had first returned to Blackheath Hall. Her face had been tear-streaked as she buried it in his shirt, the child almost hysterical with relief.

"You didn't die, Uncle Ian! You didn't die!" the child had sobbed. "Promise now that you'll keep me forever!"

And he had promised her. Knowing that, no matter what had happened with Emily, Lucy was a treasure he would never part with. Lucy. As honest in her devilment as he and Emily had been secretive. Lucy, who had stolen away his heart, just as certainly as had the woman with the haunted violet eyes. But the woman had betrayed him.

There could be no joyous reunion between him and Emily. No promises of a future together.

A slender blade seemed to twist in Ian's chest, but he crushed the pain ruthlessly.

No. It would soon be over. Right now Emily was upstairs packing her things, preparing to leave.

He wondered what she would say to the child, and whether Lucy would hate him for sending the lady away. Perhaps, now that he had decided to keep Lucy, the child would decide that she didn't want an uncle who stomped about and cursed and knew nothing about children.

Maybe Lucy would decide that she would rather be off at school, rather be anywhere away from the man who had driven away her beloved lady.

Ian's fist knotted. And maybe, just maybe, Ian had the strength to force himself to remain in this chair, listening to the hushed sounds overhead as Emily prepared to walk out of his life forever. Maybe he could keep from going to her, from telling her . . .

Telling her what? Ian thought bitterly. That watching her leave was tearing his heart out, even though he knew that he should hate her?

Telling her that he blamed himself as well as her. That he was bastard enough to hold her responsible and to exact such a horrible price because of her dishonesty, when he had been dishonest himself?

How could he admit to her that it was not her treachery with the doll or even his own vulnerability that had destroyed him, but rather the fact that a woman who had seemed like an angel had come to his bed, shared his pain, and made him believe. Believe in loving, in light, in tomorrow. And that now, he would never know for certain why she had walked down the hall to his room. Why she had pressed those soft lips against his.

He would never know if she truly loved him.

The way that he still loved her.

In spite of everything. In spite of all that had happened. In spite of grief and rage and betrayal.

Who would have believed that Ian Blackheath, scoundrel, would ever give his heart? Give it so completely that it would be lost to him forever?

The sound of the door creaking open made Ian shut his eyes tight. "I do not want to be disturbed. Leave me alone."

There was the tiniest sound of footsteps, a little voice saying softly, "I am very bad at doing what people tell me to do. I'm a most disobedient little girl."

"Lucy." Ian said her name, opening his eyes to see her, hesitating an arm's length from where he sat.

"The lady is all packed now," Lucy said, twisting her ribbon sash around her fingers. "She is going away."

"I . . . know." Ian swallowed hard. "That must make you very sad."

Lucy closed the space between them and climbed onto Ian's lap. His arms went around her instinctively, and he clung to the child as if she were the only harbor in a storm. "It does make me sad," she said, "but I was sad all the time before I came here. I was never ever happy. I used to think it was because people didn't 'preciate me enough or do what I told them. But it wasn't. It was because my mama didn't love me."

"Lucy, your mother had a . . . was . . ." Ian groped for words to explain to Lucy the tragedy that had been his sister, but the child stopped him, placing her fingers on his lips.

"I used to think she didn't love me because I was an atrociously wicked little girl, so ugly inside that nobody could love me. But now I know that's not true. You see, my mama . . . she thought you were the most despicable man in the whole world. But I don't think that. I think you are brave and good, just like the lady told me."

Claws of grief seemed to close off Ian's throat.

"I'm not brave, Lucy, and I'm assuredly not good."

"I think you are perfect. And I've decided that if my mama was wrong about you, then maybe . . . maybe she could have been wrong about me, too." She lowered her brows in fierce concentration. "Maybe I am not all dark and wicked inside me, after all."

"You are a wonderful little girl. You are everything that is open and honest, and—" Ian's voice broke. "And I love you, Lucy. So much."

"I love you, too." The child patted his cheek. "Uncle Ian, I know that you are very frightened to love anyone. I was, too. But even though the lady made a terrible mistake, you should still love her back. She won't be mean to you like everyone else. She'll love you forever and ever and not even care when you cut off horses' tails and steal dolls away."

Ian's jaw clenched. "It's too late, Lucy. I know it is hard to understand. Some things can't be fixed like you fixed my buttons."

Lucy sighed, such a sad little sigh. "That is what the lady said—that she was very bad and you can't ever forgive her. I was afraid you would get mad at me, too, someday, and you would send me away. But the lady said you never, ever would."

"I won't, angel. I swear it. But a little girl's mischief is different from adult mischief." Ian looked into Lucy's woebegone features. And he imagined the rest of Lucy's life, without Emily to hold her, to kiss her, to teach her so many, many things the child had never known.

The words that came from his mouth were pure torture. "Lucy, maybe you would rather go with the lady. I . . . I would understand if you did. I'm not very good with children. And I couldn't show you things, like how to sew. The lady loves you very much, I know."

"No, I want to stay with you. You will be very sad when the lady goes away, Uncle Ian. You'll be all lonely again and will need me to amuse you, though I'll miss the lady . . . oh, terrible bad."

Ian felt his eyes burn as the little girl's words reached right into his heart.

"When I was a very little girl," Lucy said meditatively, "I used to sing a song that made me feel all better, even when my mama was horrible hateful. It made me feel warm inside, even when I was crying. Would you like me to sing it to you?"

Ian couldn't speak. He only nodded, holding the little girl in his arms.

He closed his eyes as the child began to sing a melody so haunting it stole into his very soul. As he listened to that clear child's voice, every hope, every dream, Ian had ever dared to dream was spun out before his eyes. Everything bright and beautiful was captured in the melody; everything painful was washed away. His grief softened as if brushed by an angel's hand. His bitterness was sweetened.

The melody reached deep into his soul and pulsed there, around his own aching sense of loss.

The song held him in its hand so gently, so surely, that he didn't even feel the hot tears that trailed down his cheeks.

He didn't even sense the woman, who stood at the open doorway with her basket in her hand, her eyes wide with wonder. Her lips parted in both astonishment and resignation as she listened to the final notes of Jenny d'Autrecourt's Night Song fade away into silence.

19

Emily clutched the handle of the basket as if it were the only thing keeping her from slipping off of a precipice—a yawning chasm of joy and disbelief, of confusion and fury and grief. It was as if she were reaching out to hold a miracle, in an agonizing rebirth that stunned her, paralyzed her.

Oh, God, she thought wildly, her eyes locked upon the man who sat with his dark head bent over the child who had fallen asleep in his arms. The child who had eased herself into the sweet release of slumber with the song that Alexander d'Autrecourt had written for his little daughter eight years ago.

The song that Emily had sung to the child every night in the tiny rooms in London, but had never been able to bring herself to sing in the barren, empty years since Jenny had been taken from her.

Taken.

Not by some unfeeling deity, not by some greedy fever that had snuffed out her life.

But stolen away . . .

Emily's hands shook. Oh, God, was it possible? Possible that this child cradled in Ian Blackheath's arms was her own Jenny? It seemed beyond fantastical. Absurd. Impossible.

But how else could the child have known that haunting melody?

"Now you'll never know," Fraser had sneered at her, hinting at some secret tied to her past. "The duke would think that a fitting hell."

The duke of Avonstea had not only destroyed her life and the life of his son. In his hatred and bitterness he had made Jenny a victim of his evil pride as well.

"Emily?"

The sound of Ian's voice jolted her, and she jerked her head up, staring into his face. The firelight played havoc with his features, setting them in a stark relief that showed the devastation she had wrought upon him and the fragile peace that had been the gift of Lucy's song.

She tried to form the words, to tell him what the song had revealed. She wanted to race to the child she had loved not once but twice, the child who'd been returned to her from the dead, as if by the very angels.

Your name is Jenny . . . Jenny . . . I am your mama. . . .

Oh, God, how she wanted to awaken the little girl, whisper those words aloud.

But her gaze was fixed on Ian's face, the face of a lost soul led into the light again by the love in that little girl's eyes. A man, not gentle by nature, whose arms were curved with such tenderness about those small shoulders, whose cheeks were damp with tears Emily was certain he wasn't aware he had shed.

He had given everything during the night she had spent in his arms. Her betrayal had left him with nothing to fill the place in his heart that she had forced him to open.

Nothing except the adoration of the little girl whose eyes were filled with love and with mischief, sadness, and a very real understanding.

The child who would make certain Ian Blackheath was never again alone.

"So." His voice was soft, and Emily could sense the effect of the song on him, soothing the jagged edges of his pain. "You are leaving."

"Yes. I wanted to say good-bye."

"Lucy told me you had already said farewell."

"Yes. I wanted to say good-bye to you, Ian, and ask you if your ribs are—are causing you any pain."

"Priam wrapped them. They'll heal in time."

Emily's eyes stung. If only other things might also heal as well. "I didn't want to leave without telling you how sorry I am," she said, "for all that happened."

"I'm sorry, too."

For everything, Emily was certain. Sorry for that first kiss, for the laughter over Lucy's buttons. Sorry for tipping back Emily's bonnet in the garden to kiss her, and for calling her back when she had almost slipped out of the room the night she had come to him to make love.

Sorry she had ever touched his life.

"Where will you go now?" he asked. "What will you do?"

Emily shrugged, her eyes drinking in the sight of her daughter, terrified that if she touched the child, she would never be able to do what she must, would never be able to leave her.

"I will find some place where I can ply my needle. I have enough saved to get by."

"It's dangerous for a woman alone."

"I've been alone before, Ian. But I'm stronger this time. Because of you."

A flash of some emotion flamed in his eyes. Then he shuttered it away.

"Good-bye, Emily Rose," he said quietly. "In spite of everything that happened, I thank you for . . . this."

He laid his cheek against the golden curls of the child in his arms.

Emily's daughter.

The child who had been without love.

The child who would be Ian's salvation.

Gritting her teeth against the savage pain, Emily turned and walked out the door and out of the house. Ian's coach was waiting to take her to Williamsburg. From there, who knew where she would go.

She had run away before, fleeing England to escape her grief.

But where could she run to now? What could she hope for without Ian? Without her child?

"Emily?"

She turned at the sound of a voice and saw Tony Gray racing toward her from the stables. His eyes took in the basket and the waiting coach, and a stricken expression crossed his features.

"Emily, what the devil are you doing?"

"Leaving, Tony. You must have known I could never stay now."

"No! You can't leave! You don't understand. I just finished rifling through Fraser's belongings. I found a letter from that bastard of a duke who sired your husband. It seems that after Alexander's death, the duke wanted to drive you from the d'Autrecourts' lives forever, so he decided to do away with the only tangible reminder of your link with their noble family—your daughter. She didn't die. Avonstea gave her away to a sea captain who desperately wanted a little girl, but whose wife was barren. For God's sake, Emily, Lucy Dubbonet is really your child."

"I know."

Tony all but staggered back, stunned by the simple words. "What the hell? How—"

"There was a melody her father wrote on the day of her birth. I sang it to her every night. Lucy was attempting to comfort Ian as I left, and . . . she sang that song, Tony. That melody that no one else had ever heard."

"My God, Emily. You can't leave! I'll make Ian see reason. I know that in spite of everything he's half crazed in love with you. Or if he won't be moved, then you should take the child with you. She's yours, Emily, by right."

"Tony, do you know how many times I've dreamed of having Jenny back again? How many times my arms have ached for her? I lie awake night after night, picturing her smile, remembering the feel of her little hand in mine, so warm, so trusting. She was everything to me. The one good thing in my life when everything was going awry. She saved me from despair, Tony. If we give her the chance, she will save Ian, too."

"But . . . but you—"

"Promise me that you'll never tell him. I want to give him this gift."

Tony Gray raked his hand through his hair. "You are a most astonishing woman, Emily d'Autrecourt. A brave one. A . . . loving one. I only wish that things had turned out differently."

"I fell in love with a man who was everything I'd ever dreamed of. I shared one night with him. One magical night. And I found my daughter, Tony. Alive and well and beautiful and so . . . so wonderfully brave. There are only so many miracles out there, and I suppose I've used mine for a lifetime in this single week. But I'm glad of it. The only thing I would change is the pain that I left in Ian's eyes."

"He's a fool not to see how much he's losing."

"No. He's far richer than he was before. He has Lucy. And she'll never let him forget what it feels like to be alive. And Lucy has someone who will love her for exactly who she is. Someone who will never try to change her into something in the common way of little girls. My parents were duty-bound people, neck deep in piety. And I was never the daughter they desired. I know how much it will mean to Lucy to be able to be herself and never have to be afraid."

"And what about you, Emily? You came here to the colonies seeking . . . seeking something."

"Oh, I found it, Tony. Never doubt that. I just didn't get to keep it for very long."

With that, she climbed into the coach. Tony shut the door, leaned against it.

"You were the one who saved Ian," he said quietly. "Saved Lucy. God, it seems so damned unfair that—"

"Good-bye, Tony." She cut him off gently. "Be happy with your Nora, and take care of Ian for me. And Lucy. If I could write you sometimes to see . . . see how they fare, I . . ."

Her throat was swollen with tears, her eyes burning. In desperation she thumped on the coach roof, signaling the driver to whip up his horses.

The coach jolted into motion, and the jarring movement

seemed to shatter Emily's heart. She huddled against the squabs, her mind filled with the ethereal strains of Jenny's Night Song as the vehicle carried her away from everything she had ever loved.

Ian was alone again, the silence of the room seeming to chafe at him, chastise him. Lucy had climbed down from his lap and slipped from the room after the lady had said good-bye, and Ian was certain that the child had stolen away somewhere to cry out her private grief. A grief that Lucy would not have wanted to hurt him.

"You will be very sad when the lady goes away," the child had said. But how could a child understand this slow, painful severing of the love he had shared with Emily so briefly last night, the love that, in the space of a week, had seeped into his very soul, driving out everything that had gone before it.

But he had to kill it, had to obliterate it from his heart. It was the only way he could endure the pain she had left in him.

Ian Blackheath, the little boy whose father had never been able to love him. Ian, who had failed so miserably as a son that his father had all but murdered his mother in an effort to get another heir. Ian Blackheath, the youth who had been the terror of Hargrove's Boarding School, the boy whom all his masters had loathed. The man that boy had become, who had courted the scorn of everyone he met, because he had never been able to believe he was worthy to be loved.

To have believed for just one night, and to have that fragile hope shattered. To have been so close to dreams he'd never dared admit existed in the most secret places inside him . . .

It was the one thing Ian knew he would never recover from.

He would never know for certain whether the love in Emily d'Autrecourt's eyes had been real or just a reflection of his own desperate need for her.

Even though he had long since faced the fact that circumstances had forced Emily to carry messages to the British, there would always be that shadow, that inescapable questioning inside him.

That emptiness she had nearly filled.

"Mr. Ian?" Priam's voice made Ian straighten up. "Mr. Tony is here, insisting on seeing you."

"Tell him I'm not receiving anyone right now."

"I'd be happy to wait until tomorrow," Tony said, pushing past the servant. "Except that if I do, it will be too late."

"Too late?"

"Too late to stop Emily. Damn it, Ian you can't let her go."

Ian looked away, his mouth compressing in a white line of pain. "Don't be fooled by a pair of beautiful eyes, the way that I was, Tony. You don't have the slightest idea what Emily d'Autrecourt is capable of."

"I think I do. She told me everything while we were riding back here last night."

"She told you that she gave Fraser that accursed doll that held my identity?"

"How could Emily have known what was in the doll, Ian?" Tony demanded. "And how could she have even suspected that you are Pendragon?"

"I *was* Pendragon. But no more. Do you have any idea what I almost revealed to Fraser for her sake, Tony? To save her—"

"Damn you, Ian, you stubborn accursed ass! If you had stopped feeling sorry for yourself long enough to look at her, you would have seen what the rest of us saw! Emily is already eaten alive with guilt. Think how desperate she must have been to take Fraser's offer of that millinery shop! Think about the grief, the pain, she had suffered. She was driven to the path she took, just as certainly as we were driven to follow the one we chose. She couldn't have known where it would lead her."

"Perhaps she couldn't. Should that matter? All I can think about is the gallows Fraser was intending to build for my men." Ian rubbed at his throbbing temple. "All I can think of is how close I came to . . ." He hesitated, unable to reveal that raw place that still throbbed inside him. Looking away from Tony, he finished his admission. "All I can think of is how close I came to being responsible for the death of every man who trusted me."

"And what stopped you from exposing their identities, you ox-headed oaf? Emily! She told you that she had betrayed you. Announced it in front of Fraser and Atwood. Why would she do such a thing? Those men held her captive, helpless. She had to know that Fraser would hold her accountable if she shattered the greatest weapon he held over you—your love for her."

Ian's mind whirled with the anguished words he had choked out in the cottage, the words that had filled Fraser's face with such eagerness, such triumph: "How could I condemn my own men to death? . . . Oh, God, Emily Rose, how can I let them hurt you?"

What had it cost her to tell the truth? What might it have cost her if Fraser had gotten his blade against that velvety skin? But did that change anything? Did it change the barren spaces in his gut?

"It's over, Tony. Every time I looked at her, I would see my own weakness. I would never be able to forget how close I came to betraying—"

"You're a liar, Blackheath. What you can't forget is how close you came to believing that she loved you. How much you wanted her to."

Ian bolted from his chair, fists knotted. "Close your mouth, Tony. I won't hear another word."

"She *does* love you, you stubborn bastard! Probably more than you deserve!"

"And tell me, Tony, just how am I supposed to believe that? She came to my house searching for that infernal doll. She came to my bed—" He swore savagely.

"She came to your bed because she loved you."

"How could I ever be certain, Tony? How could I ever know?"

"Tell me, Ian, what would it take to prove to you that the

woman loves you? What price would you demand for her mistake? Would it satisfy your thirst for justice if she sacrificed her own child to you in payment for what she had done?"

"Her child is dead."

"No. Her child is alive. Lucy Dubbonet is Jenny d'Autrecourt. Emily's daughter."

Ian reeled in disbelief. "You lie. That is impossible."

"Is it?" Tony removed a letter from his pocket and jammed it against Ian's chest. Ian took it as if it were a living thing, his eyes scanning the script—a note from one Sir Jedediah Whitley, revealing the information he had recently heard at the deathbed of the d'Autrecourt butler.

The English knight had been searching for Alexander d'Autrecourt's missing widow for over a year and according to Fraser's carefully transcribed notes, had come dangerously close to finding her. So close, that the duke had enlisted his friend Stirling Fraser, to come up with a permanent solution to the difficulty before Emily discovered the truth —that her daughter had been stolen.

Sick rage rushed through Ian's veins. "Emily's daughter is alive. Those bastards! By God, if d'Autrecourt wasn't dead, I would—" Ian bit off the words, steeling himself against the outrage pulsing through him. "Still, that doesn't prove that my Lucy is Emily's lost child."

"Do you remember Emily speaking of the song she sang to her child? The one no one else had ever heard? The child was singing it when Emily came to tell you good-bye."

Ian closed his eyes. The memory of Lucy's piping voice weaving that most magical of melodies wrapped crushing fingers of guilt about his heart. The memory of Emily's eyes, so stricken as she walked away, even though she knew—she had to know—that the child was her own beloved daughter.

"Why?" Ian breathed hoarsely. "Why would she leave the girl, when I know how desperately she loved her?"

"Why do you think, you stubborn son of a bitch? She left the child with you because she didn't want you to be alone. She left the child with you, knowing that Lucy would save

you from yourself, give you a reason for living. She left the child because she loved you, loved you so damned much that she was willing to sacrifice everything for you."

The words should have brought overwhelming joy. Instead Ian felt an agony so profound that his knees all but buckled with the weight of it. He pictured Emily's face during their loving, felt the whisper of her touch, the sweet seeking of her lips. "No," he breathed, battling to beat down his raging emotions. "No."

"What the devil do you mean, *no?* What other possible reason could she have had for leaving the child in your care?"

"My care? Surely that must be it. With Fraser dead, Emily has nothing. No prospects. Doubtless she would not want to carry the child off into an uncertain future when I would be able to raise her in a manner befitting a princess."

Never had Ian seen Tony Gray's face go so still, his eyes cold and filled with disgust.

"Is that what you think this is about? Hair ribbons and jewels and everything your coin can buy? Emily knows better than anyone that you cannot place a price value on love." Gray's face was white, a muscle in his jaw ticking ominously. "I was wrong about you, Ian," he said in a low voice. "You don't deserve Emily's love. But does she deserve to be deprived of her daughter because of your selfishness and stupidity? Does Lucy deserve to be deprived of her mother because you have chosen to deaden your heart? Think about that, Ian, while the coach is carrying Emily away."

Emily closed her eyes, the swaying of the coach reminding her with poignant longing of countless dark nights alone in the shabby rooms in London when she had rocked her little daughter. How many times had she left her bed and stolen over to Jenny's cradle near the warmth of the hearth? How many times had she picked up the sleeping infant, cradling her, crooning to her, savoring Jenny's precious weight, the miraculous warmth and wonder of her contented little sighs as that tousled golden head nestled against her breasts?

She had marveled over Jenny's tiny, perfect hands that curled instinctively into the loose fall of Emily's hair, as if to hold on forever. She had been enchanted by the bow shape of the child's lips, the rosy blush of her round little cheeks. And Emily hadn't cared that Alexander was off gaming with his friends or even if he was with some woman, trying to spare his wife the conjugal duties that embarrassed them both. The pain of her own guilt, her own sense of failure had dulled, seeping into a warm golden glow as Jenny rooted against her so trustingly. And Emily had known that no matter what the cost, she could never regret having married Alexander, for their union had resulted in their beautiful, winsome child.

The coach jolted over a rut, and Emily wrapped her arms tight against her ribs, aching to hold that child again. And she battled the emotions that were only now beginning to seep into her consciousness. But her fury at the duke of Avonstea's vile deception was already paling to insignificance in comparison with the memory of Lucy's haunting stories of the barren life she had suffered in the years after she was stolen away from England.

What damage had the cruel duke done to her little daughter when he cast the child aside with no more care than he would have for a fan that did not suit his favorite waistcoat? What had it been like for Emily's cherished little girl to be ripped away from everything she had ever known —her home, her few beloved playthings, and the mother who had spent every waking hour cocooning her in love?

Could anything have been more devastating than being torn away from that love and hurled into the grasp of a woman who didn't want her, who was jealous and spiteful and cruel? Who made the child believe that she was wicked . . .

How savagely had that woman crippled the little girl who had been cradled on Ian's lap, her eyes huge with secret sorrow, her voice tremulous but so beautiful, so clear, like that of an angel drifting down to comfort them from heaven?

"Ian will take care of her," Emily whispered, feeling as if

her heart were being ripped from her chest. "I know he will. And she . . . she will take care of him."

A choked sob ripped at her throat, and she crushed it ruthlessly, certain that if she allowed herself to cry, she would never stop.

No, this was the way things had to be. The only possible way. Best for Ian. And for Lucy. She would have someone who adored her, someone who needed her desperately. Someone who could give her security, treat her like the gift that she was. And Ian . . . Ian would heal. . . .

Oh, God, please let him heal, Emily thought, remembering the devastation she had seen in his eyes.

With a suddenness that all but flung Emily to the floor of the coach, the vehicle swerved.

"Damned lunatic!" she heard the coachman roar as the coach shuddered to a halt. "What the devil— Oh, sir!"

Wild hope shivered through Emily as she moved closer to the window and caught a glimpse of a horse, its rider obscured. But the hope died when she saw that it was not Ian's stallion, but rather the mount belonging to Tony Gray.

Tony. Doubtless come to make one last attempt to persuade her to stay, when there was nothing left for her here.

She dashed the tears from her eyes, resolve striking through her as the door flew open.

Emily's heart froze as she stared at the visage framed in the doorway—the tousled dark hair, the face as tormented as that of the god Cupid painted on the wall of the *chambre d'amour,* and as filled with some emotion she couldn't name—an emotion so fierce, so primal, that she felt her hands go numb. Was it love? Oh, God, she thought with almost savage prayer, please let it be love . . .

But as he grasped her arms and dragged her from the coach, his words quelled the wild pulsing of hope inside her.

"Damn it, Emily, you little fool! Why didn't you tell me Lucy was your child?"

Emily was grateful for his hands shoring her up. She felt as brittle as a sheen of ice on a pond kissed with the first chill of winter. She shivered, tipping her chin up to meet the tempestuous blue of Ian's eyes with her own.

"Tony had no right to tell you that." She struggled to think up a plausible lie, wanting only to escape, to have done with the agony slicing through her. "There is no proof that Lucy is my child. No way of—"

"The song, blast you! Emily, the song Lucy sang for me. That was the night song you told me about."

She looked away, trying to be strong. "Ian, any number of things might have happened. I might have sung it to Lucy in the garden and been overheard without even realizing it. Or I—"

"Don't lie to me!" His hands tightened. "Damn it, did you really think I would just let you walk away? Did you think for a moment what the truth would mean to Lucy? To know that Celestia wasn't really her mother? To know that she has a mother who adores her?"

The words gashed Emily's spirit like jagged stones. "It might hurt her even more deeply to know the truth. She has you, now, Ian, to love her."

"Damn you to hell, woman, you owe Lucy the truth."

"I can't tell her! I'd break down crying and frighten her. I won't do it, Ian. I can't."

"Then I will."

"And then what?" Emily cried. "Have you thought about that?" She tried to pull away, but Ian's hands were bruising manacles about her wrists. "What happens after we tell Lucy that I am her mother?"

"I don't know," Ian snapped, his eyes darkening with anguish. "I don't know. I— Son of a bitch, I don't know anything anymore!"

With a furious oath, he lifted her up on Tony's stallion and mounted behind her. Emily almost sobbed at the feel of his body pressed tight behind her, the hard wall of his chest against her back, his thighs curved beneath hers, the steely prison of his arms around her as he spurred the horse to a breakneck gallop.

She let the tears sear her cheeks as she thought of how differently she had hoped things might be in those first moments after she saw Ian's beloved face through the coach window.

She closed her eyes, picturing Lucy's small face, the thought of what she must reveal to the little girl filling her with dread and hope.

Hope mingled with the agony of knowing that this was the last time she would ever feel Ian Blackheath's arms around her, feel the precious heat of him, the strength of him, taste the recklessness, the danger, that she now knew was just a disguise for what really pulsed beneath that hard body, behind those fathomless blue eyes.

The stark emotion called despair.

20

Emily's throat constricted as she walked into the sunlit garden, the rainbow colors spilling in riotous profusion all about her, blurring before her eyes so badly that she nearly stumbled. Ian's hand was clamped fiercely about her own, his hard palm and long fingers engulfing hers as if he feared even now that she would run away, when all she wanted was to stay with him forever.

Oh, God, what was going to happen? The question thrummed inside Emily relentlessly. What would Lucy say? What would she do when she was told . . . told that she had been stolen away? And that, by God's own miracle, she had been found?

Emily herself could scarce believe it. How would a child ever begin to understand?

Emily's throat ached from unshed tears, Priam's words of moments before echoing in her mind.

"The poor little lamb is in the garden," the servant had told them, with a heavy sigh. "Cook's been out there three times, tryin' to tempt her with sweets, and the housemaids, they been hovering around, beggin' her to play that pianoforte for them whilst they clean. Samuel, the groom, he even come in and asked her if she wanted to see the colt she gave that outlandish name to, but the child wouldn't hear of it.

She just sits in the garden cryin' over those scissors the kind lady gave her."

Priam's words had wrenched at Emily, and she had seen Ian's own features tighten. But he had only quickened his step, leading her even faster out into the fragrant bower bursting with blossoms.

Emily swiped at her eyes to clear them, and her breath caught as she saw the forlorn little figure in rose-pink satin, sniffling against the unfeeling stone bench. Lucy's face was buried against her crossed arms, those small shoulders that could be squared so regally shaking with broken sobs as she struggled to squeeze the melody of the night song through her lips.

Unable to bear the pain of it, Emily slammed to a halt, even Ian's strength unable to urge her forward. His gaze slashed to her face, and she saw the reflection of her own torment in his eyes. He released her hand, allowing her to draw out of sight, attempt to compose herself, so as not to frighten the little girl.

Emily's hand clenched, as if she were attempting to hold in the feel of Ian's callused palm cupped about hers. As if she were trying to catch that quicksilver will-o'-the-wisp that was hope.

Face contorting with emotion, Ian turned away from her and went to the child. For an instant he seemed to hesitate. Then he swore softly and scooped Lucy up into his arms. The child nuzzled close against his chest, totally unaware of Emily standing, as if frozen, behind a statue.

"U-Uncle Ian," Lucy choked out, her fingers locked about the scissors Emily had given her. "I—I didn't want you to see me . . . all weepy and sad. Knew that you . . . would feel sorry. But I can't help it. I miss the lady so terrible it hurts inside, worse even than . . . than when my papa sinked down into the sea."

Emily saw Ian's face twist with anguish, saw him battle to keep his voice soft, soothing. "Sh, angel, sh," Ian hushed her, rocking the little girl gently, stroking her hair. And Emily was moved to tears by the tenderness in him as he comforted the child. His eyes caught Emily's for an instant, and she saw her own fears for the child in his face before he forced his gaze away.

"Lucy, what would you say if I told you that your papa—your *real* papa—was not a sea captain at all?" Ian asked in a voice rough-edged with his own jagged emotions.

"I would say . . . that was a silly story."

"What would you say if I told you that your papa was a composer. A musician far away in England."

"A musician?" Lucy stilled for a moment. "A very good one or one who made people's ears burst?"

"I'm only familiar with one of his songs. It is the most beautiful melody I've ever heard. You were the one who sang it for me just a few hours ago."

Lucy lifted her face, and Emily glimpsed confusion, irritation, and a fragile kind of hope in her cornflower blue eyes. "My Night Song?"

"Yes. Will you let me tell you a story about your Night Song, Lucy love?" Ian traced the pale curve of Lucy's tear-streaked cheek.

"I . . . suppose that would be better than sitting here . . . sniffling and getting my sleeves all wet," Lucy allowed with a hiccup.

Ian sank down onto the bench and cuddled the child close, and Emily wondered what he was thinking, what he was feeling. Did he fear this might be the last time he ever spent with the child in his arms?

"Once upon a time," he began, his voice heartbreakingly awkward, "there was a very beautiful, very kind lady who had a baby she loved more than anything in the world. Her husband was a musician, and they were very poor, but the beautiful lady felt rich beyond imagining whenever she held her little girl. . . ."

Emily stood in the shadows, listening to the tale Ian spun in that deep, beloved voice. She watched as Lucy's expression shifted from sorrow, to astonishment, from outrage to reluctant enchantment.

But when Ian spoke of the child being taken away from her mama's arms, Lucy stiffened, her eyes glittering with tears again.

"This is a very sad story," she complained fiercely. "I don't want to hear any more."

"But, Lucy love, it has the happiest ending you can imagine. I promise you," Ian coaxed her, his own face reflecting pain beyond bearing. "It is so astonishing you'll scarce believe it."

She thrust her lower lip. "It had better be very happy indeed, for I'm already detestable sad."

"What would you say if I told you that the mama found her little girl?"

"I would say that it was a very bad story. That could never ever happen."

"But it did happen," Ian said. "You see, the mama never knew that the evil duke had sent her child away," he finished. "Until one day she came down the sweeping stairs of a grand plantation house far across the ocean and heard a little girl singing that very song. Her Night Song."

Emily trembled as she saw Lucy lift her face to Ian's, her features a study in indignation. "If you think that it is—is amusing to tease me so, you're wrong! I used to make up stories all the time," Lucy said. "I liked to pretend that my mama wasn't really my mama, that I was a princess who got stolen away and put in the house of a wicked witch." Lucy's lips quivered. "But I knew that was impossible, and you are terrible mean to say it is real."

"No, Lucy. It . . . it *was* real." Emily said, stepping out of the shadows.

"Lady!" Lucy started to launch herself from her seat. Then suddenly, as if beset by too many disappointments, the little girl shrank back against her uncle's chest.

"Lucy," Emily said, coming toward the child, "every night in London I held you, rocked you to sleep while I sang that song. When I had to leave you with the d'Autrecourts, I told you to sing the Night Song to yourself until I could come for you." Her voice broke. "And you did sing it, sweeting. You did."

"No!" Lucy cried out. "I don't believe you! I want to, but I can't!"

"Listen, Lucy. Listen to the song." The melody spun out

from Emily's lips, even more beautiful for the ragged edges to her voice. Pain and sorrow, joy and hope, a vision of a hundred tomorrows, bright and beautiful, seemed to shimmer in the air and wrap themselves about the child.

Lucy's eyes widened as the notes died into silence, the song seeming to cling to her like the fragrance of the roses all about them. Tears trembled on the child's sable lashes.

"You left me alone," Lucy said at last in a small voice. "I should be very angry at you."

Emily knelt down before the little girl, taking Lucy's hands, holding them tight. "I didn't know, Lucy. I swear that I didn't know you were alive. If I had, I never, never would have left you alone." Emily swallowed hard, knowing how terrifyingly wonderful this must seem to the little girl. How frightening. How fantastical.

Lucy chewed at her bottom lip. Her eyes narrowed.

"Would you have to call me Jenny then? I'm quite 'customed to Lucy. Though, perhaps, since I already have so many names, I shall have you call me Dulcinea instead."

Emily gave a choked laugh. "Lucy suits you quite perfectly," she said. "It's a wonder I never thought of it myself."

"Humph." Lucy seemed to consider. "You are a very strange lady. My other governesses always didn't like me and were mean to me, but you never were. Maybe that is because you would make a better mama."

The last word was hushed, as tremulous as a prayer. Emily felt her heart take flight. She opened her arms, and the child flung herself into them. Lucy embraced her so fiercely that Emily felt pain . . . the most healing pain she had ever known.

She turned with her daughter in her arms to where Ian stood. Tears were coursing down those arrogant cheekbones as he turned away, and Emily knew the agony jolting through him, because she had so recently felt it herself.

He was going to give Lucy up. Surrender her. Emily felt the certainty slam into her heart like a stone.

"Uncle Ian," Lucy piped up, "now everything will be quite perfect. We can be together for always. The lady and you and me."

"Lucy," Ian began, "you have to understand that—"

Emily felt Lucy stiffen. "Angel, your uncle Ian and I both love you very much. But—"

"I *hate* it when grown-ups say 'but.' It always means that they are going to be difficult. I don't want you to be difficult. I want Uncle Ian to be my papa and you to be my mama. And I demand that you give me baby brothers and sisters so that I can tell them what to do. And I would name them Arantha and Mahitibel and Roderigo."

Agony flooded Ian's eyes, and in that moment Emily knew just how deeply she had hurt him, how thoroughly she had destroyed the part of him that was vulnerable and needing beneath his hard layer of inner strength. And she wanted to spare him any more pain, wanted to ease the darkness in his eyes.

"Sweeting, my coming back here doesn't change what happened between your uncle and me. The fact is that I did something very wrong, and—"

"Damn it, Emily, you did what you had to do." She was stunned when Ian broke in. "Lucy, it is my fault that you can't have everything the way you might like it. But I will buy you and your mama a lovely house, with a pasture for Cristofori and a beautiful chamber for your pianoforte. And I'll make certain that you have all the lovely gowns you could ever imagine."

"But then I wouldn't have you."

Ian's hands knotted, and he looked away. "I could visit you often. You would be near enough so that you could run between the houses and terrorize both the lady and me. That way you could . . ." He hesitated for a moment. "You could keep both of us."

The sound of Ian echoing Lucy's treasured words, twisted the grief even tighter in Emily's chest.

Lucy's face crumpled into a formidable scowl, and she ripped herself from Emily's grasp. She faced them, her hands balled up and planted on her hips, her blue eyes spitting fury.

"This is very stupid. I just might decide not to keep either one of you unless you stop being despicable. Your eyes are all red and sad, lady, and you love my uncle very much, even though he is being the most detestable blockhead in the whole world right now. And you, Uncle Ian"—she jabbed a finger in his direction—"you keep looking at the lady like you want to do the kissing thing with her so bad it makes you all trembly inside. But you are afraid to."

"Lucy, please." Emily tried to cut the child off. "You don't understand."

"That is what grown-ups say when they are doing something they know is very foolish and they can't think of how to explain it to children who are very much smarter than they are. And you, lady, have already been very bad today. You went away in the coach and made Uncle Ian and me cry." She glowered. "You were going to leave me again. That is turning into a most disagreeable habit."

"I was . . . Oh, Lucy . . ." For a heartbeat Emily wavered, knowing that whatever she said would hurt either Ian or the child. Her eyes stung, and she knew that there was nothing to say except the truth.

"I love you so much, little one. You were . . . were the most beautiful thing that had ever happened in my life. When I was sad and frightened and alone, you showed me all that was good and beautiful." Her voice dropped low. "I wanted you to give those dreams back to your uncle as well."

Lucy regarded her solemnly. "When you were going away I was so sad I wanted to cry and cry forever. I wanted to run and make that coach stop taking you away. But I knew that Uncle Ian was very sad, too. He would need me to make him laugh sometimes and not . . . be alone."

Oh, God, Emily thought, stealing a glance at Ian. His whole body was rigid; his hands trembled. For him to hear this. To know that they both had seen his hidden pain.

"Are you going to leave me again, lady?"

"I . . . don't know, Lucy. Your uncle and I haven't discussed—"

"I think that you have been disgusting quite enough, and if you don't stop, I will take my cunning little scissors and cut off all the buttons of everyone I see, and I will be so naughty that you will have to do the kissing thing together just to get me to stop."

"Lucy," Ian said, "it's not that simple."

"Yes, it is. You go and at least *try* to do the kissing thing or your well will be so full of buttons that every time you sip a cup of tea, they will clink against your teeth." Lucy brandished the scissors as if they were the most menacing cutlass.

"Perhaps we could talk," Ian said, uncertainty wreathing his features. "We need to work out some arrangement." He gestured toward the path where they had walked on that afternoon when Lucy had been stitching buttons.

That sun-kissed afternoon seemed an eternity ago.

Without a word, Emily started down the ribbon of pebbles. Lucy's voice made her pause but a moment. "Do not forget what I said the day I told you about becoming Uncle Ian's mistress. If you shed copious tears he will carry you off to his bedchamber." Lucy suddenly looked nonplussed. "But I don't know what you need to do to make him want you for his wife."

Blindly, Emily hastened away from the child who looked so incredibly hopeful, so pitifully vulnerable, ensconced among the flowers.

Emily retreated to the arbor, hoping the shade would hide her expression. The coolness of the arch of beech trees kissed cheeks, which were still damp with tears. She shivered as the dimness encircled her, knowing that Ian had chosen to walk forever in such shadows, living the half-life Emily herself had endured in those long years she had spent with the Quakeress in England.

She heard Ian's footsteps behind her, heard him give a weary sigh.

"Oh, God, Emily," he breathed in a stricken voice. "What have I done?" She looked up to see him rake his hand back through his hair.

"We had to tell her the truth. You were right."

"No. I was wrong. So damned wrong. Tony tried to tell me, but I never bloody listen." He stopped, his voice a rasp low in his throat. "You would have left her here with me, Emily. Forever. Knowing what I am—a bastard, hard, cold, cynical. A devil feared and despised by decent people clear up to Boston."

"I would have left her with you, knowing that no one could love Lucy more. Knowing that she would be safe and protected from harm. Knowing that"—her voice dropped low—"you would never crush her spirit. My one hope was that someday I would be able to see her again and find out what a formidable young lady she had become."

Ian caught his hand in her own, his face twisting in pain. "Perhaps the little termagant is right. The best solution is for us to wed."

They were words she had wanted so desperately to hear. Words that painted a picture of a future so magical she scarce dared imagine it. It was almost too beautiful to believe in.

She looked down at their linked fingers, remembering what it had felt like to have them skim over her skin in passion, remembering them attempting to wield a needle under Lucy's instruction. To be Ian Blackheath's wife. To share his bed, bear his children. It was everything she'd ever wanted. And yet, would this be so much different from her first marriage?

She drew away, squaring her shoulders in resolve.

"No, Ian. Alexander married me because he felt duty bound to do so. I'll never subject myself to such a relationship again. It was . . . degrading."

He cupped her chin in his hand, lifting her face so his gaze could feather across it. "Emily, I'm no self-sacrificing hero like Alexander. You know that better than anyone. I want you for my wife because I'm a selfish bastard who isn't noble enough to send you away from me, even though I know I should. Because I . . . I love you, Emily Rose. And for some reason God alone can name, you love me, too."

"How can I be sure you love me?" she asked, her voice quavering. "How can you expect me to believe you love me, when you could not believe it yourself?"

His hands swept up to frame her face, his fingers tracing

her cheeks, his eyes glowing, soft above a breathtakingly tender smile. "How can you believe me, Emily Rose? Because you are an angel sent to save me from myself. Angels can see into the souls of us poor sinners and know things we try to keep hidden from mere mortals. Look into my heart, Emily Rose. Tell me what you see."

She let her gaze probe into those crystal blue depths, her lips parting in a gasp at what she saw—love. A love that made her soul soar in answering wonder.

"What do you see, Emily Rose?"

"Love," she whispered, "so much . . . love."

"I've been saving it for a long time," Ian said, his voice breaking. "Hoarding it away. I just never knew why. I didn't know that I was waiting for you. Marry me, lady. Not because of Lucy or some notion of honor or duty. Marry me because I love you more deeply than any man has ever loved a woman from the beginning of time."

His eyes glowed with reverence and passion and dreams for a thousand tomorrows. "Ian . . . oh, Ian. Yes. With all my heart." Emily's breath caught as his mouth closed upon hers, gentle at first, tender, so tender.

Her arms twined about his neck, pulling his mouth tighter to hers, the heat of his kiss melting away the last pain inside her, banishing the last lingering fears.

And she gasped in joy, in pleasure, her lips parting, her tongue seeking the crease of Ian's lips, tasting them, then sliding past, into the dark heat of his mouth.

With a harsh animal groan, Ian welcomed her with his own tongue, delving into the sweetness of the kiss again and again with honeyed thrusts that whispered of last night and of the far more intimate melding of their bodies, the dance of passion that they would share for so many years to come.

"I'll never get enough of you," Ian rasped, trailing kisses across her cheeks, down her throat. "My love. My lady. Oh, God, Emily," he breathed against her ear, "you can't know how much I want you in my bed right now. Want to be inside you, deep, so deep. If Lucy wasn't such a short distance away, you would be in deadly peril, I assure you."

A shiver of raw desire, pure elation, tore through her, and

Emily whispered, "Perhaps we could steal away somewhere later where we would not be distrubed."

She blushed, remembering all too well the night they had kissed in the east wing. The night Ian had explained the *siège d'amour* to her, filling her mind with such lascivious, sensual thoughts that she'd all but collapsed from the heat they spawned in her.

She knew, the instant he realized what she meant. He flashed her that irrepressible scoundrel's grin. "Emily Rose, you're thinking of my chamber of love, aren't you? Well, there is something I think you should know about that room, my sweet. Mostly, it was for show. A place where we could do our dastardly rebel business without fear of being interrupted."

"But the *siège?*"

"That was a jest. A gift from Tony. God, how we loved to shock people by describing its uses. However, I assure you that the thing has gone unchristened."

"Perhaps"—Emily blushed—"you and I might try it sometime, as long as . . . as we are alone."

Ian's eyes grew solemn, the tenderness inside them warming the depths of Emily's soul. "You never have to fear that I will take another woman, Emily."

"I'm not afraid of anything, as long as I can hold you, Ian, touch you, know that you love me." Emily clung a moment more, bathing in the glorious miracle of the love in Ian's eyes. "And now I think there is a very impatient moppet who needs to know that everything has been arranged to her complete satisfaction. As usual."

Ian curved his arm about Emily's waist, and they walked out into the sunshine together. Lucy was pacing before the stone bench, her brow furrowed, her lower lip red where she had worried it with her teeth.

When those wise blue eyes locked upon them, she gave a cry rife with satisfaction. "I am glad to see you being very sensible now. If people would only do what I tell them to all the time, there would not be so much difficulty in this world."

Ian shot Emily a devilish grin. "Blast the child, she's

enjoying being right entirely too much. You know, she'll be insufferable now."

"I was always insufferable. It's just that now I will be happy, too. And I never have been before. If you would just come here and do the kissing thing with me, too, I would like it very much."

Ian knelt down and opened his arms, and Lucy raced into them, tugging Emily down among the flowers as well.

After a moment Lucy raised her head. "While you were gone, spent a lot of time thinking," she said.

Ian laughed. "Saints preserve us. What were you doing? Plotting more villainy should we not accede to your wishes?"

"No. I was thinking about a real live villain. That duke who stole me away. I have decided that if I ever meet him I will make him very sorry for making me and the lady so sad. I will . . . I will . . ." She laid one finger against her chin, considering for a moment. "I will be quite dastardly, but I can't think of anything to do for revenge right now. The happiness inside me is too big to leave any room for wickedness."

Ian's laugh rumbled out as he kissed the child's cheek. "I am certain you will recover soon enough, my sweet."

"The duke is dead, Lucy love," Emily said, stroking back a wisp of golden curl. "He can't hurt us anymore."

"But what about that bad duchess? Is she dead, too?"

"No. The duchess is still alive," Emily said. "She is a very bitter and lonely woman. Just look at the granddaughter she lost."

"P'raps someday she will find me," Lucy said with a diabolical gleam in her wide eyes. "P'raps I will make her very sorry she has."

"Perhaps." Emily felt a sting of something like fear, then felt it melt away beneath the light in Ian's eyes, the determined tilt of Lucy's little chin. The duke and duchess of Avonstea might have banished their granddaughter from her ancestral home and deprived her of noble birthright, but nothing could rob Lucy of her aristocratic pride.

The girl was more than a match for any d'Autrecourt

alive. And when she was older, what a formidable young lady she would make!

"That was a very mean secret they kept," Lucy complained. "And I have decided that I don't like secrets at all. Uncle Ian, I think you should tell my . . . my mama that you are Pendragon now."

Ian all but dropped the little girl, his face almost comical, he was so stunned. "P-Pendragon? Where did you ever get such an absurd idea?"

"It's not a disturbed idea. I sneaked in very quietly and looked behind your clothespress, and I found that cunning little hiding place you have there for your Pendragon things. Your mask was in there and your cape and a very shiny pistol. I put it all on and played for a little while, but Priam came in and I had to climb under the bed so he wouldn't see me. I 'cided it wasn't a good game after all."

"Why, you little demon! I can't believe— Wait! I stand corrected. Of course you found my costume. You would have done so even if I had hidden it in the next colony."

"I am very glad you didn't get dead when you got that hole in your mask, Uncle Ian, though the blood made your mask much scarier. You know, you cannot be my papa if you get your brains blown out all over."

"I will be very careful when I wear my mask from now on," Ian promised gravely. "In fact, I don't think that I shall be wearing it at all anymore."

There was a wistfulness in his voice, the slightest shading of sorrow. He looked away, and Emily knew he was remembering countless night raids. Raids in which Ian had allowed what was best in himself to be revealed, the hidden strength and the fierce sense of justice that had become the entity called Pendragon.

She took his hand, held it tight.

The sound of someone clearing his throat made all three turn to see Tony Gray standing a short distance away on the path, his hazel eyes gazing down at them, his face flushed with unease.

Emily felt Ian go still. Slowly he rose to his feet and

offered his hand to help Emily rise, his beautiful mouth achingly solemn, his cheekbones touched with dark red.

Silence stretched out, neither man seeming able to speak, both seeming to understand the words that remained unspoken.

Tony recovered first, his voice more than a little husky with emotion. "I hope you don't mind my intruding. Priam told me where to find you." He cleared his throat again. "I rode off in a fury, but after I had time to think, I—"

"I know." Ian stepped forward to lay his hand on his friend's broad shoulder. "And I thank you—for all you have done for us."

"Us. That has a wonderfully permanent sound. Dare I hope that Emily has decided to sacrifice herself into marriage with the most notorious rakehell in Christendom?"

"Former rakehell. Now I am to be a husband. And father." He ghosted his hand over Lucy's tumbled curls.

"Yes," Lucy chirruped. "And we shall have a wedding and a vicar will have to come. And Uncle Ian will not be able to swear at him and throw him out the door, even though he very much likes to do that to vicars, I know."

Tony gave a shaky laugh. "I cannot wait to see that, Lucy! Ian Blackheath at Vicar Dobbins's mercy. By God, it will be rich! But before you indulge me in that pleasure, perhaps you would do me the honor of allowing me to escort you . . . ?" He gestured toward the rear of the garden.

Ian's brow furrowed, lips curving down in a frown. "What the blazes?"

"I could not be certain what would happen when you rode out of here on my stallion, so I decided to make one last, desperate attempt to make you see reason."

"But I already have!"

"Emily, you have my sympathy. You are to marry the most stubborn man I've ever known." Gray's voice softened. *"And* the bravest."

"No, Tony. No more regarding that. It's over."

"For once in your benighted life just do what the blazes I ask you to!" Tony said, in affectionate exasperation.

Ian grimaced. "I suppose I'll have no peace until I do."

He lifted Lucy into his arms. Emily tucked her hand into the crook of his elbow as Tony guided them through the garden gate and into a copse of trees that shuttered the area from the eyes of those in the house.

The dimness closed around Emily like a forest primeval, cool and ethereal, as if they had walked through the gate into another world.

And it was another world. Hidden among the trees was a score of riders, their capes billowing in the wind, everything about them screaming of courage and pride.

Pendragon's raiders. Ian's men. The men she had almost cost him. As if signaled by some unseen hand, they swept the plumed tricornes from their heads in a salute.

She released Ian's arm and went toward them, her eyes filled with regret. "Because of me, you might have died," she said softly.

A spindly man swung down from his horse, a bunch of flowers in the crook of his arm. "Because of you, Pendragon lives." He knelt before her, extending the blossoms. "For Pendragon's lady," he said, softly. "Our gratitude. Our loyalty. Unto death."

Ian stepped forward. Emily felt his hand close on her shoulder, felt in those strong fingers a trembling. "You are the finest men I have ever known," Ian said quietly. "I was honored to ride the highroads with you."

"Was?" A rumble of protest arose from the men as Tony came to face Ian.

"No, my friend. We have all discussed the events of the last few weeks, and we have decided unanimously that none of us will ride again unless you are astride Mordred before us."

"Curse you Tony. You saw what happened! I—"

"You learned the most important lesson of all, Ian." Tony said, pressing a wisp of silver cloth into his hand. "This will be a symbol forevermore of that lesson, my friend."

Ian opened the silver mask, identical to the one that had been torn by Atwood's pistol ball. He felt as if a fist had caught at his heart. There, on the shimmering fabric was the red dragon that had been Pendragon's symbol for so long, but entwined about the mythical beast was embroidered a perfect white rose.

Tony's voice was soft, like a benediction. "It is to remind you of everything you have to fight *for.*"

The woodland was awash with emotion, fierce, moving.

Until a tiny indignant voice piped up. "Has anybody noticed that *somebody* in the Pendragon family hasn't gotten any presents here? What about Pendragon's daughter? I think that is very rude."

A roar of laughter rose from the raiders, Ian and Emily joining in.

"Pendragon's daughter?" Tony scooped the child up and set her on his horse, then swept a tricorne off the head of one of the men and put it on the little girl's curls. "By God, those accursed English had best run for safety when she chooses to go to battle!"

"She will have her own battles to fight one day," Ian said, drawing Emily into his embrace. "This battle for freedom is one that I shall help to win for her—and for my lady." His gaze caught Emily's held it. "We shall win it, Emily," he said softly. "And then I shall spend the rest of forever loving you."

Tears brimmed on her lashes, fell free. "Forever will not be nearly long enough, my lord Pendragon."

Emily raised her lips to Ian's, felt his mouth close over hers in the most fervent of promises, filling her heart with Pendragon's dreams.

Dreams of a new world, a new country.

A new beginning for all of them.